MAGIC EYES

A Great Murder Mystery Novel That Will Keep You Guessing Until The Final Trick

Author
Leif J. Erickson

Cover & Interior Design
Cosmo Publishing

Copyright© 2018 - Millennium Publishing Company
UNITED STATES OF AMERICA

ISBN: 978-0-9962804-8-8

Chapter #1

The Day the Bubble Burst

No one ever likes to think about their bubble bursting. I don't mean the stock market bubble, the real estate bubble, or whatever the talking heads in the media are railing against this week—I'm talking about the bubble we create around ourselves. The bubbles we create to tell ourselves everything is going to be alright, things will work out in the end. I'm talking about the bubbles we put ourselves in to shield us from the truth, from any past sins we've committed. These are the bubbles we do not like to think about bursting, for when they burst we must suffer the consequences of creating those bubbles in the first place. Long in my past, like many other people, I created a bubble to insulate myself from a horrible situation. I placed blinders on my eyes so I wouldn't have to deal with the past, blinders that could only be removed with magic eyes—eyes that could see through the fog of lies and distortions I told myself, eyes that could see through the bubble and pierce the heart of the monster in my past. I never thought I would have to see, but fate has a funny way of giving us magic eyes when we least expect it.

The day started out like most any day ever did. I woke early so I could read a chapter of a trashy romance novel over a too-large mug of steaming hot, black-as-night coffee while nibbling on an English muffin loaded with copious amounts of strawberry jam bought from the growers themselves at a local farmers' market. After a quick shower and more time than necessary shuffling tops around in my closet trying to decide what to wear, I rushed toward the door of my one-bedroom apartment with just enough makeup on to make it look like I was wearing none. I grabbed my trusty old black satchel and my worn-out skateboard and flew down the two flights of stairs to the ground floor of my building.

I've boarded to work every day since I started working full time, so many years ago, the day after I graduated high school. I wanted to go to college, had plans to travel abroad—if those plans had panned out I wouldn't have needed to have blinders on, I wouldn't have created the bubble that haunts me to this day. Most of the people who see me on the four blocks from my apartment to the store know me—know my story.

My mom was adamant about many things, including what was right and proper for little girls to do—sports, big no-no. I wanted to try volleyball, basketball, softball, or soccer like all of my friends but *those aren't the things ladies do*, according to my overbearing mother. I was in gymnastics and ballet. Those were the only sports I could try out for. Same with my younger sister. I took up boarding to rebel against her when I was thirteen. Skateboards and boarders, especially female boarders, were everything my mom despised. A boy let me try his board just once and I was hooked. I boarded whenever I got the chance.

Whether it was the wind flying through my hair, the feeling of weightlessness on the halfpipe, the grunge look with ripped jean shorts and flannel shirts, or the complete disregard for stodgy old traditions the elderly desperately clung to, my skateboard was my place of Zen. I was never happier or prouder of my accomplishments than when I was on my skateboard.

My proudest moment ever was winning an amateur skateboarding exhibition. I was fifteen at the time—a female beauty garbed in ripped, cutoff jean shorts, an open red and black flannel shirt I'd bought at a thrift store over a tight cropped black tank top, and enough makeup to be confused with a clown. The contest was scored on points based off the tricks and skills the competitors were displaying, all ranked by age groups. It was down to myself and a boy. We'd been called back twice, each given another minute to show off. On the third set, he went first, showing off tricks I had never seen before. I was already pouring sweat in the midday sun but I knew I was closer than I'd ever been.

Standing at the top of the halfpipe, I threw off my flannel and let the sun bathe my now-exposed shoulders and stomach. I took a deep breath and went for it. I got more speed than I ever had before and nailed the perfect airwalk grab, getting more airtime than I ever thought possible. I built up speed and hit a 540 spin at the top of the other side, followed by a top backflip, followed by another airwalk grab with even more hangtime than before. Moves I'd only tried before were flowing through me, everything I had was being put into this moment. When the buzzer sounded and I stopped at the bottom, I looked at the boy hanging his head, he knew he'd lost.

Once I had been awarded the trophy, and my friends had congratulated me, the boy I'd beaten came over and shook my hand, telling me how impressed he was with my moves. We talked and he asked me out. My mind was swimming with delight. He was an impressive boy—well built, handsome, shoulder-length wavy chestnut hair, and dreamy hazel eyes. I agreed and gave him my number. My parents didn't know I was at the event, didn't even know I boarded, making the entire day even more wicked than just flaunting a few rules of my mother. I couldn't have been higher, walking on cloud nine when a voice behind me crashed me right down to earth.

"That was very impressive Imara. I didn't know you liked skateboards."

Without turning around I knew I had been busted.

"How did you know I was here, Dad?" I asked, looking at the ground, not wanting to turn around as I felt tears well up in my eyes. For all I had to do for Mom, I wanted something, anything, for myself.

"A father knows things sweetie," he said, in a soft, forgiving voice.

I turned around and looked at him. My dad, Dean Callan, was always a handsome man. Five-foot nine, tanned, with brushed back black hair showing the slightest hint of gray. Powerful dark eyes that could see through anything over a small nose and lips curled into a mischievous grin, like he was thinking of doing something naughty and loving the idea of getting caught. He always wore drab olive pants with polo shirts, today, it was red. I thought he could have dressed better but dad wasn't one to give in to whims—he had his set ways and woe to the person who tried to change him. In his left hand he was holding my flannel shirt, offering it to me to put back on, in his right hand was a print-off of an online flyer advertising the event.

"You forgot to shut the browser down on the computer, Imara," Dad said, with a chuckle, as I put the flannel shirt back on. I left it open but he buttoned a couple buttons to cover me up. "You're lucky I found this and not your mom."

"She's so mean sometimes," I protested, almost in a whine. "I'm sorry Dad, but I hate ballet. I hate it so much. The girls there are bitches, the coaches are dumb, and the events and shows are so boring. I love Mom but I can't live for her."

4

"You're wise beyond your years," Dad said, "but there's a difference between living for her and doing something to make her happy. You know what she'd say if she saw the outfit you are in right now."

"But this is what I want to wear," I said. "There's nothing wrong with it. Girls can do things nowadays, you know."

"I know," Dad said, with a smile. "I rather like it on you...as long as the flannel is buttoned. You're doing what I've wanted and feared the most, honey."

"What's that?"

"Developing into a beautiful, independent woman. Imara, you have no idea how bright your future is. If you want to be the skateboarding champion of the world, I'm sure you can do it. Think about it though, how many skateboarding competitors have had all the gymnastics and ballet training you have?"

"What difference does that make?"

"I would guess a lot! They both develop your strength, make you fearless, increase your balance, improve your reflexes...all of that is good for skateboarding, right?"

"I guess."

"I know you're thinking about being a doctor, you've only talked about it for years. You can do it. You have the brains, you have the will and determination, and most importantly, Imara, you have the heart. I've never seen you give up. Even though you dislike ballet you always go out there and give it everything you've got. What you did on that skateboard today—*amazing*. I was scared watching you, worried you were going to get hurt, but I know you can come back from anything. I love you Imara. I know you can find your happiness."

"Then why don't you shield me from Mom?" I asked with slightly too much venom in my voice. "Why don't you protect Sarah from going through the same things I've had to go through? Sarah isn't as strong as I am, Dad. She's already losing the fight to her demons."

"I know that," Dad replied. "I was the one who found her after she drank that bottle of whiskey. Your mom has...*issues*, Imara. When you're older you will understand. I love your mom, I really do, but at times things fall out of our control. I wish everything could be perfect for you, but in reality, that would set you up to fail in life. If life's too easy you don't become tough. I think back, your mom would find bruises and bumps on you and you would claim you fell in gymnastics. You never fell though, did you? Not in gymnastics anyway."

"They were from learning to board," I said, smiling sheepishly.

"Good cover story," Dad said.

"Do you still love Mom?" I asked, not realizing I had actually asked it until I looked into Dad's hurt eyes.

"That's a tough question," Dad softly replied. "That's not for me to answer to you. Just know your mother and I both love you very much...that's what matters most. What Sarah is doing to herself is tearing me up inside. I've tried everything to reach out to her but nothing works."

"I've tried too, Dad," I reply. "I don't know what else to do."

"I'm sure we can think of something if we put our minds together."

"I'd like that."

"Now, what about that strapping young feller you gave your number to?" Dad asked with that mischievous smile on his face again. "I thought you and Mark were together? Or are you just playing the field?"

"DAD!" I shout. "Mark and I have gone out a couple times. God, it's not like we're married! And if I go out with someone different he might get the hint that I'm a catch and he'll start moving faster than turtles walking through peanut butter with me."

Dad tipped his head back and let out a deep belly laugh. "Just don't let him move *too* fast with you. Maybe the speed of kittens in peanut butter, no faster though."

"Okay Dad," I said, rolling my eyes while giving him a hug.

"We need to celebrate that fancy trophy you have there," Dad said. "Come on, let's get something to eat. Anywhere you want to go."

"And you won't tell mom?"

"You tell me when these events are and I'll make sure you have an airtight cover story."

###

I arrived at my store, entering through the back entrance, placing my board in the small office, and walking out to the sales floor. I loved walking through the store before anyone gets there, and I know that today is going to be a busy day. I walked through the rows and rows of vintage clothing, specialty clothes, and costumes that were for sale on the racks. Dad started the store years ago, 'Decades of Threads' a store with vintage clothing, custom-made items, and costumes year-round. We bought and sold clothing at least twenty years old, imported specialty items from Europe and the Orient, and the Halloween costumes were a cash cow that kept us going in lean years.

Our biggest customers were the community theaters, high schools, and local production companies who needed time period and specialty clothing for plays. They were the largest buyers by far, followed by young up-and-comers in the business world who wanted to wear something outside the norm which made them stand out. We got a lot of teens in their rebellious years, and hipsters. It made for a good mix of people walking through our doors. I loved learning everyone's story, why they were here and not at the flavor-of-the-month trendy store buying the outfits some starlet was wearing the week before.

Next to the stories of the people who went through there, I loved the smell of the clothes. Some of the vintage wear had that old mothball smell, but the specialty items, the import items, had an aroma to them that was to die for. A fresh smell, like rain on a warm spring day, with just a hint of something powerful, like the first tulips to bloom. The smell was intoxicating to me, coming from the handmade clothing, every stitch carefully placed so no one would ever be able to duplicate it. Half the clothing in there would have been in the trash if they didn't know about the store, and the other half would have never made it into the country. The store was where my dad and mom met for the first time, where he asked her out. It was my first job in high school, allowing me to earn the money I needed to hire a boarding coach. It's the store that I owned, at only 26 years old, all mine, and I ran it with the passion and dedication Dad had when he started it so many years ago.

As I walked, I caught a glimpse of myself in a fitting mirror. I stopped to examine. I'd always been attractive. Throughout high school, even in middle school, I had boys chasing after me. Five-foot four, still with a gymnast's body, I carried myself with confidence and pride. I only wore black tights or yoga pants, remembering the pain of when Mom found out I was wearing denim, which according to her was only for boys. I still wore skateboarding high top sneakers, black with indigo laces that are sloppily tied well into adulthood. My top is an item from the store, a tight tank top with thin straps. It was bought from a small shop in

London. Black with a fuchsia floral pattern, showing my broad shoulders and just the smallest amount of midriff.

Atop my head was a mane of luscious curly brunette hair with hidden golden streaks flowing to my shoulder blades. My face was flat and narrow with sharp features and a square chin. Hazel eyes that sparkled in the light and ruby red lips that were always smiling. An ample chest, narrow waist, child-bearing hips, and long legs made for a stunning combination, if I do say so myself. I hadn't dated for quite some time. Sometimes the bubble just hurt so much it wasn't wise to let people get close.

I posed in the mirror for a moment, blew myself a kiss, and moved through the store. There were days I wished I could try on every outfit in the store—just wear each one for a minute then change into the next. Something about all that fashion just warmed my heart. I pushed that thought out of my head as I grabbed my smartphone and looked over the day's agenda. I had two meetings with local schools who needed costumes for upcoming plays, and a salesman was coming to try and sell me the latest must-have marketing technique. Even though it was mid-summer, I had to finalize my orders for Halloween costumes to be sure I would get everything on time for the rush of the season.

My favorite days were when I was buying. I loved looking through the 'net to pick out the best items for the store, looking at little boutiques and shops from around the world. The best was when someone gave me specific items to look for. Many people wanted amazing items but didn't have the slightest idea how to find them. That's where I would come in. It was a good system and provided me a good life. I was having a blast with the store, making money, and enjoying myself. I wasn't rich by any means, but I was comfortable. I could do what I wanted, when I wanted, and

I couldn't think of anything that would make me richer than that.

I noticed the clock on my phone, it was almost eight. I was always at the store early and even though our sign said we opened at nine, I turned all the lights on and unlocked the front doors. Many of my regular customers liked to come in early and I liked to talk with them, keep a good rapport with them. Their stories and adventures were some of the most rewarding parts of running the store.

As I unlocked the door, I couldn't help but notice a woman who seemed to be milling around the area. She was there when I boarded in. I didn't think anything of it until she walked toward the door of the store. I took a closer look at her and realized she was waiting for the store to open. Through the windows I could see a pale woman with perfect, silky skin. She was tall, even wearing Keds she stood almost six-feet tall. Many of the women who went to the store had platforms and heels, so it's hard to know exactly how tall they were. She had the most beautiful straight, blonde, almost white hair I'd seen. It was thick and looked heavy, in a ponytail that went almost to her waist.

The woman had a soft, rounded face, sapphire eyes, a flat nose, and pale lips. She wore no makeup—a pure, natural beauty of a woman. She had a muscular build, with her height she looked like a volleyball player. She wore tight jean shorts that went just above her knees with a tight black tank top of which the hem didn't touch the top of the shorts. Not the style that usually walked into the store, but the woman pulled it off perfectly. She looked to be about my age, twenty-six or so, with a nervous smile on her face.

As she entered the store, my first thought was she must be a new director for a school play, unsure of the store she was told to buy the costumes from. But as the lady noticed me, there was something in her deep eyes, a spark of recognition. In an instant, I realized I knew the woman from somewhere—but where? My memory banks were flooded, trying to piece everything together. The woman gave a big smile while she walked right up to me and hugged me.

"Imara," she said, holding me in a tight squeeze. "I knew it was you the moment I saw your hair flowing behind you on that skateboard. You haven't changed a bit."

"Anna?" I asked, pulling back and looking her in the eyes, still trying to piece everything together. "Anna Garst? It can't be."

"It is though, skater-shrimp."

It had to be Anna—the only person who would dare call me skater-shrimp and wouldn't get decked, only because she would deck me back. Back in the day, we were close friends, best friends to be exact, growing up our entire lives living next door to each other. She was one who encouraged me to pursue skateboarding, and helped me hide it from my mom. We'd been through a lot together. After high school I stayed here in our sleepy little suburb while she traveled the world. We wrote and talked but like most friends after high school, we went our own ways. Emotions flooded through me like a dam breaking. There was so much between us, the last days we saw each other had been unsettled and unanswered. I didn't know what to say, I was only glad she was near me again.

"It's good to see you Anna," I said, knowing it was true. "And damn, girl, you still look good." *Also true.*

"You're holding your own as well," Anna replied. "Store's looking good, Imara. You running it by yourself, I heard?"

"I am," I replied with pride. "I've expanded with advertising and a website with an online shopping portal. We do a lot of online sales."

"I knew you'd do well with this," Anna said. "I really mean that. Imara, I'm sorry we lost touch. I was so nervous waiting outside for you. This is awkward."

She was right about that. Two friends who hadn't seen each other in years after a horrible night were now standing still, embracing in a hug that didn't seem to end, not knowing exactly what to say.

"Why is this awkward?" I asked. "Nothing has changed between us."

"But everything about us has changed, Imara," Anna replied.

"What are you doing here then?"

"I've come back to find answers to what happened that night," Anna replied, looking me in the eyes. "I have to know...I have to know why...and I'm betting you have to know why as well. That's why I'm here. I need your help, Imara."

And just like that, the blinders were off and the bubble had burst...

Chapter #2

The Night I lost My Innocence

Never before had I cried as hard as I did that night. Everything was crashing down on me and I couldn't see a way out. I'd been thrown into the abyss and there was blackness all around me. It felt like an eternal night was surrounding me and there was no one left to shine a light, no one left to help me out of the darkness. I cried, not knowing if I would ever stop, not knowing where it would end—not knowing if I should just end everything right then and be done with it, or if my life was worth fighting for. I knew in the end I was always a fighter and I would just have to face up to that night as well. I knew I would need Anna there with me.

I took masking tape and made an 'X' in my window, shining a desk lamp at it. Anna and I had bedroom windows that faced each other and that was our signal to get to the other's room right away. It wasn't over two minutes later Anna was climbing into my window, a blue cotton robe over her pajamas of black shorts and a black tank top. I couldn't bear to look at her. We were eighteen, had just graduated high school, yet here I felt like a little girl who'd received the worst punishment of all time. It took control not to vomit as Anna hugged me tight.

"What happened here?" Anna asked, releasing me. "I heard the fight you and your mom were having. I don't think I've ever heard her scream so loud!"

"She found my skating outfits," I said, through tears. "She found the jeans and a picture of me on the board."

"She didn't take to kindly to it?"

"She pulled, physically pulled me out of my bedroom, Anna," I replied. "Locked the door and proceeded to dig through all my clothes. She found two pairs of jeans and one pair of jean shorts. She found the flannel shirts and the skateboard and all of my protective gear."

"What did she do?" Anna asked. "Imara, why were you two outside?"

"She threw them all in the fire pit," I said. "She burned them. She burned my skateboard...and the trophies."

"Are you kidding me?" Anna asked.

I fell back into my bed, looking at the ground. I was subtly shaking my head. I had four trophies from skateboarding events I'd won over the past few years. Four first-place trophies proving I was the best boarder that day. They were the world to me, everything I held dear to myself. When I was on the board, I was happy and everything was pure, now the board was nothing but a pile of ash.

"That wasn't even the worst of it," I said. "You won't believe what she said to me."

"I heard," Anna replied. "I believe the entire neighborhood heard."

"Anna," I said, trying to hold it together, "my own mother said I was a horrible kid and she should do me a favor and just smother me now so I don't disappoint her or destroy her life anymore."

"Honey," Anna said, sitting on the bed and hugging me, "your mom has issues. You know she doesn't mean any of it. She can't control herself."

"They can call it whatever they want," I snapped back. "Bipolar, manic-depressive, or just that she banged her head up bad in a car accident when she was in her twenties, but the fact remains, she said she would rather have me dead because I am such a disappointment to her. I'm never going to board again."

"Don't say that," Anna said. "You have so much fun on the board. It's your thing, Imara. It would be like Mozart not playing piano or Rembrandt not painting."

"You're comparing my skating to Mozart and Rembrandt?" I asked, with a weak smile as I wiped the tears from my face.

"It got you to smile, didn't it?"

I shrugged my shoulders. Anna always had an uncanny ability to make a person smile when they were at their worst. I loved her for it. This wasn't the first time she'd been there for me. There were no words to express how much she meant to me. I hugged her back, trying to find the words to express what I was feeling. I never had any trouble telling Mark, my boyfriend, what I was feeling or thinking, but this was different, this was Anna. I knew I had to say something.

"Anna," I said, so softly it was almost a whisper, "I love you. What you've done for me and how you've been there for me, I love you more than you could know. You're the best friend a person could ask for and so much more than I deserve."

"Stop right there honey," Anna said, pulling back from me. "You deserve so much more than I could ever give. Don't ever say that again. What you don't deserve is a mom who treats you like this. She burned your clothes, burned your trophies...did she hurt you?"

"Not physically," I said. "She pushed me out of my room but only because I allowed it. I didn't fight back. That was the only time she put a hand on me, but I am worried."

"What about?"

"Sarah. She was in her room last I knew," I said. "I believe someone was with her. They were working on a school project—or so they told mom."

"Should we check on them?"

"I've had enough drama for one night," I said. "I don't know if I could handle that as well. The last time I checked in on her when a 'schoolmate' was over I got yelled at and her little friend threw a book at me."

"You can't give up on her," Anna said. "Everyone else has. She needs someone to help her, Imara."

"I know," I said, with a sigh. "I just wish she would make it easier on us."

I was about to stand when the door to my room flew open after a single knock. I jumped to my feet, surprising Anna, and stood defensively, with my arms up, fists in a ball, ready for whatever was coming. I didn't know what was about to happen, but breathed a sigh of relief when my father came rushing into the room. He was in his drab olive pants with a black polo. His face bore a frightened look and when our eyes met, his face melted into something happier, but not altogether peaceful. He walked right to me and hugged me.

"You really should have knocked, Mr. Callan," Anna said, never one to pass on an inappropriate joke. "You never know what Imara and I could have been doing in here!"

"You two are good girls," Dad said. "I have no fears about that. Imara, my God, I got a call from one of the neighbors, are you okay?"

"Mom burned my skateboarding clothes, gear, and board," I said.

"And her trophies too," Anna piped in.

"She found out," Dad said, with a sigh. "I'm so sorry, Imara. You know how your mother is, she only wants you to do girl things, dress in girl's clothing. Anything that isn't along those lines is very bad. You knew the risks when you started skateboarding."

"So, it's my fault?" I asked. "My fault my mother hates me? She said that she would be better off if I was dead!"

"Not at all," dad said, putting his hands up. "I didn't mean it like that. Imara, your mother is a very troubled woman and I'm trying to help her but she won't take it. She needs more help than we can provide her. I thought, mistakenly, that having a mother in the house was more important for you and Sarah than to not have her there. I should have put her somewhere she could get the help she needs, but I thought it would be harder on you two. You must believe me that I thought having her in the house was more important for you and Sarah and I thought that we could handle her. I was wrong, and for that, I am sorry."

"Your heart was in the right place," I said. "Can we get her help please?"

"We can," dad said. "I've already worked it out. Tomorrow morning there will be people here to take her to a medical facility where they will help her. This should have been done a long time ago. Imara, your mom will get the help she needs. I can't promise she will get better, but she will be safe."

"Have you checked on Sarah?" I asked.

"No," dad said. "She's also getting help in the morning."

"What do you mean?" I asked.

"I've hired a specialist to speak with her," Dad said, "to convince her to go into a rehab program. I know it's going to be tough, but we need to be there for her tomorrow."

"You're planning an intervention?" Anna asked.

"Not a full-on official intervention," Dad replied. "I found a lady who speaks to troubled kids. She will hopefully be able to get through to Sarah and convince her that seeking treatment is a good thing. If that doesn't work...yes, we'll do a full intervention."

"I'll be there for her," I said.

"I will too," Anna added. "She's like my sister, too."

"I'm glad you two are willing to help her," Dad said. "I've not told your mother about it. I don't know how she would actually take news like that. She doesn't seem to think Sarah has any problems."

"We will be strong for them, Dad," I said.

I was about to continue when his phone went off. He looked at the screen and smiled at the Caller ID before going into the hall and closing the door to answer the call. I strained to hear what was being said but I couldn't. He seemed excited as he opened the door and reentered the room, a beaming smile on his face.

"I hate to do this to you now but I have to go," Dad said. "There's something at the store, an emergency for some play or something. You know how it is, they need a costume right now."

"I understand, Dad," I said. "Please, hurry back as quickly as you can."

"I will," he said, hugging me. "I love you, Imara."

"Love you too, Dad."

Dad left and closed the door, leaving just Anna and me in the room, alone. I didn't know what Mom was doing, if Dad would even talk to her, all we could hear through the vents of the house was Mom cussing a blue streak at the television, going on a string of swear words that would make a sailor blush. Something on the television must have set her off, triggered something deep in her mind to create a firestorm of anger.

"We need to check on Sarah," I said, not wanting to go into her room. "We have to make sure they are all right."

Anna nodded and followed me to the door. I grabbed a white cotton robe to throw over my gray night shirt and black shorts. I didn't tie the robe as we walked down the hallway, letting the oversized, soft, comfortable robe envelop me like a cloud. I wished so badly I could just walk away from all of this, from the pain of this family, but I knew I had greater responsibilities and family always had to come first. I reached Sarah's door, painted black in the white hallway, and gently knocked.

"Sarah," I said, softly, not wanting Mom to hear it. "It's Imara. Can I come in?"

There was no reply. I pressed my ear to the door but couldn't hear anything. Normally Sarah would have her industrial metal music blasting through a pair of Dad's old college speakers—massive floor speakers he used for house parties in his wild days. There was nothing coming from the room, which made me more nervous to open the door. The music had been there earlier in the evening and I knew she hadn't left. I took a deep breath and opened the door.

The smell of candles and incense overpowered my nostrils. I spotted four candles, all fall-harvest-scented on a desk and many jars with incense sticks glowing in the dark room. I flipped the light switch on and almost vomited in disgust. My little sister, only four years younger than me, just fourteen years old, was passed out on the floor—drool streaming from her mouth and white fluid on the corners of her mouth. She was in nothing but underwear. Her clear, normally pale skin, had an almost greenish tint to it, making her look something less than human. Anna rushed in and checked for a pulse—and for breathing. She signaled to me indicating Sarah was still alive.

19

Next to Sarah was another girl in the same state—passed out and barely breathing. Across the room, lying on the bed was a boy, not more than sixteen, in only his boxer shorts. I believed he was asleep but all three of them had needle marks in their arms and there was a used condom next to the trash. I took a step toward Sarah but instantly tears streamed down my face. This is my little sister! How could I let her fall into this type of lifestyle? I saw Anna gather up the drugs and needles that were left in the room, along with an empty bottle of wine.

I took a breath, tried to compose myself, and walked to my sister. I knelt beside her, shook her, but got no reaction. I could hear her breathing, and see her chest rising and falling. I opened her left eyelid but there was nothing there, just a glassy look with no comprehension. I felt so helpless, I didn't know what to do. I looked to Anna who had finished hiding all the evidence of what happened.

"We have to call an ambulance," Anna said. "This doesn't look good. They might make it through the night, they might not. It's not a chance we can take."

"I don't know," I said. "If an ambulance comes they will all be in major trouble."

"Come on, Imara," Anna said, approaching me. "You've studied this enough. You know they can't get in trouble for calling for help. This might be the wakeup call she needs. What happens if she dies tonight? Do I even need to go on?"

"You're right," I said, as I tossed Anna the phone off Sarah's desk. "You do it. I can't."

Anna nodded and dialed 911 while I sat next to my sister. I stroked her dyed black hair as tears from my eyes fell to her face. I picked up her head and cradled it in my lap as I leaned back against the black walls. My little sister, who used to be all pink and yellow, was now gothic black. Mom didn't say anything because she wore skirts and dresses, leather miniskirts and micro dresses, but they were what girls wore. She attracted the attention of boys and entertained them, just like a girl is supposed to. Mom didn't care that Sarah had no respect for herself, had no life outside of drugs and sex, and had no real friends who cared about her. Only fourteen years old and she could easily die of an addiction that had consumed her for two years.

"They'll be here in ten minutes," Anna said, hanging up the phone. I hadn't even heard what she said to them, didn't even realize she'd already made the call. "I told them they had just gotten back and we think that it's a heroin overdose, maybe some weed or ecstasy or other designer rave drug added in. I also told them they drank a lot of wine with it as well."

"Is there anything we're supposed to do?" I asked. "Did they say if there is something we should do for them?" I was still cradling my sister's head, looking at the tears bouncing off her face.

"Make sure they don't go anywhere," Anna said, "if they wake up before the paramedics get here. They are sending some police, too. They'll most likely ask us some questions."

"What do we tell them?"

"We tell them the truth," Anna replied firmly. "She needs to get help. Even if she goes to jail for a bit, hopefully that will scare her straight. Imara, this is the only way."

I nodded my head as I look at my sister's room. It was a mess, things had been destroyed—books ripped, old toys thrown in corners. The carpet felt wet and soiled. The candles and incense could not hide the smell of vomit coming from somewhere in the room. I don't know how anyone could live like that. A clock ticked away the seconds, the tick-tock sound filling the room like a banging drum. I could hear Mom yelling and did not even want to think of what would happen with her when paramedics showed up.

"I'm going to wait outside," Anna said. "Flag the ambulance down and get them to the room...so they won't have to deal with your mother."

"Thank you," I said.

Anna quietly left the room as I waited, my hand over Sarah's heart, praying she'd be okay and would get clean and get the help she needed. I don't know how long I waited, how long it was before the door opened again. Two men, mid-thirties, entered the room with a gurney. I motioned to them to come to Sarah first. They quickly went to work checking Sarah, injecting her with something, and placing her on the stretcher. I moved to the door where Anna was peaking her head in.

"I've told them everything they need to know," Anna said.

"Where's Mom?"

"In the living room," Anna said, although I could still hear her. "She's pretty upset at the television right now."

"WHO THE HELL DO YOU THINK YOU ARE?" Mom's voice raged from the main floor of the house.

Anna and I looked at each other and rushed down the stairs, taking three steps at a time. When we got to the landing we saw two police officers, one male and one female. The man looked to be forty, with bushy brown hair and an even bushier brown mustache while the lady was no more than twenty-five, fresh out of the academy, learning the ropes. They were polar opposites, him big, well over six-feet tall, and beefy, with muscles coming out of every part of his body while the little blonde girl was hardly over five feet with tiny delicate features.

"Ma'am just calm down," the girl said. "We got a call that there was a drug overdose in the house, three people—one of them is your daughter. Did you know your daughter was doing drugs tonight?"

"Get the hell out of here before I throw you out!" Mom screamed, throwing a pillow at the police.

I knew this situation had just gone from bad to worse. Mom had a blank look in her eyes, like there was no soul behind them. Her hazel eyes were empty, looking more like black pits than anything else. I had my mother's hair, almost identical except she never put highlights in her brown, curly hair. Our faces were strikingly similar as well as our body types. If she didn't have the stress wrinkles and black pit eyes a person could confuse us as sisters.

"Ma'am," the male cop said, taking a step forward. "We just want to help them. Paramedics are taking her to the hospital right now. We just want to know how long this has been going on. Is this her first night or does she have a tolerance?"

"My daughter is perfect," Mom howled. "Sarah is an angel. Now, that one right there," Mom's finger was pointing at me, "that little bitch is worthless. You should arrest her and haul her away right now."

It was like a prizefighter had taken their best shot right to my gut. The pain of what I just heard caused a renewed flow of tears to stream down my face. Anna stepped in front of me, shielding me from Mom and the police.

"Sarah is dying, Cassie!" Anna said, to my mom. "She's had a drug problem for two years. It started with drinking and weed but quickly moved to cocaine and heroin along with rave drug shit. She's in bad shape tonight."

"Is this also your daughter?" the female cop asked mom.

"No," Mom spat, "she's a whore who lives next door and teaches my eldest daughter how to disobey her mother."

"Ma'am," the female cop said, "are you feeling okay? Is there anything we can help you with?"

I braced myself for the shitstorm that was about to follow.

"You arrogant little bitch!" Mom screamed to the cop, her eyes as empty as ever. "How dare you imply that my children or I have problems we can't face ourselves? I want you out of my house this instant."

"That's not going to happen ma'am," the female said. "There are three minors on the verge of death from drugs in your house. We need to know what's going on."

"Fuck you!" Mom shouted as she ran toward the female cop.

The lady wasn't prepared when Mom pushed her into the wall. The male cop, however, sprang into action and as Mom's fist cocked backwards, getting ready to deliver a blow to the woman's head. The male cop took Mom to the ground and cuffed her. Mom struggled, swore, and fought with the cops as they dragged her out of the house and into the waiting police car.

I looked out the window, another ambulance was just arriving as they were putting Mom in the car. I heard the paramedics carrying Sarah down the steps. I looked over and almost fainted; she was covered with a blanket from head to toe. For a split second I thought she was dead, but then I saw her chest moving up and down, she was still breathing. They must have covered her since she was nearly naked when they found her. I looked out the window again as they started loading the ambulance. There were neighbors peeking out their windows—the bolder ones enjoying a cup of coffee with the show as they stood in their yards

The rest of the evening was a blur. I spoke to the police, the doctors, and called Dad. I couldn't piece together everything that happened if I wanted to. Dad was strange on the phone, like this didn't faze him that much. He said he would be home as soon as he could. By the time everything quieted down and the police had left, Dad still wasn't home. I didn't think I could cry anymore, like I had already cried all the tears my body could, and my eyes would just have to wait for more tears to develop before having another round.

I walked up to my room, threw my robe on the floor, and collapsed into bed, not even bothering to pull the covers over myself. It had been the worst day I could ever imagine. Dad would have to bail Mom out of jail for assaulting an officer, Sarah was going to be placed in a rehab program, and it felt like my family was being pulled apart. Just as I thought no one was left who cared about me, I saw another robe hit the floor and Anna climbed into bed with me. She wrapped her arms around me after pulling the covers over us. It was tight with the pair of us on my twin bed, but it felt good.

"I'm not leaving you tonight," Anna said, as she held me tight. "I am going to stay the night with you."

"Thank you, Anna," I said, "although you don't have to be in the same bed."

"After the shit you just went through you need me here, skater-shrimp," Anna said. And she was right. "I'm here for you, thick and thin. Let's try and get some sleep."

I knew sleep would be a rare commodity tonight, but with Anna there, things felt more relaxed—better, like there was a light at the end of the tunnel. Maybe now that Mom was in jail she'd get the help she needed. Sarah would go to rehab and get the help she needed and then we could be a family again. It could work. I was starting to think about smiling when we heard something, two distinct, loud blasts; a shotgun shooting twice. Both Anna and I sat up, looking each other in the eyes.

"That came from my house," Anna said.

We looked out the window to see a man in head-to-toe black, racing from the back of the house with a shotgun in his hands. Before I could say a word, Anna was out of the bed and running for the door. I followed as quickly as I could, neither of us bothering to grab our robes. We raced across the lawn, through the unlocked back door. Anna looked around before rushing up the stairs and toward her parents' bedroom. Anna threw open the door and screamed as she fell to her knees. I looked over her to see her parents—naked, above the covers, both with a shotgun blast point-blank on the face.

It was hard to process as I dialed 911, told the cops there'd been a murder. I held Anna as she cried by the door. With all that had happened I never knew this would be the last time in eight years we would see each other. Anna went to live with relatives in another town the next day and she started traveling the world shortly after. We wrote, but nothing more for years. That day was so horrible, but to top it off, it was the last day I'd ever seen or spoken to my father. He vanished that night without a trace.

Chapter #3

The New Plan

I had to wait until another employee showed up at the store and shuffle some of my appointments around, but within an hour, Anna and I were sitting at a quaint little coffee shop that overlooked a park just blocks from my store. We both sat down with large cups of overpriced, fancy lattes and enjoyed the first steaming sip while we looked over the shop. I was so glad we were the only ones in the shop other than the two teenage workers, I had a feeling the conversation we were going to have was going to be deep...and painful.

I could feel something strange, sitting with Anna again. It was like being in a dream where I didn't know if I was dreaming or awake. Not a day went by when I didn't think of her and all we went through that night eight years ago. I so badly wanted Anna to stay in town with me, or for me to go with her, but I had to run the store. I had to stay in town to watch over my mother and my sister and keep the channels open in case something developed in Dad's missing person's case. I looked at Anna and smiled, not knowing who should say the first words.

"You really look good," I said, meaning it. Anna still had her volleyball body; thick, muscular arms, a powerful and confident posture, and killer legs capped off with a shimmering smile. "I mean that, Anna. You still play ball at all?"

"Thanks," Anna said, blushing. "I haven't played in some time...I really can't play anymore. You look good too...and the store looked to be running well. I've never seen it with that much merchandise before."

"It's the online expansions I've done," I reply. "The advertising really helped, plus I went around to schools and theaters and really sold the store to them. We do half our business online the other half in the store, and both are way more than Dad ever did."

"He'd be very proud of you."

"Yeah right."

"What?" Anna asked as she cocked her head sideways looking confused. "Your dad loved you, Imara. You know that. He was a very good man."

"Not good enough to stick around, Anna," I said. "I knew he sounded funny on the phone when I called him that night. He knew what was in store for the family. Mom was never going to get out of the institution, it looked like Sarah would have real jail time, I mean juvenile jail, but still locked away. And at the time, I didn't even know it, but the store was falling on hard times. He didn't have the customer base he needed. The writing was on the walls, Anna. Dad left us because he knew his good life was over. I just wish I could have said goodbye to him...I wish I knew where he is now. Does he look up at the stars at night, wishing to see us, wondering if we are wishing on that same star?"

"That's the cheesiest line of bullshit I have ever heard, Imara!" Anna said, laughing. I cracked up laughing too. "You're tougher than that."

"With all the shit I've been through there isn't any other way," I replied. "But you, where have you been?"

"I had some money so I went to California," Anna said.

"You didn't even stay for your parents' funeral," I interrupted. "I was there, Anna. It was beautiful, considering."

"I couldn't bear it," Anna said. "I went to the west coast to find fame...a lame plan but I figured, 'what the

28

hell?' right? I mean anybody can be famous if they get the right break. I entered into acting and singing lessons, took some martial arts and sword fighting classes. I figured with my size maybe I could be in a superhero movie or something. I always dreamed that a producer would walk into the class looking for a girl my size for a role...and boom! I would be a star."

"Didn't happen?"

"After two years, I hadn't even met a director or producer," Anna replied. "I went to parties to try and meet people but I couldn't get in. Nothing worked. I would go to open auditions for bit parts, on-screen extras, even offered to volunteer my time but I didn't even get a single look. I'm not mad about it, just a little disappointed. I really enjoyed the martial arts training I was doing, so I packed up and headed to Tibet."

"What?" I almost choked on my coffee. "You were in Tibet?"

"For two more years," Anna replied calmly. "I trained in some amazing schools. Some have been teaching the arts for thousands of years. I lived in the mountains, had no possessions, and I spent my days training and meditating. It felt so good, so relaxing. I found that place you found on your skateboard. I was entering mixed martial arts competitions, using Lama Pai, White Crane, and Hop Gar styles blended with the karate and kickboxing that I'd learned in California. I was doing okay, planning a Carano style career, be a fighter then transition to films. It would have worked but in a meet I destroyed my knee and ankle."

"How bad?"

"I can't do martial arts anymore," Anna replied with a frown. "I can't move anywhere near as fast—my left knee can't take the hard jumps, and my ankle can't pivot and twist like it used to. Imara, I can't even play volleyball anymore. It was bad."

"What did you do then?" I asked.

"I went to India to get better," Anna said, as she sipped more of her coffee. "I'd heard yoga could heal bad injuries. I trained in yoga with monks at monasteries in the highlands. I was there for a year, learning all I could about yoga. I used that to naturally heal my body. I don't take any painkillers. After I left there I went through Europe. I did everything there that I could—museums, history, art, culture, and religion. I listened to anyone who would talk to me. Listened to the stories of the older people who'd lived through the wars, listened to the historians talk about the culture, and just interacted with anyone who would have me."

"How the hell could you afford all of that, Anna?" I asked stunned. "What did you do for money while you were traveling the world?"

"I'm not very proud of what happened," Anna said. "But hey, walking into your parents' bedroom to find them dead, you need to live a little."

"What happened?"

"Remember Dad was super mad at that developer who wanted to build that mall thing, whatever it was?" Anna asked.

"Wasn't that Jimmy Nelson, the mayor, and Eddie Hayes, the real estate developer?" I asked. "They kept hounding your dad to sell them land, right?"

"Dad owned a number of rental properties," Anna said. "He did all the work on them along with running his handyman business. Jimmy and Eddie wanted to build the Front Street Gallery and Entertainment Complex, The gallery for short, but some of Dad's properties were in the way. When he died, everything was passed to me. I owned

30

everything. What I didn't know was that Dad's handyman business had made a lot of money and all the money had been put into the properties.

"I only made a few thousand dollars selling the tools and truck of the business, but the money the business made had paid off all the rental properties. I sold about half of the properties along Front Street so they could build their thing, whatever it is. I kept the rest and hired a company to manage them for me. That's where I got the money from, Imara. I sold my parents' house and bought a different house to rent out. Dad taught me a lot about the real estate business. I've done well with the money they left me. I was able to live off the interest while I was abroad, so I still have all the properties and all the money I made from selling the real estate on Front Street."

"I'm very happy for you," I said. "You deserve something good after that night."

"Honey," Anna said, in a serious tone, "you deserve a hell of a lot more than I got. I mean, I saw the pain in your eyes that night, girl. Don't deny it."

"It was hard," I said, annoyed. "But I made the best of it. The past is in the past and nothing I can do will ever change it. Sarah got help...it didn't last, she relapsed and got help again, and relapsed, then got help again. But now it's been five years clean and sober for her and she's doing incredible things. She's big into running marathons now. She competes in like, five full marathons each year."

"That's amazing," Anna said. "How's your mom doing?"

"Anna please," I said, looking away. "I can't talk about her now. It's just too messed up. All the things she's said to me, everything that happened... another incident destroyed any value my mother ever had to me. Please don't make me relive that now."

"I'm sorry, Imara," Anna said. "Forget it. Tell me, what's the old town like? You have a man around here?"

"No," I said, as I could feel the blood rushing to my face, blushing. "I haven't had a real boyfriend since Mark. He and I dated through his first year of college but then he transferred and we broke up, not wanting to do such a long-distance thing. He begged me to come with him but I couldn't. I had no money at the time and was struggling to pay all the bills. I fought tooth and nail to keep the store. I knew I could make it profitable and successful but I needed money to buy inventory and money to promote the place."

"What did you do?"

"I started doing everything," I said. "The first thing was visiting every theater and school in the area. I did a slight trick with that. When I told them about our period and vintage clothing, I also told them subtly about Halloween costumes. Gave the directors coupons for 10% off costumes and told them to give the coupons to the actors. Stuff like that, 'underground marketing' I think they call it. I volunteered at local city events so I could get promotion acknowledgement. Anything that was free, I was all over."

"I wish I would have known, Imara," Anna said. "I could have given you the money you needed."

"I wish you would have known too," I said, sarcastically. "Because it would have been nice...not to have the money, which I would have never taken, but to have a friend there beside me as I was fighting to keep everything together. It would have been nice to have a friend to talk to when I was going to the soup kitchen every other day to eat because I couldn't afford to buy food. It would have been nice to have a friend by my side when I was pawning Mom's jewelry to make payroll and keep the lights on..."

"I get it," Anna interrupted. "Imara, I know that I was a horrible friend to you, taking off without saying a word, only writing a couple of lame letters. You were the stronger out of us."

"I'll sleep better knowing that," I said, my words dripping with venom. "Why are you back, Anna? To tell me how sorry you are about leaving me?"

"No," Anna said, deadpan. I could tell I'd cut her deep with that comment, I thought about apologizing but Anna cut me off, "I've always had a problem with the official story...the police story."

"What about it?" I asked.

"There's nothing there," Anna said, pounding her fist on the table. "For God sakes, a man enters our house and shoots my mom and dad point blank in the face with a shotgun. Their faces were gone, no open caskets, that's why I didn't go Imara. I wanted to remember them alive, not see the boxes they were buried in. My dad had contacts and connections throughout the town. He was well-liked and respected in the community. Neighbors heard the gun going off, twice, but yet not one single person can give any more than 'there was a man dressed in black, from head to toe'? There were all the police investigations and everything else and not one person, Imara, not one damn person was even brought in for questioning. About a year ago the case was shelved. I got a letter saying they were no longer looking for suspects. Not one clue in the house, not one shred of evidence. That doesn't seem fishy to you?"

"My father vanished without a trace," I replied. "*Nothing* seems fishy to me."

"I can't sit back," Anna said. "Obviously they wanted either my father or mother dead. Dad's wallet and Mom's purse weren't touched. Dad had a gun in the headboard of the bed, which is really strange. They were having sex...gross, right? Then a gunman walks in but yet Dad made no effort to get a loaded 9mm pistol not inches from his head...why? There's so much to this that bothers me. The guy...I guess it was a guy, he ran like a man but we didn't get a good enough look to rule out it was a chick, rushes into the house, shoots them, and leaves. I want to know why."

"Did anyone ever contact you?" I asked. "Maybe looking for information or something?"

"The only one who contacted me after the shootings was Mayor Jimmy Nelson," Anna said. "He expressed his condolences and offered to help."

"The mayor?" I asked skeptically. "I thought your dad didn't like him."

"He didn't," Anna replied. "Dad told Jimmy many times he would never sell the land to him for the Front Street Gallery."

"Why did you sell it to him?" I asked.

"Unlike my dad," Anna said, with a smile, "I had no reason to compare dick sizes with Jimmy, which is what the feud was all about really. Jimmy took care of a lot of funeral planning for me and paid me well over market price for the houses. He even offered me a job with him but I turned it down. I told him Hollywood was calling."

"Do you think Jimmy was involved?" I asked.

"No," Anna replied. "I have a different theory."

"What's that?"

"Dad had been doing work for a big family on the south side of town," Anna said, lowering her voice and leaning in. "He had over twenty-five thousand dollars' worth of materials into the job, and over three hundred hours, yet he hadn't been paid. He was extending them credit. I believe he was going to go to court to force them to pay him for the work. That was the one place Dad really failed. He was always too trusting. Remember the stories he used to make up for us when we were little?"

"Oh my gosh!" I exclaimed. "I'd forgotten about them. He was so creative. He should have written children's books."

"Right," Anna replied. "I thought that too, but one common thread through all the stories was that a very trusting person was burned by trusting too much. He even admitted it was a problem for him."

"So, you believe that to save twenty-five grand, a family had him killed?" I asked.

"Yes I do," Anna said. "Or not...I don't know but I refuse to believe they were never questioned. Think about that Imara. The police, who knew they owed my dad a lot of money, never questioned them. There's something wrong about that, isn't there?"

"I guess."

"I'm going to start digging," Anna said. "And I'm not going to stop until I have the answer of who killed them."

"Then what?" I asked harshly, interrupting Anna. "What are you going to do? Bring them to justice? Kill them yourself? What can be gained by opening this past wound?"

"I'll be able to sleep at night," Anna said, firmly. "Look, maybe I didn't have the best relationship with them but they were my parents. I want to know what happened to them, why they died. I have to get closure on this. I have to know why."

"You know how much pain that will bring up?" I asked. "Are you ready to handle that? Have you even been to their graves since they were buried there?"

"No, I haven't," Anna replied. "It burns me inside to think I haven't been there. They raised me better than that. They meant a lot to me. I know how much pain I'm going to have to deal with. Maybe I'll even find a skeleton in their closet...but I have to know. Imara, I have nightmares about that night, every night in my dreams. Seeing them in bed without faces, it is burning me inside. I can't accept that the police, with all the forensics and science we have today, couldn't make a single arrest, didn't even have a suspect. Someone out there knows something, and I swear to you right now, or I will go in the Goddamn grave, I will find out what happened to my parents."

"That's a big commitment," I replied. "Are you sure you can stick to it or will the world be calling to you? Will you want to go off on some amazing adventure?"

"I will find out what happened to them," Anna said. "I'm not leaving our town of Prairie Rapids until I do."

I smiled. I knew when Anna set her mind to something, she couldn't be talked out of it. Nor would she be stopped. Anna was going to figure this out or die trying. I just didn't want to be involved. I wanted my life the way it was. I was happy and had put all of this behind me.

"I'm glad you're back, Anna," I said. "I hope this doesn't sound too cheesy, but I hope we can reconnect and make up for lost time together. We were such close friends."

"I hope so, too."

"I would offer you a place to stay but I only have a one-room apartment," I said. "Without a sofa."

"We've shared a bed before," Anna said, with a wink. "Granted, we were only there for about five minutes before the gun went off."

"Was that all that was?" I asked. "Hey, there's something to go on!"

"What?"

"All the police and ambulances and stuff," I said. "I wonder if the killer was waiting, hiding somewhere and hoping everyone would leave."

"That's why I need you," Anna said.

"Need me?"

"Yes," Anna replied. "You are going to help me solve this case."

"I am?" I asked.

"You have a good mind for details," Anna said. "I need that. In return for helping me, Imara, I have something for you."

"I don't want anything from you, Anna," I said. "I take that back, I do want something from you...your friendship."

"In exchange for helping me," Anna said, firmly, "I swear to you I will not rest until I have found out what happened to your father, too. I will find him for you. What do you say, Imara? Will you help me and help yourself?"

My mind was blank. I had pushed all of this out and hadn't thought about it for so long I didn't even believe it could be brought up again. The last thing I wanted was to go frolicking through the past, looking at all the problems. Anna was looking at me, waiting for a decision. I said the first thing that came to my mind, "No...the past is dead and buried. As far as I'm concerned, my father died. He'll never return and I see no reason to dig up the past. I'm sorry, Anna."

With that, I stood up, gave her a half-hearted smile, and quickly walked out of the coffee shop.

Chapter #4

Wasted Days

I sat down on a park bench that looked out over a children's playground. Within the grounds were all kinds of swings, slides, sandboxes, merry-go-rounds, and teeter-totters. There were a few children playing with their mothers watching over them closely. I was surprised there weren't more children there. The weather was perfect. The temperature was in the upper 80s with a gentle breeze that felt so good—so pleasing as it touched my face and skin. The air was ripe with the smells of flowers and trees, the fresh cut grass, and the warm air.

The park was a large area near a river that ran through Prairie Rapids, within the park grounds were the rapids from which the town got its name. The park was large, with lots of other areas, but this place was my favorite. Beyond the playground was the river and past that was the downtown skyline, skyscrapers rising up out of the Midwest prairie to touch the sky. Prairie Rapids had a beautiful, well-known skyline, one that looked clean with the cloudless blue sky behind it. I always felt the skyline view was truly one of the greatest things about living in Prairie Rapids, along with the natural, nature feel of the city.

Behind me was a jogging and biking path, paved, extending through the city along the river but also had branches that stayed in the park, offering a challenge going up and down the rolling hills following the river. I glanced at my watch, knowing my little sister Sarah would be emerging through the tree line on the trail soon. She ran every day to keep herself in shape for the marathons, and to keep herself from falling back into old patterns of destructive behavior.

I hear footsteps racing from behind the trees and as I looked. Sarah emerged, dripping with sweat, her tanned olive skin glistening in the midday sun. Her skin was perfect, her body too, standing only five-feet tall with ample curves in all the right places. Sarah had always been attractive, and now with all the running she'd been doing the last five years, she'd developed a supple layer of muscle under her entire skin, she looked fit but feminine, with owl-bright brown eyes under a cap of straight brunette hair always pulled into a ponytail. She was so sweat-soaked in that moment it looked like she'd taken a shower.

Sarah was the fashionable one of the two of us, always wearing designer dresses and skirts with amazing tops made from the world's best designers. She was a stark contrast to my black tights and vintage tops. Even when she went running, in her shorts and cropped running top, everything had designer labels, and she looked amazing. Almost perfect...the only blemish anyone could see was an ink-vine scar that ran from the top of her left eye, over the eye itself, extending down on her cheek and almost touching her mouth. It was a brutal scar that took away from how attractive Sarah could be, but she'd never have it removed or covered up; the night she got it was the last night she ever did drugs, and the person who gave her the scar would have killed her had it not been for a freak set of coincidences. She kept it to remind herself what would happen if she fell back into the drug game.

Sarah lit up when she saw me sitting on the bench. For the past five years we'd been working on our relationship with each other, helping the other when we could. Things had been very good between us and we were acting like sisters should act, encouraging and helpful. I didn't know how she'd take the news about Anna being back and wanting to look into the deaths of her parents and the disappearance of our dad, but I owed it to Sarah to tell her and get her opinion on the matter. Sarah drank from a fountain in the park before walking over to me, giving me a hug before we both sit down on the bench.

"I know that look," Sarah said, in her angelic voice. "You've either got boy troubles or there's something really weighing on your mind. Out with it 'Ara. Don't make me wait."

"Anna came back today," I said, bluntly.

"Anna, like, Anna from next door, Anna?" Sarah asked. "Anna Garst?"

"That's the one," I said.

"She was always so pretty," Sarah said. "She still looks good?"

"Like you wouldn't believe," I replied. "She's been staying active and is pretty ripped."

"Where has she been all this time?"

"All over the world. California first, where she tried to become a star but that didn't work so she was in Tibet and then India before traveling around Europe."

"That sounds amazing," Sarah said. "So jealous. I really want to travel around and see what else the world has to offer...I know you do too, 'Ara. It's something you and I should do together before we go off and get married and have kids and stuff. Just think about it, you and me, traveling country to country, not a care in the world. The store must be to the point where you could leave it for a month. You've trained Jack well enough to handle it."

Jack Spangler was my assistant manager at the store. A short man with a sandy beard and long hair. He was book smart but had as much common sense as an over-energetic puppy at feeding time. What I liked most about Jack was that he was a smooth talker and could connect with anyone, just like a puppy. Everyone liked him. Sarah was right, he could handle running the store, but I didn't know if I could handle not being there that long.

"We can see," I replied, realizing Sarah was waiting for an answer. "I do want to get away but things have really taken off. I don't want to risk anything."

"I understand," Sarah said. "We can't wait too long though, otherwise it will never happen. I don't want to look back at a life of wasted days...I've had enough of them the way it is. But Anna coming back, that's exciting. What's she up to these days?"

"She's back. I'm not sure for how long, but she's back to investigate the death of her parents."

Sarah looked like I'd punched her right in the gut with an iron fist. Her face contorted liked she'd smelled something rancid and she swallowed deeply. She had already put everything together. I didn't even need to say it.

"And she wants our help," Sarah said. "I'm betting in return she will look into what happened to Dad."

"Right."

"What did you tell her?"

"I said no and walked out."

"Just like that?"

"She was waiting for an answer and I said the first thing that came to my mind. It was my gut reaction."

"How did she take it?"

"I walked out before she replied."

"That was cold," Sarah said, with a smile. "I believe I would have had a few choice words for her before walking out. Anna is a good girl who deserves to know what happened. Now that you've had time to think about it, what do you think?"

"I don't know what would be gained by it," I replied. "If Dad was alive he would know where to find us, if he wanted to be found. He walked out on us that night, Sarah, and if he wanted anything to do with us at all he would have called or visited. Things are more complicated than that though...money things."

"With the business and house and stuff?"

"Exactly," I replied. "The police declared him dead so his estate could pass to us, since Mom wasn't fit to be the executer. I still feel horrible about suing to keep Mom out of his will."

"You had no other choice," Sarah said. "Nor did you have a choice in what you did to me. You were right to force my assets into an asset trust to be frozen so I couldn't touch them. It's a good thing you did or I would have snorted and shot every penny of it. 'Ara, I believe if I would have had access to that money there would have been no stopping me. I would be dead right now. You know what I had to do to get my fix? Just think if there was nothing in the way of getting high! I thank you for it."

"I know you do," I reply. "But the thing of it is, if I wasn't friends with the cop, and if certain strings weren't pulled, Dad's assets would still be frozen and in limbo. Let's say we find him and somehow, someone else finds out about it. I could be going to jail for fraud, along with the cops and doctor who signed forms for us. We would most likely lose everything."

"I doubt it would be that bad," Sarah said. "They would look at the situation and realize you didn't have a lot of options. You kept four people employed while taking care of me and Mom. That's gotta count for something."

"It's not a risk I'm willing to take."

"So let me get this straight, 'Ara," Sarah said, with a sly grin. "You don't want to look for our father because we may have committed a little estate fraud? Really? Why don't you tell me the real reason?"

"Damn it Sarah," I said, with way too much frustration in my voice. "I loved him and I know you did too but he walked out on us. When we needed him the most he was gone. You know how much I cried after Anna left? How hard it was on me when you went into relapses? There were times when I had no one left to turn to. Not a single family member or friend was there to help me out. I want to find him, push him up against a wall, and demand to know why he fucked us over like he did...but that still won't bring back the past. It won't solve anything. The best we could ever hope for would be a long-distance relationship where we couldn't even mention him around here and we'd always be fearful of being discovered."

"That's not true," Sarah said. "That's not true and you know it, Imara."

Sarah was staring daggers at me. She, even more than myself, wanted to know what happened to Dad. She always wanted to ask him why he never tried to control her drug, drinking, and sex problems. She was so young when she got into the lifestyle; he knew, but was always a hands-off kind of guy. He was the type of father who would let us fall and then ask us what we learned from the experience. We both loved him but not as much as we should have. There was resentment because he wasn't there many times when we needed him and also because he was there when we didn't need him.

"Say we find him, Sarah," I said, slowly, "...then what? Do we demand to know what happened? Do you think he'd tell us? Do we forget all of it and play 'happy family', like he never left? What's the answer?"

"You did some investigation on your own," Sarah said. "I know you did even if I wasn't in the right mind to help you. What did you find out?"

"The quickest and easiest way to find someone is through the DMV," I replied. "Eventually, they need to renew their driver's license. I made friends with someone who works at the DMV here in Prairie Rapids and they've been checking once a month to see if Dad has renewed his license or if he transferred it to another state. There's been nothing. I read at least ten different books on how to find anyone and they all say start with the license. It's very hard and expensive to get false documents to obtain a new social security number and name. It can be done, but it's tricky and has its own set of risks. The next thing is to follow his social security number. He's applied for no new loans, credit cards, or opened a bank account. His number is dead. His cellphone, which has never been found, was shut off the night he disappeared and has not been reactivated since then. He never attempted to clean out his bank accounts, nor did he take the contents of the safety deposit box."

"What was in the box?" Sarah asked. "I've always wanted to know. I know I wasn't in a state of mind where you could tell me when you opened it and cleaned it out."

"There were deeds to the house and store," I replied. "Lots of legal documents regarding the store. There was some of Grandma's jewelry and a few hundred dollars in cash. Nothing giving any indication as to what happened or where he could have gone."

"So, everything you tried was a dead end?" Sarah asked. "There wasn't even a clue or something to go on?"

"Nothing," I replied. "Not a single trace. Once the store started getting some money I did hire an actual private investigator. He did some work and gave me some information but it was more confusing than anything else. He was baffled by the case...couldn't believe there was no information anywhere, no trail to follow. He said that by all accounts he would consider Dad to be dead."

"What information did he give you?" Sarah asked.

"He said Dad was a very secretive person," I replied. "So secretive that he was certain Dad had some major secret to hide. The investigator said there was no way a normal person who wasn't hiding something would be taking the actions that he did."

"What was he doing?"

"It was difficult to understand," I replied, shrugging. "I was so frustrated at that point I didn't really care. Dad wasn't home at night. It seemed like every night he would go to the store to work, and something would 'come up'— problem was, he was never at the store. The investigator found out that the store was always closed at five; no one was thereafter. A lot of money had left the store accounts that couldn't be accounted for. The investigator said the most likely scenario was that Dad was gambling, illegally. He got in over his head, couldn't pay the debt, and he's at the bottom of the river. But he also said that scenario doesn't make sense because no one has come after us. He says they would have gotten their money somehow and no money was taken right before his disappearance. He said the whole thing was very strange."

"Are you comfortable with what we know?" Sarah asked. "Or possibly never knowing the real answer? Is that something you can live with?"

I looked at the ground. I couldn't look at Sarah. I didn't know what my answer was. I wanted to keep the store moving in the right direction. I wanted to live my life, have some fun, and have a family of my own. I looked up to the parents who were watching their kids play on the jungle gym. A mom was scolding her daughter for sharing her Cheerios with the birds flying nearby. Another mom was brushing sand off her son, who'd somehow managed to get sand into every piece of clothing he was wearing, along with plenty of sand in his fine blonde hair. I could feel Sarah's stares on me. I knew she was waiting for an answer.

"It tears me up inside, okay?" I said, perturbed. "I can't stand not knowing what happened to him. I want more than anything to know, but we're not going to *know*, Sarah. I believe he is dead. I don't think we'll ever be able to really know what happened to him."

"Can you live with yourself not looking into it?"

"I don't know, Sarah," I said. "What do you want me to say? We've been through so much shit in our lives and we're both doing really well now. I think we should keep it that way. Could you handle it, Sarah? Let's say we start looking into this and we find a secret life, maybe another family. Would you be able to handle it, or would you go back to the blow?"

I had spoken out of concern to my little sister but she took the comment the wrong way as there was a resounding crack as Sarah's hand connected with my face. My cheek stung as I looked at the tears welling up in Sarah's eyes. She was beginning to cry but trying hard not to. I knew I'd crossed a line with that comment.

"I can't believe you think that of me now," Sarah said, as people were looking at us. "'Ara, look at how I'm doing. I'm getting better times at each marathon, work is great, and I've been starting to date a little. I'm back on track and there's nothing on this earth that could make me get involved in that shit again. I can handle it. My guess is you're too frightened to look. You know that no matter what we find it's going to destroy your image of Dad. He will be forever tarnished by what we uncover. That's what you don't want."

"You know what the investigator said was his most likely scenario?" I asked. "You know what he said he would bet money on happened?"

"What?"

"That Dad has another family somewhere," I replied. "It's possible to have a pair of social security numbers, even multiple names. The investigator has never seen one this elaborate and secure but he said with enough money and the right connections, it could be done. His guess was that Dad had two wives, two sets of kids, and that he chose the other ones over us. That's what I really believe, Sarah. I just tell everyone I believe he's dead because it's far less embarrassing."

Sarah was silent for a moment, looking at the ground like I had been doing before. I never wanted to tell her that, the final thing the investigator had told me. I never wanted her to have to know about it, but there it was, out in the open for all to see. Sarah brushed tears out of her eyes as she stood up. I stood with her. Sarah didn't even look me in the eyes as she hugged me, moved back to the running trail, did a couple of quick leg stretches, and without a word, took off running. When she was out of sight I sat down on the bench and watched the families have a wonderful day in the park.

Chapter #5

The Front Street Gallery and Entertainment Complex

A few days had passed since talking with Sarah on the bench. She'd called me and apologized for how things went that day, not that she needed to, but she wanted to make sure we were okay. I had a sneaking feeling she was attempting to get in contact with Anna, maybe offering to help in the investigation. I still couldn't decide what path was right. It would be nice to know, but on the other hand, it would be going through a lot of painful emotions that didn't need to be dug up.

I was surprised I hadn't heard from Anna in a few days. I didn't know where she was staying or what she was doing. I wouldn't even know where to start if I was her. How could she pick up a trail of clues that were eight years old and had been poured over by police and investigators? She was right though, something didn't add up with the official account of the evening and the way the police handled everything. I knew that one day Anna would return but I didn't expect it to be like this.

It was a Friday afternoon at the store and I was dealing with a frantic play director for a community theater. They had a performance that night, opening night, and the star's costume they had bought from a different costume shop had been destroyed by him not cleaning it properly after rehearsals. The director was my least favorite kind; a parent who'd made their kid the star of the production thinking they could parlay this into a three picture Hollywood deal. It was nearing five o'clock, closing time, and I had a feeling this was going to last longer than a normal day.

"It has to look perfect!" the director exasperatedly exclaimed. The director was a tall man with black hair and darker skin. He had a thick body that was turning to fat. In his mid-forties, the man had enough stress wrinkles to be in his sixties. He was wearing a gray suit with a black shirt, and sweating profusely, having a miserable day. "I tell you this now, we go on in just over two hours. I have to get back and we need a perfect costume. It has to be a dress a hippie would wear in the 1960s on the streets of London."

"I've shown you these four," I said, pointing to the four hanging on a rack, four he didn't even look at before dismissing. It was for his daughter, so it had to be perfect. "They all match the time period perfectly. Any one of these would work."

"But they are all giant-sized," the man protested. "My daughter, Hannah, the star of the show, is only a size two."

"This *is* a size two," I said, holding up a red dress that was genuinely made for hippies in the early 1960s. "This dress was made in London."

"But the male lead is also wearing red," the man almost shouted. "Don't you know anything about the theater? They can't clash! They have to shine. What else do you have?"

I thought about telling him to check some stores on the other side of town, or buy something off the internet, or maybe, just maybe, be more careful with the costumes next time, but I didn't feel like getting yelled at even more by this man. I smiled and walked to the back, trying to remember what else I had that would work for his precious little Hannah.

When I got to the back room, I noticed Jack was rummaging around in the clothing. He'd already set out three more dresses that would work and was looking for more. I watched Jack before he noticed I had entered the store room. He was wearing black jeans with a short-sleeved button-up flannel shirt, embracing the lumberjack look with his sandy beard. With his short size he looked comical, like a kid dressed up for Halloween. I noticed my outfit in the mirror, black tights with a black vest and knee-high boots. The vest was from the 1970s, a velvet material home-sewn into a sleeveless vest having French dart bodice shaping and large brass buttons up the front. It was V-necked and showing more midriff and cleavage than should be allowed in a retail setting. I realized Jack was watching me pose in the mirror, smiling at me.

"Imara," Jack said, in his high-pitched voice, "that outfit wouldn't work on anybody but you."

"It doesn't work on me Jack," I reply with a laugh. "This vest is made to be worn with a white shirt underneath with bell-bottoms. My tights and designer boots don't really match. Contrasting styles, you know."

"I still say you look stunning in it," Jack said. "Still dealing with Mr. Jackass out there?"

"Needs to see more dresses for the star," I replied.

"I figured. Here are three more I could find that should work. They are all period correct but they might be a size or two too big. If they have any kind of decent seamstress they will be able to fix it in a minute or two."

"What would I do without you Jack?"

"Be miserable and alone."

"I DON'T HAVE ALL DAMN DAY," the man shouted from the sales floor.

"I hate drama queens like that," Jack said. "His daughter probably sucks as an actress, too. The only way

50

she could get a part is if Daddy was the director. Good luck out there."

"You can take off at five," I said, looking at my watch. "I'll deal with him and lock up."

"Thanks."

"Big plans for the weekend?"

"Not going to his play!" Jack said, with a laugh. "Just hanging out with some of the guys. Maybe catch a game somewhere."

"Have fun," I said, as I scooped up the dresses and headed back to the sales floor.

I started setting out the dresses in the sales floor while director supreme looked on in disgust. He was bound and determined to veto everything I brought him. As I was straightening out the dresses, I noticed movement in the store; someone else was in the building but I couldn't see who they were. The last thing I wanted was another customer, but sometimes that's how it was. The man glared at all the dresses before shooting me a look that could have killed a lesser person.

"And this is all you have?" he asked sarcastically.

"This is it," I replied, not knowing if it was true or not, but I'd reached my limit. I wasn't going to search for him anymore. "These dresses are all the right time period and will work for your play. Some may be a size or two too big, but a seamstress can fix that simple enough."

"Fine," the man said, looking them over. "How much for these three and the red one on the rack?"

"$525," I said, after a moment of adding them up.

"What?" the man asked, shocked. "Boy, you sure have a racket here, don't you? $525 for four dresses, are you sure?"

"They were all flown over from shops in London," I said, not wanting to debate about it with him. "That's the price for them."

"Fine," the man said. "Ring them up."

I rang the four dresses up and the man paid with his credit card. The entire time I was dealing with him I was scanning the store, trying to figure out where the person who'd entered when I was in the back went. The man left and I walked around the sales floor, certain I'd seen another person. I hadn't heard the door open, so no one could have exited the building while I was working with him. For the briefest of moments I thought someone might have snuck in and was getting ready to rob the store, but with the little amount of cash I kept on hand I doubted anyone could be that desperate.

I took one last look around the sales floor before I locked the front door. I walked toward the back, still looking for any sign of anyone but there was no one there. I opened the door to my office and almost had a heart attack; Anna was sitting in the chair behind my desk. She was smiling, knowing she'd gotten me. Anna always liked to play simple practical jokes on people, just like her father had.

Anna looked stunning tonight, short designer jean shorts with a designer tank top and decked to the nines with accessories and ribbons in her straight, blonde, almost white hair. Anna looked like she was ready for a night on the town, and something told me I was going with her.

"You closing up for the night?" Anna asked.

"I was in the process, yes," I replied.

"Good," Anna said, standing up. "Hurry your skinny ass up. I'm taking you out tonight."

I quickly shut the store down, locked all the doors, and followed Anna to the parking lot. She had a rental car, a silver Chevrolet Sedan, so I tossed my skateboard and trusty black satchel in the backseat and hopped in with her. Anna didn't say a word as she took off, driving toward the heart of the downtown area.

"Sorry I've taken so long to get back to you," Anna said. "I was busy trying to lay the foundation for this investigation. I'm doing a lot of planning and everything as to be perfect."

"What are you doing?" I asked.

"Making friends with some of the new police," Anna said. "Touching base with old friends and relatives. I've been at the library for the past two days doing nothing but looking through old newspapers and reading up on detective techniques."

"You're not going to stop until you have something, are you?" I asked.

"Not a chance, honey," Anna said. "This investigation is mine. I will not rest until this is settled. I think I may have a starting point already. This is what we are doing tonight."

"So, I don't even get a say in whether I'm going to help you or not?" I asked with a firm tone. "You're just dragging me along?"

"You'll like this tonight," Anna said. "I'm not going to force. I just want to run something past you. I just want you to hear it and tell me if I'm crazy or not. Once tonight is over I'll let you make the decision for yourself whether you want to help or not."

"Serious?" I asked.

"Serious," Anna replied. "I don't know, Imara. I started putting pieces together...started looking at the puzzle, and asked the first question, 'who would benefit the most from my parents dying?'...and that led to a very strange answer."

"What answer was that?" I asked when Anna didn't finish her thought right away.

"That's what I need to talk to you about," Anna said. "That's why we're going here."

I looked to where Anna was pointing—we were pulling into the main parking lot for the Front Street Gallery and Entertainment Complex. The parking lot was massive but the buildings beyond were even bigger. There was a main gate with an arch over the top, proclaiming the name and the names of the people who made the complex happen, with Mayor Jimmy Nelson being at the top with Eddie Hayes, the real-estate developer and construction-magnet right below.

Anna parked the car in the front of the lot and we started walking in the beautiful evening air toward the arch. There were fountains on both sides, sprinkling water over statues of what looked like Greek Gods. As we passed through the arch, there was a block-long cobble-stone path with stores on both sides, hanging lanterns, and trees and flowers everywhere. It was designed to look very old school Main Street, almost a blending of 1950s Americana and something that came from the 1800s in London. The stores, most of which were open, although the grand opening celebration was still a few weeks away, were all new and higher-end. This Gallery wasn't for discount shoppers.

Past the first block of shops was an open area that had an outdoor amphitheater dug into the ground. To the north was an indoor theater with seating for five thousand and to the south was a larger stadium, ready for a professional basketball game. Both the theater and stadium could be accessed from the outside of the gallery, each with its own parking ramp connected to the facility with entrances that led to the gallery itself. Surrounding the rest of the open area were all kinds of restaurants and snack shops.

Beyond the open-air area of the gallery was a four-story, ultra-modern shopping mall. It had more stories than anyone could imagine and looked like something directly out of the future. Shimmering stainless steel glittered in the setting sun as the mall rose above us, glass and steel in the once green prairie. The entire place smelled of flowers and trees, with modern pop music being piped in through hidden speakers throughout the area. There were a few people around, taking in the sights and sounds of the area—very few people, since there was much in the mall that hadn't opened yet. Once the grand opening event took place, I would bet the mall was going to be the absolute social center of Prairie Rapids.

"They did a hell of a job here," I said, looking everything over. "And I heard there are four different hotels connected to the skyways linking the mall to the stadium and theater. This place is going to make a lot of money."

"I'm surprised you didn't want to move your store here," Anna said. "That entrance street we walked through would be a perfect location for your shop."

"Moving is never good for a store," I replied. "Especially a little store like us. I'm happy with where we are and I wouldn't even want to know what the rent is going to be in a place like this."

"Jimmy and Eddie are going to make plenty of money with it," Anna said.

"How so?" I asked.

"They own most of it," Anna said. "The parts they don't own they had the city and taxpayers finance. It's all a giant scam to line their pockets."

"I don't think I've ever heard you talk about the government like that," I said, looking at Anna. "What gives?"

"You know the entire footprint of that mall is sitting on where Dad's houses used to be?" Anna asked. "He owned the whole area."

"I knew he had houses here but I didn't know how many," I replied. "You don't think the Mayor and Eddie were behind his death, do you?"

"No," Anna said. "That would be too simple."

"Occam's Razor," I replied. "The simplest explanation is usually the correct one."

"Jimmy killed Dad so I would sell him the land and he could build his mall?" Anna asked.

I simply shrugged my shoulders, still overwhelmed by the beauty of the place.

"I think it goes much deeper than that," Anna said. "This wasn't the first idea of what they wanted built here. Going back a few more years, this area was supposed to be a massive satellite complex for the university downtown. They wanted to get out of the downtown area, somewhere more accessible and cleaner, and this fit the bill perfectly."

"I never knew that," I replied.

"Dad didn't buy those houses until the rumors started to circulate," Anna said, lowering her voice. "He sat on some advisory board to the university. He knew about it and went and bought up all the houses before word got out, I'm sure he was hoping they would skyrocket in price and he could make a bundle selling them. Problem is, Eddie owned some of the bars around here back then."

"Eddie owned bars?" I asked.

"He owned six bars and nightclubs throughout the city," Anna said. "He was a real sleazebag too. There's talk he had people pushing drugs and running prostitutes out of them. He was busted a number of times for gambling but never got in any real trouble."

"What happened to the bars?"

"He did get busted for a large deal of cocaine being sold and the money being laundered through the bars. He was forced to sell the bars and clubs, at a pretty good profit, and used that money to start his real estate development and construction firms. He never even got a slap on the wrist. The rumor is his first wife was a hooker he fell in love with, but after a couple years she took him for everything he was worth."

"I never knew any of that," I said. "What's it got to do with your father? Why didn't the university build here?"

"See, that's the thing! The university was dealing on the land but it fell through. They found out Dad bought the houses and decided if they built here they could get in trouble. He blew it for them. They ended up going to the south of town, which was empty and open into the prairie, surrounded by farms, but in the last few years it has been surrounded by urban sprawl. I'm betting it was someone from the university who wanted revenge for what happened. They could have had an amazing campus here, something very distinct in a pleasant setting but instead they got a cheap, franchised version of it."

"That's quite a leap," I said. "I mean, it could be possible, but would you even know who to start investigating?"

"There are some names I'm going to look at."

"Why was your dad so opposed to this complex?"

"He always hoped the university would come back," Anna said. "I don't know, but it's a start. Come on, let's get some drinks and dinner. Maybe we can find a couple of good men in these places tonight."

Chapter #6

The Prairie Bar

Anna led me into a bar with old western saloon-style swinging gates on the entrance. The inside was decorated to look just like a bar from the old west; wood floors and walls, knotty pine, wagon wheels, and antlers decorated the walls, and there was a mechanical bull in the corner ready for all comers to challenge it. A player piano was wailing out a western tune while the bartender and wait staff were milling about as there were no other patrons in the Prairie Bar yet.

Anna looked over the décor of the place and smiled. A place like this, something weird and out of the norm, was right up her alley. This was not the bar for me. I would much prefer polished mahogany, plush carpets, lounge music, and red wines. Anna walked over to a taller table with four seats and sat down. I took one more look over the interior of the bar and restaurant before taking my seat next to Anna.

Our waitress walked over with the menus and I had to hold back from laughing. She was a very pretty girl—tall and Asian, with straight black hair and tanned skin. Her outfit looked very comical though—cowboy boots, jean shorts, a black tank top with the Prairie Bar name and logo on the chest, a deputy's badge, and a pair of holsters on her belt with a toy six-shooter in each. Anna could have pulled off the look, I could have too, but this was a mock western bar that was staffed with Asian college kids.

"What you'll have 'night y'all?" the waitress asked as she gave us menus.

"A water and a dirty Martini," Anna said.

"Water and a Tom Collins," I said, as I took the menus from the waitress.

The waitress smiled and rushed over to the bartender—a young black man, college-age, who was dressed in a gray suit with a matching ten-gallon hat and sheriff's badge. Anna saw what I was looking at and smiled.

"It worked in 'Blazing Saddles'," Anna laughed. "What do you think of this place?"

"I give it two years," I said, looking around, "before it's closed down and turned into a normal bar. This gimmick isn't going to last long. I doubt they will get any regular customers. This is a gimmick bar for bachelor parties and parents with unruly kids to visit once for a lark, but it's not a place a husband and wife who go out twice a week are going to have in their regular schedule."

"I find it charming," Anna said. "It's got character...and a lot of characters working for it. If the food is good then I bet a lot of people will be coming here. I bet after games at the arena this place will be packed."

"I wish them the best," I said, looking at my menu, everything was beef and looked to be very large meals. "But it's not a place I would want to own."

The waitress returned with our drinks, setting them in front of us before pulling out a pad and a pen, "Ladies know what y'all want?"

"We'll both have the Prairie Burger and fries," Anna said, not even looking at the menu. "Cooked medium for both."

"Coming right up," the waitress said, taking the menus away.

"What's the Prairie Burger?" I asked.

"No idea," Anna said, "but everyone I talked to said I had to order it and have it cooked medium. They all said this place has the best burgers in town."

"Well," I said, raising my glass in a toast, "here's to new restaurants and rekindling old friendships."

"I'll drink to that," Anna said, as we clinked our glasses together.

We both took a sip of our drinks. I could tell from Anna's expression that her drink was strong, as was mine. They were almost too strong—the bartender had burned the drinks. I could tell from the way he was moving that he wasn't a very experienced bartender. It made me nervous for the food. It's always a drag when a promising restaurant messes up your food, especially when it's something as easy as a burger.

"So, where do you start?" I asked as I put my drink down. "You have some information, where will you go from here?"

"I've been talking with a new cop on the force," Anna said, leaning in and lowering her voice. "Plus one who was investigating when it happened. I think with this new cop, he's open to certain ideas, exchanges for information..."

"Don't tell me you're going to sleep with a cop to gain access," I interrupted.

"It crossed my mind, but this guy, I mean for crying out loud he's only twenty-four and he's already got money problems," Anna said, with a laugh. "Married and a couple kids, bought a big house, filled it with crap they don't need, and bought her a sports car. He's swimming in debt with no chance of ever being able to get out without a little side action."

"So, a bribe here and there to find your way?" I asked.

"It's what makes the world go round honey," Anna said. "Even in cultures much more ancient than ours, things like that go on, yet for some of them it's the natural order of things. Each person has to make their own path in the world. Some choose to follow the path laid out for them, others follow paths that were created long before their time, and some make their own path. It's interesting to see how in some cultures, sex is viewed as a pleasure and therefore the more you have, and the more people you have it with, is viewed as a very good thing. Although, other places I've been I would have been beheaded when I was seventeen.

"The same goes for bribes and money. When I was with the monks, who had no money, they grew their own food and bartered for anything else they needed. They received gifts that they either used or traded with, but there's no waste, *nothing* goes to waste. I can't think back to how many times I've bought a top then never worn it, or something like that. Those people use everything they have, and I'll tell you this honey, they are a hell of a lot happier and more relaxed than we are. Nothing bothers them. Every day is a gift to them, a gift to enjoy. Even people are gifts to them, whether it's just talking to someone, spending a day together, or a sexual encounter, they view every person who comes into their life as a gift to be cherished. And I tell you this, it was very hard to leave after being treated like that."

"So, they weren't celibate?" I asked with a smirk.

"Not the group I was with," Anna replied. "But sex was very different, over there. It was an experience, something that was to be remembered. They don't have toys or weird positions and hang-ups about it. It is two people, connecting on a spiritual level, so much more than just a physical act. Much more than propagating the species. They teach that we can have enjoyment without attachment."

"If you found your Zen, or Nirvana, or whatever it is, then why are you back here?" I asked.

"I don't want to let myself grow stale," Anna said. "That was a big teaching I received in Tibet. You cannot rest, you always must be learning a new style. The soul will lose power and abilities if you allow yourself to get in a rut. The further you push, the stronger you become, until you are invincible...at which point, you will meet your God—and if you're not humble, showing gratitude and humility, you will be cast out. If you don't become strong then you will never meet God."

"What religion are you?" I asked.

"I'm still Christian," Anna replied. "But I have a broader view of what religion and God means. It can't be contained to a little box that says Catholic or Protestant. There's so much more out there you've not been exposed to."

"And have you found your happiness?" I asked.

"I have," Anna replied. "But there is a stirring in my soul. I'm doing this not to bring someone to justice, not to extract revenge on the people who did this, but to let my parents rest in peace. Imara, they deserve to have their deaths answered. I still have to ask the question, when the gunman came in, he simply walked into the room. The door wasn't broken down or anything. My parents didn't lock their room. There was a loaded gun in the headboard of the bed, inches away from Dad's hand, yet he didn't reach for it. Why? Anyone who knew Dad would have known he kept a gun nearby, so if he didn't know the person, why didn't he reach for his gun? I have to know the answer."

"Maybe there wasn't time," I said. "Maybe he thought he could talk his way out of it. He was telling the person to take whatever they wanted. Maybe he was trying to distract the gunman before grabbing it."

"Could be," Anna said. "But I've meditated on this for a long time and something doesn't sit right with me. I have to know."

"I understand your pain, Anna," I said. "I really do. I want you to know that I don't think you're crazy for digging into this. Say you bribe the cop...what information are you expecting to get?"

"He's going to bring me anything that's in the police station about the case," Anna said. "I want to know everything that happened, I want to see every form they filled out. There's a file that has all the notes, even the notes that were written down as the crime scene was being investigated. I want to see everything in that file. I want to know why no leads were followed, why no suspects were ever brought in for questioning. There has to be a clue there somewhere."

"And what about your dad's business connections?" I asked. "What about the university and what happened with the land?"

"I'm going to keep my eyes and ears open," Anna said. "Somewhere along the lines something will break. I know I should be able to uncover this. Once I have the information from the police file, I will have a lot more to go off of. That's why I want you with me. Imara, you could be really helpful looking over all the data. You have an eye for detail that doesn't miss a thing. I really need you to help me with this."

I smiled and took another sip of my drink. So far, I hadn't committed to helping and I wasn't sure if I wanted to. I thought it might be fun tagging along, helping out, but then Anna would try to find Dad—try to find something that explained what happened to my father and I wasn't sure I wanted to know. I smiled again and was about to speak but Anna beat me to the punch.

"There's something else," Anna said, softly. "This is the big one. I didn't know about it when I was younger, I didn't put the pieces together, but there is one clue that guarantees that this is a big situation. The morning after my parents were killed..."

Anna stopped as she was looking at someone who walked through the door. She had a very quizzical look on her face. I turned around and was taken aback by what I saw—well, by *who* I saw entering the bar. Even the bartenders in their western costumes were stunned at the pair walking in.

The first was a man—tall, over six feet, but I instantly noticed he was wearing black boots with platforms and heels, so he may not be all that tall after all. He was muscular though, a bulky body that was being carried in a dominate and confident posture. On second glance, I realized his bulk may have been from his costume—black trousers, a white long-sleeved shirt with a black vest, and a hooded black cloak with the hood thrown back. The man had white satin gloves and black mirrored sunglasses. He had the most wonderful mane of long jet-black hair that extended to his shoulder blades and matched the color of his full, thick beard.

His partner looked even stranger—a five-foot-nine strawberry-blonde whose curly locks dropped almost to her waist, wearing only a deep blue velvet leotard with black sheer stockings and black velvet gloves that extended to her defined biceps. On her feet were black, flat, over-the-calf slip-on boots made of the same velvet as the rest of her outfit. The girl, who looked to be in her mid-thirties, had an abundance of makeup on, all of it with glitter incorporated, she painted her lips ruby, blushed her cheeks pink, and formed a deep-blue glitter mask around her eyes. The pair looked very strange indeed.

As Anna and I gawked at these strangers walking into the bar, the man, who looked to be in his early fifties, scanned the bar. When he saw us, he almost did a double take. He looked almost shocked to see us sitting there, almost as if he had recognized us but in an instant I realized he thought the bar was going to be empty, like he didn't want people to see them around. The man smiled and walked over to us.

"And on this fine summer's eve I saw two ladies enjoying a drink while waiting for their supper," he said, in a deep, raspy voice that had a broken quality to it, like he'd suffered vocal damage in the past. His voice was so deep, and he spoke in a slow, fluid rhythm, like your head was being drenched with warm syrup. "Can you two lovelies help out poor, lost travelers like ourselves tonight?"

"And who might you be?" Anna asked.

"I am Malenko Pendragon," Malenko said.

"Aren't you great?" Anna asked with a smirk.

"Greater than you could ever imagine, my child," Malenko said. "Greater than anyone that you have ever met, or will ever meet in your lifetime."

"Interesting," I said, trying to contain my laughter. "Who's your friend?"

"She is Princess Aine," Malenko said, "and she is my assistant."

"You seem familiar," Anna said, looking at Malenko. "Why do I know you?"

"Malenko has traveled the world," he said, "seen many crazy things. You may have seen me on the internet though, as I have one of the most popular video channels, showing magic which the people in this country have never seen."

"That's it!" Anna exclaimed. "I remember the name. You were doing street magic in Bucharest Romania last year. You are really good."

"Romania is a very magical place," Princess Aine said, in an ethereal, heavenly voice. "The only place in the world to hold more magic than Romania is our Celtic homeland of Ireland."

"Is it in poor taste to ask you to do a trick?" Anna asked. "You were so good, Mr. Pendragon. My mind was blown at the stuff you were doing."

"Malenko is not a simpering pup who performs because some fan girl asks him to," Malenko said, with a crossed tone. "You may have seen Malenko Magic on the street but I can assure you that the people there had given me something in return. You wish to see Malenko's powers? What do you offer in return?"

"You want money?" Anna asked.

"I would think that someone like you," Princess Aine said, "with all your meditative and worldly training could offer us something more than money. You spent all that time in India training with monks and money is the best that you can offer us?"

The color left Anna's face. She was stunned, trying to string words together. The fact that this strange woman, and even stranger man, who'd yet to remove his sunglasses in the bar, knew where she'd been, that she'd been training with monks, left her shaken to the core. But I didn't jump to conclusions. I'd seen enough magic tricks to know that every magician was nothing but a con artist with a conscience.

"How did you know that?" Anna finally sputtered out.

"I have an eidetic memory," Aine said, softly. "You told us about your training when you watched The Malenko perform."

"Oh," Anna said, softly. "For a show of your magic, Malenko, I will tell you one of the five truths I learned during martial arts training in Tibet."

"Malenko accepts your terms," he said, producing a deck of cards almost out of nowhere. "I will shuffle and you will select one card, showing your friend, but no one else."

Malenko shuffled the cards. He mixed them up, then cut the pack four times, showing that he cut to an ace each time. He then reshuffled the pack, cut four times, showing the kings each time. He shuffled the pack a third time, using motions to make the cards almost look like they were cascading down a waterfall. The speed and skill in his hands had spoken to years of practice with cards.

He held out the pack and offered Anna the opportunity to choose one card. Anna pulled out a card and showed me the five of diamonds. Malenko shuffled the deck again before allowing Anna to place the card anywhere she wanted back in the deck. Malenko did some strange shuffles and weird cuts before he handed the deck to Princess Aine and stepped back.

"I'm going to test your poker face," the princess said. "I'm going to show you three cards while asking you if it is your card. I want you to say 'no' every time I ask if it's your card. Do you understand?"

"Yes."

"Okay then," the princess said, as she cut the pack into three piles and set them on the table before holding up the first pack, showing us the bottom card, a two of hearts. "Is this your card?"

"No," Anna said, with a smile, as Aine took the two and placed it face down in front of the pack.

"Is this your card?" Aine said, holding up the middle pack showing a king of spades.

"No," Anna said, as Aine placed the pack back on the table, with the king facedown in front of it.

"Is this your card?" Aine asked, showing Anna the third pack with the five of diamonds, her card, on the bottom.

"No," Anna said. "That's not my card."

"Interesting," Aine said, as she placed the five facedown in front of the third pack. "You've revealed much to me Anna, in fact, you've given me everything I need to have you figured out. You see, this isn't your card," Aine flipped the two of hearts over, "and this isn't your card," Aine said, as she flipped the king of spades over, "and this, certainly isn't your card," Aine said, as she flipped the third card over, which had changed into the five of clubs.

Anna's eyes went as big as dinner plates, looking in confusion as to how the five had changed from her five of diamonds into the five of clubs. Aine had a smug smile on her face, knowing that she'd taken Anna in hook, line, and sinker on the trick. I was as confused as Anna. Aine picked up the three packs, gave them a quick shuffle, and looked into Anna's eyes.

"Pick a number between one and ten," Aine said.

"Seven," Anna replied.

"One...two...," Aine started counting as she peeled a card off the bottom of the deck of cards for each number she counted, "three...four...five...six...and seven."

Aine flipped the seventh card over; it was the five of diamonds.

"This is your card, Anna," Aine said, with a smile. "You have a horrible poker face. Please don't play cards in Vegas, I'd hate to see you lose your money."

"Does our magic meet your standards?" Malenko asked.

"That was amazing," Anna said. "How the hell did the five of diamonds get buried so deep into the deck? It doesn't make any sense."

"It doesn't," Malenko said. "But explaining the magic wasn't part of the terms nor will it ever be. We upheld our end of the bargain Anna, do you uphold yours?"

"I learned in training that one should never attack offensively for gain," Anna said. "The man who is fighting for what he has to lose will fight harder and more aggressively than the one who is looking to gain riches. Position yourself as a fierce opponent who defends their ground at all cost. This way, attackers looking to get rich will learn of your tenacity and seek out lesser targets."

"A wise lesson," Princess Aine said. "You and I look to be of comparable size, although you have the height and weight advantage, I have the age and experience advantage. Would you welcome a contest against me? Winning terms to be discussed?"

"I cannot," Anna said. "An injury prevents me from competing again. If I was healthy I would love to test you."

"Princess Aine," Malenko said, firmly, "Malenko must remind you that we are here on business, not pleasure."

"Business?" I asked. "What kind of business would you two have here?"

"Word has traveled through the land that this fine Front Street Gallery and Entertainment Complex is opening its doors very soon. A grand opening that will be remembered for the ages."

"That's the whole point of this place," Anna said. "To be remembered through the ages."

"What do you mean?" Aine asked.

"Mayor Jimmy Nelson and Eddie Hayes," Anna said. "They plastered their names all over this Gallery. The Nelson Theatre, Hayes Arena, Jimmy Nelson Avenue, please, it's disgusting the proverbial blow job these guys are giving themselves so their names will live on in the community."

"You are cynical," Malenko said. "One would think that with all your training and world experience you wouldn't hold such hostilities toward such an innocent place like this."

"Nothing about this place is innocent," Anna said. "And I'm not going to discuss my reasons with you. My reasons for hating this place are my own."

"Fair enough," Malenko said. "Malenko and Princess Aine are here to unveil a new breed of Malenko Magic. Malenko has traveled the world for many lifetimes learning everything there is to know about magic. Malenko and the princess have seen all the greats, read all the classics, and we've developed a routine that will be remembered in the annals of magic history forever. It is here, in the Front Street Gallery, on the grand opening night, Malenko wants to take the stage and show the world the new, Malenko Magic."

"Back up and hold the damn phone, place the president on hold, and watch the family gold," Anna said. *"Malenko has traveled for many lifetimes?"*

"Malenko is the tenth reincarnation of the greatest wizard to ever live...Merlin, from the Arthurian legend," Malenko said. "Merlin was born of the queen of magic. Each lifetime he takes a new form. This lifetime the form is Malenko Pendragon."

"So, Malenko...do you suffer from insanity...or do you enjoy every minute of it?" I asked, trying not to laugh.

"I assure you Malenko is not insane," Princess Aine said. "He is the greatest magician to ever walk the earth."

"So, what's your story?" Anna asked Aine. "How many times have you reincarnated?"

"None," Princess Aine said. "I was thirty-two years old—an average girl by all measures, except for my stunning beauty. I was a farm girl in the highlands of Ireland when Merlin came looking for the rock to build Stonehenge. He didn't find the rock he wanted in my land, but he found me. We made love under a sky full of shooting stars and since then I have never aged. Never died. When Merlin dies I must walk the earth alone, waiting for him to come back, to reincarnate, and to grow of age where our love can blossom again. Sometimes I find him, sometimes my heart is so heavy with sadness that I cannot go on."

"Okay..." Anna said, raising her left eyebrow. "This is kinda creepy. Imara, isn't that *so* a story that my dad would come up with?"

"It is," I replied with a laugh. "Except your dad would have a part about someone being too trusting and getting cheated over."

"Right."

"Mock if you will," Malenko said. "Malenko cares not. All Malenko requests is to know who he would have to talk to about booking the opening night in the theater!"

"The Mayor," I said.

"Yeah," Anna chimed in, "Jimmy Nelson. He hangs out at city hall. There may be some crime there you can help them with, Merlin."

"Malenko does not answer to Merlin," Malenko said, with a ting of rage in his voice. "You can jest all you wish but Malenko is not an entity to be trifled with. You have not seen magic like Malenko Magic before. Be warned, Malenko has arrived."

"We'll consider ourselves warned," I said.

With that, Malenko and Princess Aine spun on their heels and strutted out of the bar. Anna and I couldn't contain our laughter until they were out the doors, both of us roaring with laughter until we were crying, making fun of the spectacle we'd just seen. Even the bartender and waitresses of the bar were joining us in laughter. We laughed until our food showed up. Prairie Burgers—a half-pound of hamburger, four strips of bacon, two slices of ham, four slices of American Cheese, lettuce, pickles, black olives, peppers, mayo, mustard, and ketchup. More than either myself or Anna could have ever dreamed of eating in one sitting. It took all of our control to stop laughing and start eating; *Malenko had arrived.*

Chapter #7

Memories

It was a quiet afternoon in the store. Jack was handling the floor while Sarah and I were looking through the books. After Sarah had gotten her life cleaned up she got an accounting degree from a community college and worked in the accounting department of a smaller office supply company. She still came in part time and handled the books for the store, which was something I could never keep straight on my own. I loved having her work with me. I only wished we did enough business that I could employ her full time.

We always worked swiftly together, with her pouring over the documents and entering everything in the computers, giving me a sheet at the end that told me how the store was doing. I would be there to answer any questions that she had, to help make sure everything was entered in the right area, and to make sure our tracking system showed which larger groups bought what clothing and when. It was a good system that kept the store running smoothly and kept the clients very impressed when I pulled up files showing exactly what they bought and when. I suppose there were software programs and other systems out that could handle it, but with so many specialty items and not a lot of money for systems like that, handling it with Sarah seemed best.

"You've had a good month," Sarah said, looking over a sheet that had just been spit out of the printer. "If I'm not mistaken, last month was the best month for the store, ever."

"We had some big productions in the area," I replied. "The local college needed over one hundred different outfits. They completely restocked their theater department. It's good for last month but they blew their budget and won't be back this year. It's a tradeoff."

"You got some real capital to work with, 'Ara," Sarah said. "Now would be the time to put some more into the online division. You could really take this store to the next level."

"I don't know about that," I replied.

"What do you mean?" Sarah asked.

"I spend so much time here the way it is," I said. "There's really not much else in my life. I want to get away from the store from time to time, not chain myself to it further."

"I understand," Sarah said. "But the numbers come up a little more and you could hire another full-time worker. Right now it's just you and Jack, with your four part-timers filling in. Another full-time worker and you could start getting more time off."

"And if things slowed down?" I asked. "There isn't enough of a cushion to absorb a slowdown in business. Not if we hire another full-time worker."

"That's why you need to push further," Sarah said. "You could possibly kill two birds with one stone. See, thing of it is, these books are getting to be more than I can in the ten hours a week that I'm doing them. If I was hired on full time here, with an agreed upon forty-five to fifty hours a week, I could do the books and work sales."

I was stunned. Sarah had never before asked to come to work full time. It was something I'd dreamed about—she and I, sisters, running the store together. I could make her a partner and we'd share control and operations of the store. I knew there would be problems here and there, it wouldn't be perfectly smooth, but I also knew we could make it work and make our parents proud. I smiled at Sarah.

"You want to work here full time?" I asked. "What about your job? I thought you really liked it. Why are you looking to leave?"

"It's complicated," Sarah replied after a brief pause.

"Try me," I said.

"There are two coworkers that are getting into drugs pretty heavily," Sarah said. "They can handle everything now, but it's only a matter of time before they are out of control. I've caught one of them snorting in the bathroom. The manager has developed a thing for me, always wanting to be near me, asking me weird questions. Another lady who works there, one of the sales gals, she told me that even though he's married, he gets kinky on the side...weird stuff. I want no part of it."

"You need to go above their heads," I said. "Let them know about drug use on company time. Tell your HR rep that the manager is being inappropriate around you."

"Ya know," Sarah said, not hiding the annoyance in her voice, "that's what everyone says to do but it really doesn't work that way."

"What do you mean?"

"I tell the company about the drug use," Sarah said. "It's not their fault, they are victims of a drug culture, so they get a free month in rehab to learn about new drugs and better ways to hide them before they come back to work with the bitch who turned them in. Their dealers, who lose money, are now looking for the reason their good clients are no longer there. 'Ara, I've been through this game on their end. I turn the manager in and he's pissed and tries to shit-job me until I leave, making it hard to find a job elsewhere when my future interviewers talk to him.

He shows them my record and I'm out the door, no chance of getting hired. The world is a shit place. I mean, look what we've been through...look what Anna went through. There are a lot of bad people in this world and it seems like the world is setup to protect the bad guys and the not innocent. We have to make our own way and can't rely on anyone else. What do you think, Imara. Do you think there could be a spot in the store for me?"

"I'm not going to say no," I reply. "I need to think about it. If we start expanding more, what can we get into? I mean, most years the two months before Halloween make us enough money to fund the rest of the year...we have to hire extra help and have extended hours. I'll think about it, Sarah. I really will."

"Thank you, 'Ara," Sarah said. "Hey, I know a great way to earn some extra business, let's find that Malenko jackass you were talking about and give him free costumes for his show in exchange for advertising during the performance."

"I bet he would take it," I said, with a smile. "He was so strange, talking in the third person, claiming to be reincarnated from Merlin. It takes all kinds, I guess."

"What did the area look like?" Sarah asked. "The Front Street Gallery, I mean. Is it pretty nice?"

"It's amazing," I said, thinking back to it. "If you like that fancy, flashy style. It had a certain character to it, but no warmth, no soul. It was like it was saying, 'Hey, I'm here, all flashy, and I want you to spend all your money here, right now!' I guess you could compare it to, like, when you see a really attractive woman, who's got a killer body, amazing features, a great look along with a great energy, but then she's wearing some trashy, whore-like come-fuck-me outfit to make sure all the desperate losers are staring at her the entire time. It's like, they're trying way too hard and projecting everything they want right out there but it's not that great of a deal. Make sense?"

"I think I get what you're saying," Sarah said. "It's the modern world—cheap and flashy, no concern for the humans, just the technology behind them."

"Something like that," I said, as we looked back to the books.

As we continued going through the books, I looked over my little office. The wall with the door had four four-drawer filing cabinets. Along with the door, the cabinets took up the entire wall. There was a secondhand metal desk from a thrift shop, with a new leather office chair I had bought for myself. A pair of laptop computers and two utilitarian chairs on the opposite side of the desk were the only other major items in the office. It was a tiny space, painted a strange shade of brown with a tiled floor. There were old movie posters from the fifties and sixties on the wall, Dad's collection of classic sci-fi memorabilia, and a hand-made wooden clock on the wall behind the desk Dad received as a gift from a customer from overseas.

With both Sarah and myself in the office, the room was cramped. The desk wasn't a big desk, simply a standard size, but one side was pushed up against the wall and the other was so close to the wall on the other side that I had to turn sideways to get around it to my chair. I liked my office, it had a charm, a warmth that was inviting and spoke to the character of the people who used it. It would be nice to have a large office, to not have stacks of old papers around, since there was no place for them. I could use old cardboard boxes as extra filing drawers, but it was my home and I liked it. A new store in the gallery would have more room, but this place has memories and it's where I wanted to be.

"So, how was Anna in there?" Sarah asked, bringing me back to the room. "She was okay being in the gallery?"

"It didn't bother her," I said. "I really couldn't tell. She's not exactly the same girl I used to have sleepovers with, Sarah. She's really grown up and changed."

"I just meant," Sarah continued, "that with everything that's gone on, I didn't think she would want to be in that area. Her father had those houses and that real estate there and all."

"If it bothered her, I didn't notice it," I said.

"So, she thinks it might be because of the university?" Sarah asked. "There could be some bad blood from when her Dad bought the houses."

"They were going to expand there," I said, trying not to sound annoyed. "Mike knew they were going to be expanding there so he bought up some property while it was still cheap. If plans would have moved ahead, the university would have announced their expansion plans then started to make offers on the land. They would have offered a good price and Mike would have made a good bundle of money in a short timeframe. They found out he had bought the land there, and they backed out. If someone found out about it there could be accusations and other problems. They thought it best to walk away and find a different location."

"He did okay though," Sarah said. "I don't remember Anna ever needing anything. They always had money."

"They did."

"What do you think Dad would have wanted us to do?" Sarah asked. "Would he be happy with the way things went down with Mom? Is this the life he wanted for us?"

"It doesn't matter what he wanted for us," I said. "It only matters what we want. I keep thinking back to that night. He sounded so strange on the phone, like he was in a

78

hurry to hang up. He sounded like he'd been working out—he was breathing heavy. I just wish I knew what it meant. He didn't take his car that night, so I thought he was just out of breath from running to the store and there could have been some major client throwing a fit and he didn't want to keep them waiting...but then again, it could have been something else."

"I just wished I knew why he didn't want us," Sarah said. "I mean, I guess, I can understand not wanting me, with all the problems I was having at the time."

"Don't say that," I said, looking Sarah in the eyes. "Don't ever say that. He loved you just like he loved me. We talked about ways to get you help. He hired that person to talk to you. We were planning a full intervention if that didn't work."

"I know," Sarah said. "Some days I wonder though. Maybe he just had a lot of secrets to hide. What do you think he'd say to us if he walked into the store today?"

"He'd be pleased as punch with your recovery," I said, with a smile. "And I would have to think he'd be very impressed with the store and how well it's doing. I think Dad would be proud of us."

"Do you ever wonder if he checks in from time to time?" Sarah asked. "Like, in disguise, or maybe from a distance? Do you think he watches what we're doing, making sure we are okay?"

"It's a nice thought, but then he would see how much pain he's caused us," I said. "Sarah, do you want to have Anna help us find him?"

"Yes I do," Sarah said instantly. "And he's your father...Dean is your dad, too. You should want to find him, 'Ara. No matter what happens, we should know what happened to him. We deserve that much."

"I suppose you make a good point," I said. "The only problem is I have nothing to go on. I've exhausted every lead I ever had. There've been no new developments in eight years. That's why I think he's dead, there's been nothing for so long. Even if he were alive, I don't know at all where to start."

"Anna said the cops have files they didn't release to us," Sarah said. "About her father's death. Maybe there was something there they know about. We could have her cop friend get information for us."

"I have a real problem bribing officers," I said. "It sounds all well and good, the guy's in debt and needs help, but if we got caught we could get into a lot of trouble. You know damn well he would sell us out, too, if anyone ever found out about it. He would just say he was setting us up for whatever reason. You cannot afford to get in trouble again. If you get tangled up in something like that and a judge sees your prior record you will never see the light of day again."

"'Ara, they're not going to throw me in jail for getting information from a cop," Sarah said. "I just don't know what other ways we can go about this. If we are going to find the information, we need to get into those files."

"Do we even know if those files contain anything useful?" I asked. "Anna has yet to see anything from them. Who knows, maybe we already know everything there is. One other problem, let's say this is the big conspiracy everyone thinks it is, what happens when the locked files start to go missing? The people involved in the cover-up will know someone is trying to expose them. Wouldn't that make them take extra steps to cover their tracks and possibly begin to take more extreme measures to make sure their secrets aren't found out?"

"You make a good point," Sarah said. "But on the other hand, no one knows we're doing this yet, so we have the advantage. If there is murder and kidnapping, or something along those lines, we owe it to our dad to let him rest in peace. Maybe he's still being held captive somewhere. Would you just sit here if you knew he was in pain?"

"There are so many things that could have happened Sarah," I said. "And 'Occam's razor'...the simplest answer is usually the correct one. There was another family, another woman, and he chose her and them over us."

Sarah was about to reply when Jack quickly knocked on the door and entered the office before I had a chance to answer him. Jack was in rare form today, his suspenders over his flannel shirt with his scruffy sandy beard made him look like a mountain man, minus the axe. He had a flustered look on his face.

"Imara," Jack said, speaking softly. "There's a man here who says he needs to talk to you. He says it's very important."

"Okay," I said, with a sigh, as I got up. "Keep running the numbers, Sarah. I'll think about what you said...everything you said."

I walked out of the office and quickly slipped into the bathroom to check my hair and makeup in the mirror. Like always, I had just enough makeup on to look like I wasn't wearing any. I teased my curly brunette hair as I looked myself over. I had my black tights with a black sleeveless tunic, something I'd found that was made to resemble clothing worn in the middle ages. I gave myself a wink, ready to sell, and headed out to the sales floor.

As I walked out I saw a distinguished looking man in a dark gray suit glancing over some of the clothing. His back was toward me but I could see that he had jet black hair, trimmed short and neat, a powerful body, tall, and was one hell of a snappy dresser. The suit and his dress shoes were top rack all the way. I got close to him before I said anything.

"Excuse me," I said, with a smile. "Good day to you, sir. I'm Imara. Is there anything I can help you with?"

"How about a broken heart?" the man asked in a deep smooth voice.

"Pardon me?" I said, getting my hand ready to slap his face when he turned around. "I think you're in the wrong location for that."

"Am I?"

The man turned around and my heart skipped a beat. It wasn't the flat, squareish face, not the blocky head or the perfect nose. It wasn't the bushy eyebrows that needed to be plucked or the large hands. It was the eyes, the emerald eyes so dark they almost appeared black, yet twinkled with an excitement that said something wonderful was about to happen. I recognized him the second I looked into his eyes. It was my ex-boyfriend, the man who meant more to me than any other man, save for my father, Mark Lewis. It had been almost seven years since we'd broken up, and that long since we'd seen each other. Without thinking, running on pure emotion, I rushed to Mark, embraced him, and planted a kiss on his lips.

Chapter #8

Lost Love

My mind was swimming as I pulled back from Mark. His eyes—his perfect emerald green eyes, were huge. The kiss had surprised him as much as it had surprised me. I took a step back from him as the silence that hung over the entire scene became unbearable. I didn't know what to do or say. I could feel the warm blood rushing to my cheeks. I was blushing with a confused look on my face. Mark's face looked like mine, blushing and confused. He was the one who came here, he should be the one prepared for the consequences of his arrival. I wasn't going to speak until he spoke first.

"Not what I had in mind sugar, but I believe that works," Mark said, with a smug grin.

"Don't ever call me sugar again," I said, as I punched Mark in the arm, half playful, half serious. "You lost the right to call me that when you left me here alone."

"Oh," Jack said, way too enthusiastically. "This must be the infamous Mark. You were right, Imara...he does have dreamy eyes."

I shot Jack a look that could have frozen boiling water, "his eyes aren't *that* dreamy...I mean, this isn't *that* Mark. This *is* a Mark, not *the* Mark."

No one was convinced by the sound of my voice. Mark had a smile on his face and he knew he had me.

"Look Imara," Mark said, holding a hand up. "There's no reason this should be awkward. Why don't you and I go get a cup of coffee or something? I just want to talk to you."

"Careful, 'Ara," Sarah said, emerging from the back office. "He's got a habit with you. *Talking* leads to so much more."

"Thank you, Sarah," I said, rolling my eyes.

"Sarah?" Mark said, looking at my little sister. "Is that really you? My, you look a lot better than the last time I saw you. How are things going?"

"Sober," Sarah said. "Thank you."

"I think a cup of coffee would be fine," I said. "Jack, show Sarah some finer points of running the store. I may be moving her up from doing more than just the books."

"Sure thing Imara," Jack said.

"'Ara," Sarah said, with a serious voice. "Thank you...and call if you need anything, okay?"

"I will."

I took a quick look around the store then walked out the front door, hardly waiting for Mark to keep up with me. I started walking down the street toward the coffee shop that was just a little over a block away. As I was walking, I looked at my reflection in a shop window and realized Mark was walking two paces behind me. He was keeping his distance, but following me nonetheless. I smiled, realizing how much I still liked him but wanting to make sure I kept my head around him.

I walked into the small coffee shop that was almost empty, save for two college-aged kids who had their faces buried into laptop computers. The two workers were in their own conversation and barely paid attention to us when we walked in. I ordered a large house coffee, not feeling the mood for anything special. Mark ordered the same and paid for both. I smiled when he paid but picked up my cup and walked over to a table that had a good view of the busy street that the coffee shop sat on. I took my first sips of the scalding hot, very strong coffee in silence as Mark just looked at me. Again, I wasn't going to say the first words.

"I've missed you so much, Imara," Mark said, with a smile.

"Not enough to call or keep in contact with, apparently," I retorted. "Why now? What is it about this time on this day that makes you walk back into my life? I've fallen for your eyes so many times but I just don't think I have the strength to do it again."

"You've got more strength than you could ever know, Imara," Mark said. "There isn't anything you couldn't handle."

"You look good though," I said, ignoring his comments. "Tell me, what's going on? What brings you back to steady old Prairie Rapids?"

"I've finished," Mark said. "I actually finished."

"Finished?" I asked. "You mean, like, medical school?"

"Yes," Mark said, excitedly. "I'm a doctor now."

"I'm never calling you 'Doctor Mark'," I said, with a smile. "You can forget about that right now."

"I'm not excepting you to," Mark said. "I just finished my residency out in New York and I've been hired at the new hospital they built right outside the Front Street Gallery."

"Is there anything that place doesn't have?" I asked. "I didn't know they were putting a hospital there."

"Well," Mark said, shyly. "It's only a clinic. I'll be doing physicals, checkups, things like that. There's a walk-in clinic for sick people who can't wait but don't want to go to the emergency room. And it's not *in* the gallery, it's a couple blocks away, past the mall. I'm excited though. Now I get to start paying off all those student loans that I acquired."

"What happened to being the world's foremost child surgeon?" I asked. "I thought you wanted to be a pediatrician?"

"Dreams come and go," Mark said. "The competition to get into that field is intense right now. I thought this would be the best way to go...start small and work from there."

"I'm happy for you," I said. "I really am. I'm also glad you're back in the area. I know your parents missed you while you were out in the real world."

"Hey," Mark said. "Don't start with that shit again. You could've come with me if you wanted to. You didn't have to stay here. I know you wanted to be a doctor with me. You were going to travel the world being a doctor for the World Health Organization."

"That was the dream of an innocent little girl," I said. "And that little girl had to grow up in a real hurry."

"I couldn't stay at state college here," Mark said. "You know that. I wanted to stay with you but I had my own dreams. They didn't have a good enough pre-med program. I had to go for myself."

"You didn't have to go to New York though," I said. "There are schools that are closer. We could have been a couple hours away, not half a country away."

"I know," Mark said. "But I wanted to be the best, so I had to go to the best school...look, I don't want to argue. That's not what I came here for. The store looked to be doing well. I've never seen so much stuff in it. How's it been going there?"

"Amazing," I said. "I've expanded and moved online. We're doing much better than when Dad had the store. I really enjoy it."

"So, in a way it's worked out well for you?" Mark asked.

"I don't know if I would say that," I replied. "But I have found my happiness. You know, it's really strange, not two weeks ago, guess who walks in the store? Anna Garst. I haven't seen her in over eight years. The last time I saw her was the night everything happened. She's back in town, and now you show up. The three of us need to get together and hang out one night, it will be like old times again."

"That would be great," Mark said. "I don't know about Anna though. She was always weird around me."

"That's because she really liked you but didn't do or say anything because you were with me," I replied. "I mean, she *really* liked you back in the day."

"She was always a nice girl," Mark said. "A little strange but nice. They ever find out what happened to her parents?"

"Never," I replied. "That's why she's back. She's trying to figure out who killed them and why. She's got some leads and is looking into some things."

"You ever hear from Dean again?" Mark asked.

"No," I said, shortly. "He never made any attempts to contact us. As far as I'm concerned, my father's dead."

"I'm sorry to hear that," Mark said. "But what about you? How are you doing?"

"I'm good," I said. "I've dedicated myself to the store and fashion. I still do a little boarding but no more competitions, it's just for fun. What about you? How are you doing? Do you have a girlfriend or wife following you here?"

"No, I don't," Mark said. "I broke up with a great lady two weeks ago. We'd been dating for almost seven years."

"Seven years?" I asked confused. "I need to know the whole story. No skimping on the details."

"You sure you want to hear this?" Mark asked.

"Yeah," I said. "I need to hear every word of it."

"When I got to New York she was living in my apartment building," Mark said. "She was studying to be a registered nurse. Things started off hot and heavy between us, couldn't keep our hands off each other, were always together, planning on how we were going to live our lives together, we'd be working together in the hospital. It wasn't four months and we were living together, picking out an apartment to make our own. It was a really good time."

"Was she hot?" I asked with a smile. "What was her name?"

"You couldn't believe how hot Amanda was," Mark said, with a grin. "She was a university cheerleader, five foot five, fire-red hair with the sexiest freckles on her soft white skin..."

"Sexiest freckles?" I asked, skeptically. "Really?"

"You have no idea," Mark said. "Amanda was a real pistol. She was a football cheerleader and was the tumbler. She could do flips in the air and get caught on the ground— totally fearless, absolutely flawless. It was breathtaking watching her preform. We were so in love and everything was wonderful."

"Why do I get the sense that something tragic is about to happen?" I asked.

"Amanda got pregnant," Mark said. "Ya know, sometimes condoms break. It happens."

"Why is that tragic?" I asked.

"Have you ever seen a cheerleader flying through the air pregnant?" Mark asked.

"Good point," I said.

"Her family couldn't afford college and without her scholarship she couldn't stay in school," Mark said. "Amanda got a job as a licensed practical nurse, as we started wondering how we were going to fit a baby in our one-bedroom apartment. I had my academic scholarships but it wasn't enough. I was thinking about dropping out of college and getting a job. We knew it would hold us back the rest of our lives, but we had to do what was best for the baby."

"What happened?" I asked.

"About seven months in, Amanda started having stomach pains," Mark said. "It started slow but within a couple hours the pain was so great she couldn't stand it. I rushed her to the hospital where they tried some things but the baby was gone. Dead. Just one of those things, ya know? They really don't even know what happened, could never give us an explanation."

"That's why you didn't study as a pediatrician, right?"

"Exactly," Mark said. "Amanda worked her ass off and got back into shape to get her scholarship back but it never worked out. Something with the way the rules are set up, I don't know. Amanda had her tubes tied so she would never have to go through that again, saying that we would adopt when we were ready, if I wanted a child with my blood we could work something out, find an egg donor to work with or something. Our relationship was never the same. There was always this black cloud hanging over us. It was a horrible time."

"My God," I said. "I'm so sorry. I couldn't imagine something like that happening."

"About a year after, we went to counseling together," Mark said. "Things improved...not like they were in the beginning but we were feeling better, seeing that there was some good in the world and we were both moving on. We had some good times together. About a year or so ago, Amanda started getting the urge to have a child. We were engaged and had been planning a Vegas wedding sometime this summer.

"We started looking at adoption agencies but they wouldn't put us on the list until we were married. I was starting to look for work, which is hard to find right now. With graduation approaching there was a lot going on. I found the job out here but Amanda pitched a fit, she didn't want to move to Prairie Rapids. I'm not sure when, but she started seeing another man on the side. He was divorced with full custody of three kids. The kids were there and she could step in and be their mother.

"I tried everything I could to hold us together, but with finals and interviews and everything else, there wasn't enough time. I knew Amanda was lost to me but I wasn't going to give up without a fight...literally. I kicked the guy's ass in front of his kids. He didn't know about me or that Amanda was with someone else. It turned into a huge mess and I walked away. I don't know what happened to them."

I sat stunned, sipping my coffee as I tried to think of something to say. There was so much pain and suffering that didn't need to happen. At one time I loved Mark with every fiber of my being and would have gladly married him on the spot had he asked. Too many years and too much life had passed for me to keep those feelings for him though.

"I'm so sorry," I said. "And here I thought *I* had been through a lot. You really had the shit kicked out of you out there."

"I think it's karma," Mark said.

"Karma?" I asked. "For what? What could you have done that was bad enough to deserve all the stuff you got out there?"

"The way I treated you after your father disappeared," Mark said. "The way I left you here to go live my life while you had to take care of your mother and sister, wondering what happened to your father. It was a cowardly thing for me to do, Imara, and for that I'm sorry."

"You had to live your life," I said. "No harm, no foul. Was I pissed at you? Hell yes. I hated you for a long time but that's in the past, Mark. There's no reason we can't be friends again. With you in the area, and Anna back, it will be like old times."

"I wasn't thinking *friends*, Imara," Mark said, as I swallowed in a throat that was suddenly dry, I knew what was coming. "We should pick up where we left off."

"What?" I asked, cutting him off. "Drinking cheap beer your brother got us while doing blowjobs on the sofa in your parents' basement? Acting like teenaged fools while keeping one ear to the stairs to hear if they're coming to check on us? I think we're past that stage in our lives, thank you very much."

"That's not what I meant Imara," Mark said. "We loved each other at one time and there's no reason we couldn't love each other again."

"We were too young to know what love was, Mark," I said. "Yeah, it felt great but we were teenagers screwing around, hoping not to get caught. There's a big difference between that and two adults who are in love with each other."

"Will you at least give us the opportunity to see if there is anything there?" Mark asked. "If you have someone I will understand, but if not, there's no reason not to give love a chance."

"Why do people have to have love?" I asked. "I haven't dated since you, Mark. I'm happy with myself. One day, I do want to get married, but he needs to sweep me off my feet...not tell me that he loved me once eight years ago and now that he's had his heart crushed by someone else he wants to give it a try again. I'm no one's second place Mark."

"Imara," Mark said, trying to sound sincere, "I didn't mean it like that. All I want is the chance to see what is here."

"Nothing," I said. "Mark, there is nothing here. There hasn't been for seven years. You didn't write or call or visit. That tells me everything I need to know."

"Don't be mean about this," Mark said. "We had something great, don't deny it. I'm trying to find happiness in my life, a purpose in my life. Isn't that something that you want to? I can give that to you. I want to rekindle our lost love."

In one fluid motion I used my left hand to take the cover off my cup of coffee, and with the right I dashed the contents of the cup in Mark's face. Luckily it had cooled enough so it wouldn't burn him, but he still let out a scream of shock as the people in the little coffee shop looked at us. My eyes were burning fire through Mark. I was so mad I wanted to jump across the table and slap him. I knew I had to walk away before I got myself in trouble. Mark simply looked at me with sad eyes, not knowing at all what to say. I knew this time I would have to speak first.

"My life has a purpose," I said, with venom injected into every word. "I have happiness. I don't need some jackass like you coming in, warming me all up, just to leave again. You had your chance and you made your decision. Live with it."

With that, I strutted up to the two women who were working behind the counter. I dug into my wallet and pulled out a twenty-dollar bill. I tossed the bill on the counter and winked at the workers who were silently clapping for what I had just done.

"Sorry about the mess," I said, as I pushed the twenty toward them.

Without waiting for them to reply, and without looking back at Mark, I held my head up high as I did the most arrogant power strut that I could out of the coffee shop. Once I was clear of the windows of the coffee shop, I started running toward the costume shop, starting to cry about halfway there. I wasn't sure what brought it on—was it the way Mark had acted, or did I still love him and just resented the way he thought he would come back here and I would fall into his arms? Either way, once I got to my store, I slipped in through the back door so no one would see me. I locked myself in my office, and stayed there, crying, for over an hour.

Chapter #9

The Blood Begins to Flow

I had hoped to stay in my office all day, allowing Jack to run the store while I tried to figure out everything that was swimming in my head. The instant I saw Mark there was a spark—a connection that remembered all the fun and pleasure we had in the past, but in talking to him, I couldn't help but feel that we had gone in very different directions— not in our professional lives, but as humans. It felt like we were as different as a Manhattan Aristocrat and a suburban girl-next-door.

I knew that one day I would meet Mark again, see him and speak with him, but I didn't think it would go like that. He was always so strong and powerful before, the leader of the pack and never one to simper or ask. It was one of the things that drove me wild with passion when we were together as teenagers; he went for what he wanted without worrying about the consequences. He could light my heart on fire with his emerald eyes and make my soul dance with his mind-blowing kiss. But now he was just...something less.

I wondered if I was being too hard on him. To lose a child and discover that your fiancée is cheating would be a terrible blow to take, but I believed the Mark I knew and loved wouldn't have allowed things like that to destroy him. He would have made sure his fiancée was treated so well, so fulfilled there would be no way she would be looking for other men. I looked at the clock and it was almost five. I thought the best thing to do would be to go home, light a group of candles, draw a nice bubble bath, and soak while listening to some smooth jazz.

"You're not going to believe this shit," Anna burst into my office, not bothering to knock or anything. Her face was flushed and she looked frazzled. "This shit is major."

"What is it?" I asked as I tried to wipe the tears away from my eyes. Luckily, Anna was so worked up with her information that she didn't notice. "What's the deal?"

"Do you remember a man named Tim Krause?" Anna asked.

"Rings a bell," I said, thinking. "Why do I know that name?"

"He's a stooge for Jimmy Nelson," Anna said. "He's a whimpering lapdog of a pathetic man who doesn't have a single original thought in his brain. He hangs around guys he thinks are macho, in hopes that some of it will rub off on his pansy-ass."

"Why don't you tell me what you really think of him," I said, with a smile. "What's got you all worked up over him?"

"He's been a city council member for many years," Anna said. "About twelve, I think. He always does exactly what Jimmy wants, always reports to Jimmy on what the council is doing."

"So?"

"He was murdered," Anna said, coldly. "Not that the world is experiencing a great loss over it but there are some...complications. The cop that I've been seeing...working with...his name is Lund Grimes..."

"Lund?" I asked. "Really?"

"Lund has been giving me some information," Anna said. "He's a newer addition to the force, wasn't around when shit went down, but he's got access. He called me the second he left the scene. As I said, there's something you need to know about this murder."

I shifted in my seat, uncomfortable. I had a feeling I was about to be dragged into this whether I wanted to be or not. Anna was excited but beneath that excitement was distress, unmistakable fear. Something had gotten her worked up and I was guessing it wasn't Lund but something he had told her.

"What could possibly be important to me about some city council member getting killed?" I asked.

"There were some papers left at the scene," Anna said.

"Do they have a suspect?" I asked.

"Two, actually," Anna said.

"Who?"

"You and me."

And just like that, my mind went blank. I couldn't think—couldn't focus. How on earth could anyone suspect me of a murder I'd just heard about? I didn't even remember Tim Krause. I don't think I'd ever met the guy—if I did, he didn't leave enough of an impression on me for me to remember him. I simply fixed my eyes on Anna. She was wearing black sweatpants today, with a plain tank top. Her hair was in a ponytail, messy, and not styled. She wore no makeup and had the slightest bags under her eyes. Her clothing was wrinkled, she'd either just woken up or just gotten out of bed. The question was whether anyone was in the bed with her.

"How deep are you in with this cop?" I blurted out, probably the worst question I could have asked considering what she'd just told me.

"I'm not doing anything sexual with him," Anna said. "I swear to you. I've just been bribing him. I gave him $5,000 to tell me everything he knew and could find. He's keeping me informed."

"How did you transfer that much money to him?" I asked, still not getting on the right subject.

"We wrote a contract saying he was my bodyguard for an event," Anna said, flustered. "Damn it Imara, didn't you hear what I said? He called me while I was napping and said that you and I were the prime suspects. They are going to come and question us."

"I heard you, but I don't get it," I said. "Why are we the suspects?"

"Because of what was found with the body," Anna said. "Tim was supposed to be meeting people at the gallery today. He no-showed, so when they told Jimmy he called his contact on the police force and had them go to Tim's house. The doors and windows were locked from the inside. His wife and kids had been out all day. Tim was shot pointblank in the face with a shotgun…"

"Oh my God!" I exclaimed. "How could they know it was him? I mean, his face must be gone…just like your parents' faces were. How did they ID him so quickly?"

"He has some tattoos," Anna said. "His family said he was also in the same clothes. But the thing is, the room he was in was locked from the inside. There was no way anyone could have gotten out of the room after he died. The weapon hasn't been found. It was taken with the killer."

"That is tragic," I said. "Think of those kids, having to grow up without a father. I know what they are going through, no one deserves that. But it still doesn't explain why we are suspect."

"It fits with my parents' deaths pretty well," Anna said. "Same setup."

"That's not enough to link us to it," I said. "There has to be something else. You said something was found there, right?"

"There were two newspaper articles left with the body," Anna said. "The first was my parents' obituaries and the second was the write-up about your father's disappearance."

"Why the hell would anyone leave those on a dead body?" I asked.

"Very good question," Anna said. "Lund said there was something else. In them there were two names circled...yours and mine. The cops have nothing else to go on yet and they are under a lot of pressure from the mayor to get this handled quickly. He doesn't want a raincloud hanging over the grand opening of his Gallery."

There was simply too much to process. My mind froze up and I started to cry. I didn't know why I was crying nor could I control it, but the tears rolled down my cheeks. Anna rushed over to me and hugged me, trying to comfort me but there was really nothing to be said—no way to control what was happening. I had been at the store all day, except when I went to the coffee shop, so Jack and the workers at the shop would be able to account for my whereabouts all day. There was no way I would be in trouble over this.

"Do you have an alibi for the day, Anna?" I asked. "Can people account for you all day?"

"I was at the gym early this morning," Anna said. "Was lifting weights for about two hours before getting breakfast. After that I went to the hotel I've been staying at and have been in my room ever since. I was going over old articles and police files."

"The hotel has hall cameras, right?" I asked.

"It does," Anna replied. "Yes."

"Then we should both be good," I replied. "We will be able to prove we were nowhere near Tim when this happened."

"I hope you're right," Anna said.

I was about to reply when there was a knock on the open office door. I looked past Anna to see a man in a city police uniform standing next to a man in a plain gray suit with a white shirt and boring mauve necktie. The man in the suit had gray hair to match the suit, a gray mustache to match the hair, and many stress wrinkles in his leathery skin. He looked like a tough old brute, a no-nonsense man who did his job. I knew instantly that it was a police detective, an American Flag pinned to his lapel. Captain America was going to be the man investigating the crime. I swallowed in a dry throat, trying to dry my eyes again.

I noticed something that gave me a glimmer of hope though, a look exchanged between the police officer, a young lad in his mid-twenties, and Anna. His nametag said Officer Grimes. It was Lund, the man on Anna's payroll. He was cute, in that mid-twenties-buff-guy way, with a shaved head and rusty goatee. He looked over-enthusiastic yet seemed a good fit for a police officer. The detective simply stared at us for a moment.

"Interesting to find you two together," he said. "I'm sure you know why we're here but I bet you didn't think we'd get here this quickly. Why are you crying?"

"We're having an argument," I said, quickly, as I stood up and placed my arm around Anna's shoulder. She gave me a confused look. "Things haven't been going well for us. Why are you here? What's going on?"

"I'm detective Travis Lukens," Detective Lukens said. "There's been a murder and we want to ask you a few questions."

"Who's your puppy dog?" Anna asked, looking at Lund. "What right do you have to question us?"

"This is Officer Grimes," Travis said. "He's here in case things get out of hand. I need to know, what have you two been doing all day?"

"What right do you have to question us?" Anna asked. "Are we under arrest?"

"Not yet," Travis said. "Look at it this way, you're Anna Garst, right?"

"Yes," Anna replied.

"Well Anna," Detective Lukens continued, "the simple fact is that we have reason to believe you may know something about this crime. We want to, informally, I might add, question you to clear your name. By helping me here you will be helping yourself. Everything you say will be written down and kept for further investigations. Helping us is helping yourself."

"I've been here all day," I said. "I arrived at quarter-to-eight and have been here ever since, except for about a half hour while I got a cup of coffee. The shop is just a block to the west. They know me very well there and can vouch for us."

"And you, blondie?" Travis asked Anna.

"The name's Anna, Detective," Anna shot back with a glare. "I went to the gym at six, was there for two hours before getting breakfast at a nearby restaurant then went back to my hotel room, where I've been until I came here."

"Interesting," Travis said, as his hand scribbled down notes.

"What is this about?" I asked again. "Who was murdered and why would you would be coming to find us?"

"Show them the papers," Travis ordered Lund.

Lund reached into his pocket and pulled out two photos of the papers found at the crime scene. They were Anna's Parents' obituaries and the story of my dad's disappearance, written about two weeks after he'd gone missing. Just as Anna had said, our names were circled with ink. I looked from the picture to the detective.

"What does this mean?" I asked. "Why would you come to us with this?"

"Seems that someone thinks you might know something," Travis said. "I want to know what. Why would someone murder a person and leave these papers?"

"You're the detective," Anna said. "You tell us."

"Is there anyone out there that would want to hurt either of you?" Travis asked.

"Someone shot my parents eight years ago," Anna said. "I wasn't home, but in Imara's house. Maybe whoever did that, because they were never caught and I've never gotten closure from the case, maybe they are coming after me, wanting to finish the job, and they are going to kill Imara too, since she was the reason I wasn't home that night?"

"Interesting," Travis said. "I thought of that too."

"I know you!" Anna shouted, standing up straight and taking a step toward Travis. "You were nothing but a beat cop...a city police officer who was investigating my parents' deaths. I remember being questioned by you before, the night it happened. I remember you promised me you would find the killers."

"I remember that too, Anna," Travis said. "And I'm very sorry I've never brought anyone to justice for you. You have to understand, we did everything we could, Anna."

"It wasn't enough," Anna said.

"No," Travis replied, "it wasn't. But if this leads us to the killers, you'd want to help, correct?"

"Who was it that was murdered?" I asked.

"His name was Tim Krause," Lund said. "He's a city council member and sat on the board of directors for the Front Street Gallery and Entertainment Complex...and he sat on some other boards as well. He was a very important and respected member of the community."

"There are some...anomalies in how he was found," Travis said.

"Anomalies?" Anna asked. I was impressed with how well we were doing, not giving away that we knew this information and asking Detective Lukens to clarify.

"There is no discernible exit," Detective Lukens said. "It's like the killer escaped by magic or something. I've never seen anything like it before."

"How is Tim's family holding up?" Anna asked.

"Not very well," Lund said. "His wife found him in the upstairs bathroom."

"So, other people had been through the scene before police got there?" Anna asked.

"There were some," Travis said. "The wife and kids."

"You said there was no way anyone could have gotten out," Anna replied. "If they went through the house before you got there, isn't there a chance they could have changed things? Maybe they are so distraught that they don't even remember. I remember what I was like in the first few days after Mom and Dad died. I couldn't keep anything straight then."

"We've got a reconstruction team at the house now," Travis said. "They don't miss anything. Leave the police work to us, Miss Garst. I'll ask again, do you know anyone who would want to hurt you? A competitor with the store...an old enemy? Anything that you can think of would be helpful."

"There's no real competition that would care about me," I said. "Nothing that would do anything on that level. I can't think of anyone else who would hold a grudge against me."

"And your father was never found, correct?" Travis asked.

"That's correct," I replied.

"Is there any chance it could be him?" Travis asked.

"Yes," I replied as Travis's eyes got big. "The same percent chance that it was Bigfoot and Elvis working on a new murder novel so they decided to see what killing was really like. I haven't seen my father in eight years. As far as I know or am concerned, my father is dead."

"I'm sorry to hear that," Travis said. "If you two can think of anything, anything at all that could help in the investigation, please call right away." Detective Lukens reached into his pocket and pulled out two business cards, handing one to Anna and one to me. "My office and cell are on there, along with e-mail. The entire force is going to be working on this, so let me give you a small piece of advice, the mayor wants his grand opening to be perfect. If you are withholding anything that could help us or you get in the way, the consequences will be very severe. Thank you for your time."

With that, Travis and Lund walked out of the office. I was stunned, looking at the card he'd handed me. I couldn't believe they would think we would be behind something like this or that we would hold information. Anna had a smile on her face, something that told me she knew something.

"What is it?" I asked.

"Did you hear the fear in his voice?" Anna asked. "The desperation in his eyes? There's more to it. Lund told me. I was going to tell you before they came in. There was a note, words cut from old newspapers that said, 'the show is just beginning.' They know there are going to be more murders. Imara, this isn't over. The blood begins to flow and the victims will fall like ripened wheat."

"Do you think we are safe?" I asked.

"I don't know," Anna said. "Someone wants us to be afraid though. Why else would they put those papers there and circle our names. I'm wondering if we are going to have a police tail on us. That would make my investigation much harder."

"What if it *is* my dad?" I asked. "What if he was kidnapped by the city council and has now escaped and is extracting revenge?"

"Then they would know he's escaped and would be looking for him," Anna said. "Lund told me we are suspects yet also on a victims-watch list."

"Victims-watch list?" I asked.

"They made a list of everyone they thought could be next," Anna said. "His wife and kids were at the top, followed by the mayor and the rest of the council, and finally us."

"Nice to know we're not at the top," I said. "But what about Sarah? Why isn't she involved in this?"

"I don't know," Anna said. "I wonder if they are going to question your mother."

"Anna," I said, softly, "my mother died four years ago."

Anna fell into a chair, looking like I'd hit her in the gut. There'd been so much pain in the past and Anna knew all that I had been through with Mom. The last Anna knew, Mom was being taken to jail and was going to be placed in an institution for her own safety. Anna and I had just reconnected and there hadn't been time to explain the details of yet another painful chapter of my life. A night, four years ago, that now that I think about it, could shed some light onto our present situation...

Chapter #10

A Doorway Opens

I waited until Jack left the store and brought Sarah into the tiny office with myself and Anna before I told Anna the story of what happened to our mother. I had made sure earlier to double check all the doors in the store, making sure they were locked. I didn't want anyone to disturb the conversation. I had done my best the past few years to make sure I never had to relive that night. I badly wanted to forget it ever happened, not only for the pain it caused but the unanswered questions. No matter how hard I tried, I could never forget.

It was a summer's night four years ago, warm and lovely following a bright sunny day, the type where everything in the world just seemed brighter and better. I had been planning a party to celebrate Sarah's first full year of sobriety and we were even able to get Mom out of the institution for the evening, just for a couple hours, to have supper with us. We had to pay for one of the institution's guards to be with her, but she got to join us in my apartment for supper.

Everything had been going well for me. The store was hitting new highs, I was making better contacts in the business world, and Sarah was well on her way to an accounting degree at the community college. It had been four years since Dad disappeared and I was starting to accept the fact that I would never see him again. It wasn't a pleasant thought but it was a thought of closure—finality. I had already exhausted every lead I had and there was nothing left to go on. I had made my peace with it and was moving on with my life.

The dinner itself went well. Everyone was in a good mood—even Mom seemed pleasant—happy actually. Her doctors said she was making good progress although the scar-tissue and brain damage from the car accident she had when she was younger guaranteed she would never be able to live on her own. She would always need trained care around. Her brain no longer functioned right and they never knew when she would have a meltdown and throw a fit. We wouldn't be a full family again but we could be there for each other. I was trying to see the positives in everything and thought that maybe, just maybe, a new corner had been turned. After the meal, however, things took a turn for the worse.

"Have you spoken to your scumbag father recently?" Mom asked. "Has he been slinking around?"

"I told you before, Mom," I said, softly. "We haven't seen Dad in years. Not since the night you were taken away."

"He had me taken away, Imara," Mom said, with a hint of rage in her voice. "I know it was him that did it. He was always trying to get rid of me."

"Dad never wanted to get rid of you," Sarah said. "He loved you."

"Love," Mom scoffed. "That's what you call it? He was okay with me having slight mental problems. He knew about them when we were dating. The imbalances and the depression. I felt so good when I was with him. It was the only time I felt normal...loved. Then came the car accident"

"Mom," I said, trying to sound sympathetic, "you've had a long day the way it is. Maybe it's time for you to go home. Would you like to go to bed?"

"Don't treat me like I'm a damn baby!" Mom shouted. "I'm not some loony in that place dear. I know why I'm there. After the accident I was in real trouble but because of you two, Dean kept me around. He didn't keep me there as a favor to you two, he didn't have me there because he didn't want you to grow up without a mother. He kept me in the house so I would take care of you—feed and clothe you. He didn't want to have to do all the housework himself. You see dear, it's much easier to find a mistress on the side than to enter into a full relationship with two young girls. That's the truth of your dear, precious father. I hate him and I hope he's rotting in the ground somewhere."

Mom quickly stood up, standing so fast she knocked her chair over. Sarah and I instantly stood as Mom's guard took a step forward.

"Calm yourself," Mom said. "I just need to go to the bathroom. I can still function in there by myself—or do you want to come in and watch?"

No one said a word as Mom made her way to the bathroom. I looked to Sarah who had tears in her eyes. I was fighting to keep my tears in. I could only imagine what the guard was thinking, what he must think about our family. We waited for ten minutes until we heard a loud thump come from the bathroom. I knew before I even stood up—I knew what had happened.

I looked over the room. Sarah was nodding her head while Anna's eyes were wide with shock. It had been a story I'd replayed many times in my head but still had trouble believing. The end of my mother had been shocking to me. I never thought she would kill herself. Mom had never given me any indication that things were that bad. I don't know why it happened but she was gone.

"What did she do in there?" Anna asked.

"Used a scissors to slit her throat," Sarah said. "She was standing in the tub when she did it. The thump we heard was her hitting the ground."

"The guard broke the door down and we saw her lying there," I said. "It was a messed up night."

"Wait," Anna said, piecing the story together. "That happened in your apartment? The one you're living in now?"

"God no," I said. "I packed my bags that night and found a different place. There was no way I could stay in the same place where my mother died."

"But what did she mean by what she said?" Anna asked. "Was your dad seeing someone on the side?"

"I'd never even thought about it before," I replied. "I never had any idea but after she said it, I couldn't help but think of all the times he was at the store late or would come home for supper and then return to the store. I guess it could be possible, and after she said that it lent credence to the theory that he left us for another family."

"You really think that could happen?" Anna asked.

"I don't know," I replied. "I mean, I know I built an ideal image of him in my mind. I know there were family problems I never knew about until after they were gone. But I still don't think he could have been that cold to us. I mean, Sarah and I, how could a man walk out on his daughters? That's stone cold right there."

"With my drug problems it was probably pretty easy for him to walk away," Sarah said. "It was only a matter of time before I would overdose or get killed, the way I was going. I should be dead, honestly. There is no reason that I am alive."

"What do you mean?" Anna asked.

"This scar on my face?" Sarah said, pointing to her scar, "was given to me the night I should have died. I relapsed and was on a horrible bender. I had no money so I was doing whatever I could to get my fix. My dealer was starting to pimp me out but we were in someone else's territory. I'd just finished with a guy and my dealer gave me a syringe of heroin. I was injecting it when three men rushed in. They shot my dealer in the head without a word. They pinned me down...started beating me.

"One used the syringe to give me this scar. He was going to rape me before killing me. The other two guys, they were strung out pretty bad...most likely meth. They started goofing around, saying they wanted me first. The guys got into a playful fight which turned deadly when a gun accidentally went off. One was shot in the stomach.

"He killed the other two before he died. When they opened fire, there were at least five bullets that hit inches away from me, so close that I don't know how I didn't die. I felt like there must have been something there to save me. Some power intervened. That was the last time I've ever done a drug and there is nothing on this earth that will ever make me go back to them."

"Oh my God," Anna said, as the color left her face. "That's horrible. I couldn't imagine going through something like that."

"It was the absolute worst night of my life," Sarah said. "I made myself a promise that I will never go back to that kind of lifestyle. I've found a better way to live and am doing much better. The fact remains though, the question is, why did Mom think that Dad was cheating? There must have been something going on to make her believe that."

"I can't think of anything," I said. "There was never anything that led me to believe he was cheating. It could have been Mom just having problems. She did tend to always think things were much worse than they were."

Sarah nodded in agreement and Anna contemplated what we were saying as she shifted in her chair. I didn't know what to believe. It had been such a big day already and I just wanted to go home and relax. Getting questioned by the police was the last thing I needed. I knew I had to let Anna know what happened. Anna and Mark were always good friends and she would be interested to know he was back.

"You'll never guess who came in yesterday and talked to me," I said, looking at Anna with a smile.

"Mark Lewis?" Anna replied.

"How the hell did you know that?" I asked stunned.

"I didn't," Anna said, as stunned as I was. "I just took a shot in the dark. He's back? I thought he was married out in New York."

"He just finished up college and got a job at the new clinic near the gallery," I said. "There were some problems with his relationship out there. It's a long story."

"Got a date with him tonight?" Anna asked with a wink.

"Not a chance in hell," I said. "Not after what he did."

I told her the story of our coffee meeting, how he acted so strange and how I threw my coffee in his face. I got madder and madder as I told the story, having to relive it again, still so disappointed in how Mark acted. Anna and Sarah listened to every word and they were having the same reactions to Mark as I was.

"So, that's why you were crying when I got here," Anna said. "I was wondering what had set you off."

"I didn't know you noticed," I said.

"Please honey," Anna said. "Imara, you were a mess when I got in here. I knew something was wrong but didn't have time to ask you. What are you going to do about him?"

"Nothing for now," I said. "I'm going to wait it out. I'm sure he'll talk to me again, try to make amends for what happened or demand that I apologize for what I did. Either way, I'm going to feel him out and see where it goes. Maybe he just didn't know how to talk to me since we'd been away so long."

"You still like him?" Sarah asked.

"I really do," I said. "But I like the man he was. I don't know if I like this new version of him. I kind of want to just get to know him again."

Anna was about to say something when there was a loud knock on the front door. I looked at my watch and it was quarter after five. My regular customers know I'm willing to meet them anytime at the store, all I ask is that they call me and let me know. I motioned Anna and Sarah to stay where they were, but to listen in case I needed them.

I walked out through the sales floor as the loud knocking started again. Someone was acting impatient as they were waiting to get into the store. I turned the lights to the sales floor on as I looked out the window. It was still a bright and sunny day out. The mid-summer's weather had been perfect, a great summer day to be outdoors.

I saw a man standing by the door. He was a tall and lanky man—gangly with a thin frame covered with an expensive gray suit. His face was reptilian, like a viper ready to strike. He had shifty black pits for eyes and narrow lips with a tongue darting out and licking the lips quickly before retreating back behind his glaringly-white teeth. Above the mouth was a thin black mustache, perfectly groomed to match his thinning black hair.

I opened the door, ushering the man in, realizing that his each of his fingers were covered with a gold ring, some with diamonds, others with other light-catching stones. His gold watch looked stunning, an expensive piece that matched the cufflinks on his starched white shirt. It took me a moment to put it together, but it was Mayor Jimmy Nelson himself, walking into my shop.

"You must be Imara Callan," Jimmy said, in an almost hissing, snake-like voice. "I was told you were a beauty beyond measure. The rumors don't do you justice."

"Thank you, Mayor," I said.

"You know me," Jimmy said, with a smile. "Please, you can call me James."

"I thought most people called you Jimmy," I said.

"Some do," Jimmy replied, annoyed. "Mainly people who represent backwards thinking. The old ways of doing things has been proven to not work. You can call me James."

"Okay James," I said. "Welcome to Decades of Threads. How can I help you today?"

"I've got the grand opening of my new Front Street Gallery and Entertainment Complex opening up very soon," Jimmy said. "It is going to be amazing. I put the entire deal together. It's going to be an amazing boon for the city of Prairie Rapids. This will bring in tourists and help the local economy. This will allow us to show the world that we have refined culture and taste here. The gallery will be the shining jewel of our fair city and I was the one who put it together and made it happen."

"It's impressive," I said. "I was there the other day. The Prairie Bar."

"You have a Prairie Burger?" he asked.

"I did. Very good but I couldn't finish the thing by myself. I was there with a girlfriend, we could have ordered one and split it and it still would have been too much."

"The grand opening of the gallery has to be an event that makes history," Jimmy said. "We are going to have media from all over, people from all over. It will be the biggest event for this state this year. There's so much planned...a four-day weekend of events. The governor is even going to be here. My youngest daughter, Carla, was the winner of an essay contest so she will get to cut the red ribbon to open the gallery."

"You've worked very hard on this," I said. "You must be very proud, James."

"Here's the thing, Imara," Jimmy said, lowering his voice, "I was approached by a strange man...Malenko Pendragon. He's a magician who's toured the world, headlined Vegas, and done it all. He's a bit eccentric but amazing nonetheless. He made me a great offer. He's going to do the opening show, opening night in the theater. They have already started to work on the stage, I guess it's going to be a huge setup. He actually offered to do it for free so he could show the world his Malenko Magic...whatever that is. He's going to be recording the show."

"It should be amazing."

"I'll get you tickets," Jimmy said. "As many as you need, that's not a problem. They are not going to sell them to the general public, it's going to be for VIPs only."

"Thank you," I said. "But why am I a VIP?"

"I need you," Jimmy said. "Actually, I need your store. See, he wants this old Hollywood theme. I need authentic clothing for myself, my wife, and our two daughters. I shall be dressed as a director, my wife needs elegance and grace, and our daughters will be starlets. There may be one more, a boy who's been seeing my oldest daughter, but I don't know if she's going to bring him or not. Is that something you can do?"

"Absolutely," I said. "No problems there. Just have everyone come in and get measured and let us know what colors they want and I can find it. I may have some dresses that will work for your daughters, depending on their size."

"Both are very slender," Jimmy said. "Tall and slender, elegant and graceful."

"I'm sure they'll look very beautiful," I said. "When do you need them by?"

"The opening is in about three weeks," Jimmy said.

"No problem," I replied. "You will all look stunning."

"Thank you so much," Jimmy replied. "I wasn't going to come here first. I really didn't know about this place. I was just planning on having an aide find the clothing off the 'net but then it was brought to my attention that we have a specialty clothing shop right here in Prairie Rapids."

"I'm glad you found out about it," I said.

"Then I found out who you are," Jimmy said, taking a snake-like step toward me, locking his eyes onto mine. "I've heard you are good friends with Anna Garst."

"I am," I said, swallowing as he got even closer, backing me into a corner with no way to get out. I was starting to sweat, starting to show fear and get nervous. I couldn't figure out why he was pressing in on me. "Anna and I go way back."

"Interesting," Jimmy said. "I'm sure that two girls such as yourselves tell each other everything. Answer me this, why is she looking into things that happened in the past?"

"I don't know what you're talking about," I replied quickly.

"Yes you do, Imara," Jimmy said. "I'm not the guy you want to lie to. One of my cops, a young man who just happens to have money troubles, gets paid five-thousand dollars to be a bodyguard for one evening to a complete nobody who didn't even go out that night."

"She thought someone was after her," I interrupted. "The same people that killed her parents and were never caught. She feels the need to have protection. I don't know why, but she thought they were going to go after her that night." I lowered my voice and leaned toward him, "Anna really hasn't been right in the head since that night. She's still pretty disturbed."

"Are you telling me the truth?" Jimmy asked.

"I am," I replied.

"There are files that have gone missing," Jimmy said. "Files that no one should be looking at. There's no reason for them to be looked at. Not now anyway. I hope for her sake, and yours, that you are telling me the truth. Some things aren't meant to be investigated. A doorway opens and everyone rushes in not knowing what they are going to find."

"Why are you so concerned about it?" I asked. "How did you discover that the files were missing if no one was supposed to be looking at them?"

"There are many questions that have no answers," Jimmy said. "And those questions will have no answer tonight. Just be warned, I don't want my cops getting tied up in old crimes. All the reporters coming to cover the gallery will start looking into it. They will find no story but they will make something up and run with it. Then, instead of being known for this beautiful, amazing gallery, Prairie Rapids will be known for some urban legend that isn't real. Understand?"

"I believe I do," I said.

Jimmy smiled a bone-chilling, snake-like smile as his tongue darted across his lips. He winked at me before slowly taking a step back, turning around and walking out of the store. Once he was clear of the store I rushed to the door and locked it, wondering just what the hell Anna had gotten herself into.

Chapter #11

Money Can't Buy Truth

It had been two days since Mayor Jimmy Nelson cornered me in the store. Anna and Sarah heard every word that was said. We knew instantly that he found out Anna was attempting to get information on a case that had been unsolved for eight years. We couldn't help shake the question whether Jimmy was truly concerned with the grand opening of the gallery and just didn't want all this old murder and heartbreak brought up, or if he was somehow involved in the murders that took Anna's parents from her eight years ago.

It was a question we'd asked ourselves hundreds of times in the two days since then. Having copies of every story about the Garst murders and the Callan disappearance from the library, Anna, Sarah, and I poured over every article, sifted through all the files Lund had taken from the police station, and tried to piece together a plausible scenario—but no matter what we tried, no matter how we pieced things together, nothing seemed to work. As far as we could tell, no one on the face of the earth knew anything about what really happened that night. To say we were frustrated with the situation would be a vast understatement.

Until Jimmy cornered me in the store, I still wasn't sure if I was going to help, if I wanted to get involved in the investigation, but after he did, I knew I no longer had a choice. There was something going on and someone knew. I developed a resolve as strong as Anna's. This case was going to reveal its mysteries to us. There would be nothing standing in our way to stop it. Even if Jimmy knew that Anna had hired Lund, there's nothing he could have done about it. The police didn't have a contract saying they couldn't do for-hire work when they were off the clock. Unless Lund was caught stealing the files, there was nothing they could touch us with.

It had been a busy day at the store when Jimmy came in with his wife and daughters to get measured. I had two different production companies come in for outfits and had started to inventory the Halloween merchandise. Jack had the day off, so I had two of my part-time workers in the store with me all day. They were both good girls, just out of high school. I enjoyed working with both of them and I had been teaching them a lot about the fashion and business worlds. Both girls were socialites, very popular in their schools and had much going for them.

The first was Janet Thompson, a tall stringy girl with chopped black hair. She had a very narrow face and tanned way too much, but she was pretty, with smoky eyes and a sinister grin always locked on her face. She was a fashion hound, always wearing the latest brands and hottest styles.

The other girl was Tina Smith, a party girl who liked to call herself 'fun-sized' since she was only four-foot eleven. She was a small girl but projected such an energy that people always took notice of her. Tina was slightly different from Janet in the clothing department. During the winter, Tina only wore jeans and hooded sweatshirts. In the summer it was jean shorts and plain tank tops.

Tina had a round, flat face, soft and innocent that contrasted greatly with her personality and party style. She had fire-red hair that was always pulled into pigtails and matched the freckles on her face. I was excited that both girls were going to the state university right here in Prairie Rapids and would be able to stay on and work here during school. Both girls wanted to do something in fashion, so working in a store like mine was the perfect opportunity for them. I really enjoyed both of them and was glad to have found them.

"Hey Imara," Janet called out as I looked at the clock, realizing it was almost five. "We need to talk to you."

I looked over and saw Janet and Tina walking toward me. They both looked to be extremely nervous about something. I couldn't imagine what would have them upset, they were both girls that could handle themselves in any situation.

"What's up, girls?" I asked. "How can I help you today?"

"We need to talk to you about the schedule coming up," Janet said, looking at the ground. "There's a problem with it."

"Anything you need, you can come to me," I said. "Is there a big party coming up that you two want to go to?"

"Nothing like that," Janet said. "See, the thing about it is, you know, we both are really appreciative of you giving us jobs and giving us all the training that you have. You've been really great, ya know?"

"I enjoy both of you," I said. "You're smart and talented and hard working. Anything that you need to talk about you can always come to me with anything. What's up, girls?"

"The thing about it is..." Janet said, trailing off.

"We both accepted new jobs," Tina blurted out in usual Tina fashion. "There was a big offer on the table. They came to us...you have to understand. We weren't looking for this but they came to us and made us both offers."

"Where at?" I asked, stunned.

"In the mall at the gallery," Tina said. "There's a high-end clothing store and they offered both of us almost double the hourly wage, plus commissions, plus during the summers they will set it up as an internship so we get college credit. It was a deal we couldn't pass up."

"That's amazing," I said, my mind still swimming at what I was hearing. "Congratulations. girls, you have to do what's best for your futures. I wish I could offer you something to keep you here but there's no way I can compete with that. I could offer you a little more money, but nothing on the level that they are talking about."

"I'm so sorry," Janet said. "I told them no, twice, and they kept making the offer better. They really wanted us. It was the guaranteed internship that sold me. They are so hard to come by right now. And paid, as well. We had no choice."

"I understand, girls," I said. "I'm very sorry to lose you but you cannot pass something like that up. Can I ask you a question though? How did they find out about you?"

"The manager of the store said the mayor gave him our names and said he was supposed to hire us," Tina said. "Mayor Nelson knew about us somehow and said we would be perfect for the job. They made us the offer right away."

"I'm really happy for you," I said, as I hugged both of them. "Don't worry about me. I can always find people to work here. I'll never be able to replace you two. Remember, the door is always open. If that store doesn't work out, you are always welcome back here."

"Thank you," Janet said.

"Thanks," said Tina. "That means a lot. I was worried about how you would take the news. I'm just wondering why the mayor was so keen on getting us hired. I guess it doesn't matter. It's a boom for us."

"No matter," I said. "You got the jobs and it will help you with your careers. It's about quitting-time ladies. I've got some friends coming over and I need to get ready for them. You two can take off. Thanks for everything."

"Not a problem," Janet said. "Thank you for understanding."

Tina hesitated a moment, waiting for Janet to grab her purse and head out the door. Tina moved to me and hugged me tight. I hugged back. There was a tear in her eye as she smiled at me.

"Imara," Tina said. "You've got the coolest name. I know I've said that before but I'm naming my first daughter after you, when I have one."

"Thanks Tina," I said.

"Imara, you're so pretty...I mean, you're *hot*. Why do you spend so much time by yourself? You could land any man you wanted. I know you've had some trouble in the past...some hard times, but you need to live a little. Party it up and have some fun. Don't wait until life passes you by and you're left with nothing but this store and regrets. You've got money...go have some fun!"

"Money can't buy truth, Tina," I said, looking her in the eyes. "When you get a little older, have some more experience under your belt, you'll know what I mean. You're right though, I do need to loosen up. Who knows, maybe I'll find a nice man at the grand opening party for the gallery."

"If you need to know where a party is to take him," Tina smiled, "you've got my number. I always know where the parties are."

"Thanks Tina," I said. "Keep in touch with me. Don't become a stranger."

"I won't," Tina said, as she gave me one last hug before heading out the door.

Tears rolled down my cheeks as I dropped into my office chair. I hung my head, losing those two hurt. The business would be fine, I always had people stopping in asking if I was hiring. I could find people to work the store, but I would never be able to get two like that who I got along with so well—who meant so much to me. I don't know why Jimmy sniped them away from me, but he was throwing haymakers early on. It was clear I had been entered into a battle.

I heard the back door to the shop open. I tried to dry my tears, but I didn't have anything nearby that would work. The box of tissues on my desk was empty and I was wearing a blue satin cropped tank top that I didn't want to get wet. I quickly rubbed my hands over my face as Sarah and Anna entered the office together. Anna was carrying a red backpack she draped over her knees as both she and Sarah sat down on chairs. They looked at me for a moment as I tried to compose myself.

"What happened?" Sarah asked. "Is everything okay?"

"Janet and Tina quit on me," I said, with my voice cracking. "Jimmy told one of the stores in his mall to give them whatever it takes to hire them. They are getting almost double the wages, commissions, and it's set up as an internship. Jimmy's taking off the gloves and not fighting fair."

"Then we need to kick his ass," Anna said. "He won't get away with this."

"What can we do, Anna?" I almost shouted. "We've been over every news article about the incident and we have nothing. There isn't one shred of evidence that can lead us in the right direction. Where do we go from here?"

"I have something here," Anna said, as she opened the pack.

Anna shuffled through some papers in a folder and handed me a sheet of white paper. I looked at the sheet. It was a small notebook page, like a pocket notebook, that had been copied onto a standard white sheet of copy paper.

The small sheet had been written on with a pen in sloppy, hastily-written handwriting. I was stunned at what I was reading. It was a list of suspects that Detective Travis Lukens, when he was Officer Lukens, had written down as possible suspects in the killing of Anna's parents. None of them had ever been officially questioned. At the top of the sheet was none other than Mayor Jimmy Nelson.

"They never even questioned him?" I asked.

"Never," Anna said. "And look at the date, it's at the beginning of the investigation. That's what interests me. See, everyone knew a few months later that Dad refused to sell the property to the gallery development, but this was before that knowledge came out. This was early on, so there should have been no reason to suspect Jimmy, unless they know something we don't."

"The other names on the list," I asked, looking over the other three names, "I recognize Eddie Hayes, but the other two I don't know. Who are they?"

"They are people involved with the gallery," Anna said. "They were behind-the-scenes people. One of them has since passed away and the other doesn't live around here anymore. They were big with the planning stages. I think this is something we can go on. We may need to get Detective Lukens and question him. Find out why these people weren't questioned."

"That's going to be tough," I said. "Has there been any word on Tim Krause?" I asked. "Have there been any arrests made?"

"They're clueless," Anna said. "Lund says that everyone is walking on egg-shells at the station and that Jimmy has been there raising hell, yelling at everyone. Word on the street is that Jimmy has someone tailing him, security that's staying hidden, just in case."

"He's paranoid," Sarah said. "He knows someone knows something. I think we can forget about the university connection, and as 'Ara said, 'Occam's Razor'—the simplest answer is the right one."

"We need more to go on but I agree this is the direction we start looking," Anna said. "How do we get information out of Travis? We could get him drunk but that has its own set of risks to it and then he knows. Would it be possible to force something out of him?"

"Anna!" I almost shouted. "Are you seriously talking about forcing information out of a police detective? Do you realize how serious that is? Let's pretend for one second that you do that but it turns out we were wrong; do you know how long you'd be in jail for? It wouldn't be pretty."

"Okay," Anna said, giving me a glare, "what's your idea then?"

"Well, I don't have one off the top of my head," I said. "But there has to be a better idea than that. What else have you learned from Lund?"

"He says everything at the station is tight now," Anna said. "There's no one willing to talk about what happened and a lot of files got moved. He can't help us much anymore. I'm keeping him around to tell us what moves they are making but we have to assume he will be reporting back to them on what we are doing. I fed him some lines about the university and how I found an angry letter written from a board member to Dad. I told him that's the direction we are looking. It'll be interesting to see where that information ends up."

"A nice move," a voice said, from the doorway, causing all three of us to almost jump out of our chairs.

I looked to the doorway to see Princess Aine standing in the doorframe. Aine had a bright smile on her face but was wearing the strangest outfit I'd ever seen a person walk around in daylight in. She had black, over-the-calf boots with six-inch heels, black sheer stocking, high-waist black briefs, and a crushed velvet, haltered and cropped sapphire top that looked like it was for a dance recital. She had nothing covering her arms or most of her stomach, but she sported a sparkling silver tiara on her head that complimented all the glitter and makeup she had on.

"What are you doing here?" I asked, almost stuttering. "Before that, when did you come in? I never heard the bells on the door ring."

"I arrived just before your workers quit," Aine said. "I witnessed the entire event."

"I never saw you in the store," I said.

"You weren't meant to," Aine said. "I didn't want to be seen by the other two, so I kept myself hidden. Malenko has taught me much of his magic. Amazing how often one would need magic eyes to see what was right in front of their face."

"Who the hell is this?" Sarah asked.

"This is Princess Aine," I said, as the princess bowed. "She's the one I told you about, the one with Malenko Pendragon."

"That's right," Sarah said, snapping her fingers.

"So tell me something Aine," Anna said, "do you always dress like you're ready to perform? I mean, come on, that outfit is probably comfortable and you look hot in it, but really? Wearing something like that out in the open?"

"I don't understand," Princess Aine said. "Why wouldn't this outfit be practical for today? It's a hot day and this allows my body to cool itself."

None of us could answer. There was something about her that was unspeakable. She carried herself so powerfully, so confident. There wasn't a hint of fear or doubt in her voice or movement. This was a woman who lived her life under the mantra of no fear.

"How can I help you Princess Aine?" I asked, realizing that we would never get anywhere trying to figure each other out. "Is there something that you need?"

"There is," Aine said. "I will require costumes for the big magic show. Malenko has some incredible feats planned. Things that no other magician has ever been able to do...well, no one has performed these tricks in *this* realm anyway."

"I have all the costumes that you could ever need," I said, ignoring the last part of her comment. "What types are you looking for?"

"Before we get to that," Aine said. "I heard your conversation. Malenko knows much and has many contacts. That's how he found out about the gallery opening. I believe that we can help you gather information."

"You can help us?" Anna asked. "Why would you want to help us?"

"When you've lived as long as I have," Aine said, with the softest of smiles, "and as many lives as Malenko has, you realize that the important things in life can't be bought."

"Anything can be bought," Anna said.

"Money can't buy love," Aine said. "Not the true form of love. You can buy lust, pleasure, and companionship, but that is not love. Money can't buy happiness..."

"Then sister," Anna said, with a grin, "you don't know where to shop."

"You misunderstand me," Aine said. "You can buy things that make you happy, but once those things are gone then the happiness is gone. You can't go to the store and buy a pound of happiness."

"I guess," Anna said.

"Money can't buy truth," Aine said, as she winked at me. "And truth is the most important thing in our lives. Without truth, nothing is real."

"Says the woman who makes a living deceiving people," Anna said.

"But we are honest about the deceit," Aine said. "I swear to you...all we are interested in is the truth. We will help you but there will be a cost."

"What cost is that?" Sarah asked.

"One of you will need to help with the show," Aine said. "We will use you on stage."

"I'll do that," Anna said, instantly. "That would be awesome."

"We will pick," Aine said. "When the time is right and we find the right fit. It will be one of you though. I will be back with Malenko, soon, to obtain the outfits we require. Thank you and I leave in peace."

Princess Aine bowed to us, bending at the waist and lowering her upper body until it was parallel to the ground. She held her hands in a praying position as she stood statue-still for a moment. Aine slowly raised her upper body and smiled at us as she left the office. I heard the bells to the door jingle as she left. I looked to Anna then to Sarah. We were all skeptical about what we'd just seen, but maybe someone from the outside was exactly what we needed to get the information that would help us.

Chapter #12

A Haunting Past

I walked past the mock main street and into the promenade area of the Front Street Gallery and Entertainment Complex. There were a few people around, shopping and checking out the gallery before the place became eternally packed after the grand opening, but for the most part, it was quiet. I couldn't help but wonder what a university would have looked like here, or what the houses would have looked like had they remained. The relentless march of progress never ceases though, and all old things must make way for the new.

I'd received a message earlier in the day from Doctor Mark. He wanted to meet with me there, just to talk. I wasn't sure if I should or not but I figured I would give him another chance. He'd meant so much to me in the past, I wasn't ready to cast him away yet. But I knew for sure he'd better have a better attitude and be more realistic about his intentions. As I looked around the gallery, I saw a woman sitting on a bench. Even though it was a warm day she was in a heavy old trench coat with a stocking hat and massive sunglasses. It was Anna, positioned perfectly if I needed her.

I saw Mark sitting outside the small coffee shop that sat between two fancy restaurants. He had a cup in his hand and one other cup on the table, sitting in front of an open chair. It was already a strike against him. He should have remembered I'm very moody about my coffee and I can decide to order four different things while waiting in line for a minute. Coffee is an extension of me, so he better have gotten it right.

"Hey Mark," I said, as I walked up to the table and sat down.

He stood, getting ready to give me a hug but I didn't give him the chance to. I took a sip from the cup, decaf that was watered down. I almost spit it out as I set it down. Mark had a stunned look on his face. He sat down as a hand reached from behind me for the cup. I was startled but turned to see a dignified man in his forties standing behind me, drinking from the cup I had just sipped from. He was in a brown suit with trimmed hair the color of polished bronze. He had a high forehead with big features. The man had a warm smile as he looked me over.

"This must be the infamous Imara," the man said, in a smooth tenor voice. "Very pretty, but you'd better watch out Mark, I don't know if you can handle this one."

The man smiled and winked at me as he turned and left, coffee cup in his hand. I didn't know what to say but I knew my face was a red as the red polo shirt Mark was wearing with his khaki pants. Mark watched the man walk away before turning to me.

"That was Doctor Andrew Dumas," Mark said. "You might remember him as the doctor who performed the autopsies on Anna's parents."

"I didn't know that," I said. "Why are you having coffee with him?"

"I talked to Anna and your sister," Mark said. "I made them promise not to tell you we talked. I'm so sorry for the way I came off last time. I wasn't thinking when I was talking. I was speaking from the heart, Imara, and my heart tells me that I still love you; I never stopped loving you, but I know I hurt you in ways that can never be repaid."

"Admitting that is a start," I said.

"It's like there's a haunting past behind me," Mark said. "I don't want to allow that to continue. It wasn't right.

Anna told me about what you guys are doing. I think that you all deserve closure on the cases. I sought out Doctor Dumas and made friends with him. He's coming to the new clinic, too. I'm hoping that through him we can gather some information that could help you."

"That's very thoughtful of you Mark," I said. "Thank you."

"You deserve better than what you got," Mark said. "The hand you were dealt was a crap hand but you've made the most of it. I'm impressed. I knew you could do anything you set your mind to."

"Mark," I said, leaning in, "can the after-school-special shit. I don't need to hear how tragic my life has been and how I'm a fighter or a role model or anything like that. I just want to live my life, have fun, and leave a sexy corpse, that's it. When I first fell in love with you it was because of how strong of a man you were…not this pathetic, apologizing, simpering lapdog looking for approval. I understand your last relationship ended badly, but man-up and bring back the Mark that could make my stomach do summersaults just by smiling at me. Understand?"

Mark turned his head to the side as he furrowed his brow, looking deeply at me. I think he understood what I was trying to tell him but he didn't know how to get there. There was a lot of pain in his past but he had to find a way to move past it or it would haunt him for the rest of his life. I decided to see if Mark had found out anything from Doctor Dumas.

"How long have you been talking with Doctor Dumas?" I asked.

"A few days," Mark said. "He's got a real ego problem. He's been married four times and each time it ended because he was sneaking around with a younger woman, but he's never married any of the girls he was messing around with. I've been using his ego to my advantage. I approached him and started asking questions. At first, he didn't want me to bother him but I explained how I heard that he's the best doctor in the state, he's won some medical awards, and how I really wanted to learn from him. He took the bait and opened the floodgates to me. All I had to do was act like he's as important as he thinks he is and now Doctor Dumas will tell me anything."

"Nice work, Mark," I said. "I'm impressed."

"You've got an in with him too," Mark said.

"How so?"

"When you walked up, sat down, and drank from his coffee cup," Mark said. "He loves really sassy women. Top that off with your outfit and you could be his next mistress. He remarried earlier this summer."

I looked at my outfit, my black tights with designer black boots, a posh black belt, and a black with cream-colored drawing patterned strapless top that looked like it was from an ancient Native culture. It was a snappy, attention-getting outfit.

"He'd like this?" I asked. "I figured he would want a woman in a business suit or something."

"No way," Mark said. "He'd be all over you. Just something to keep in mind if you ever need a way to extract more information from him."

"I'll keep that in mind," I said. "Thank you."

"I don't really have anything else to say, Imara," Mark said. "I'll help you and Anna anyway I can with your investigations. Just let me know. I want to be involved with you and maybe being around you will bring the old Mark back out and things will get better. All I'm asking for is a chance."

"You get *one*, Mark," I said, firmly. "One and that's it. Do not test me on this. If you do anything that even slightly harms my heart, you'll be out in the cold. Don't try to move too fast either, let's just let this develop naturally and see what happens."

"Agreed," Mark said. "I'd love to stay and chat with you but I have a meeting tonight for the clinic. I'm a junior on the board of directors. It's a good position, it will help me with my career. I'll call you soon though, let you know how things are going and if I'm finding anything from Doctor Dumas."

"That sounds good," I said, as Mark and I stood up. "Remember one thing though Mark, you have to call me soon to setup a date...and it better be a damn good one."

"I will," Mark said, giving me a hug.

I watched as Mark walked away. I didn't move until he was out of sight. I slowly walked over to the bench where Anna was sitting. As I walked up she removed her jacket and hat, revealing that she'd been sweating profusely underneath her heavy coat.

"You didn't have anything other than a heavy wool coat for me to wear in the middle of the summer?" Anna asked as I sat down next to her. "This jacket was made for Russians to keep warm in the winter. You know how cold it gets there?"

"The man that was with Mark when I arrived was Andrew Dumas," I said, ignoring Anna wiping the sweat from her face. "Doctor Andrew Dumas."

"That son of a bitch," Anna said. "That prick messed up the autopsies and never filed the right paperwork. Had I known who that was I would have walked over there and beaten the lies of out him right there and then."

"Calm down," I said. "Mark has an in with him. He also told me that he likes to cheat on his wife with younger, sassy, funky dressed women. He has a real weakness for them."

"We're both younger, sassy, and funky dressed women," Anna said, lighting up. "But what good would that do?"

"Information, I guess," I said. "Find out if someone was pressing him to come up with certain results, find out if he was paid to ignore or add things to his report."

"That could come in very handy to us, Imara," Anna said. "I really like the way Mark was thinking there."

"Why didn't you tell me he talked to you?" I asked.

"He made me promise," Anna said. "And I knew that he realized he'd screwed up. I had to let you meet up with him again. I didn't want you to know what he said."

"What did he say?"

"That when he saw you it was like he'd never left," Anna said. "That you were even more beautiful than before, and that he realized the moment he saw you what a mistake he'd made, and that he still loved you."

"Pouring it on thick," I said. "I don't know. I told him to ask me out on a date and to make damn sure it's a good one. I'll give him a chance. I told him he needs to bring the old, powerful Mark back. I think he got it."

"I'm happy for you," Anna said. "Life is too short not to have someone who you can share your soul with."

"What about you?" I asked. "You found anyone since you've been back?"

"No," Anna said. "I haven't been looking either. I'm here for a specific reason. I need to uncover this, so I cannot be distracted by romance and love. I'm not going to turn fun down, but I must stay focused on what the goal is."

"I think closure will be good for Sarah, too," I said. "She needs something to hold onto in her life. I'm going to offer her a full-time position in the store. Now with Janet and Tina leaving, I can have Sarah there full time. I could use another full or part-time worker there as well."

132

"I'm not going to make any promises," Anna said. "Once this is over, I don't know where I'm going to end up, if I stay or go. Thank you though."

"I'm just glad we're back together," I said. "I missed hanging out with you. We always had so much fun together."

"We did," Anna said. "I remember the sleepovers at your house when your dad would bring us fresh-baked cookies at two in the morning."

"I loved that," I said. "But hated the upset stomachs we would have in the morning."

"Those were brutal," Anna said, with a laugh.

"How do you like living in the hotel right now?" I asked.

"It's fine," Anna said. "Not having to clean up is nice."

"I know I don't have a lot of space," I said. "We could figure something out though, if you wanted to live with me while you are staying here."

"Thank you, Imara," Anna said. "I'll consider it. It's nice to have a place they don't know about, you know, just in case bugs or something start turning up."

"Bugs?" I asked. "What do you mean?"

"Listening devises," Anna said. "Who know how deep this goes. The hotel is much more secure and I can switch every couple weeks. That way we can stay ahead of them and have a place to hide out if need be, somewhere with a lot of other people around."

"Ya," I said. "That makes sense, I guess. You really think things could get that out of control?"

"He's already hired away your workers," Anna said. "It is out of control already. They are trying to scare us out and we haven't really gotten anywhere yet."

"The other day you told me you had information," I said. "Something you didn't know back when everything happened, but later on found out about. We got interrupted and you never had the chance to tell me what it was. What did you find?"

"Oh, this is good," Anna said. "I can't believe I wasn't made aware of this right away. I mean, this proves something strange went down…"

Anna took a deep breath, getting ready to tell me her news. As she was about to speak, two men walked up to us and started talking.

"Hey there, what are a pair of gals like yourselves doing here today?" one asked.

I looked at them. They were comically identical. Both in Front Street Gallery security uniforms of a black shirt, with the words 'FSG Security' written in bold yellow lettering, and black pants. They had belts with handcuffs, a Taser, flashlights, and other items concealed inside closed cases attached to the belts. The men were both in their thirties, shaved bald, cleanly shaven faces, and buff. The only real difference I could tell was one had a rounder, softer face with blue eyes while the other had a narrow, hard face with hazel eyes.

"We're just having a conversation," Anna said. "That isn't a crime, is it?"

"With as good as you two look we should make it a crime," the narrow faced man said. "You're distracting everyone with your hot looks sitting here on the bench. You really should be more cautious."

I smiled. I knew that Anna was going to chew this man up and spit him out. She hated it when guys used cheesy lines thinking they were slick. I was certain that Anna was ready to pounce on him like a hungry cat seeing a slow mouse.

"Ahh," Anna said, with a smile. "You're sweet. Nobody's ever called me hot before. Most guys don't pay attention to us. We never really dated before."

"It's their loss," the rounded face man said. "I'm Darrel and this is Todd. I'm amazed you've never been chatted up a lot by guys. As security guards we get to see a lot of women but we never do anything like this. We just saw you two and were compelled to come over. You're so attractive."

"You're so cute," Anna said. "Handsome and buff. I'm Anna and this is Imara. Have you two always been security guards?"

"We were cops before," Todd said. "And good ones, too. We worked hard and got promoted. This offer came to us and you wouldn't believe the money they are paying us. Darrel and I have been together since grade school. We dominate everything we do...be it football or police work."

"I bet two studs like you tore through all the cheerleaders," Anna said. I couldn't figure out why she was playing with these guys. By now they should have been on their knees crying and begging Anna to stop. "You must have had all of them."

"We each had our fair share," Todd said. "You two must have been cheerleaders, as attractive as you are."

"We never did the cheer thing," Anna said. "We studied, mostly. Neither of us has ever been with a man before, if you catch my drift." Todd and Darrel almost leapt out of their skin with joy and excitement when they heard that. "We want to, but no guys ever talk to us."

I knew something was up. Anna had just hooked these guys so there was no way they could get away. She had a trick up her sleeve. They were ours now and would do anything to get what they thought we had. Anna promised me she wouldn't use sex as a weapon in this game, but I was certain we'd never have to engage these guys, the whiff of being with a pair of virgins had cleared their heads. They would do anything for us if they thought it would lead to the bedroom. Although, one look at either of us would tell them that unless we had a time machine to go back to high school, they weren't going to be deflowering us any time soon.

"I think we could talk to you," Darrel said, after a moment of silence. The guys were so stunned and excited they didn't know how to continue. "We would be very gentle with you."

"That's all we ask," Anna said. "You have to ask us out though. We need to have at least three proper dates before we can move forward. You know how the game works, so we have to play by the rules."

"We'll take you out," Todd said. "It will be a great time. We'll just see how things go from there."

"Sounds great," Anna said. "Give me some paper and a pen and I'll write down our numbers."

Todd handed Anna a pocket notebook and a pen. Anna quickly put our numbers down and handed it back to him with a wink. The men smiled as they waved and walked away. Anna had a smug smile on her face but I didn't want to ask until the guys were well out of earshot.

"Unless we go back about ten years for you, and eight for me, those guys won't be getting us as..."

"It's all part of the game," Anna interrupted me. "They are so blind. So dumb."

"What do you mean?"

"First, to think that we are virgins," Anna said. "But I said that because I know who those two are. I remember them but they don't remember me...or you."

"I don't remember them," I said. "Who the hell are they?"

"They were cops on the force when all the shit went down," Anna said. "I remember them because I was scared around them. They were investigating on the murders. They were at the house a number of times. They were there when I was questioned. I remember them because they had gotten kicked off the high school football team for nailing the coach's twin daughters. They got caught in college for being with high school seniors. The girls were eighteen so they didn't get into real trouble, but they were obsessed with being a girl's first man. I remember because during the questioning they were both trying to hook up with me."

"Trying to hook up with a girl whose parents were just murdered?" I asked. "That's got to be a new low of some kind."

"They thought I was a virgin then, and they still do, I guess," Anna laughed. "We go out with them, play up the sex thing, and get them to tell us everything. You think it's by chance they just happen to be working here as security guards?"

"Point taken," I said. "They screwed up the investigation and were given a plum job with big pay. This is getting interesting."

"Come on," Anna said. "I want to find out everything I can about those two."

I stood up with Anna, smiling. It seemed like we had all the leads we needed, now if we could just get some real answers out of them we would be getting somewhere.

Chapter #13

The Magic Begins

Anna and I had begun to walk toward the exit of the gallery when I thought I heard my name being shouted from somewhere. I just barely heard it floating on the gentle summer's breeze in the hot humid air. I turned and looked, realizing Anna had done the same, indicating that she had heard it too. There were a few people around but I didn't notice any trying to get my attention until I looked to the theater and saw a figure coming toward us, waving. It was Princess Aine. Her outfit today was, oddly enough for Princess Aine, completely normal.

Aine approached us wearing a black skirted business suit with a white blouse underneath, black pumps, black sheer stockings, her hair up in a twisted style, and very elegant earrings, gold neckless, bracelets, and a fancy gold watch. She rushed toward us, waving. It took a second to recognize her without all the trashy glitter makeup on. In this outfit, Aine looked like she could sit in any boardroom and be taken seriously. She also looked amazingly attractive. I knew that the costumes were an act but it was nice to see she had an amazing sense of professional dress.

"Anna, Imara," Aine said, as she reached us. "I'm glad to have spotted you here. Malenko was going to call you. We are starting to do some test runs of the magic and we wanted you two to come individually and do some tryouts. See which one of you would be better for the show."

"I'm feeling a little tired," Anna said. "But Imara, if you're up for it, go ahead. I'm just going to head back to the hotel."

"I'd love to," I said.

"Hey, Princess Aine," Anna said. "You look really good. What's up with the outfit you're wearing? Got a business meeting or something?"

"Oh, God no," Aine said. "Malenko has people who handle his business meetings for him. I'm in this uncomfortable, strange outfit because of the show. It's all part of the act. As people walk in, I dress in this and welcome them, acting like I'm with the theater. When the show starts, I give an introduction speech and relay some of the history of magic while Malenko shows some very basic tricks. The show really starts when this outfit disappears and I'm back in my normal clothing. It's very stunning and catches people off guard."

"Sounds great," Anna said. "Call me when you get home, Imara. We'll talk then."

"Okay," I said, as Anna took off by herself.

"You will really enjoy the spectacle of what we've prepared," Aine said.

"What kind of name is Princess Aine?" I asked, blurting it out. "I've been trying to figure it out but I can't place it."

"Aine is the name of the Celtic Goddess of love," Aine said.

"Was that the name given to you by your parents or did you choose that name for yourself?"

"Malenko gave it to me," Aine said. "When he was Merlin, so many years ago."

"3000 years?" I asked.

"Yes."

"I thought the King Arthur Legend took place in the Middle Ages," I said. "Only like a thousand or so years ago."

"It did," Aine said. "We spent many lifetimes together before we had to help the king of Britain. We've done many things. Come, we are wasting time with idle chat when there is work to be done."

Aine started walking toward the theater. I tilted my head, trying to figure her out. Everything she'd said to me she said with complete conviction, looking me in the eye and speaking in a steady tone. If it was a lie, she'd practiced it so many times she must've really believed it in her mind. I didn't know what to make of her, only that I needed to be careful and watch what I say around her and Malenko.

I quickly followed and rushed into the theater behind Aine. I was amazed at the lobby and hallways of the theater. They were reconstructions of an old Hollywood-style theater. Everything looked like it was from the 1920s. There were brass chandeliers hanging from the ceiling with dim bulbs casting a glow on the crimson carpets, original playbills and advertising posters from the 20s and 30s. In one corner was a perfectly restored 1927 Cadillac 90-Degree luxury car, and in another corner was a bar designed to look like a speakeasy. It was incredibly overwhelming. Everything looked shiny and new and completely transported a person back to the '20s. Every little detail was done to perfection to make the ambiance complete, even down to the two-pronged mock electrical outlets in the hallway.

"They are only covers," a hissing male voice said. "You can remove the top and the normal, three-pronged outlet is underneath. Just one way we went the extra mile to make this theater authentic."

I looked up to see Jimmy Nelson standing in the hallway. He'd noticed I was looking at the outlets. He was in a dark gray suit, looking as snake-like as ever. I shuddered as he looked at me, his eyes were so cold, like there was no soul behind them.

"It's an amazing theater," I said. "The people of Prairie Rapids are really going to love it mayor."

"So many more than just the people of Prairie Rapids," Jimmy hissed as his eyes fixed on me without moving, like a cobra studying its prey, getting ready to strike. "Opening night I have reporters and publicity coming from all over the state and country. This is going to be national. When the people of the state see what I have done here, when the country sees how I single-handedly turned this decrepit area into a thriving community that brings in people from all over the world, then they will know that I am the one they want leading them."

"You want to be Governor Nelson?" I asked. "This whole idea was nothing more than a play to get the governor's mansion?"

"Please, Imara," Jimmy smiled. "Think bigger than that. President Nelson has a better ring to it. But I suppose I will need to spend a term or two in the Governor's mansion. My advisors think it would be best. They don't think a mayor can jump right into presidency."

"Has this always been your goal?" I asked.

"Ever since I watched my first presidential inauguration when I was five," Jimmy said. "Richard Nixon. You see, with this event, Imara, I'm going to have reporters from all over and the rumors are going to start floating around that I am considering running. I'm going to brush them off, saying the city of Prairie Rapids needs me right now. I have to lead and guide them. Then as more people start pushing for me to run, I can gain momentum in a campaign fueled by the internet and social media. I'll be elected before I even enter my name in the race. It will already be a given. The magic begins and I will see my dream of the White House come true."

"Sounds like you have it all planned out," Aine said. "Please sir, Mayor Nelson, we have much work to do on our show."

"Of course," Jimmy said. "You need anything just let me know. Anything at all."

Jimmy winked at both of us before walking out of the theater. Aine shuddered just watching his swaggering, arrogant walk before taking me by the hand and leading me toward the main theater. When we passed through the massive double doors that were covered in the softest red velvet I'd ever touched, my breath was taken away. The theater was magnificent.

Rows and rows of plush red chairs on black carpeted floor with polished bronze everywhere. There was subtle lighting showing where the walkways were and illuminating the row number at the end of each row. There was a massive balcony area above us and the stage rose up out of the ground majestically, shrouded in red curtains.

Upon the stage, the orchestra of construction rang out. The buzz of power saws, the driving beat of hammers on nails, and the chatter of workers. There was a wooden frame standing on the center stage. Two-by-four studs had formed a rectangular structure that stood in the direct center of the stage. There was string and markings everywhere, indicating where things were to be placed. Piles of lumber, some cut spare pieces, others fresh, ready to be used, were haphazardly sitting all around the frame on the stage.

Working in the thick of it was Malenko Pendragon. His hair and beard looked amazing—such a thick, shiny black. He was wearing black garments that looked to have been cut for someone living in the Middle Ages. Malenko was going over blueprint plans with a construction worker, but when he saw Aine and I enter the theater, he halted all the work and told the workers to take a break. The workers quickly scurried away and a silence fell over the theater. Malenko motioned for us to come onto the stage.

"The theater is such a magical place," Malenko said. "Nowhere else can one be hero or villain...conqueror or conquest. On this stage, dreams become reality. We can hang a star to wish upon or we can create a new star that will shine for the ages. It is in the art of the theater one truly discovers oneself."

"I never knew that a magic show needed such a big set," I said, looking at the frame that stood over twice my height, at least twenty-feet long, and ten-feet deep. "What is all this for?"

"This is what's going to change perceptions," Malenko said. "Watch and learn."

Malenko picked up a blanket and walked toward Aine. Aine braced herself, like she was getting ready for him to push her, or apply pressure somehow. Malenko smiled and tossed the blue blanket over Aine's head. To my total shock, the blanket fell to the floor, Aine was no longer there. In my momentary shock, Malenko picked up the blanket, shook it, and held it like a curtain. He shook it once and let it fall to the ground. I was stunned, Aine was standing there again, but she was in a black tank leotard, her hair down, her face covered with glitter makeup, no stockings, and only black dance slippers on her feet. Her earrings and other jewelry were gone. There was no sign of her business suit. I stood with my jaw hanging open for a second before I gathered enough wits to speak.

"I will pay you anything," I said, trying to be coherent. "I mean *anything*...do anything to learn how to do that."

"What do you mean?" Malenko asked.

"Do you realize how quick I could get ready in the morning?" I said. "Just wave a blanket and I'm dressed, hair and makeup done, just like that. I have to know."

"The magic begins," Malenko said. "When I walked the earth I learned many things, met many people. Once I heard the story of a woman who'd become the best magician in the land. Everyone was going to her shows. You must understand, this was over a thousand years ago, so a woman performing in that capacity was something strange. She didn't wear the clothing of women in that era and the Church had cast her out as a witch.

"I went to see her show and it was some of the most incredible magic of the time. I was certain she had studied under some powerful wizard who'd broken a cardinal rule...never teach magic to people who do not understand the fundamental powers of magic. She had no regard for the safety and power of the magic. It would only be a matter of time before she would find herself in trouble.

"I stayed in that village for two years, watching her magic from afar, watching her power grow. One day, a man came walking though and happened to see the magic. He was a very angry and bitter man, having been driven out of his village for cruelty while his wife and children stayed, to be taken in by his arch-enemy, his brother. This man saw the magic and thought he could use it to take back what he'd lost.

"The man cornered the woman, demanding to be taught the secrets. She refused, saying that he didn't want to use magic for good or to entertain, but to harm others...the highest crime under magical law. The man got aggressive with the woman, forced her to the ground and attempted to lie with her in the way a husband would lie with his wife. Physically, she wasn't powerful enough to overcome him as he threw her onto the bed and climbed on top.

"Using what magic she could conjure up, the woman cursed the man, making him impotent and afraid. Others had heard the commotion coming from the magician's dwelling and had rushed in, getting there just as the curse took effect. The townsfolk seized the man and held him while she explained what happened. They hanged him in the town square.

"The entire village showed up to witness the event but there was no satisfaction that day. As the rope dropped, the man, having obtained some magical power from the woman, disappeared the instant the rope was about to pull taught. He was gone and the townsfolk were worried...*what if he comes back?*

"Time passed and passed again. Every member of that village spread to the four corners of the globe. The woman swore off magic and took her own life, knowing that staying in this realm would be more punishment than what would be waiting for her on the other side."

"Wait," I asked, interrupting. "Why would she do that? What was she afraid of?"

"The man who cheated death," Princess Aine said. "He is the greatest foe in any realm, in any time, in any setting."

"You see, Imara," Malenko said. "The man who cheats death has survived an ordeal meant to take everything from him. He's marked, and everyone who deals with him thereafter is cursed. The man from this story, well, he came back to get revenge on the town that tried to kill him but there was no one there. He spent the rest of his life trying to track them down, killing them off one by one.

"He was driven mad with rage, only seeing revenge in his magic eyes. He finally found the woman who had denied him her magic and made him impotent. He found her grave and his heart was so broken by the fact that he couldn't take revenge…it stopped working right there and he collapsed, dying on her gravesite."

"I don't get the moral of the story," I said. "What's the point?"

"Have you ever met anyone who's cheated death?" Aine asked.

"Not that I know of," I said.

"The question you need to ask yourself," Malenko said, with a grin, "is who else was supposed to die that night? Who else was supposed to be in that house with her parents and get murdered?"

"How the hell do you know about all of this?" I asked. "Why do you care about it?"

"There are reasons," Malenko said. "Who else?"

"Anna?" I asked.

"Anna," Aine said. "She left the next day, walked the earth and learned many things. She learned how to kill. Do you think in her fighting that she only learned to fight by the rules? Do you think she could kill?"

"But Tim Krause was shot in the face," I said. "Not beaten to death…wait, Anna couldn't have killed anyone. She doesn't have that kind of instinct in her. You don't know her like I do."

"And she escaped Death," Aine said. "She trained to be a killer. You have no idea what she is like since she got back."

"But we're investigating what happened," I protested, refusing to believe that Anna could be a killer. "We don't know who's behind it yet."

"What if Anna found out before?" Malenko said. "What if she already knows?"

"She would have told me," I said. "We may have lost touch for a few years but I know Anna. She would never kill and she wouldn't keep things like this from me."

"We could go back and forth all day and not get anywhere," Malenko said. "What you need to know is that anyone who has cheated death is cursed and they will seek out those who've killed them. Once you have cheated death by murder, revenge is the only thing on your mind. Those that killed will not be allowed to go unpunished. Karma has a funny sense of humor about that. Look into Tim Krause, Imara. He's the key. You might find his connections to be broader than you first realized."

"Okay," I said, frustrated, "we'll look into him but you have to tell me something first."

"Anything you want to know," Malenko said.

"How do you know so much about the case and why do you care?" I asked. "Give me the real answers damn it, don't brush it off with some mystical bullshit about knowing much or being here for some karmic reason. What's in this for you?"

Malenko just smiled at me, a sinister grin that chilled me to the core. As our eyes were locked, he winked at me. Before I could do anything, I heard a voice from the main entrance.

"What are you doing up there?" Princess Aine shouted from the back doors of the theater.

I turned and looked and my world view changed. Princess Aine was standing by the doors I had walked through to enter the main theater just moments before, but she was back in her business suit. She'd been standing not three feet from me in her leotard a split second before. I looked back on the stage but Malenko wasn't there either. I was the only one on the stage. I didn't know what had just happened, only that it was strange.

"How the hell did you do that?" I asked as I walked toward Aine.

"Do what?" She asked.

"You were on the stage," I said. "In a black leotard and had glitter makeup on your face. You were there literally a split second before you appeared here in your business suit looking normal."

"This outfit may be normal for you, Imara," Aine said. "But it isn't for me. I don't know what you're talking about. I escorted Mayor Nelson out of the theater, and I distinctly remember telling you to stay right where I left you in the hallway. Why did you come in here?"

"I followed you in here," I said, more confused than ever. "We were talking with Malenko. He did a trick where he changed your outfit in the blink of an eye."

"Malenko isn't even here right now, Imara," Aine said. "Come on, I need to talk with you in the office I set up for myself. The stage is off limits until the production of the set is complete...are you feeling okay?"

"I don't know," I said, as I started to follow Aine out of the theater. "I really don't know."

Chapter #14

The Best Kind of Promotion

Although Anna had questioned me many times about what had happened at the theater two nights prior, I refused to tell her. I told her I saw the first trick, the quick outfit change that defied all reason and logic, but I didn't tell her about the warnings and what happened after the second outfit change. I didn't know whether I should believe them or not, but I still couldn't even piece together what had happened, how Princess Aine changed so quickly and how she got to the back of the theater when she was standing right next to me.

I did tell Anna that I had a hunch, something that told me we should be looking into Tim Krause and why someone would want to kill him. We discovered that he was a totally unremarkable man who only did what those above him told him to do. He was loyal to Mayor Nelson and never spoke out of turn. We also discovered that he sat on a board of trustees for the state university right here in Prairie Rapids. That position allowed him to sit on a number of oversight boards for the university, including a property board.

What that meant, I still wasn't sure. But the connection to the university was confirmed. We had compiled lists of all the people on the same boards as Tim and Anna had instructed Lund to put his ears to the ground to see if he could hear anything about them—did any of them leave town, are they looking for protection, or are they making backdoor deals? As far as we could tell, there was nothing going on with them yet, but Lund did say that the police didn't have any leads and there were still far more questions than answers.

Anna and I had been working with Sarah, going over more papers and files. Trying to find something to go off of when we had to leave for our date with the security guards. We both dressed up, Anna in a tight black halter dress with a swooping neckline, me in my tights and a black designer tank top, both decked to the nines with accessories. We were going to play with these cops as much as we could, get them so amped up they would tell us anything. Anna and I were feeling confident about it but when we arrived at the gallery, our date didn't start exactly as we thought it would.

We walked into Donny's, where the guy's told us to meet them. They said it was a refined cultural dining experience for the higher-end customers. It was actually Donny's Sports Den, a sports bar and betting den that advertised they had four 300-inch projection televisions and over one hundred other televisions throughout the bar so customers can watch every game that's currently being played anywhere on the planet. The bar was clean but rowdy, full of middle-aged men eating wings and slurping down cheap beer from plastic pitchers.

As I scanned the room, I couldn't see any other women. It was all men who were so engrossed in the baseball, soccer, tennis, rowing, boat racing, cricket, polo, boxing, and the dozen other sports that were on random televisions they didn't notice that two hot, sultry-dressed women had just walked into the bar. I had a glimmer of hope for the place when I noticed two college-aged women moving about, but the hope was lost when I realized they were workers, almost all the waitstaff and bartenders were college girls, all wearing various lengths of compression shorts with random sports jerseys, each tied up to show a tip-changing amount of midriff.

On the far side of the bar was an arcade area with four pool tables, four foosball tables, a pair of air hockey tables, a shuffleboard setup, at least twenty different arcade games, and even an arm wrestling table with the rules posted on the wall for any contest. Any person in the bar could challenge anyone else. They each paid ten dollars and the winner would receive a free drink and the loser would get nothing. They both would get their picture taken together, one holding a sign saying winner, the other with a sign saying loser, and the picture was placed in a slideshow that was running on a screen near the arm wrestling table. There were already a couple pictures in there of people who had tried it.

I felt Anna's arm nudge me and I noticed that she was pointing. I looked and saw Darrel and Todd, both wearing faded ripped jeans and New York Mets shirts with Mets baseball hats. Anna and I knew we'd overdressed but that was to our advantage and we needed to keep every advantage that we could get. Anna led the way to the guys' table—a booth in the far corner of the bar that was out of the way and quieter. Todd let us slide into the middle of the booth so that one guy was on each side of us, trapping us in.

"You two look amazing," Todd said, before he looked Anna in the eyes. "Damn, I don't think I've ever seen a honey as sexy looking as you."

"You're too sweet," Anna said, clearly disgusted with the compliment. Todd put his arm around Anna and Anna played along, moving closer and snuggling up with him. I shot her a look—I knew we couldn't push these guys along too fast or they would know. Anna smiled back, "Just remember that you promised to be gentle."

"We remember," Darrel said, as he put his hand on mine. "We ordered for you. They have the best wings in the state here. We got a couple pitchers of beer, too."

Darrel took a pitcher off the table and filled two more glasses, giving one to me and one to Anna. I took a sip and winced—it was a cheap, watery beer with no real flavor. Anna took two big gulps. I really hoped she knew what she was doing.

"Okay," Anna said, as her eyes lit up. "We need to get this party rolling. Truth or dare time. Todd, you go first. Ask Imara, *truth or dare.*"

"Really?" Darrel asked. "Like the little kid game we played when we were in sixth grade?"

"Is this with adult rules?" Todd asked.

"Come on, guys," Anna said, in a party girl voice. "Like, it will be fun."

"Okay," I said, with a sigh. "Truth."

"Tell me something about yourself that no one at this table knows?" Todd asked, confused.

"Okay," I said, smiling, "I only wear yoga pants and tights, nothing else, always solid black. What you don't know is there's a reason for that. My mom wouldn't let me wear denim as a kid, *jeans were for boys* is what she told me every time we were shopping. She would only buy me skirts and dresses. That is, until I was in the seventh grade. I was ice skating when I fell and damaged my knee. It was really messed up and there's all these scars on it. It got infected and my knee got discolored. My mom was so freaked out because I was no longer perfect that she made me start wearing tights under my skirts. When I would get to school, since I hated skirts, I would take the skirts off and just wear the tights then put the skirt back on before I went home, my way of giving the finger to my overbearing mother. I still can't stomach the thought of wearing jeans or letting my knee be seen in public."

"Fuckin' awesome," Todd said, as he finished his beer and poured some more. "What about, like, when you're swimming? Do you wear tights with a bikini top, or what?"

"I've worn swimming tights," I said. "The kind that surfers wear. But I really don't like them. Mom got me a waterproof knee brace. It's like a black sleeve that goes over my knee and covers the damaged area. It makes it look like I've got a bad sports injury or something...okay, my turn. Darrel, truth or dare?"

"Dare," Darrel said, with a big grin.

"Okay," I said, with a smile. "I dare you to walk over to any table you want, and just take a couple wings from their bucket and start eating them."

"Damn!" Todd almost yelled. "Chick's got a bite to her. Come on, Darrel. Don't let me down man."

Darrel smiled a nervous smile before sliding out of the booth, adjusting the hat on his head, and started walking toward the nearby tables. He got to one that had four guys, all eyes glued to a boxing match on a big screen television that was going from a match to an all-out war. Darrel quickly grabbed two wings and rushed away from the table. No one saw him take them. He had both wings devoured before he got back, grinning ear to ear as he sat down.

"Anna," Darrel said, wiping the sauce from his face, "truth or dare?"

"Truth."

"If you could have sex with any man on the planet, living or dead, and he could be whatever age you wanted, who and how old?"

"Interesting," Anna said. "I would say Elvis Presley, right after he came back from the army."

"Nice choice," Todd said.

"My turn," Anna said, excitedly. "Todd, truth or dare?"

"Dare," Todd said.

"I dare you to challenge a special someone to an arm wrestling contest in the arcade over there."

"No problem," Todd said. "I'm a champion arm wrestler. Who's the chump?"

"The bartender," Anna said, with a sinister grin.

We all looked at the bar to see a five-foot-tall petite blonde woman wearing a mid-1990s Minnesota Vikings jersey that had the sleeves cut off. Todd just smiled.

"I fail to see what the challenge is going to be," Todd said.

"There will be no challenge," Anna replied. "You challenge her, go to the table, and you have to lose."

"No way!" Todd said. "Then my picture would be up there of me losing to her! I'm security around here. What happens if I have to come in here one night to break up a fight and they see that? I lose all credibility."

"Then I guess you are screwed," Anna said.

"No way," Todd said. "Pass, truth. Whatever you want to know."

It took me a second to realize it, but Anna had known what she was doing all along. The second she saw the arm wrestling table she'd been putting this plan together. She backed Todd into a corner. He would have no problem winning, but the dare was to lose, he couldn't have that here. I could only imagine what kind of questions Anna was going to be asking.

"Tell me exactly how you two got the jobs here," Anna said. "The security jobs. You said you were police, right? Mall cop is a step or five down from being actual police, right?"

"It's not like that," Todd said. "See, there was a case a few years back, a really big, high profile case. They needed things handled quietly so they called us in. We did what they needed to do and in return, we got these jobs. Think about it, we're not out risking our lives on the street. I mean, you never know who's got a gun or is looking to take out a cop. We're security here. We point old people to the bathroom and tell children not to swear, yet we're paid higher than guys who've been on the city force for ten years. It was the best kind of promotion."

"What did you have to do?" Anna asked. "You're still on truth remember."

"We had to take statements from people who'd seen a suspect flee a murder scene," Todd said. "And then make sure to lose those statements in the shuffle of papers."

"Where are they now?" Anna asked.

"There's a locked file on the case," Todd said. "Somewhere at the station. I'm not really sure but that's where they kept all the secret information on the case."

"Who ordered you to do that?" Anna asked.

"I'm not sure who it was," Todd said. "Some guy from the university or something. I don't know how he got involved. That's enough truth though. Imara, truth or dare?"

"Dare," I said, quickly, not wanting them to ask why we were asking those questions. "I pick dare."

"I dare you to kiss Anna," Todd said, with a smile.

I reacted before I thought. I leaned over and planted a kiss on Anna's lips. I surprised her almost as much as I surprised myself. It was a stupid game and this would make sure they forgot about the questions Anna had just asked them. As I pulled back from Anna's face, she had a smile and the guys were completely blown away. They started giving each other high-fives as other people looked over to see what the commotion was about.

"Okay Darrel," I said, looking to him. "Truth or dare."

"Dare," Darrel said. "Come on, double dare. Let's get this game moving. Make it interesting."

"I dare you and Todd to go to the competitive dance machine in the arcade," I said. "Have a dance-off with each other."

"That's not that daring," Darrel said.

"I wasn't finished," I smirked. "Do it in your boxers."

"Our what?"

"Strip to your boxer shorts," I said. "You know, your underwear. Don't tell me you're a whitey-tighty kind of guy."

"I've got boxers on," Darrel said. "Todd?"

"Boxers it is," Todd said. "Nothing but the best for my boys. Um, I'm down with this. Darrel, what do you think?"

"You think we could get fired for this?"

"Hell no!" Todd said. "We drank too much, started dancing, and got hot. They just said boxers, nothing about going naked, so we'll be safe."

"Better get a move on boys," I said. "This party is just getting started and we've got a long night ahead of us."

"Come on," Todd said. "I know what the next dare is going to be. You two girls are going down...if you get my drift."

Todd and Darrel stood up and marched over to the dance machine. Darrel put in a ten-dollar bill and the machine came to life, the music and announcements of the upcoming match overpowering the sportscasters on the televisions. Todd and Darrel started cheering and yelling, getting everyone in the bar to look at them. When most of the bar had their eyes on them, Todd and Darrel stripped down to their boxers and started the game.

The crowd in the bar went nuts, some of them cheering the two guys on, most of them catcalling and throwing popcorn at them, making fun of them. Both Darrel and Todd got into the game, dancing their hearts out. I looked at Anna as she was watching. We leaned close but still had to yell to hear each other.

"It's time to bail," Anna shouted. "We got the information we needed. I'm not blowing one of these losers only to find out that's all the information they have."

"How do we find out the name of the guy who told them to hide the interviews?" I asked.

"That's a good question," Anna said. "Let's go and we can think it over...or do you want to stay and think it over while sucking Darrel's..."

"I get it," I said. "Let's go."

We started to sneak out of the bar. Everyone was paying so much attention to Todd and Darrel on the machine that no one even noticed that we were leaving. We kept our eyes toward the arcade area, making sure the guys didn't see us. At first they would think we went to the bathroom, but when enough time had passed, they would know we ditched them. Once we were outside we ran through the well-lit gallery.

Anna led me to the coffee shop that was on the other side of the gallery. We rushed in, each grabbed a cup of the house coffee, and took a table that allowed us to see the entrance to Donny's Sports Den. We took sips of our coffee as we watched the door.

"How did you put that together so fast?" I asked Anna. "How did you know Todd would balk at losing arm wrestling?"

"I didn't," Anna said. "I took a bet on that one. Most guys, especially as arrogant and wannabe macho as he was, would rather lose an arm than lose in arm wrestling to a girl. Even if he did it, I had a ton of dares that eventually would have gotten us to where we wanted to be."

"Nice work," I said.

"Thanks," Anna replied. "Now, how do we find out who gave that order? There's got to be someone who knows."

"Maybe you could have Lund look for the secret file," I said. "If we could see the interviews then we might be able to figure out who left your house that night. That could be something."

I hadn't told Anna about the 'cheating death' story I either heard from Malenko or dreamed I heard from Malenko. I'm still not even sure how to classify that event. I didn't want to worry her further, so I just pushed past it.

"But the problem is that it goes back to the university," Anna said. "We've got a good lead with Jimmy, but I don't know anyone from the university..."

Anna was cut off by her phone ringing. She pulled her phone from her pocket and grimaced. "It's Todd."

"Don't answer it," I said.

"I have to," Anna replied, hitting the answer key on her phone. "Hello...I'm sorry, Todd...Imara and I got scared...we saw you in your underwear and we thought the next step would be you seeing us in our underwear and we're not ready for that yet...you understand...I'm sorry...we can meet up again soon but you have to promise not to push...Imara is crying from that comment you made...about going down...okay...bye."

"They bought it?" I asked as Anna put her phone down.

"I think so," Anna said. "I said you cried over that comment and he said they were only joking, they don't even like getting them."

"Liars," I said. "They'll say anything to move this along."

"We got information," Anna said. "We can avoid them. Let's get out of here and get back to the papers. Maybe we can find the university connection somewhere there."

I grabbed my cup of coffee and followed Anna out the door, taking a look around the empty shop to make sure no one was listening to our conversation. There was only one other person there, a college girl with headphones on. I was pretty sure we were in the clear but something told me the night wasn't over.

Chapter #15

The Haunted Case

Anna and I left the coffee shop and walked toward the exit of the gallery. I looked toward the bar but couldn't see Todd or Darrel through the windows. I wondered if they'd stuck around and kept drinking or if they were going to leave. I wondered how much trouble they got into for stripping down to their boxers and dancing for everyone. It would make a good story for them one day. I didn't care for either of them and knew that Anna didn't either. If we met them again we would have to be careful to make sure it didn't get pushed too far.

The gallery was quiet, no people around. Anna seemed to be constantly looking over her shoulder, looking around like we were being followed or something. I couldn't figure out what she was looking at. She stopped walking and held up her hand before I could say anything. I scanned the area but couldn't see anything that would be reason to stop. I looked at Anna who had her brow in a scowl, like she was pissed at something she was seeing. I tried to ask but before I could get a full syllable out she held up her hand to quiet me.

"Ladies," a powerful man's voice said, from the shadows, "don't you look all dressed up and fancy tonight."

Detective Travis Lukens stepped out of the shadows, throwing his spent cigarette to the ground and stamping it with his foot while blowing smoke rings our way. The wispy smoke seemed to frame his face as he walked toward us.

"Detective Lukens," Anna said. "You enjoy scaring the daylights out of two unarmed women at dusk? Is that your idea of a good night?"

"Hardly," Travis said. "I just thought it best to keep an eye on you two. You never know when you are going to need a hand."

"I think we are safe now," I said, looking over the detective in his three-piece brown suit. He did look stunning, in that gentleman type of way, but he had no reason to be watching us. "Why do you think we'll need a hand?"

"I have my reasons," he said.

I wanted to scream. I was so sick of people telling me that they had their reasons and not elaborating on what those reasons were. That is one of the reasons I didn't want to get involved with it—it was going to be a royal pain in the ass every step of the way.

"What are your reasons?" I asked. "Just tell us and not use all that secret, cryptic message stuff."

"You're dredging up the haunted case," Travis said.

"The haunted case?" Anna asked, skeptically. "You've got to be kidding me."

"A haunted case is any case that has ghosts following it," Detective Lukens said. "The case you are looking at has hundreds. There were many people, as it seems, that never wanted this case to be solved. Any answer we could have gotten was hidden before it could be asked. There's nothing that can be done to solve the case, but if you want to know why I'm really following you it's because I believe that the reason your names were circled on those old newspaper clippings we found on the body is because the killer is coming after you next."

My head started swimming, like I was treading water and something was pulling me down so I couldn't think clearly. The thought had never crossed my mind that the killer would be coming after us, if this even was a case where the killer would kill multiple times. So far there'd only been the one death and nothing to indicate that there would be more.

"Why us?" Anna asked.

"Why not?" Travis said. "Two attractive young women, there's always a reason."

"That's a horrible thing to say, Detective," I said, almost in a shout.

"I don't practice much tact," Detective Lukens said. "There's not much use for it where I come from. I'm just curious, what were you doing with Todd and Darrel tonight?"

"On a date," Anna said.

"Must be a quiet night if you ditched them to go get coffees," Travis said. "Didn't you like the way they were dancing?"

"No, I didn't," Anna said. "They didn't dance well enough for me to stick around. That isn't a crime, is it?"

"No," Detective Lukens said. "But it should be, breaking their hearts like that."

"They are probably hitting on the waitresses right now," Anna said. "They'll find someone stupid enough to fall for their lines. Their balls won't go blue tonight."

"Interesting," Travis said.

"Can we go?" I asked. "I don't like this. I think it would be best if Anna and I left right now. Unless you need us for questioning or something there's no reason for us to be sticking around here."

"You can go," Travis said. "Just know that you will be watched."

"Have we been watched for a while now?" I asked.

"You have."

"Then you can explain something to me," I said, smugly. "Explain to me just how the hell Princess Aine changed outfits so quickly, twice, then went from one second standing right next to me to the next second being across the theater."

"I would love to explain that," Travis said, "but alas, I can't. I wasn't able to get inside the theater. I tried to follow you in but the doors locked behind you. There was nothing I could do. I didn't see you again until you left."

"So, you didn't see the magic?" I asked.

"There's no such thing as magic," Detective Lukens said. "Magic is an illusion. It's what bored people do to pass the time. Magic isn't real."

"Tell that to Malenko," Anna said.

"See, there's another thing," Travis said. "This Malenko character. I've done some checking and as far as I can tell, the guy doesn't exist. There's no one by that name and I can't find out anything about him. Hell, we don't even know where he and his little pet are staying while they're in town. That's the real mystery about the guy."

"This could all be over if the police would just tell me who killed my parents and why," Anna said. "That's all it will take. I'll even sign a form saying I won't press any charges to the people who did it or to the police for the cover-up. They'll also have to tell Imara what happened to her dad. I know you people know what's going on and you're all just having one big fuckin' laugh at us as we scrape around, following little clues that get us nowhere."

"The haunted case is best left alone," Travis said. "I'm warning you. You follow the case all the way to the end and what you discover is that no one is who you think they are. Take Malenko for instance. Who do you think he really is?"

"I have no idea," Anna said.

"Could he be one of the people who were forced out of their houses here?" Detective Lukens asked. "Could he be someone from the university who was forced out of a job because of the disaster of the expansion plans? Could he be one of the cops forced out of the police force after the case? Who knows? That's one of the questions that I'm trying to figure out."

"But I saw him in Romania," Anna said. "I saw Malenko and Princess Aine in the capital when I was in Europe. They were doing a small street performance to raise awareness about a show they had coming up. They were booked in a theater over there for a weekend. I wanted to stay and see it but I had to keep moving. I was shocked when I saw them here."

"Interesting," Travis said. "Anything else you remember about them?"

"Just that the story was the same," Anna said. "He was Merlin and she's never died. That's not a story you forget hearing, ya know. The shit those two could do with cards on the street though—my God, you'd think they could do real magic. My mind raced for a week trying to figure out the tricks."

"Interesting," Travis said. "You two stay safe. Remember that we are keeping people close to you, just in case."

"I can take care of myself," Anna said. "And I can take care of Imara, too. We don't need your protection on this."

"As you will, ladies," Detective Lukens said.

With that, the detective gave us a smile and started walking away through a grouping of trees and disappeared from our sight. I looked to Anna who had a grin on her face. She had a look in her eyes that told me that we were going to be getting into trouble whether I wanted to or not. I knew better than to protest when she had that look, that glimmer in her eyes like anything was possible and she was ready to conquer the world. I only had to wait until she spoke to realize how crazy it was going to get.

"I need to change," Anna said. "I've got extra clothes in the car. You brought other shoes, didn't you?"

"I threw a pair of sneakers in your car," I said. "I hate wearing pumps for long stretches."

"Every woman does," Anna said. "Sneakers are good. We will be doing some sneaking. The rest of your outfit should work but I would recommend taking all your jewelry off, just in case."

"In case of what?" I asked as Anna started walking toward her car.

Anna didn't reply to me. She waved me along and I had to rush to catch up with her. We got to her car and Anna opened the back door, reaching for a duffel bag on the seat. She motioned for me to turn around and block the view so no one could see her changing. Anna quickly changed before handing me my shoes. She slipped out of her dress and into black tights with a plain black tank top, put on a pair of black gloves, and handed me an identical pair as I put my pumps in the car.

"Want a tee-shirt or is that top okay?" Anna asked.

"Okay for what?"

"Running and sneaking around," Anna said.

"Give me a shirt," I replied.

Anna reached into her bag and took out a plain black tee-shirt. I took my tank off and put the shirt on. It was a size too large but I tucked it into my tights as I looked at myself in the reflection of the car windows.

"Perfect," Anna said. "We are ready for a little breaking and entering."

"Wait a second," I said. "We can't do that."

"You don't even know what we are going to break into," Anna said.

"The answer is no," I replied firmly. "We could go to jail, Anna."

"Detective Lukens said we were being watched at all times," Anna said. "He was implying we could get away with things like this as long as it helped him solve this murder. We figure out who killed Tim and I'm sure we will have found our answers as well."

"And if we don't?" I asked. "Then what? We go to jail. Anna, I can't go to jail."

"Would you trust me?" Anna said. "No one is going to jail. He said they don't know where Malenko and Aine were staying, right? I'm willing to bet they are living in the theater. Maybe if we sneak in there and find their stuff we can find something out about him."

"What are we going to find?" I asked.

"Identification," Anna said. "He must have either flown or taken a boat across the ocean, Imara. He needs a passport for that. No other way. We find that, maybe a social security number, and we can know exactly who they are."

"Who knows what he would do to us if he caught us," I said. "Anna, if they're living there he's probably watching the place. I think this is a really bad idea."

"Point taken," Anna said. "But unless you want to go back to Darrel and get on your knees, pleading for him to just open up to you, this is the best way."

"Can't we solve this without sex or criminal activity?" I asked. "It's a haunted case, can't we bring in someone to help with this?"

"Come on, Imara," Anna said, as she closed and locked her car. "We're going to that theater."

I grudgingly followed Anna as she started jogging back through the parking lot toward the entrance of the gallery. I couldn't help but take in all the fancy lighting that was placed on the entrance arches and fountains as we jogged toward it. They had spared no expense in putting this place together.

As we were almost to the entrance arch, a man stepped in the arch, blocking our way. He was a tall man, very buff and built, tight jeans and a white tee-shirt. He had big muscles all over, arms covered in tattoos, a shaved head with a handlebar mustache. The man had giant eyes that didn't seem to focus, almost like they were covered in glass. From first guess, I thought the guy was either drunk or stoned, but his movements were precise and tight, he wasn't stumbling or having trouble. He motioned for us to stop.

"Evening ladies," the man said. "I know that I'm new to these parts but I was wondering if you could tell a feller where he could find a good time."

"Any number of the bars inside this Gallery will suffice," Anna said. "We're in a hurry, if you don't mind. Could you please move?"

"You two look like you're about to have a good time," the man said. "Could I have some fun with you?"

"Look buddy," Anna said, getting rage into her voice. "I don't drop into bed because some muscle-bound oaf smiles at me. Get out of the fuckin' way, you jerk."

"There's no reason to get mad," the man smiled.

"Yes there is," Anna said. "Beat it, loser."

"Now you're starting to piss me off," the man said, advancing a step forward.

Anna was almost blindingly fast as she moved into a crouched defensive position. The man stepped toward her as Anna shot her hand straight up, catching the guy in the chin and forcing his head back. The man was surprised but Anna kept pushing forward, trying to kick the man in his shin. The man grabbed Anna's arm, and using his size, forced her hard to the ground. He took a step back.

"Looks like you've had some self-defense training," the man said. "That's good. It's good that a lady as pretty as you can defend yourself. Hit me in the chin, snap my head back, kick my shin, and I'll be disoriented enough that you can trip me, knee me in the groin, and run, correct?"

"Not exactly," Anna said. "I won martial arts tournaments."

"But for that everyone is the same size," the man said. "I outweigh you by well over one-hundred pounds. You should have known better. That martial arts stuff is cute and all, but it's nothing compared to this..."

The man reached behind his jeans and pulled out a small silver revolver, aiming it right at Anna who was still on the ground. Anna breathed a deep breath and slowly stood up. She positioned herself in a fighting stance, almost a boxing position, her right foot ahead of her left and both of her arms up, fists balled up protecting her face. Anna was lightly bobbing and weaving, ready for action.

"Seriously?" the man said. "I pull a gun and you get into a fighting stance? You do know how a gun works, right? I pull this trigger and you cease to exist."

"You're not here to kill us," Anna said. "If you were going to kill us...if you had reason to kill us...you would have done it already. You want something from us. Tell me what I think you're going to say and I'll bite it off while it's in my mouth, I swear to God."

"You're a perverted little one," the man said. "I could like that. You're right though. I am here to warn you about something. This case you've been looking into...well, people know. The wrong people know. And unless you want to end up buried next to your parents real damn soon, I suggest that you leave the dead in their graves. Nothing good can come from digging up the past. Consider yourself warned."

"I'll consider it," Anna said, as she quickly moved forward.

With one fluid motion, Anna kicked the man in his hand and the gun went flying. Anna spun and kicked again, connecting her foot with the man's jaw. There was a sickening thud as her foot connected. The man took two steps back, screaming out and grabbing at his jaw. Anna moved in again as I rushed for the gun. The man used his elbow to nail Anna in the side of the head as she was trying to attack him. Anna fell to the ground in an unconscious pile.

The man rushed toward me as I was going for the gun. I picked up the gun as I felt his hands on me. I tried to scramble out of his grip but he was massive, bearing right down on me. He cocked his fist back, ready to level a blow that surely would have knocked my head clean off. He stopped and grabbed the gun out of my hands as his left hand went around my throat. The man picked me up by the throat with his left hand, sadistically smiling as he slammed me into the water of a fountain.

I tried to gasp for air as the warm water covered my body. I was thrashing about with all of my strength but the man was holding me down with one hand on my neck. I couldn't see anything, the water was covering me and I could only sense a blackness enveloping my body. I thought he was going to kill me. There would be nothing left. As my body quit moving about, even though my mind was still screaming at my muscles to move, a blanket of peace and blackness started to cover me. I was scared but felt okay with that.

At once, the hand left my throat and I tried to gasp for air but only got water into my mouth. I felt hands tugging at me, pulling me out of the water. I was out of the water and my back slammed against something hard and someone was pressing down on my chest. I spit out more water than I thought I had swallowed as I looked up. The hands were from Anna and Princess Aine. I tried to sit up but pain shot through my body. The last thing I could focus on before blackness covered me was that I couldn't see our attacker anywhere.

Chapter #16

Beyond the Law

I was wrapped in a blanket even though I wasn't cold. The police station was hot as police officers passed by in a blur of blues and blacks. I couldn't concentrate, couldn't focus my brain after having almost met my end. I never thought some punk trying to warn us would almost bring about my demise, but I was certain that if Aine hadn't shown up he would have killed me, then Anna. That was the only thought in my brain. I couldn't shake it. I was almost killed that night, drowned in a fountain.

I heard Anna explain it to three different officers. Anna was struggling to get back to her feet when Aine rushed to the area and told the man to let me go. He simply laughed but Aine rushed toward him and produced a fireball that shot into the man's eyes. The fire seemed, as Anna said it, to shoot right out of Aine's hand. Aine was wearing a black leotard, arms completely exposed, and Anna had seen nothing in Aine's hands as she was rushing toward the man. The fire, like Aine, had come from nowhere.

I was in the process of being interviewed by the fourth cop of the night. I wasn't answering any questions. I only gave a description of the man, telling them what I could remember. I didn't want to say anything until they caught the guy. I hoped they would be able to find him quickly. The police said they had the entire Front Street Gallery and Entertainment Complex on lockdown—police everywhere searching the area for the man. I was certain Mayor Nelson must be beyond upset, this close to the opening and two women almost raped and killed at the front entrance of his complex. The media would love that story.

"Let's try this again," a bland young cop asked me. "What did the guy want?"

"To rape me and kill me," I said. "Nothing more than that. He saw two young women walking alone and he wanted to take us."

Anna had given me instructions when we were brought to the station to stick to that story. I was not to mention a word about the investigation or why we were going back to the gallery after we'd left from our date.

"He didn't talk to you?"

"He tried to pick us up," I said. "He wanted to have sex. We refused him and he got angry. I don't remember anything after he attacked me."

"And your friend...Anna?"

"Get the hell out of here, rookie," Detective Lukens said, as he entered the room.

Travis had a glare on his face that could have split stone. His face was red and there was a snarl in his voice. He slammed the door behind the cop and didn't even give me a smile as he sat in the chair.

"What the fuck happened out there?" Travis shouted. "Can the bullshit, Imara. Start talking."

"I was almost raped and murdered," I said, with tears in my eyes. "That's what happened out there. Thanks so much for keeping an eye on us, Detective. You really came in handy while that guy was choking the life out of me under water. So glad you're there for us."

"Damn it!" Detective Lukens screamed as he threw his coffee mug against the wall, shattering the mug and spilling steaming hot coffee all over the floor. Some of the drops hit my blanket and I was glad for the cover up, I could feel the heat of the coffee through the blanket. "Don't give me some line of B.S., Imara. You and Anna both changed clothes. You were coming back to the gallery after you'd left. You were in the parking lot. I want to know exactly what happened from the time I left you until you were negotiating with your maker."

"I don't remember," I said, with venom in my voice. "I don't remember what happened. I remember the guy and that's it. Why is it so damn important what he said? Just find the bastard and lock him away."

"I want to know what you two were doing," Detective Lukens said. "We're not leaving that point. Anna says she was knocked silly, that must've been pretty easy, and you claim that you don't remember. How convenient. You think I'm a rube? You think I can't draw up some charges on you? Tell me what I want to know."

"Draw up charges on us?" I scoffed. "For what?"

"The way you're dressed," Travis smiled, "and how you look, I'll book you both for prostitution."

"Go ahead," I said, confidently. "I'll say that you were my best customer. I'll say I finished with you before this client came around...what do you want, Travis? I don't remember what happened. Threaten all you want but I don't ever recall hearing of a person's memories coming back to them because they were threatened. Just catch this guy."

"You're lucky Aine came when she did," Detective Lukens said, as he stood up and made his way to the door. "Men like him are beyond the law."

Detective Lukens shot me one last cold glance before he walked out of the small room. I looked at my surroundings. I was in an office, with a plain wooden desk that had every drawer locked. I could see through a window into the main part of the station where cops were running in all directions. There were a few other chairs in this office,

I was sitting in the comfortable leather chair behind the desk, but there were three utilitarian chairs on the opposite side.

The door opened to the office again and Anna and Aine entered the room. I hugged both of them, taking my blanket off and setting it on the desk before we all sat down. I wasn't sure what to say, only that I knew I had to tell Aine what I felt.

"Thank you Princess Aine," I said. "I can't thank you enough for saving my life. I don't know what would have happened if you hadn't gotten there when you did."

"Think nothing of it," Aine said. "There is no greater honor in the world than to save a life. I would have done it no matter who he was choking. Life is not something for us to take. We can give, we can save, but to take is the greatest evil imaginable."

"How did you know?" Anna asked. "I mean, what were you doing there?"

"Magic has a funny way of directing people to the proper place at the proper time," Aine said. "I had been out for a stroll and just happened to be walking by."

"You went for a stroll in that?" Anna asked, referencing Aine's black leotard, dance slippers, and face covered in glitter makeup. "That's the outfit you wore to go on a stroll at night?"

"There's nothing wrong with this outfit," Aine said. "It is quite comfortable for strolling in. You wouldn't know because your mind is so closed off that you've never even tried wearing something like this for a stroll. Oh, Anna, you and I should really spend time together. I would really enjoy that. We could be such good friends."

"I don't know about that," Anna said. "You seem nice enough but I don't believe for one second that you were just walking along and that magic somehow told you to be there to save us. I want to know what we've really stumbled into here."

It was then that a flashing light on the desk happened to catch my eye. At first I didn't pay any attention to it, but something, intuition perhaps, told me I needed to look. It was on the phone system that was on the desk. There was a light flashing, indicating a conference call was taking place and that this handset had the hands-free speaker on. The light wasn't flashing when it was just Detective Lukens and myself in the room...someone was listening to us.

I quickly used small hand gestures to indicate to the others that we were being listened to. Anna got a grin on her face—an evil, dastardly grin that I knew was going to get us into more trouble than we were already in.

"So we know what this is all about," Anna said, loudly and clearly. "The police and mayor are using the Front Street Gallery as a front to move drugs and weapons. We've seen cops pushing the drugs on the teenagers that were in the gallery. We have the evidence that it comes from the mayor's office and all we have to do is get a photo identification of who is doing it and we can have all of them arrested."

Just like that the light went out.

"It's out," I said. "Are you sure that was a wise move?"

"They had no right," Anna said.

"Why were you coming back to the gallery?" Aine asked. "I know about the date to gather information. I know about..."

"How the hell do you know that?" I asked. "And why won't you answer me when I ask that question? And how the hell did you do that trick in the theater the other day?"

"I'm sorry, Imara," Aine said. "I don't think I can answer any of that. I told you before that the trick you described is impossible. I was never on the stage with you, neither was Malenko. I know much because those beyond us want me to know much. That is the way of things. I'm sorry I can't tell you more."

"You know what?" I said, "I'm out. Screw it. I don't care what happened to my dad, I don't care who killed yours, Anna. I just want to run my shop and not get tied up in all of this madness. I almost died tonight. It's not worth it...not for me it isn't."

"Don't say that," Anna said. "We have things to go off of, we have leads. We are close to piecing this together."

"If we're dead then we're not solving anything," I said.

"Please, Imara," Anna said. "Don't do this to me, not now. I know you're stronger than this. This was just a little hiccup. We can get through this."

"I'm not helping anymore unless I get one thing," I said.

"What?" Anna asked.

"Aine," I said, "you have to give me one straight answer. How did you know I was in trouble? I want to know everything behind it."

"I was following you," Aine said. "I was hiding in the bar when you were on your date, I was in the coffee shop while you waited to see if your dates were going to leave, I watched you at the car, and finally when you came back to the gallery."

"You watched me change?" Anna asked.

"Very nice," Aine said, with a smile.

"Why were you following us?" I asked. "What possible reason could you have to be following us around like that?"

"It's for the magic show," Aine said. "We have to gauge which one of you is most in tune with the natural world. Which one of you has better magic flowing through her. I'm leaning toward Anna, she seems more open-minded but I haven't ruled you out yet, Imara. I think you could surprise us yet."

"I still don't get you, Princess Aine," I said.

"And you never will, Imara," Aine said. "I'm not for you to figure out. Just know that I will protect you as I protect all good things."

"I'm a good thing?" I asked.

"A very good thing," Aine said. "You have seen much, worked hard, and have come out a better person for it. Opening night of the gallery will be a night to remember—a night beyond comprehension. Malenko is going to try magic that hasn't been attempted for hundreds of years...things that can only be dreamed of today."

"What do we do next though?" I asked. "How can we keep looking, knowing that people are willing to kill to make sure this stays hidden?"

"We have to dig even faster," Anna said. "Look even harder. It's time you got Mark and put him to good use. We have to know what that doctor knows. What was his name?"

"Doctor Andrew Dumas," I said. "He did the autopsies."

"There must be something," Anna said. "I have ideas of what we can do. We should also look around the station here and see if we can find those locked files."

"Where would they be?" I asked.

"Has to be in records somewhere," Anna said. "I don't know, is there a restricted file around here somewhere? Aine, can you get through locks?"

"Very easily, yes," Aine said. "Only as long as we are not stealing for monetary gain or personal profit. I cannot use my powers for such tasks."

"We are trying to find the identity of a murderer," Anna said.

"For that, I am willing to help," Aine said. "There isn't a lock on the face of the earth that could prevent me from getting in."

"That's good to know," Anna said.

I was about to speak when Officer Lund Grimes entered the room. He shut the door behind him and smiled at all of us. He winked at Anna.

"Everything okay, ladies?" Lund asked. "Can I get you anything?"

"We're fine," I said. "A little shaken up, but other than that, okay."

"There's a lot of pressure on us right now," Lund said, sitting on the desk. "This is the last thing Mayor Nelson wanted in the weeks leading up to the opening of the gallery. He's told anyone that if they leak a word of this to the media that he will fire them. He's hiring more security for the gallery opening and is going through the security tapes right now. There was a camera on the fountain area so we should have a good look at the attacker."

"That's good to know," Anna said. "Anything else you can tell us?"

"Funny you should ask," Lund said. "Seems that some troublemakers have been digging into an old unsolved case. For some reason, all the files pertaining to that particular case have been locked away. No one gets any access to them. There's been no word as to why."

"Any developments in the Tim Krause murder?" Anna asked.

"Officially, no," Lund said. "Off the record, there is a traffic camera that was near Tim's house. Get this...a black car. They don't know exactly what it is because all the markings had been pulled off of it and a different grill was put in the front, so they think it's an older Dodge but they're not sure the model. The license plates were gone, too. No way to identify the car. The driver even went so far as to remove the vehicle identification number in the front dash..."

"Don't tell me those traffic cameras are good enough that they could pull a VIN number from a moving car," Anna said.

"They can," Lund said. "They are powerful cameras. But the thing is, this car is seen stopping on the street near Tim's house. Man got out dressed all in black, mask on, and not one person can remember a thing about the guy."

"I thought I read one time that even with a mask," Anna said, thinking, "that there's software that can recreate the face underneath it. Couldn't you do that?"

"We tried that," Lund said. "Didn't work. He was wearing a paintball mask, not a ski mask that's tight on the skin. The mask he was wearing has its own shape, not following the skin, so there's nothing to go off of. It's like the guy is beyond the law. He thought of everything."

"And it was done during the day?" I asked.

"Correct," Lund said. "This is very disturbing ladies. There is a lot of talk about what steps come next and as a police officer, I don't like it."

"Like what?" Anna asked.

"They are talking about giving us more power to apprehend and detain people," Lund said. "It would cause a lot of problems, I think. It would upset a lot of people while not really helping. They think they know who it is but no one wants to say it."

"Who is it?" Aine asked.

"It has to do with business deals gone badly," Lund said. "Mayor Nelson always wanted the gallery on the edge of town...easier to get to. He owned some land out there but the university decided to build out there. Mayor Nelson made a fortune off selling his land and bought the land for the gallery at a deeply discounted price. There was a member of the university board who was involved somehow. He's been involved with a lot of things but I can't get a name out of anyone."

"Keep trying," Anna said. "There are hidden files locked away somewhere. We have to get them. We have reason to believe there's more information than we first thought."

"I don't have access," Lund said.

"Could you tell us where they are?" Aine said. "We could take it from there. I can get in anywhere."

"You really think you could steal locked, secure documents from a police station?" Lund asked.

"I've stolen more from places more heavily guarded than this," Aine said. "I've stolen jewels and gold from royal vaults because they didn't pay us for our show."

"Even if I did know where they kept the files," Lund said, looking around. "I wouldn't know how to get in."

"We don't need you to get in," Aine said. "Just tell us where."

"Third floor," Lund said. "The room on the northeast corner of the building."

I smiled. I knew that Aine would get the files for us, nothing to worry about. I didn't know if she would need our help but I was certain we could get them. Once we had the locked files, we would be able to crack this case. There would be nothing in our way. Just then the door opened. Mayor Jimmy Nelson, Todd, and Darrel walked in. Todd and

Darrel were in their security uniforms. None of the three men looked very happy.

"Stand down, Officer," Mayor Nelson said, as he handed Lund a piece of paper. "We are taking over this investigation."

"What?" Anna asked as Lund read the paper. "How can you do that?"

"It happened on Gallery property and is therefore Gallery business," Jimmy said.

"We've checked over the tapes," Todd said, glaring at Anna. "There's nothing on them. No attacker."

"How did I get wet then?" I asked.

"Maybe from the date," Darrel said, with a smug grin. "Or maybe you just jumped in the fountain yourself. Anna could have choked you to put the marks on your neck. Maybe you were going to blame one of us for it. There's a million possibilities."

"I was attacked in your gallery," I said, standing. "You cover this up and you're as guilty as the man you hired to kill me."

"Watch your mouth or I'll have you arrested for those lies," Jimmy said, in a hissing voice so sickening that I shuddered from the sound of it. "Get out of here...I mean now! And you'd damn well better watch yourselves."

"Just like that?" Anna asked.

"Interesting what happened when we did a search on you," Todd said. "Seems you spent some time overseas. Also seems like you were arrested in Austria for having sex in the backseat of a parked car."

"And the sex was fucking awesome," Anna said, winking at Todd. "Too bad you'll never get it. Come on, let's go."

I followed Anna out of the office and through the police station. She was walking with her shoulders back and arms swinging, her head held high. She was grinning from ear to ear. I would have been mortified if that had happened to me, and the Anna that I grew up with would have too. Time changes so much about people that it's hard to tell the difference between who people are and who they were when they come back into your life after a long absence.

Chapter #17

The Valley of Darkness

It had been two days since I'd almost died. I was still shaken by the experience in ways that I could have never imagined. Anytime I heard a noise behind me, I jumped. I was startled all the time. I had to put music on at night to sleep, otherwise every noise in the apartment would snap me awake. I felt horrible. Even when I did sleep it wasn't a good or deep sleep. Anna had moved into my apartment that night, knowing there was no way I would be able to stay alone. We stuck together ever since that night.

Anna was helping in the store, along with Sarah. It was the one bright spot in the valley of darkness that had become my life since the incident. The three of us working together was great. Anna had already proven her worth to me by calling all the production companies in nearby towns, getting more clients coming to the store. Sarah was streamlining the accounting and billing systems, something she always wanted to do but didn't have time while she was working her fulltime job. I never thought losing Janet and Tina would be a good thing. I still missed them but business was starting to pick up even more than I'd expected.

No matter how much good I tried to view in my life, all my mind could focus on was that man and his hand around my throat, choking the life out of me. I'd woken both nights after the incident, screaming, feeling his hand on my skin, my body submerged in water, frantic from the nightmare I was having. Anna comforted me both times as I cried. She said that in time it would pass and I would go back to normal sleep. I prayed she was right but didn't know how long it would take.

As Anna escorted the final customers of the day, a pair of teenaged girls who needed outfits for an upcoming costume party, I looked over the store. There were so many clothing racks that it was getting hard to move around. I was almost out of room in the warehouse with all the Halloween costumes, and merchandise was turning through the store faster than ever. Both Anna and Sarah thought it was time to start looking for a bigger store, but I didn't want to do that, it had been the location of Decades of Threads since Dad started the store in his twenties. I liked our little space and didn't want to leave it.

As Anna was about to lock the front door, I heard a knocking at the back. I walked to the back, excited. I knew it would be Mark Lewis. He was meeting us here tonight and I had a longing to see him. After the attack, I had thought more about relationships and what I wanted to get out of life. Maybe solving this crime wasn't the most important thing, but having good people in my life was. I knew that making time for good people would be something to help me out of this valley of darkness.

I opened the back door and ushered Mark in. He looked as handsome as ever in his dark gray suit. He smiled as he walked in, a twinkle in his eyes. He gave me a hug and a small kiss on the cheek. I smiled as I locked the back door and led Mark into the main part of the store where Sarah and Anna had already gathered with all the newspapers and documents we had. Anna was looking through a notebook where she'd started writing down all the information and events that were happening to us. She said we had to document everything, no matter how small, to make sure we didn't forget a single detail.

"Looks like you have a lot of papers," Mark said, as he set his briefcase down and opened it. "I have a couple others for you."

"What did you get?" I asked.

"I brought the official autopsy for Anna's parents," Mark said. "But there's a lot of inconsistencies with them. They haven't been filled out correctly."

"Why would that happen?" Anna asked.

"I don't have an answer for that," Mark said. "There must have been something in the files that would have indicated who the killer was, or maybe who hired the killer. Your mom's file is complete, but your dad's is not the original, nor was it filled out when the autopsy was completed. The document on file was filled out later on that night...hastily."

"What do you mean?" I asked.

"Compare the two," Mark said.

Mark pulled out two autopsy reports, both signed off by Doctor Andrew Dumas. Anna's mom was listed as dying at around 10:30pm but her dad was listed at 12:30am. The report for Anna's mom was done with very nice handwriting that had been written slowly and looked professional. Anna's dad's report was in the same handwriting, but sloppy, like whoever was writing it was writing fast and shaking. It was a strange comparison.

"That's Doctor Dumas's handwriting," Mark said. "I know that for a fact. Why he didn't fill them out at the same time is the real mystery."

"Is he a drinker?" Sarah asked. "Does he do any drugs?"

"I know he drinks," Mark said. "Couple glasses of wine every night, some mixed drinks on the weekend. I've heard rumors that he's got this amazing lake cabin that he hosts parties at. Some people have made heroin references but I don't think he does that very often. Why?"

"What if he filled them out," Sarah said, "then got buzzed. Someone comes in and tells him that he has to redo one of them. That could explain the handwriting."

"It also could explain the time difference," Anna said.

"What do you mean?" I asked.

"Most doctors that I know are creatures of habit," Anna said. "He most likely always fills out the form the same way, glancing at his watch and writing down the time. He did that not even thinking about what he was doing. He's just done it that way so many times that he didn't think about it."

"Strange that no one else caught it," I said. "But the question is what happened to the original? If it contains information, then we need to find it."

"I know that in the main hospital there are locked files," Mark said. "I don't know how to even get into the room. There's security on that floor—a locked door, then the files themselves are locked."

"If we could get Princess Aine in there she would get them," Anna said. "I believe she could get through any door or lock."

"Even with security?" Mark asked.

"I'm sure there would be some form of diversion," Anna said. "You don't know the talent and power of this woman."

"She's the one who saved you from the attacker?" Mark asked me.

"She is," I said. "We were very lucky she showed up when she did."

"And the mayor said they saw nothing on the tape?"

"That's correct," I said.

"Then he's got to be our prime suspect," Anna said, interrupting Mark's thoughts. "There has to be something that can link him to all of this. We should hire a private investigator to tail him, maybe do some digging."

"I don't know," Mark said. "If the investigator gets caught we could be in a lot of trouble. Jimmy doesn't seem like the type of guy that would just leave information around. I doubt we would be able to get anything from him."

"It wouldn't hurt to try," Anna said. "We have to figure out what's going on here. I still say we should try and figure out who Malenko and Aine are. They seem to be way too deep into this."

"I don't think so," Mark said. "Something tells me Malenko and Aine are scam artists. I think they heard about the gallery and the murders and are going to somehow incorporate that into the show. I mean, they said that they wanted one of you in the show and they are following you. I'm very skeptical of those two."

"She saved my life," I said. "Anna's too. We don't even know her real name. I doubt I can ever pay her back for what she did."

"I just wish I knew how she made that fire appear," Anna said. "I know there are stage props and such that can make a fireball like that but there was nothing in her hand— no way she could have had anything concealed in her outfit."

"Magicians are not to be trusted," Mark said. "I don't know if I like the idea of her working with us, the more I think about it. I mean, sure, what if she gets into the files but gets caught? If she turns us over to the police, I'd lose my job and would be out of luck. I get fired for something like that and there wouldn't be a hospital in the country that would take me. I can't risk it."

"She wouldn't even know you are working with us, Mark," Anna said. "We would make sure to keep your name out of this. Look, we have all this information but it's incomplete. We need to find out what's being hidden if we are going to crack this case."

"I still don't know, guys," Mark said. "There's just too much that could go wrong with it. Imara, I just don't want to see you get hurt."

"I won't, Mark," I said. "I believe more than ever that we have to finish this. I hate to say it but that man who attacked us opened my eyes. Look how much they are willing to sacrifice for this gallery, if that's what it's about. Now we know that there's a university connection and a connection to the gallery. We know that police are on the payoff and it looks like doctors too."

"You said Doctor Dumas likes to have parties at his cabin?" Anna asked.

"He does," Mark replied.

"That's a route we could take," Anna said. "Sarah, you know the party scene. If we could use your knowledge..."

"No," Sarah said, firmly. "Absolutely not. I don't ever want to be near that shit again. You have no idea the power drugs can have over a person. Nothing else mattered, just getting that next fix. The things I had to do were horrible. I don't ever want to go into that valley of darkness again."

"You wouldn't have to go into the valley," Anna said. "Just use what you know to pump some information out of the doctor."

"I can't," Sarah said. "There's nothing you could say or do that would make me want to get anywhere near that stuff again."

"Okay," Anna said. "We can figure out something else. We have to get those reports though. If we can see what the differences are then we would have a better place to start from."

"Anna," I said. "Twice now you were going to tell me about something you'd found out that you said changed the entire game on this. Something had happened. What was it?"

"This is unbelievable," Anna said. "I mean, this is..."

Anna was cut off by a loud pounding on the front door. I wasn't expecting anyone to arrive here tonight but there were always people dropping by for this or that. As I moved toward the door, I got a look at the man who was standing there. He was big, tall and bulky, but his mass was held in a very powerful frame. The man looked strong as a bull, not someone to be messed with. He wore jeans and a tee-shirt, work boots with gloves hanging from his back pocket. He had a three-day growth of beard on his face but his head was smoothly shaven. I knew before I opened the door that this was Eddie Hayes, Mayor Nelson's partner in crime.

"Hello," I said, smiling as I opened the door. "How may I help you tonight?"

"I'm supposed to get measured up for this goddamned Gallery opening BS," Eddie said, as he pushed his way into the store. "And make it snappy toots, I ain't got all damn night."

"You must be Eddie Hayes," Anna said, stepping forward. "Pleasure to meet you."

"Who are you?" Eddie asked, eyeing Anna up and down.

"I'm Anna Garst," Anna said, with a smile.

Anna and Sarah had taken to copying my outfits, making almost a store uniform. We all wore black tights to work, with a top from the store, and Anna's top today was beyond stunning for her fit body. She was wearing a yellow floral patterned top from the early seventies that was cropped and haltered, exposing much of her upper body. Anna was using her assets to hook Eddie in.

"Why don't you measure me up?" Eddie asked, licking his lips, eyeing Anna like she was a treat to be eaten.

"I hope we got a tape that's long enough," Anna said, with a smile, and winked at her obvious innuendo. "What are you going to be wearing for the opening?"

"A suit from the twenties," Eddie said. "Mayor Nelson has this all figured out, some old school Hollywood crap. I'm just supposed to be there."

"And why are you going to be there?" Mark asked. "You're a contractor, right?"

"Real estate development," Eddie said, as Anna started to take the measurements. "I developed the gallery project from start to finish. It was perfect timing since I'd just finished the university expansion project."

"You did both of them?" Sarah asked. "Impressive."

"I got more money than I could ever spend in this lifetime," Eddie said. "You should come with me to this party I'm going to in a couple days. It's at this doctor's cabin. You'd know him, Mark...Doctor Dumas. His parties are always fun. He invite you?"

"No," Mark said. "I don't know him well enough yet."

"I do," Eddie said.

"I didn't know you two knew each other," Anna said.

"I'm on the board for the hospital," Eddie said. "We hired Mark and Doctor Dumas."

"I didn't know the board did the hiring," Anna said.

"We'll make the final decision for all the doctors," Eddie said. "HR handles all the nurses and other personnel. I believe you would fit right in at his parties, honey."

Anna smiled as she moved to the counter to write down some of the measurements. As Eddie was looking at her, he reached into his pocket and pulled out a tin of chewing tobacco, taking some and stuffing it in his lips. The sight and the smell of it turned my stomach. Anna tried not to wince but even she shuddered at the disgusting sight. I'd heard Eddie was a strange guy, rough around the edges, and I was beginning to see why. Anna slowly moved back in to continue measuring.

"I'm always up for a party," Anna said. "Never know what kind of people you're going to meet there. Do these parties get pretty wild?"

"You have no idea," Eddie said. "Honey, you and I at that party would be amazing."

"I thought you were married," Mark said. "Wife and kids and all."

"I'm always married," Eddie said. "From time to time. But that doesn't mean that my pipes only work at home, does it? Hell, you're young at that stud age. You should have a different chick in your bed each night. Trust me, look at my brother, the dumbass. He married his high school sweetheart when they were eighteen. The only woman he's ever been with. He looks at me now and just wishes he could have a taste of what I've got. I told my wife when I married her that she'd better not expect me to be in our bed every night. You gotta put a bitch in her place from the start. Nobody tells me what to do."

"Except, of course, Mayor Nelson," I said. "He tells you what to do all the time, doesn't he?"

"That's different," Eddie said. "That's business. As long as we're making bank together, I really don't care. What do you say little chick-a-dee? You want to go to that party with me?"

"I'll think about it," Anna said. "My only concern is that I'm not woman enough to handle a man like you. I think you'd eat me up and spit me out."

"Just like you thought Todd and Darrel would eat you up?" Eddie asked. "I give you compliments for what you did to those two nitwits. I don't know why in the blue hell James keeps them around, they are good-for-nothings. Damn boys get themselves into more women problems than they know what to do with. I'm always bailing them out but James says we have to keep them happy."

"Why?" Anna asked.

"When we're on our little date I'll tell you all about it," Eddie said, as Anna finished up with the measuring. "I think you'll really enjoy this date but don't think for one second that I can be manipulated by you like those two pups."

Anna smiled as she stood straight and tall, arching her back slightly, and pressing out her breasts. She posed a little bit before writing the last of the numbers down. Eddie had his eyes glued to her. Anna smiled more as she licked her lips and moved closer to Eddie. Anna got close to Eddie, placed her hand on his chest, and gently moved it to his stomach as she leaned in to whisper something into his ear. Anna leaned far enough in so that her chest was rubbing against his. Eddie was glowing he was getting so excited. Anna kissed him on the cheek as she moved away. Everyone had their eyes on Anna and Eddie, not paying attention to what I was doing.

"I'll see you 'round then, big guy," Anna said, with a wink.

"Anytime, honey," Eddie said, as he made his way to the door. "Just remember that if you want to spend some time with a real man, I'm the guy you need to talk to."

Eddie waved as he walked out the door. Anna smiled a smug grin. I didn't know what she said to him, and I didn't think I wanted to know, but Anna noticed I was smiling too. I had a smug grin on my face.

"What did you do, Imara?" Anna asked.

"Malenko and Aine aren't the only ones who know a little magic," I said.

"What do you mean?" Sarah asked.

"While Anna was doing her misdirection," I said, smiling as I held up a black leather wallet, "Eddie's wallet magically appeared in my hands."

I smiled as I opened the wallet. I wasn't going to steal anything from it, and once we were done looking through it I was going to put it in a box and mail it to him with a note saying I found it on a street, but I thought that maybe, just maybe, there would be something in there that could help our cause. I mean, it wouldn't hurt to take a few risks, would it?

Chapter #18

The Moment of Magic

It had been a calm day at the store. Anna was in the back working through all the papers while Sarah and I were on the sales floor. There had only been a few customers in today, just browsing through the selection to see what had come in. No major sales. I always hated days like this and hoped it was just a one-off deal, and that tomorrow we would see customers beating the doors down, rushing into the store to buy whatever we had on the shelves.

Anna emerged from the back, holding Eddie Hayes's wallet that I had snagged from him the night before. I didn't feel any remorse for stealing his wallet. I told Anna she had to document where everything in the wallet was before she could take anything out. I also told her to wear a pair of gloves when handling it and to make sure that none of her hair fell into it. Anna had her hair pulled back into a ponytail with a blue baseball cap on her head.

"Find anything?" I asked.

"List of phone numbers," Anna said. "An interesting list to say the least. These are numbers he doesn't want stored in his phone. Jimmy's, a number of council members, and the numbers of the boards from both the hospital and university."

"That's interesting but doesn't really prove anything," I said. "Could be he loses his phone a lot and doesn't want anyone stumbling onto those numbers. Were there any other interesting numbers on the list?"

"Todd and Darrel," Anna said. "Along with Tim Krause...and the governor."

"Why would that number be on the list?" I asked.

"It's his personal cell number," Anna said. "Beyond that, there's a lot of business cards, a little over five hundred in cash, food receipts, couple condoms, credit cards...and this."

I looked at what Anna was holding up. I wasn't sure at first but as I looked closer my heart skipped a beat. It was a keycard used in electronic locks. The front indicated that it was for the hospital and writing on the back indicated that it was a master keycard, good for opening any lock in the hospital.

"You know what kind of trouble we could get in with this?" Anna asked. "We could have access to all the files. We could know exactly what happened."

"Why the hell would Eddie Hayes have a master keycard to the hospital?" I asked. "That makes no sense at all. He shouldn't have that."

"But he does," Anna said. "And now we do. Think of it like a magic trick, Imara. You set everything up, get people looking in the wrong direction, and as Princess Aine would say, you execute the moment of magic to wow everyone watching."

"If we use that card," Sarah said, "won't the hospital have cameras in those areas? I mean, they'll know that we're not Eddie."

"No one will ever know," Anna said. "Think about it, we'll go tonight. Use the card to breach the security and get the files. Then tomorrow morning we ship the wallet, along with the keycard, back to Eddie. No one will know that we accessed the files."

"If we could get Mark to come with us," I said, excitedly, "then we would have a reason for being there. I mean, he could say that it was hospital business."

"It's a different hospital than the one he works in," Anna said. "How would that help us?"

"At least he's got a knowledge of the building," I said. "Plus, he knows a lot of the people that work there. This could be the best way. Mark and I will go and get the files tonight. You find anything else in the wallet?"

"Nothing that helps us," Anna said. "All standard wallet stuff."

I was about to ask another question when the door to the store opened. I was excited to get a final customer of the day since it was so close to five but when I turned to look my heart sank; Detective Travis Lukens and Officer Lund Grimes were walking into the store and the detective did not look happy to see us.

"Interesting that I always find you three together," Travis said, as I noticed Anna hiding the wallet in a rack of clothing. "I figured that you three would be here. I have some questions to ask you."

"We don't know anything," Anna said.

"And please tell me, blondie, what don't you know about?" Travis asked with a harsh tone in his voice. "I haven't even told you what happened and you already don't know about it. I think I should bring you and Imara in right now. Arrest you here on the spot, drag you downtown, and question you there. Then maybe you'll remember something."

"Okay, Detective," I said. "What is going on? What happened?"

"Your little adventure two nights ago," the detective scoffed, "what happened when you left the station?"

"We went home," I said. "Anna's been staying with me. We were at my apartment all night."

"And last night?" Travis asked. "What did you do after work last night?"

196

"Went home," I said. "We hung out, played some cards and went to bed. Nothing out of the ordinary, Detective."

"Are you sure that's all you did?" Travis asked.

"Yes," I said, mad. "What else do you want me to say, Detective Lukens? We didn't go anywhere, we ordered food in, and we hung out in my apartment. What happened?"

"The man that attacked you," Lund asked.

"*Allegedly* attacked her," Travis interrupted.

"Allegedly," Lund continued as he held out a photograph. "This him?"

I looked at the picture. It was the man, almost the same outfit he'd attacked us in. He was standing in front of a park, smoking a cigarette. It looked to be some kind of police surveillance photo.

"That's him," I said. "Where did you get this picture? Did you arrest this guy?"

"He's dead," Detective Lukens said, coldly. "He was found dead not long ago."

"Where?" Anna asked.

"Classified," Lund said. "We cannot let that information get out right now."

"So, he was murdered somewhere in the gallery?" Anna said. "Otherwise you would tell us where he was at. How did it happen?"

"Shotgun to the face," Travis said. "The place he was found was locked from inside, no way anyone could have gotten out. It would be called a suicide but there was no weapon found at the scene. It's as baffling as Tim's death."

"And you think that we did it?" Anna asked.

"You had motive," Travis said. "You were afraid for your life. I've seen women do worse when threatened like this. Did you kill him?"

"You were supposed to be watching us," Anna scoffed. "Didn't you see where we were at? Wouldn't you know if we were at the gallery when he would have been killed? You tell us...did we kill him?"

"Very cute, Anna," Travis said. "And I fuckin' hate cute. Don't push my buttons girl, not right now or I swear to God I will have you in a cell tonight."

"You've got nothing on us," Anna said, taking a step forward. "You pathetic slob. You've got no leads and a mayor crawling up your ass. You know that you will be canned if this isn't figured out by the time the gallery opens. A murder in the gallery under your watch? You must be sweating bullets right now, Travis. I would hate to be in your shoes."

"Watch your fucking mouth," Detective Lukens roared as he knocked over a clothing rack, sending specialty clothing flying over the floor. "I mean it, Anna. I don't need some punk girl lipping off to me right now."

"And Imara doesn't need some punk detective who got his job from blowing the right case, screwing this one up. She almost died because you were sitting on your ass and now you've got another death on your hands. What are you going to do, Detective?" Anna asked with a smug look on her face.

Travis looked ready to destroy the entire store. His face was red, he was sweating, and it looked like his entire body was shaking. If Anna wanted to get him wound up and pissed off, she'd succeeded perfectly, although I couldn't figure out why she was doing it. He could arrest us and most likely would if she kept lipping off to him. I knew Anna had a plan but I couldn't see what it was.

"Nothing to say, Detective?" Anna asked after a moment of silence. "I figured that. You've got nothing to hold us on, you couldn't even arrest us if you wanted to.

You've had people watching us, so you know full well that we were nowhere near the gallery yesterday or today. Am I right?"

"You are," Lund said.

"Who was the guy then?" I asked. "Who was he and why did he try to kill me?"

"We're working on that," Lund replied. "We found him hanging, which had been done after he'd been shot. Not sure why the killer did that. We guess the guy was killed not long after he got into the altercation with you. The real question we need to ask you is who else is watching you?"

"No one that I know of," Anna said.

"Nobody's watching us," Sarah said.

"Imara," Lund said, softly, "care to add anything?"

"If someone is watching us," I replied, "I don't know anything about it. They haven't made it known to us if they are."

"You find out anything on Malenko?" Anna asked. "You know anything about him?"

"We know enough about him and Aine to know that they are not to be messed with," Travis said. "We are keeping a very close eye on them. They didn't kill anybody. Aine was at the station with you and Malenko was working on his little show. He works almost non-stop. I've never seen such dedication before."

"It's good that someone takes pride in their work," Sarah said. "If we could have that out of all the cops in the area maybe we wouldn't be experiencing a killing spree."

"I think they need to knock off a few more people before we can call this a killing spree," Lund said. "But just know that not a word of this is to get into the media."

"How can you do that?" I asked. "The public has a right to know they are in danger."

"The public has a right to know what we tell them," Travis said. "Now, I came here for a specific reason. There is something that happened with this murder, like the last, that drags you into it. This time we need something from you, Anna."

"What do you need with me?"

"There were notes found again," Lund said. "Same as last time, your parents' obituaries and the write up about Imara's father disappearing."

"Were our names circled again?" I asked.

"Not this time," Travis replied. "But there was something else left there. A piece of paper written on with words cut out from magazines. It said, 'three bodies rest in two graves. When the third is found, all questions will be answered...but remember, answers will only lead to more questions.'"

"They are implying that Mom was pregnant when she was murdered," Anna said. "Three bodies in two graves...that's what they mean, right?"

"It could," I said.

"Mom couldn't be pregnant," Anna said. "She'd been fixed a number of years before. There was some trouble...Dad thought that Mom had cheated on him, which was absolutely ridiculous, Mom loved Dad and would never do anything to hurt him. Dad wanted to trust her but he also wanted to be safe. They didn't want any more kids, so Dad had Mom get a procedure so she couldn't have any, just in case."

"What difference would it make if her mom was pregnant?" Sarah asked. "I fail to see how that would change anything."

"She makes a good point," Anna said. "What difference would it make?"

"We've gone through your dad's medical files," Travis said. "He also had a procedure. If she was pregnant, maybe this has to do with jilted lovers and nothing to do with your dad's connections among the city."

"Okay," Anna said, shaking her head. "What do you want from me then?"

"I have this form," Detective Lukens said, handing Anna a few pieces of paper. "It is a standard contract that allows us to dig up your parents' graves and exhume the bodies to do some testing on them."

"Dig them up?" Anna said. "You want to see if she's actually pregnant? Are you kidding me? Fuck you and your papers." Anna threw the papers on the ground. "Dig up my parents to see if my mother was really cheating on my father. Go to hell, Travis. You're not touching that grave."

"We are, actually," Detective Lukens said. "We just have to do it the hard way now. Well, not even the hard way. See, those graves could potentially include evidence that could catch a murderer. If we bring this evidence to a judge he'll grant us the necessary papers to get a backhoe out there before it gets dark tonight. Lund, call Eddie Hayes's brother."

"Eddie's brother?" I asked. "What does he have to do with this?"

"Eddie's brother, Fred Hayes," Detective Lukens said, "is a good friend of ours...and the local judge. He'll gladly come down to the station to help catch a murderer. I'll remember how well you cooperated with us later on, Anna. You could have made this a much cleaner investigation."

Detective Lukens and Lund walked out of the store. Anna was stunned. I rushed over to hug her but she pushed me away. She was thinking, trying to remember something that had happened long ago. Anna started to pace and motioned for us to remain silent. Finally, she stopped pacing and looked at us.

"She could have been pregnant," Anna said. "I remember that she went in to have the procedure but didn't go through with it. She even had something else done at the hospital, I don't remember what, so that she had to pay them, there was a trail of bills and whatnot so that Dad would believe her. I remember a fight between them when Dad found out later on. She had a miscarriage about six years before she died. She very well could have been pregnant."

"And if she was, I'm sure it was your father's," Sarah said, trying to be helpful.

"I don't know," Anna said. "I always thought I had the perfect family but there was always tension under the surface. I never really understood where it was coming from. Maybe this is all about lovers."

"There is nothing more powerful than love," Princess Aine said, seemingly emerging from a clothing rack, scaring all of us in the room. "Love can cause people to do very strange and unnatural things."

"Damn it, Princess Aine," I said. "Where did you come from? How long have you been hiding here?"

"I arrived not long ago," Aine said. "Enough to hear most of the interesting parts of the conversation. It's funny how deep this mystery is getting. I just wish I knew who was behind it all. I suck at reading mystery novels. I always turn to the end to see who did it."

"Why spoil the surprise?" Anna asked. "If you hate mystery novels then how can you be in a magic show? All that is, is mystery."

"I don't hate mystery books," Aine said. "I love them. I simply said I suck at reading them. Magic is different, it's like a well-played chess match. All the pieces are put into place, you try to get your opponent to look in a certain direction, and then the moment of magic happens and they are blown away...*checkmate*. If they had magic eyes they could see. If you had magic eyes you could see. But you don't."

"But you have magic eyes," Anna said. "Tell us, Aine, what is going on here?"

"I see a terrible feud that happened many years ago," Aine said. "There was bad blood on both sides. Loyalty and dedication were changing by the day, sometimes by the hour. Someone knew the only way to stop the feud would be to kill the other side. Your father couldn't do that and that's why he is no more."

"My father's dead in the ground," Anna said. "And the police are going to dig him up like a dog goes after a forgotten bone. It's so wrong. I don't want them dug up."

"It's going to be okay," I said, hugging Anna. "You won't have to see them."

"I don't even want to hear about it," Anna said. "I'm sure, however, that once they find something out they will come running to us to rub it in. If Mom was pregnant, would they be able to tell who the father was?"

"I don't know," I said. "You would think that the autopsy would have shown whether she was expecting or not. That's not something an autopsy would miss...unless the doctor giving the autopsy was instructed to miss it."

"It just adds more layers to this mystery," Anna said.

"It's a mystery that deepens by the day," Princess Aine said.

I looked at the princess. She was in rare form today, wearing a black leotard that was covered in sparkling sequins. She had ribbons in her hair that matched the color of her leotard with black dance slippers. There was a tiara in her hair and her face was covered in glitter makeup.

There was glitter in her hair and on her upper chest, shoulders, and arms. It looked like she'd taken a shower in glitter.

"Do you need something, Aine?" I asked.

"I just wanted to check in on you three," Aine said. "And I also wanted to invite you to stop into the theater soon. The show is rapidly approaching and Malenko wants to speak with all three of you. There might be spots for all of you in the show, if you're willing. But please, stop in soon."

"We will," Anna said.

Aine bowed to Anna before smiling and waving at Sarah and me. She calmly strode out of the store and into the street. I wondered what her angle was in all of this, almost half expected her to still be in the store, wearing a normal outfit with no glitter. The trick still bothered me but not as much as her not admitting that she'd done it.

I knew the time had come where I had to call Mark to let him know about the key and what we were planning to do. I hoped that he would come with me, no questions asked, but if he wouldn't, then I would have to go alone. I couldn't risk the others getting caught as well. If we were arrested, nothing would get solved—this was something that needed to be taken care of. I took a deep breath as I picked up the phone and dialed Mark's number.

Chapter #19

Secret Lies

I felt strange...*bad*. Like karma was going to extract some form of bizarre revenge on me for what I was about to do. I didn't know why I felt like that, we were trying to obtain information to solve a murder case. Maybe it was the clothes I chose to wear—black tights, a matching long-sleeved top, and my hair pushed into a black stocking hat. Maybe it was how easy Mark agreed to come with, but he wasn't here to solve the case—he wanted to solve me. Maybe it was the fact that we were breaking into a hospital at night. I kept repeating to myself that we were doing this to solve a murder.

Mark had opted to wear blue jeans and a plain white tee-shirt. He looked as good in that outfit as he did when we were seniors in high school. We both wore gloves but he thought I was going too far with the long-sleeved shirt and the hat on such a warm summer's night. He said it was a dead giveaway that we were up to something. We both were wearing glasses we'd gotten at a local dollar store, designed for people who needed help reading. Mark had a fake brown mustache on his upper lip while I had a press-on butterfly tattoo on my neck. We were both nervous about getting caught on film while attempting to solve this murder.

We approached the hospital, the entrance bathed in the humming yellow light of the streetlamps, the sun having disappeared over two hours earlier. The entrance to the majestic hospital was empty, no vehicles or people around. There was ornate landscaping and flowers, making the place look so bright and cheerful. The red brick building was tall and imposing, a bastion of the community that had been sitting in downtown Prairie Rapids for over fifty years. Both Mark and I breathed a heavy sigh as we walked through the automatic doors and into the main hallway.

The walls were a bright white, illuminated by overpowering fluorescent lights that lined the ceiling. In front of the doors was a large reception desk, with stations for six different people to sit. Each station had a different sign hanging over it, telling incoming people which station they were supposed to go to. Beyond the station was a guard desk and another reception desk large enough for a single person. All the desks were made from a cold metal, very sterile and plain. There was no one at the desks, no one in the waiting room.

Mark motioned toward a set of double doors leading past the security desk. They were closed and had no windows to look through; no way to know if anyone was waiting on the other side for us. Mark walked to the doors and tried to open them but they were locked. I pulled out the card I'd gotten from Eddie's wallet and held my breath as I slid the card through the electronic card reader next to the door. After a second there was a clicking noise from the doors and a light on the card reader flashed green.

Mark pushed the doors open and peeked his head through. When he was sure the coast was clear, he motioned for me to follow him through the doors. The hallway was dimly lit but the floor and walls were very white. It had a clean smell to it, like someone had just mopped the floors with a powerful bleach. The scent of the cleaning agent burned the eyes with every breath. Mark led the way as we moved quickly though the hall. At every door and every hallway intersection Mark would move slowly and glance around the corners, making sure no one would see us. He said the elevators were on the far end of this hallway, but with each door we passed, my heart raced faster and faster, almost pounding out of my chest. I was certain it was loud enough to give our location away.

Past the doors and hallways, through another set of locked doors, and to the back of the hallway, we finally reached an elevator. Mark pressed the button to go up, which illuminated when he touched it but the elevator didn't appear to be moving. We waited for a moment before Mark pressed the button again. I looked around but there wasn't a card reader near the door, the elevator wasn't locked out. I was trying to stop my hands from shaking, trying to steady my breathing as Mark pressed the button more and more, before finally, the elevator started to come down.

When the elevator reached the bottom floor, there was a chime that went off right before the door started to open. My heart stopped because I could hear voices coming from behind the door. I wanted to run, wanted to hide, but there wasn't time, there would be no way for us to get into the clear before the doors were fully open and we'd be exposed. As the doors opened I felt a rush of relief flooding over me like a warm tidal wave.

Inside the elevator, pushing cleaning carts, were a man and a woman, both in their thirties who were so busy in their conversation about how much they hated their boss that they didn't even notice we were there. Mark and I moved out of the way as they pushed their cleaning carts past us, not even bothering to acknowledge that we were standing in the hallway. Mark and I entered the elevator and pressed the button for the third floor. The doors closed as the elevator jerked. The ride was noisy and rough, an old elevator in an old building. I'd thought that the hospital would have taken better care of their building but the elevator didn't seem like it had been worked on in years.

We arrived at the third floor, stopping with a jolt. When the elevator door opened we saw a yellow hallway. The carpet was yellow, the walls were yellow, and even the lighting seemed to have a yellow tint to it. The hallway smelled of vanilla, a poor vanilla air freshener that clearly needed to be changed. Mark led the way as we moved down the hall. Every door we passed was locked, with no windows in it or any markings other than the room number to indicate what the room was for. Mark knew what room we needed, I just hoped that our luck would hold out and no one would spot us in the hallway. I wondered if security guards were watching us right now, watching our every movement on cameras and just waiting for us to do something big they could arrest us for, besides breaking in.

Mark arrived at a door and tried the handle. It was locked, so I took the card out and slid it through the reader. There was the click of the lock opening and a light on the reader flashing green, so we pushed our way into the room. The room we entered was large and very cold, like the room had its own high-powered air conditioner. The room was long and narrow, with file cabinets lining the walls with an island of cabinets in the middle. The wall cabinets extended to the tall ceiling and there was a moveable ladder attached to each side. Mark pulled the door shut behind us and manually locked the doors using a short rope he pulled from his pants' pocket.

"Is that really necessary?" I asked. "If someone tried to open that door they would know someone is in here."

"I'm not taking the chance of getting caught," Mark said. "Let's just find what we came here to get and then get out of here. Look under the 'G' for Garst. That's where they should be."

I scanned the files and found the G's. I had to move the ladder over to reach the file that would have Anna's parents in it. I opened the file and quickly shuffled through them until I reached Anna's dad. I pulled out his file and opened it. The first page made me want to hit something. I swore out of frustration.

"What is it?" Mark asked.

"It's the exact same page that you found," I said. "The false one. This is only a copy of what you had before."

"That's strange," Mark said. "The original should be there. What else is in the file?"

"There's a number of papers here," I said, paging through everything. "But nothing looks helpful to us. It's just his basic medical files."

I handed his file to Mark and pulled out Anna's mom's file. I flipped through the file but didn't find anything that appeared to be helpful. I found the papers about the procedures that she had, found the information on the past miscarriage, found the documents for Anna's birth, but there was nothing that helped us. Everything was what we thought it should be.

"You see anything in that file that's out of the ordinary?" I asked Mark.

"Nothing," Mark said. "All of this is in order. Imara, this looks to be a bust."

"Now here's something you don't see every day," I said, stunned, as I was looking at a paper that was in the mother's file. "Did you know that Anna died at 10:30 that night as well?"

"What are you talking about?" Mark asked.

"There's a death certificate for Anna here," I said, handing him the document. "It says that Anna August Garst died at 10:30, the same day and time as her mother. Cause of death is shotgun blast to the face."

"This is strange," Mark said. "It's signed by Doctor Andrew Dumas. Why the hell would he have filled this out?"

"Maybe they were supposed to kill Anna too," I said. "They wanted to get rid of the whole family. She doesn't have any other family elsewhere, both her parents were only children and her grandparents are dead. What would have happened to all her dad's property if Anna would have died?"

"I suppose it would go into probate," Mark said. "Then the state would auction it off. If there's no one willing to come forward to claim it, I would assume they pay off all debts then keep the money. It would simply be considered taxes."

"And with the amount of connections Jimmy has," I said, "I'm sure he would end up with the land at a very good price."

"That is a safe assumption," Mark said. "This is very strange. Why would he sign this before it even happened? I wonder if they wanted everything to be rushed through so they had all the documents in place. They would have to leave the estate in probate for a month, so the quicker they had this document in, the quicker they could rush everything through and sell the land."

"This document alone should be cause to get Doctor Dumas in trouble, correct?" I asked.

"That document could do a lot of damage to his career," Mark said, "if the board found out about it. It implicates him in the murders. It proves he had something to do with it. The main question is, why was it in Anna's *mom's* file? Check Anna's file."

I shuffled through the folders until I found Anna's. I opened it up, looked everything over, before I handed it to Mark. I didn't notice anything out of place. Everything, as far as I could remember, looked right.

"Nothing wrong there," I said.

"Except this," Mark said, looking over a form. "This says that Anna was a blood donor for her sister. Anna doesn't have a sister."

"No, she doesn't" I replied "Anna is AB negative blood, very rare. She's never mentioned a sister."

"It says here that one of her older sisters was involved in a horrible crash and that Anna donated blood...and a kidney."

"No fucking way," I said. "That's impossible. Anna...I don't know how that's possible. I mean, I've seen her in a bikini, she doesn't have any scars. When did it say this happened?"

"Anna was only twelve," Mark said. "The sister was eighteen."

"Can they do that with an age difference like that?" I asked. "Wouldn't Anna still be developing while the sister was, for the most part, fully grown?"

"If she needed it to survive and Anna was the only match," Mark said. "They would risk it. Look in the mom's file, does it mention anything about other children?"

I tore the file apart, looking at every piece of paper with critical eyes. I was certain I didn't see anything but I had to check and double check. I went through her dad's folder again, there was nothing at all to indicate that Anna had a sister.

"Nothing," I said. "What does this mean?"

"I don't know," Mark said. "But there's indications here that Anna had plastic surgery to cover the scars. There'd be no indication of them ever being there. She's never mentioned any of this to you?"

"No," I said. "I thought that I knew everything major about her. We told each other everything growing up. Even thinking back to then, I really don't remember her being out for surgery or ever missing sports or anything. How could she have kept this silent?"

"There's really no way," Mark said. "I say we take all these files with us and look though them more at your apartment. We need Anna's death certificate. With that we can confront Doctor Dumas and he may be willing to give information in exchange for it."

"I've got a different plan for getting information out of the doctor," I said. "In case that doesn't work. We need to get back to the apartment though. They should have finished exhuming Anna's parents. I should be there for her if there's any phone calls. Anna is tougher than she looks but I don't know how much more she can take."

"How are you holding up with all of this?" Mark asked as he rubbed my arm with his hand. "You're tougher than you look, too, ya know."

"You saying I look weak?" I said, as I pulled my arm away from him.

"No," Mark said, stunned. "What I meant was..."

"Got ya," I smiled. "You never could tell when I was playing with you."

"Never could, Imara," Mark smiled.

"I'm holding up okay, I think," I said. "I just wish I knew how there was so much information I never knew about. I really want this to be over. I mean, with Sarah involved full time at the store, and possibly Anna working there full time too, and with you back in town, things could be really good again Mark."

"I just hope we find your father in all of this," Mark said. "I mean, he vanished into thin air. Maybe Malenko can wave his hands and make him reappear."

I was about to respond when the doorknob started to rattle. Someone was subtly trying to get into the room. They had already used the keycard and unlocked the door.

The rope Mark had placed around the doors was the only thing keeping them from getting in. My eyes went big and my heart raced as I couldn't focus on anything. Luckily, Mark sprang into action. He quickly closed the files we'd opened before pushing the ladder away from the area we'd been at.

Mark jumped up on the middle cabinets and stood on his tippy-toes. He opened a grate that led into the ceiling vents and hoisted himself into the vent before motioning me to do the same. I stood on the cabinets as the door was being more violently shaken. The person on the outside really wanted to get in. I handed the files to Mark and tried to hoist myself up. It was a struggle; I didn't have the upper body strength to do it. Whoever was at the door was starting to put their weight into it, slamming against the door. I could hear the door slamming back into the doorjambs as the rope held tight. I knew the rope wouldn't hold for long as I struggled to get up.

Mark reached his hand down, grabbing me by the arm, but my spandex shirt was too slippery and he couldn't hang onto me. I fell down, landing on my back on the cabinets as the doors were really getting pushed in. I felt a pain shooting through my right hip and leg. I forced myself to stand up and jump, getting further into the vent. Mark grabbed my hands and helped me into the vent. We were both exhausted by the time he finally got me in.

Mark jumped over me and replaced the vent cover just as the rope on the doors broke and the person slamming against it fell into the room. It was Eddie Hayes followed by Jimmy Nelson and Detective Travis Lukens. Eddie stood up as they looked around the room, trying to see if they could find our hiding spot. I hoped they didn't know we were in there, that they wouldn't be able to figure it out, but there weren't many other places we could have gone. Travis grabbed the ladder and went right to Anna's files.

"They're gone," Travis said. "They must have taken them."

"There's nothing there that could affect us, is there?" Jimmy asked.

"There is," Detective Lukens said. "Doctor Dumas did what he was instructed to do, filled out all three death certificates. They will know Anna was supposed to die that night."

"How the fuck was that not destroyed?" Jimmy asked. "Anything else?"

"Not that I know of," Travis said. "Even with that form they won't be able to get anything. Doctor Dumas has enough standing in the area to say that he signed it before a name was written. It was a mix-up which is why he made another."

"We already had to get a fake certificate for the father," Eddie said. "That was screwed up once already. We never did figure out why. We can't have more screw-ups on this. Tim was our contact on the University and now he's gone. He did all the work there. If the rumors about tonight are true, then who knows what this means."

"It can't be," Jimmy said. "There is no way the body found tonight is who you're thinking. I don't know what that's about but it's not him."

"And if it is?" Eddie asked.

"Who could have done it?" Jimmy yelled. "Anna? An eighteen-year-old girl physically beats up and kills one of the toughest gang-bangers in the city? I doubt that. Did Dean Callan do it? Imara's dad? That skinny little pansy couldn't hurt a flea. I'll bet you a hundred bucks that we just found Dean Callan. That's whose bones were above Mike Garst's casket. We're in the business of secret lies gentlemen. Whoever the poor bastard is, I'm not going to worry or speculate about it until we know. The teeth were still usable to get a dental record. We'll have it by the morning, no later. We need to find where they went and what other files were taken."

"We need to get my wallet back," Eddie said. "I'm going to kill that little bitch that took it. I know it was Imara. I hope she and her friends show up to the party at Dumas's tomorrow. I'll take all three of them out back and teach them a lesson they'll never forget."

"Don't get yourself in trouble over them," Travis said. "You lay a finger on them and they will go to the police and there'll be nothing we can do to protect you. Think about it, they are going to take this information to Andy and try to blackmail him. Let's go. We'll meet up with them soon enough. Get Andy on the phone and tell him to meet us at the gallery. Tell him to talk to no one and stop for nothing. We intercept Andy first and they have no bargaining powers."

Jimmy led the group out of the room. They relocked the doors as they left, letting the rope that tied the doors hang down. Mark motioned to me, moving and I started to follow. We weren't going back into the file room. I had to talk to Anna—they found someone in her dad's grave, bones above the casket. My mind was swimming. I had to ask Anna about her sister, this mystery just kept getting deeper.

Chapter #20

Blood in the Streets

Mark and I raced back to my apartment as quickly as we could. We crawled through the ventilation system to avoid walking through the hallways of the hospital. Once we exited the vents, we were dodging security guards who were patrolling the grounds. We'd been safe to make sure no one got a good look at our faces. The first thing I did when we returned to the apartment was wash the tattoo off of my neck. I thought that with my hair up, the tattoo would stick out on camera. Mark took his fake mustache off as Anna and Sarah hounded us on what happened.

I didn't know how to proceed. We'd learned so much but there was information that we didn't know. How do I ask Anna, my best friend who told me everything, to tell me about an older sister I didn't know she had? There was no easy way to explain this. I was trying to figure it out, trying to understand, when the phone rang. Everyone jumped at the ringing and looked at their phones. It was Anna who was receiving a call. She took the call, looking sicker and sicker as the conversation continued, Anna not saying a word. She thanked the caller and hung up.

"They found bones above my dad's casket," Anna said, slowly, sinking into a chair, staring blankly at a wall. "That was Lund. I'm going to be questioned about this."

"Who was it?" I asked quickly. "Was it my father?"

"They just got the report back from forensics," Anna said. "They rushed it through. They had a dental cast made from the bones and they searched everyone in the area."

"Was it Dean?" I asked impatiently. "Did they find my father?"

"It was Christopher Trellis," Anna said.

"Chris, who was known on the street as the nightmare?" Sarah asked. "Of the Trellis Family?"

"That's the one," Anna said. "His bones were found in my father's grave. As best they could tell, someone must have dug into the grave within a day or two of the casket being placed. They placed the body there and covered it up. It was a great idea. How could anyone ever think to look there or find it? If they wouldn't have needed to look at my parents his bones would have never been found."

"Do they think they know the cause of death?" Mark asked. "Did they notice bullet holes or anything like that?"

"Lund said it looked like someone took a baseball bat to him," Anna said, "before they shot him in the face with a shotgun."

"Who is this guy?" I asked. "Sarah, how do you know him?"

"His father, Anthony, was the biggest drug runner in the town," Sarah said. "I partied with some of his family. I was fourteen when I met Chris, this was right before he disappeared. Chris was ambitious. He was moving drugs, running prostitutes, and it was rumored that for fun, he was a murder-for-hire guy. Wherever this guy went, there was blood in the streets. He was a bad dude—but one day, he was gone. The sick thing is, police had him under constant surveillance. No one knows how he slipped out of police sight before getting killed. Many people thought the only thing possible was that he went into the witness protection program after providing information about his father's operations. Everyone who worked with him knew he was watched so they worked around it. It was a strange situation."

"That's what Jimmy meant by Anna not being able to do what they found," Mark said. "No way Anna could have beaten the guy to death."

I quickly explained what we'd overheard when we were in the vents of the hospital. Anna couldn't understand what was going on. We were all trying to make sense of it.

"Did Lund say anything else?" I asked. "Anything about your parents?"

"They have the caskets out but haven't checked them yet," Anna said. "They were too worried about the bones. Why would a killer be in my father's grave? What does this mean?"

"He was the one who killed your parents," I said. "I think we can gather that. The real question is how he got into the grave. Did the people who hired him do that so he could never tell?"

"Interesting thought," Mark said. "But let me pose this, if Jimmy is behind this, or even the university with Tim sitting on the board feeding Jimmy information, then Jimmy should have known Chris was the killer. I'm sure that if Jimmy hired someone to take Chris out after the murder had been committed, he would have known where the body was and would have never suggested digging up the graves. There's no reason for it. What this leads me to believe is that someone saw the murders happen. Someone knew and followed Chris as he left the house. He killed him and waited for after the funeral to bury him where no one would ever find him. I remember the police and feds searched the area for Chris. They brought in rescue dogs trained to find dead bodies. How could the dogs work in a graveyard? It's the perfect dumping location. The dogs searched the riverbanks and some abandoned lots but the case was never solved."

"But who could have seen him?" Anna asked. "We rushed to the house and didn't see anyone else there. Where could they have been?"

"That's a good question," Sarah asked. "They said Chris killed over twenty people. That was the rumor going around. He had contacts all over the world to move drugs into Prairie Rapids. It was a member of his former crew that gave me this scar." Sarah pointed to the scar on her face. "They were not guys to mess around with."

"How soon until the police get here?" I asked.

"Lund said they should be here soon," Anna replied. "What did you find? Is there anything in those files you have?"

It was the moment of truth. I set the files on my small coffee table and took a deep breath. I didn't know what to show Anna first, her death certificate or the evidence that she has a sister. I didn't even know how to proceed. There had been so much dumped on Anna tonight and I didn't want to pile it on, but we had to move forward. I knew she might have known something she hadn't told us.

"We found some strange things, Anna," I said. "We found your death certificate."

Anna had a confused look on her face. I pulled the document out of the folder and handed it to her. Anna read over the paper many times as Sarah looked over her shoulder.

"What does this mean?" Anna asked. "I was supposed to be killed to?"

"That's what we think," Mark said. "What we heard Jimmy say would indicate that Doctor Dumas was in this from the start. They paid him to file these documents."

"Why wouldn't the killer have waited for me?" Anna asked. "We are quite certain that whoever killed my parents were watching, waiting for all the police and ambulances to leave Imara's house. He should have known that I was over there. Why didn't they just wait for me to come back?"

"That's a good point," I said. "Maybe there was someone else in the house."

"What do you mean?" Anna asked.

"Maybe somebody else was in the house and chased Chris away," I said. "Maybe they killed Chris that night even, chasing him out of the house."

"This is just too frustrating," Anna said, hitting a pillow in disgust. "I just wish I knew what happened."

"Well," I said, not knowing how to continue, "that isn't the worst part about what we found...there were some other papers in the files that are...sensitive, to say the least."

"What do they say?" Anna asked.

"That you're not an only child," I replied.

There was a silence in the air. Anna's face contorted and crunched up as she tried to process what I had said. She looked at me with a blank expression. She'd heard what I said but it was so far removed from what she knew that she didn't even know how to respond. After what seemed like an eternity of silence but was only a few moments, Anna spoke.

"What do you mean, not an only child?" Anna asked.

"There are documents here talking about how you were used as a donor to an older sister," I said. "It's quite clear they are talking about an older sister. She would have been eighteen when you were twelve."

"I don't have an older sister," Anna said. "Hold the phone a minute, she was six years older than me? Not possible. Mom and Dad had only been dating for four years when Mom got pregnant and they got married. That girl would have been before Mom knew Dad."

"Then it's a half-sister," I said.

"You have AB negative blood, Anna," Mark said. "That's passed through your father. If he had a daughter with another woman before he met your mother, then once they got married, your mother made him promise not to mention her to you..."

"My dad would never," Anna said, quickly interrupting Mark. "He would never keep something like that from me. He would have told me if I had a sister. I always wanted one, always asked for one but they never wanted more kids."

"There's more to it though," I said. "When it said you were a donor for her, it wasn't just blood. The forms say that she was in a horrible car accident and she needed a kidney. They say that one of yours was used."

Anna was speechless. She began rubbing her hands on her sides, feeling where her kidneys should be. She was so shocked by the statement that she didn't even know what to say or do. Mark stood up and smiled. He pointed to the floor.

"Lay on the floor," Mark said. "There's an easy way to figure this out."

Anna reluctantly got onto the floor as Mark pulled her shirt up to expose her stomach. Anna was fidgety as Mark felt around on the sides of her body. He had a strange expression on his face as he thoroughly studied one area on Anna. Mark stood up with a frown, "Right kidney is gone. She's a donor."

"How the hell is that possible?" Anna almost screamed. "There's no scar, I don't remember them taking anything. How could they harvest me without me knowing?"

"This would have happened in June when you were twelve years old," Mark said. "Think back, is there anything you can remember about that time? Anything that would have been strange or out of the ordinary?"

"I can't remember that far back," Anna said, tears in her eyes as she looked over the papers in the file. "There's nothing...wait a minute, there is one thing. How the hell could I have been so stupid?"

"What is it?" I asked.

"I had my tonsils removed," Anna said.

"That's normal," Mark said. "Nothing wrong with that."

"No, it's not normal," Anna replied. "I had them removed two years earlier. I remember one day that Dad came to my room and said that the tonsils had grown back. Mom was crying, really hard. They took me to the hospital, to the emergency room. I was out. I guess that I never really thought about it before. They could have taken it then. I remember they gave me all these rules I had to follow. I did get all the ice cream I wanted for a week after we left the hospital, but other than that, I think I just brushed the incident off and tried to forget it. Why don't I have a scar though?"

"Plastic surgery," Mark said. "They could have completely covered the scar. What else do you remember about it? What about your parents, any conversations they had at that time?"

"That was when Mom went on a real health food kick," Anna said. "I remember she was super concerned about what I was eating but I knew she and Dad were sneaking food I wasn't allowed to have. That always pissed me off. I also remember Mom was really mad at Dad for something, she took it out on him. That summer, like in August, she made him rent a cabin on a lake for a week. She always wanted that for a vacation but he didn't. I thought he was just being nice but maybe he owed her something."

"You think she didn't know he had a daughter from another woman?" Sarah asked. "Was your dad ever married or engaged before he met your mother?"

"No," Anna said. "At least I don't think so. How could I have a sister or half-sister out there and not know about it? Why wouldn't Daddy tell me? This is beyond frustrating."

"There's something I missed before," Mark said, looking at a document from the folder. "I know who we can ask about the situation."

"What do you mean?" Anna asked.

"Doctor Andrew Dumas," Mark said. "He was one of the doctors who assisted in the car accident. He didn't do the surgery but he signed off saying the victim needed an immediate transplant or she would die. He even suggested you because of the blood types...interesting, there's a reference here that the closer relative would be better but that she wasn't available, that another medical problem excluded her from donating."

"What does that mean, Mark?" Anna asked. "I can't think anymore...just spit it out in plain Goddamn English!"

"This is implying that your half-sister is a twin," Mark said. "The twin would be a perfect match for a kidney but I'm guessing she was also in the accident, that's why they didn't want to risk it. She couldn't survive an operation and they didn't want to risk losing both of them in surgery. I can't think of anything else this could mean, unless maybe she wasn't in the area. Maybe they couldn't get her there in time to do the operation. Something is very fishy about this. Doctor Dumas will be the one to answer all of our questions."

"All we need to do is show him the death certificate with his name on it and he's backed into a corner," Sarah said. "This will be easy."

"They've thought about that," I replied. "They have already figured out ways to get around that. They are not taking chances anymore. We need to get something on the doctor that will force him to tell us everything."

"It all goes to Jimmy," Anna said. "Think about it, the connection to the university, Tim Krause, who was a lapdog for Jimmy. The connection to the hospital, Doctor Dumas, who's also a lapdog for Jimmy. Jimmy runs this town. In the last election the opponent accused him of being soft on crime and gangs. Jimmy hired Chris Trellis to kill my parents. Jimmy has his hooks in all of this...the question is, how do we prove it?"

"We get Dumas to crack," I said. "We need his story He can tell us what is going on with your siblings, how that all fits together, Anna. Maybe he knows the full story. The problem is he knows Anna and me. He would never fall for anything we did. Sarah, on the other hand, you might be right up his alley."

"I don't know 'Ara," Sarah said. "If I go to that party I'll be way too close to drugs and booze. I can't fall into that again. There has to be another way."

"What did you have in mind?" Anna asked. "How do you think we can get the information out of him?"

"He relies on his standing in the community for his power and respect," I said. "We have to find a way to challenge that. We need something to blackmail him with. Pictures of him with a woman who's not his wife. Something along those lines that will force him to tell us."

"I can't do something like that," Sarah said. "You want me to go in there like a hooker and tease him into telling us his life story? He's going to know that something is up."

"No, he won't," Anna said. "We can get him drunk before he meets you. Heck, we get him drunk enough and he'll go with us."

"We have to be careful," Mark said. "You get him drunk and he could claim that he didn't know what he was doing...he was tricked by you. When we get him he has to be lucid and coherent. We also have to be careful not to break any laws, otherwise he can charge us, while once again saying he was forced to do everything we tried to blackmail him with."

"I can't do it," Sarah protested. "There's no way. I haven't even been to a party since I became sober. I'm scared the smell of booze or the whiff of a drug would set me off on a spiral again. You know how many times I almost died?"

"You're right," I said. "We can't risk you. I could try it...I suppose he doesn't know me as well as he knows you, Anna. It's worth a shot."

"Imara," Mark said, in a stern voice. "You're good looking...sexy as hell, but, and I'm sorry to say this, you don't have that naughty-girl attitude in you. There's no way you could pull off what needs to be done."

"Oh," I said, grinning, "I can be naughty Mark. I can make him want me so bad he'll do anything."

"Imara," Sarah said, looking at me, "Mark is right. Andy has experience with these types of women. He'll see through you in a second."

"Anna," I said. "Back me up, I can get down and dirty, right?"

"I love you, honey," Anna said, "but you could never pull off acting like a hooker. You don't have it in you."

"I'll do it," Sarah said. "I don't want to see you get hurt. But you guys have to be there, making sure I don't get too close to anything that could harm me."

"I promise you, Sarah, I won't let you fall back into old patterns," I said.

I was about to continue when Anna's phone rang. Anna quickly answered it, not saying a word but just listening to the person who was talking a mile a minute on the other end. Anna was confused by the caller but listened to them without asking questions. When she hung up the phone she paused for a moment.

"There was an attempted murder tonight," Anna said. "Another council member. Lund wouldn't tell me who, but they dodged a serious bullet. No one is coming here tonight to interrogate us."

"What do they know?" Mark asked.

"Whoever did it tried to burn his house down," Anna said. "The guy was paranoid so he had a massive security system on the house, no way to get in and all the locks were controlled electronically. The killer started a fire on the outside of the house and threw bottles of gasoline at it. The house lost power and the guy couldn't open the doors. He got out by luckily having a chainsaw in the house. He used the saw to cut a hole in the wall big enough to get out of. He did that on the second floor and jumped off the roof."

"Amazing," I said. "When is this going to end? How many deaths are enough? There's blood in the streets and we're just getting started."

I knew the next few days were going to be intense. I didn't know how we were going to continue but I was certain that Sarah had a plan and could pull it off. Once we had the information we needed from Doctor Dumas, we could take Jimmy down.

Chapter #21

The Power of Lust

I rode with Anna to the party knowing that Sarah was already there. Mark had arrived early to view the lake home of Doctor Andrew Dumas, to find out who was attending, and to introduce Sarah to Doctor Dumas. I was nervous, not knowing what to expect. What we'd heard so far about these parties was that there was drinking and drugs, possibly even some prostitutes, and gambling. It was about powerful, well-connected, wealthy men having a good time without their wives, children, or conscience to bother them. I knew Sarah could handle what we planned, I just hoped it wouldn't have to go too far.

The first sight of the house took my breath away; a sprawling, three-story mansion that sat as close to the lake as the law would allow. The house had mock-log-cabin siding, which looked very tacky on a house so large. The middle of the house was all floor-to-ceiling windows through which we could see many people already inside. The landscaping was professionally done and could have been featured on any Homes magazine cover. As Anna parked the car I got a twinge of fear that we may be in over our heads with this place.

We walked toward the house slowly, trying to take the impressive place in. Between the house and the lake was a grassy area that gave way to a beach. There were people everywhere on the grass, some near the smoking grills where piles of meat were stacked, some ready for cooking, others for eating, some in the grass playing croquet, bocce ball, and lawn darts, and others relaxing on the beach, or watching a group of six bikini-clad college girls playing volleyball. I looked to Anna who was as stunned as I was. This party was all about pleasure and fun.

There was a bar setup close to the grills with a handsome young man in a suit tending bar. I felt sorry for him—almost triple-digit temperatures and he had to be outside in a suit. Even though the sun was almost set, the temperature was still in the low nineties. Anna and I walked to the bar and looked over the selection. There was beer, wine coolers, rum, and vodka with an assortment of things to mix them with. Anna and I both opted for a fruity wine cooler, tipping the bartender, and walking around trying to spot anyone we knew. We settled in near the volleyball game, watching the talented girls having a fun game.

"I don't know," Anna said. "There's something about this place."

"I was thinking Gatsby," I said.

"More than that," Anna laughed. "What kind of man throws parties like this? I mean, look at how much money he's spent. What is the reason?"

"I don't think I follow you," I said.

"I get the feeling he is trying to impress people," Anna said. "Which is dumb. Everyone knows he's a well-respected doctor who has an impressive regional patient list. He sits on charity boards, is advisor to the hospital board, and from what I've heard is a wiz in the stock market. Look at those girls playing ball. They are good. I would guess that every one of them played varsity ball in high school, and some of them played in college."

"They look to be in college now," I said.

"That's my point," Anna said. "Why are they here? What possible reason could those girls have to be here other than to meet people and make connections?"

"What do you mean?" I asked. "What kind of connections?"

"There are powerful men here," Anna said. "Look around...there are doctor's, business owners, politicians, the crooks from the local school boards, all people who could give those girls jobs when they are finished with college...*if* those girls do a job or two tonight. It's the power of lust, honey. I bet we go into that house and we can find all sorts of job opportunities, if we're willing to pay the price."

"You really think those girls would do that?" I asked. "I mean, they look so powerful, so confident in themselves. To balance your entire future on a drunken sex act, you really think that is going on here?"

"I'll bet you anything Imara," Anna said. "This type of behavior goes on all the time, it's the way the world works. Money is exchanged for pleasure, pleasure is exchanged for power, and power is exchanged for money. Circle of life and all."

"No way," I said. "They could never get away with anything like that."

"And every guy here has a wife at home watching the kids," Anna said. "He told her it was a business gathering and they are discussing expansion plans or fiscal policy. We need to be very careful. I'm sure they are on the lookout for cameras and such. Being seen in a place like this could be very dangerous for these people. Look, most businesses and people are good and they hire people the right way, but there are some in every bunch that use their power and station to do things that people like us only see on scrambled late-night television."

"I suppose," I said, looking over the crowd. "How much further ahead do you think those girls on the court are going to get for coming here?"

"He has parties like this all summer," Anna said. "They come here, show off, get drunk, play around, and are given guaranteed jobs when they graduate in the spring...the university connection at work. Those girls were recruited here by Tim Krause. Somehow he was able to entice them to come. I bet he promised a lot. If you didn't notice, we didn't pay for our drinks, but the men are paying for the ones they drink. Not really a question as to why."

"I never knew this went on," I said. "Sad, really."

"Why?"

"That these girls can't rely on their brains and intelligence to get ahead," I said. "They have to rely on their bodies and other *talents*."

"The world can be a shitty place sometimes," Anna said. "Come on, let's find Doctor Dumas and Sarah. Let's see how far she's taken him already."

I followed Anna as she walked into the house. The interior of the house was just as impressive as the exterior. Inside, all the walls were knotty pine and the floors were hardwood. Everything was rustic and cabin-like, except the massive size. There were chainsaw-carved figures of bears, ducks, deer, and squirrels that lined the hallways, paintings and pictures of pheasants and deer, and different animal hides hanging on the walls. It was an outdoorsman's paradise.

Many of the people looked out of place, wearing fine suits or slacks and polo shirts while the women all wore party dresses. Anna fit in perfectly with her tight little black dress, strapless with a short hem. I, on the other hand, was in my tights with crimson and gray sleeveless button-up from the seventies. I felt out of place at the party, not just from my outfit, but personally, I would much rather be curled up on the sofa with a good romance novel than get chatted up by the drunk men at that party.

We passed room after room, most of them devoid of people but full of things—arcades, media centers, pool tables, and even a first floor hot tub. The majority of the people were in the center of the house which was open and sprawling—music was being played as people mingled around bars and buffets of fine finger food. The ladies who were inside looked more professional than the ones outside, they were older and dressed more dignified in their dresses with high-end jewelry, but something told me they weren't there just to enjoy the all-you-could-eat caviar.

Anna nudged me, pointing out where a group of interesting people were. It was Doctor Dumas, Mark, Jimmy, Eddie, and Sarah. They were together, intently discussing something, pausing every few moments to break into laughter. The group had cocktails in their hands, and Eddie looked to be drunk already. He noticed two women walking by in tight red party dresses. Eddie stopped them but when he placed his hand on one of the girls' rears, they both took off with Eddie cussing at them. I noticed Anna smugly smiling at the incident.

I wondered how we should play the night out as I looked over Sarah. I wasn't the only one noticing her. Sarah had committed to her role. She had on fishnet stockings, a tight black miniskirt, a skimpy black leather top, neck choker, over-the-forearm designer gloves, and over-the-calf black boots. Sarah had her hair teased out frizzy and wild and was wearing way too much makeup. She had a press-on tattoo of a very colorful green and red dragon which covered most of her back and was very visible. She walked aggressively, with power. One look told everyone that Sarah was there to make some money.

Sarah was standing close to Doctor Dumas, her hand on his arm. I wanted to move closer so we could hear what was being said but I knew I couldn't give myself away to Jimmy and Eddie. When Sarah realized we were there, she and the doctor spoke for a moment before he began to escort her toward a flight of stairs. Sarah motioned for Anna and me to follow. We rushed up the stairs to the second floor, followed behind them in the hallway, then took a back set of stairs to the third floor. The second and third floor were just like the first, hardwood floors with knotty pine walls and ceilings.

As we followed Sarah and Andrew, I could smell the cigarette and cigar smoke that was lingering in the air. It was a powerful aroma from the remains of many parties. The slightest hint of candles tried to mask the older scents but they were no match. The third floor was empty of people but we could still hear all of them from downstairs.

Andrew led Sarah into a room and closed the door. Anna and I stopped outside the door, not knowing if we should go in or wait. We didn't have to wait long before the door opened and Sarah welcomed us into the room. It was a bedroom, large, with a king-sized bed that had a post in each corner that looked like a tree. The canopy of the bed looked like tree branches over the bed, giving the illusion of sleeping in a forest. The walls were decorated as trees and shrubs. There was a massive window that looked out over the beach area. On the far wall was a dresser and some extra chairs. Doctor Andrew Dumas exited a closet with a wine bottle and two glasses in hand—he had a wine closet in his bedroom.

"I didn't know we were going to have company," Andy said.

"I like to have my friends with," Sarah said, in a sultry voice. "You don't mind if they play with us, too, do you?"

"I think that could be arranged," Andy said. "You ladies want some wine?"

"Of course," Anna said. "She'll have a glass too."

Andy opened the bottle and poured two glasses. He handed one to Anna and one to Sarah before going back into the closet. Sarah made a motion, indicating us to be ready to start videotaping when he got back out. Andy returned with two more glasses, filled them, giving one to me and taking a drink from the other.

"'98," Andy said, savoring the wine. "Damn good year for French wine, don't you agree?"

"It's amazing," Anna said, taking a sip. "So good."

"Now," Sarah said, pulling out a chair and pushing Andy into it, taking his wine glass and setting it on the dresser, "what are we going to do with you?"

"I can think of a few things," Andy said. "I can think of many things."

I got my cellphone out and started recording. I was sure to get Andy's face clearly in the video while trying to stay to the side so he couldn't see what I was doing. Sarah was keeping his attention, sitting in his lap, and kissing him. As Sarah kissed the doctor, Anna moved behind and started massaging his shoulders. They were really getting him excited as Sarah reached into her top and pulled out a small vial. My heart sank. I hoped all my life that Sarah would never return to drugs but I remembered that vial. She always had it with her.

"I've got something for you," Sarah said.

Sarah opened the vial and used the little spoon attached to the top to scoop up a small pile of a white, powdery substance. Sarah quickly inhaled it with her right nostril before taking another scoop and inhaling with her left. She handed the vial to Andy and left his lap, and seductively danced on the other side of the room. Sarah motioned Anna to join her. The pair started dancing together while Andy held the vial. I understood what Sarah was doing. I'd have a shot of Andy snorting cocaine with neither Sarah nor Anna in the shot. A very damning video that could force Andy into talking.

"You have to take some," Sarah said. "Both nostrils. I know you're a big, strong man. Show me how tough you are. I'm just a little thing and you saw how much I can handle. How much can you handle?"

"It's just straight coke?" Andy asked. "No synthetic or designer shit?"

"Just straight Colombian snow," Sarah said. "You're not afraid, are you?"

"Not afraid," Andy said. "I've never snorted before...I only shoot up."

"You saw me do it," Sarah said. "Be a man, take twice what I did and I'll kiss you like this."

Sarah pulled Anna in close to her and the pair started kissing. I was as stunned as either Andy or Anna, but Anna just rolled with it. I kept the camera on Andy, who proceeded to inhale two blasts in each nostril, wincing and squirming after each hit. Andy took off his suit jacket and over shirt, leaving just a white undershirt on with his suit pants as Sarah and Anna finished their kiss. Sarah looked at Andy and smiled.

"Where you keep your toys?" Sarah asked.

"Toys?" Andy asked innocently.

"Don't play coy with me," Sarah said. "I know you've had more women up here than you can remember. Trust me, big guy, when we're done you won't even remember your wife's name. Where are the toys?"

"Top drawer of the dresser," Andy said, as a smile came across his face.

"Get on the bed," Sarah said, as she opened the drawer.

Andy quickly moved to the bed as Sarah dug through the drawer. She pulled out two pairs of handcuffs. Andy swallowed hard as Sarah swaggered over to him, climbing over the foot of the bed and kissing Andy as she moved up his body. Sarah took the vial that Andy set on the nightstand, took another hit herself and gave Andy some more, a hit in each nostril. Sarah set the vial down, took Andy's shirt off, and began kissing him. Andy and Sarah were all over each other, but Sarah made sure that Andy stayed on the bottom. After a minute of kissing, Sarah cuffed Andy's arms to the bedposts. Andy just smiled.

"Three girls and one tied-up guy," Andy said. "I love that. Why don't you take her dress off? Yeah, that would be hot. Take her dress off."

Sarah looked at Anna while I kept the camera rolling. Anna moved to the foot of the bed as Sarah slid off the bed. They looked into each other's eyes and kissed again while Andy laughed with glee. I had Sarah and Anna out of the camera, only Andy, his face perfectly clear and well lit, in the frame.

"Tell me," Sarah asked as she turned Anna around and began running her hands up and down Anna's back, teasing that she was going for the zipper. "Tell me Doctor Dumas, you like playing with hookers?"

"I love hookers," Andy said. "Fuck my cow of a wife. That bitch went cold after our last kid. I haven't fucked her in ages."

"What do you like hookers to do to you?" Sarah asked, playing with the zipper.

"I love it when they suck me off," Andy said, "chain me to the bed, and go down."

"You like fucking college whores?" Sarah asked.

"I love it," Andy yelled. "I love women. I love getting fucked by complete strangers and paying them lots of money. I make millions of dollars and I love using it to buy women."

"You buy women," Sarah said. "How many hookers have you fucked while high on heroine?"

"Hundreds," Andy said. "I've fucked hundreds of hookers on weed, ecstasy, heroine, and any other drug you could imagine. Baby, I got some high-class LSD in this room. I've been saving it for a very special person. It makes everything so amazing. You haven't had sex until you've had it on this stuff. I think you could handle it. You up for it?"

"I'm up for anything," Sarah said.

Sarah smiled and pulled the zipper down on Anna's dress. Sarah pulled the dress down to Anna's waist, exposing her strapless black bra. Andy cheered them on, loving it as Sarah and Anna kissed again. It was perfect. You could hear Sarah talking but couldn't see her. Andy had said everything that we needed. As Anna and Sarah finished kissing, Sarah pulled Anna's dress back up and turned with a serious face toward Andy.

"Oh, don't tell me you're one of those bitches," Andy said. "You want your pay up front? Look in the second dresser drawer. I keep money there for when I'm entertaining."

Sarah walked to the drawer and opened it. The drawer was full of hundred dollar bills wrapped in stacks of ten thousand.

"Lots of money," Sarah said, as she lifted a couple stacks then put them back.

"You should be worth a thousand," Andy said. "Total...not each. The LSD is in the bottom of the drawer in a glass container. Get it and come on. I'm so ready, you don't even realize."

"Your balls are gonna be pretty blue tonight doctor," Sarah said.

"Oh, fuck you," Andy said. "Fine, a thousand a piece. Hell, two thousand a piece. I've got a hundred grand in that drawer that I can replace in the blink of an eye. Take five each just get that dress off her and get into bed...both of you."

"Not going to happen, Andy," Sarah said. "We've been recording this."

Sarah pointed to me and Andy realized what I was doing. His face flushed red and he looked ready to ravage all three of us.

"What the fuck?" Andy asked. "Don't you dare try to blackmail me."

"Too late," Sarah said. "All we want is information. You did an autopsy on Mike Garst, where is the original?"

"Oh," Andy said. "It's you three. Jimmy warned me that you would try something like this. No matter. I'll have Detective Lukens plant some drugs on you and you three will be gone."

"This video of you talking about screwing hookers and showing you doing cocaine will be sent to your wife, children, and the board at the hospital," Sarah said. "Not to mention we now have you saying you're going to frame us."

"What do you want?" Andy asked.

"The original autopsy report," Anna said. "And we want to know what happened."

"Your dad got in the way," Andy said. "But you three need to think...they killed your parents, Anna, you think they'll just let you walk away with this information? All three of you are dead."

"I've got connections," Anna said. "Imara's already uploaded that video to friends of mine that you will never have access to. Anything happens to us, it goes viral."

"Look," Doctor Dumas said. "The original had a flaw in it, something was wrong and I don't know what. That's why I created the fake."

"What was wrong?" Anna asked.

"There was a mix up at the lab," Andy said. "We sent in blood and tissue for testing, see if they were drugged or drinking or poisoned or something. The lab sent the wrong results and we didn't get the originals back."

"Why did the death certificate change then?" Anna asked.

"I did some basic tests and filled it out. When the tests came back wrong I threw them out and just made a new certificate."

"What about my kidney?" Anna asked. "What was that all about?"

"Your dad had a girlfriend before your mother," Andy said. "They had twins together. The mom took them and raised them. I don't know any specifics about that. All I know is that they were both in a car accident and one needed a kidney to live. The other was in such poor shape that they didn't dare open her up. The mother came and pleaded with your father to use yours. They hadn't spoken for years...again, I have no idea what happened. He agreed, but your mother didn't...this was the first time she'd heard about the twins. They told me they didn't want you to know, so we went with the tonsil story."

"Where are they now?" Anna asked. "Where are my sisters?"

"That I don't know," Andy said. "Please, let me go and we can work this out. I can't have that video getting out."

"Where is the original death certificate?" Anna asked. "I have to see it."

"I'll give it to you tomorrow," Andy said. "I'll stop by your clothing store first thing and give you the original. Please, you can't show that video to anyone."

"What else can you tell us about this?" I asked. "Who is behind it?"

"It's deep," Andy said. "And believe me, with Tim being killed, you almost getting killed, the suspect getting killed, and Chris's bones turning up in the grave, everyone is on edge. You have no idea how much security is around. I won't tell Jimmy about this because he suspects you three already, but I swear to God, you show that video, it will be your death."

"We are committed to each other through the power of lust," Sarah said. "You lusted after us and we lusted after information. If the death certificate hasn't arrived by noon, the video goes live."

"Agreed," Andy said. "Now untie me."

Sarah moved toward the bed and removed the cuffs. The three of us quickly made our way to the door. Sarah paused, looking back at Andy who was on the bed, looking dejected.

"Hey big guy," Sarah said, looking back to him holding up her vial of coke. "You don't do many drugs, do you?"

"A little," Andy said. "As I said, I've never inhaled before. Always inject...that was mostly talk."

"That's obvious," Sarah said, with a smile.

"Why?"

"This was sugar and flour," Sarah said, with a wink.

My heart skipped a beat as we walked out of the room. Sarah had me convinced she was using something real. I felt so relieved as we walked out of the party. I couldn't wait to get out of there and make for home. Something told me we needed to be careful. As we got to the parking lot, I stopped and looked back.

"What's wrong?" Anna asked.

"I don't know," I said. "Something feels unfinished with this."

"That it does," Sarah said. "Anna, thanks for playing along but that was all in the interest of getting information out of a guy. Everything in there was to manipulate him."

"Agreed," Anna said. "That was the weirdest feeling I ever had. We did it to get information and that was it. It was acting that meant nothing."

"Agreed," Sarah said. "Now let's never speak of it again."

"I can live with that," Anna said, as she and I got into her car.

As we took off from the house I couldn't help but shake the feeling that something wasn't right. I was certain we'd scared Andy enough so that he wouldn't tell the others about what happened. I felt like he was holding back. All I knew was that I was damn glad to be leaving that party.

Chapter #22

Magic Never Dies

Decades of Threads hadn't been open an hour and already I'd made three big sales. All three of them were sales that we'd gotten thanks to Anna and Sarah doing more active sales work, calling around and getting the word out about the store. I was pleased as I waved goodbye to a group of teenaged girls who'd just bought a number of outfits for a dance competition they were participating in. Not only had they bought costumes for their show, each girl bought some clothes to wear daily too.

Even though the day was going so well, I couldn't shake all the information we'd gathered from last night. It was Jimmy, we knew he was behind everything but now we had to prove it. We needed to find out exactly how it was done. Since Jimmy had Christopher Trellis do the actual murders, it would be hard to link the crime to Jimmy. Even with Doctor Dumas's confession, there would still be loose ends and it would only take one well-placed bullet to destroy the only witness that could confirm the entire story. I told both Anna and Sarah to be on the lookout, who knows how far Jimmy will go to protect his Gallery, his one place that cements his name into the future.

Anna was at the library this morning, going through articles trying to find out about the accident and who her father was dating before. The thought of having twin sisters excited her, even if they were only half-sisters, but Anna was still determined to find them and reach out to them. Sarah was at her other job, having only a few days left before she was completely done working there and with me full time. I was waiting for Doctor Dumas to bring the real death certificate, and I had instructions from Anna that if noon rolled around and I hadn't seen or heard from him yet, I was to send the video to his wife and the police.

As I was waiting, the door to the shop opened and a young woman walked in. She was pretty, with bobbed red hair and a round, freckled face. I would guess she was in her mid-thirties with a petite body in a gray, skirted business suit. She had a pleasant smile underneath warm hazel eyes. The woman was carrying a black briefcase. She walked right up to me, not bothering to look at anything else in the store.

"Welcome to Decades of Threads," I said, smiling. "Can I help you today?"

"I am here to help you, Imara," the woman said, setting the briefcase down on the counter. "Doctor Dumas asked me to bring this document over here."

The woman quickly worked the lock on the front of the briefcase, spinning the three dials on the left, then the three dials on the right before the case clicked open. She opened the case and pulled out a sheet of paper and a sealed envelope.

"You'll need to sign this," the woman said, handing me the sheet of paper.

I looked it over. The document was a legal form, acknowledging that I received whatever she was dropping off. It was very generic, like a form that could have been downloaded from any legal website and printed off. I signed the form and the woman signed it for Doctor Dumas. She put the form in the case and handed me the sealed envelope. The woman locked the case, smiled, and without another word, walked out of the store.

I quickly opened the sealed envelope, hoping it contained the documents we were looking for. I pulled the single sheet of heavyweight blue paper out and looked it over. It was an official death certificate for Anna's father. At first, I didn't notice what the issue was. I couldn't figure out why Doctor Dumas had made a new certificate and gotten rid of this one. I studied the form but its secrets eluded me.

"Is that something interesting?" a female voice rang out behind me.

I almost jumped out of my skin, thinking I had been alone in the store. I quickly turned around to see Princess Aine and Malenko standing in the store. I don't know when they entered, I never heard the chimes on the door, and they weren't in the store before the lady walked in.

"You scared me," I said, to Aine. "Please stop doing that."

"Part of the job," Malenko said. "Magic never rests, never stops...magic never dies."

I looked at Malenko. He was dressed like an aristocrat; a stunning black suit, top hat, gloves, and cane, all looking like it came straight from 1850s London. Princess Aine wasn't disappointing either. She was wearing an indigo leotard with black sheer stockings, indigo over the calf boots, topped off with a matching top hat. Her face was almost completely covered in glitter makeup and her amazing hair was in two tight braids. The pair looked so comical I had to stifle laughter.

"This isn't a magic store," I said, smiling. "How do you keep doing that, Princess Aine? How do you keep getting into the store without me hearing you come in?"

"How does the wind move through the forest?" Aine asked. "How do the waves move to the shore? If you look for an answer to present itself, nothing will. But if you present yourself to the answer, it will find you."

"Lovely," I said. "How can I help you today?"

"Malenko needs more fashion for the show," Malenko said. "This show will be Malenko's finest achievement. Malenko has guests from all over the world coming to attend. This will be a magical gathering not matched since the times of Merlin, when Malenko called a conference to council on the Galahad and the Grail."

There were so many questions I wanted to ask Malenko about what he'd said. I knew he wasn't telling the truth, there was no way he could be, but there was something about the way he said it that just made me want to believe that everything he was saying was true. I didn't know how to respond, so I just remained silent until he started to speak again.

"What Malenko has planned for this show," he continued, "will be written down in the annuals of magic for millennia to come. Everyone will know that I, Malenko Pendragon and my assistant Princess Aine are the best magical team in this realm."

"Once you've proven that," I asked, trying not to laugh, "what are your plans? Once you've proven you are the best, do you have to defend that title or what?"

"Then Malenko and Aine are going to a different realm," Malenko said. "One that you and others from here cannot get to. There, Malenko will practice more magic and prepare for a challenge that one day will come."

"Interesting," I said. "What kind of fashion do you need today? I can get anything, but right now I have a lot of stock, more than I normally have."

"Malenko needed another assistant for this venue," Malenko said. "Another female to bring about a surprise to the mix."

"I need something to complement them," a female voice said, from behind me.

I spun around, not surprised to see another woman had quietly entered into the store. The woman was a haunting beauty. She was of Mediterranean decent, dark olive skin that looked smooth as silk, black-as-night straight hair that flowed to her mid-back. Lifted cheekbones and a high forehead on a narrow, pointed face made her look almost royal. Black makeup surrounded her black eyes, forming a mask on her skin. Behind ruby sparkling lips were perfectly straight, perfectly white teeth.

For a woman I guessed to be in her mid-forties, she looked very good. She had a dancer's body, shorter and muscular. She stood with her feet apart, hands on her hips, allowing me to get a full view of her. She was dressed as comically, or magically, as the other two; a black leotard partially covered by a sleeveless, rose-colored vest. The vest had what looked like golden clasps that held it together in the front. She had black dance slippers on her feet and a glove on her left hand that matched the suit.

"I need something that will allow me to perform the 'Count of the Highlands' illusion," the woman said.

"Never heard of the 'Count of the Highlands' illusion," I said.

"It was performed many centuries ago," the woman said.

"Let me guess," I interrupted. "It was performed by the count of the highlands?"

"No," the woman said. "It was performed *to* him. The Count had a daughter who was the most beautiful woman in the land but he would allow no man to ever get near her. No matter what was tried, no man could meet this stunning beauty. One devilish duke got a novel idea and posed as a woman in the fanciest of ball gowns. The ruse worked and he was allowed to speak in the gardens with the lass. She was every bit as stunning as the rumors had been. After an hour of making her laugh and speaking to her heart, the man revealed himself for what he was. The Count's daughter, ecstatic to finally get a taste of what love was, made love to the duke right there in the garden.

"When the Count discovered what happened, he went on a rampage like none had ever seen before. He killed everyone the duke had passed when he was dressed as a woman. He blamed everyone for what happened. When he found his daughter was with child, the Count was beside himself, saying he would rather have a daughter in a grave than a grandchild conceived in deception and born out of wedlock.

"The Count gave the order to kill his daughter but none of his generals would obey the order. They all told him that he was overreacting. The Count spread the word through the land, if someone would do the deed, if someone would kill his pregnant daughter, he would give them part of the county that he controlled and make them a landowner.

"Of course, the first person to answer the call was the Duke. Once again, in disguise, the Duke arrived to claim the prize. He wanted to be the one to kill the Countess. Here's where the trick comes in. The Duke and Countess were in the courtyard with the Count and his entire court looking on. The Duke approached the Countess with sword unsheathed. As he raised his sword in preparation of the killing blow, the skies erupted in anger, lightning and thunder violently appeared on the formally sunny day. The sky went black as night—as quickly as the sun had disappeared, it reappeared. It was once again a pleasant summer's day...except that the Duke and Countess were gone, never to be seen again."

"So, it's a disappearing act?" I asked. "The lights are going to go out and you are going to disappear?"

"It's so much more than that," Princess Aine said.

I turned around to look at her but was stunned, beyond stunned, at what I saw. Malenko was gone and Aine was in a professional suit; black form-fitting pants, an indigo and white top, and a black suit-jacket. She had black pumps on her feet and no glitter makeup on her face. Her hair was down as she stood there like nothing happened.

"How the fuck did you do that?" I asked, actually mad.

"Do what?" Aine asked.

"You switched outfits," I said. "And you're not wearing your glitter makeup. It's the same thing that happened at the theater."

"I've told you before," Aine said, firmly. "I told you to wait but you went ahead. I was never in the theater with you. I have no idea what you are talking about. I also have no idea what you are talking about now. I've been wearing this since I arrived in the store."

"No, you haven't," I protested. "You were in a leotard that was indigo colored. You actually looked really good in it. But that's what you were wearing and you had glitter makeup all over your face."

"I'm sorry, Imara," Princess Aine said. "I've only been wearing this outfit since I got ready this morning. I only wear my leotards when I'm on stage."

"Tell me..." I paused, realizing she would never actually explain it, "where the hell did Malenko go?"

"I'm right here," Malenko said, from behind me.

I turned around to see the woman was gone and Malenko was standing in her place. I looked at him where he stood, in the aristocrat suit he was wearing before. There was no trace of the woman anywhere.

"Stop that," I said. "Where did the woman go?"

"The Count of the Highlands," Malenko said.

"How the hell am I supposed to measure her for an outfit if she disappears like that?" I asked, realizing that her measurements should be the least of my worries right now. "What do you people want?"

"Here are her sizes," Malenko said, handing me a sheet of paper he'd pulled from his jacket pocket. "We only wanted you to see her for a moment so you knew the body type and could visualize what you're working with. She needs an outfit that would match the highlands of Scotland, circa 550 A.D."

"Okay," I said, looking at the sheet. "What is her name?"

"Anna-Sophia," Malenko said. "She is very important to the entire show. You must have her outfit ready soon."

"I'll see what I can do," I said. "The other items you ordered should be here either today or right away in the morning. You can come in anytime tomorrow and do a fitting. Just pop on in. I'd ask that you let me know how many people would be coming and how you'll be popping in...but I doubt that you'd tell me."

"You must know one thing," Malenko said. "Imara, magic never dies. The illusions you see magicians do now are only modern updates of what men and women were doing in my time. The magic stays constant. Sure, it might be in a suit, leotard, or fur coat, but that's the beauty of magic, you never know when or where it's coming. You believe what you see...what your eyes tell you to be true...but we deceive your eyes. You believe what we show you to believe. In the end, when the show is over, you'll understand, I hope. There isn't anything else I can say to you right now, but all you need to know is we are here to help you."

"Help me?" I interrupted. "Why do I need help?"

"Your father does," Aine said. "He needs to rest at last. You need to know what happened."

"How the hell do you know about my father?" I asked. "Tell me right fucking now what you know."

Before either could say anything, the lights in the store went off. The window shades, controlled by a computer in the office, shut, casting the store into complete darkness. I couldn't see my hand in front of my face. I froze perfectly still and closed my eyes. I waited until I heard the electric motors of the curtain humming, opening the shades. When they stopped, I waited a moment before opening my eyes. I would have been surprised if there was someone in the store, but as I thought, the store was empty, except myself.

A flash of an idea came to the front of my mind. I have security cameras in the store that feed video to a hard drive recorder. Certainly, I should be able to see the outfit that Princess Aine entered the store in and there should be footage of how they were moving around and switching positions. I rushed to the back warehouse of the store, squeezing my way through all the mess of clothing and costumes that I had to get ready to move, making my way to the little metal desk that had the security system on it.

I turned on the monitor and brought up the current video feed. Using the keyboard, I entered in the time, telling the machine to take me back to just before Aine and Malenko entered the store. I watched the camera and to my surprise they entered through the back, but I knew the back door was locked. I locked it after I entered that morning. Aine was in her leotard, not the suit. I knew I hadn't been crazy.

A moment after Malenko and Aine had entered, Anna-Sophia entered. She was in the same outfit she'd been in when I was talking to her. Malenko, Aine, and Anna-Sophia positioned themselves into clothing racks, hiding on the shop floor where I couldn't see them. It was a clever trick I hadn't thought of. It was so simple. Aine had told us that she could get through any lock. They hid until needed.

I was feeling confident I had broken their magic and I knew their tricks. There was only one thing left that really bothered me; Aine's clothing switch.

I reasoned that Anna-Sophia must have turned the lights off and operated the window shades, maybe even doing it remotely, controlling my computers somehow. That could have been enough of a time gap to get all three of them out of the store. I watched as I started speaking with Malenko and Aine, them coming out of clothing racks at the same time, scaring me in the process. My heart was racing and I was sweating, in just a moment I was going to see how the clothing trick was done. I couldn't even imagine how she could have gotten all that makeup off and changed her hair in the brief moment I looked away, but I was about to find out.

With my excitement at a maximum, my eyes glued to the security screen, I counted down the seconds until the switch. On the screen, Anna-Sophia emerged from a rack, I turned around, and then the screen goes blank. I screamed out. The video didn't come back until the lights came on. Somehow, they'd even gotten my security. They were good.

Chapter #23

Family Ties Run Deep

I lost track of how many times I watched the surveillance video of Aine doing her clothing switch. It was so frustrating. At the moment the switch happened, the footage goes black and doesn't come back until the lights come back on a few minutes later and everyone is gone. I didn't even know it was possible for the security system to be manipulated like that. Every time I watched, I hoped that something would appear, something would come through, but it was simply a blank screen each time. I knew there had to be some strange trick going on, but I couldn't figure out what was taking place.

I was at the store with Anna and Sarah, waiting for Mark to arrive once he was done with work. The past few days with Mark had been good, even though we hadn't really had any alone time, he was helping as much as he could and I thought we'd gotten past the unpleasantness of our first encounter since he'd gotten back. I wasn't fully ready to let him in, he still had to show some of that fire that drove me wild when we were younger, but he was moving in the right direction. I wished he would move a little faster but with all that had been going on, we were lucky to see each other at all.

Anna had tried but was unable to find out anything about the accident or her half-sisters. It seemed like every direction we turned there was a new brick wall in our path. We'd break down one wall only to find two more standing in our way. As the day of the grand opening and the magic show got closer, the mysteries of the murders piled up. We could finally safely assume that Jimmy, the Mayor of Prairie

Rapids, was behind it in a vain effort to create something to carry his legacy, while at the same time propelling him to higher levels of power. But we had no way to legally prove it in a court of law. We needed to find the smoking gun that could put all of this to rest.

"There's one thing I don't get on here," Anna said, as she looked over the death certificate the strange woman had brought me earlier in the day. "I don't get how they could have made this mix-up."

"What mix-up is that?" Sarah asked.

"They messed up Dad's blood type," Anna said. "He was AB negative."

"Is it possible to get a false reading?" Sarah asked.

"No," I said, "Doctor Dumas did say there was a mess up at the lab. They probably sent the wrong results. I mean, everything else checks out."

"It does," Anna said. "I just wish we could find something that proved it wasn't my parents in that bed. You know, I wish they were still alive out there somewhere. Some nights I pretend they are...that they did it for some scam or something, and they're living the high life on a Caribbean Island somewhere. It's a nice thought."

"You do realize, Anna," Sarah said, "like our Dad going missing...that means your parents didn't want you around anymore."

"I know," Anna said. "Still...I'd rather have them alive and not wanting me, than dead. Know what I mean?"

"I know the feeling," I said. "I would give anything to see Dad again. I would sell the store and everything in it just to know what happened to him that night. I mean, how does someone vanish?"

"It's strange," Anna said.

"You've been trying to tell me something," I said to Anna. "Something about when your parents were killed. Every time, you've been interrupted. What was it?"

"This is good," Anna said. "In the days after my dad died...someone drained some of his bank accounts."

"What do you mean?" I asked. "They stole the money out of them?"

"They did," Anna said. "It wasn't a lot, something around fifty-thousand dollars, but still, that's a good chunk of money. The way they were transferred was that someone logged into Dad's accounts and did a wire transfer with the money. They knew his passwords and login questions. The money was pulled out of the country, that's why it could never be traced."

"That's the damnedest thing," Sarah said, as I tried to wrap my head around what Anna was saying. "We had something very similar. In the three days after Dad disappeared there was about fifty thousand pulled from Dad's accounts. We didn't know how it had been transferred."

"What do you mean?" Anna asked.

"Since the accounts were Dad's personal accounts," I said, "the bank wouldn't let us view them or have access to them until we had a death certificate or something that said that power of attorney had changed. It was a couple months after when we received the statements showing the money had been transferred. We even tried to get the police to pressure them to tell us where the money had gone but they wouldn't tell us a thing. It was a corporate bank, so no one there knew Dad or his family personally. There was nothing we could do. Once we finally got the information out of them, so much time had passed that it was impossible to track. All we know is that the money went to Eastern Europe."

"Now that is the damnedest thing," Anna said. "The money from Dad's account went to Eastern Europe as well."

We were all silent for a moment. The implications of what had happened were astounding. The fact that both of our situations were so similar was causing me to rethink what might have happened. What if Dad had been the one to kill Christopher? What if he killed him and ran? I could tell Anna was having similar thoughts.

"Whoever killed Christopher would have known their life was in danger," Anna said. "They would have to run."

"That much money in Eastern Europe," I replied. "About a hundred grand...a person could live very well over there. Get them set up in a small house, find them a job...there's no way they could have stayed here."

"Impossible to stay here," Sarah said. "I would think the money went to pay the Trellis family to not hunt the killer of Chris, but they would need millions to live through that, if they found out who killed him. Once they knew, they wouldn't stop hunting them. Remember, with guys like Chris, family ties run deep. If our Dad killed Chris and they knew or found out about it, they would have come after us."

"You're right," I said. "There's no way they wouldn't have. The only possible answer is that either our Dad didn't kill him or that he did and they never found out. His body being found in your father's grave, Anna...it makes me nervous. Will they come after you simply by association?"

"I'm not going to worry about it," Anna said. "We have too much going on right now to think about them. We have to figure out how we can link everything to Jimmy, expose him for what he did and get him behind bars, where he belongs."

"He's covered his tracks very well," I said. "There's nothing we can use against him. They ever find out what Andy told us and I'm willing to bet that he's dead, too."

"What I really wish would make sense is that Malenko character," Sarah said. "What are they up to?"

"I'm wondering that myself," I said. "They know something and there's no reason for them to know anything about this."

"And you said there was another one?" Anna asked.

"Anna-Sophia," I replied. "She looked to be in her mid-forties but really took care of herself. She needed an outfit for some weird trick they're going to be doing."

Anna nodded as the chimes from the door rang out. I looked to the entrance of the store to see Mark walking in. He looked dead-on-his-feet tired from a hard day at the hospital. He smiled when he saw me though—an encouraging sign, but the bags under his eyes and the stress on his face said he wouldn't be up for much tonight. Before he could even say anything, Anna shoved the death certificate into his hands. Mark looked it over.

"They messed up the blood type," Mark said. "Other than that, everything looks good."

"How could the blood type get messed up?" Anna asked. "They are trying to cover something up, aren't they?"

"It was a lab error, Anna," Mark said, yawning. "They told them to rush. You can't tell these labs to rush things. They have a process...if you rush, you get rushed results. Don't read into it more than that."

"You sure?" Anna asked. "We went through a lot to get this form."

"It looked like it," Mark said. "Doctor Dumas was thoroughly disturbed when he returned from the room with you. He took Jimmy into a private room. There was some yelling and cussing behind the door but neither would talk about it later. Whatever you three did, you stirred the pot something fierce."

"Something has to give us a break in this case," Anna said. "We have all the information about Mom and Dad's murder but we don't have anything that can put the people involved behind bars. We are no closer to locating Imara and Sarah's dad, although we think he might have gone to Eastern Europe right after it happened."

"What leads you to believe that?" Mark asked.

"Money trail," Anna said.

"You know," I said, starting to pace as I was thinking. "The people I talked to, about how to find missing people, they said that if they went out of the country, they could get false documents much easier than in America. If Dad was able to change his name and come back to this country as an immigrant, there would be no way we could find him. The trail for Dean Callan would be dead cold somewhere halfway around the world."

"I'm just going to say what we've all been thinking for some time now, Imara," Anna said, stopping my pacing and looking me right in the eye. "What if Malenko, with all his Merlin-magic horseshit, is actually your father?"

"If that is the case," I said, slowly, "what is his reason for being here now? I mean, what is he going to do?"

"Maybe he's going to take out members of the Trellis family," Anna said. "What if members of the audience are Trellis, and that structure that they were building on stage is nothing more than a chamber of death? How would anyone ever know? How could they follow a man like that?"

"I've looked into Malenko's eyes," I said. "That is not my father."

"He's heavier than your dad," Anna said. "But men can add weight and muscle. It sounds like something happened to his throat, like he was in an accident or something, that's why he doesn't sound the same as he did before. He's interested in all of what's going on and he knows about it. It's uncanny how much that would explain."

"Impossible," I said. "I know that when Dad comes back Sarah and I will be the first to know. He would tell us. But I can tell you this, Anna, I've looked into his eyes. I looked into his eyes when he was in the store earlier, those are not my father's eyes. Unless he had an eye and soul transplant...that is not my father."

"I know that family ties run deep honey," Anna said. "But how else would he know what he does?"

"Maybe he was hired by Dad," Sarah said. "Remember the story Anna-Sophia told? A man disguised as a woman to manipulate people? What if the woman with him was Dad?"

"Unless he's had a lot of equipment removed," I said. "Or they are masters of illusion, that wasn't a man. She was in a leotard for crying out loud. If she would have been in a dress or shorts, then yes, I would concede that there would have been a way to hide his manhood, but in a leotard? It was a woman."

"Maybe they were hired by Dad," Sarah said. "Think about it, how else would they know everything that's going on?"

"Maybe they are members of the Trellis family," I shot back at them. "And the reason they want us in the show is to kill us. Maybe this is a setup to get back at Dad for what happened with Chris, whether Dad did that or not."

"You three can run around in circles all day debating theories about what happened and you'll never get anywhere," Mark said, sounding annoyed at our talking. "The only way you can solve this is with hard evidence. Every avenue we've investigated has led to either dead ends or more confusing information. I want to help you solve this, I really do, but I'm already starting to feel pressure at work. They know I'm involved and I was told by a superior that I need to keep my nose clean. They don't want any bad press about the gallery. If the gallery fails, then the hospital will most likely fail too. There's a lot of money and power behind this."

"If you follow the money you can always arrive at the answer," Anna said. "The question is, where is this money going?"

"It all flows into Jimmy's accounts to run for higher office," Mark said. "That's where this is all going. I hate to break it to you, if everything we think is true, that Jimmy is behind this to set himself up for a higher office, then nothing we can do will result in anything good for us. Do you think for one second that they will let us bring him down?"

"What do you know?" Anna asked Mark. "Somebody got to you today, didn't they?"

"It's not like that," Mark said. "Really...I was just told that I need to steer clear of anything that would make the hospital or the gallery look bad. I mean, my contract contains a ninety-day probationary period where they can terminate me without cause. If that happens, I'm done. It's really hard to find another hospital that would be willing to take a chance on me if I was let go of this one."

"You want out?" I asked. "Look Mark, this isn't your battle. It's ours. There's no point in risking your career over it."

"I promised you I would help," Mark said.

"And you have," I replied. "There's no reason for you to destroy your life with this. You still owe me a real date though, and it better not be to the grand opening of the gallery. Make it a good one Mark, I really am looking forward to it."

"You sure you're okay with this?" Mark asked.

"I am," I said. "Just don't forget our date."

"I won't," Mark said, giving me a hug. "I wish you the best, I really do. I want to help with this. If you need information from the hospital I can still get it, but we have to be careful about how we pass it back and forth...thank you, Imara. I'll call you soon."

Mark left the store. I felt tears welling up behind my eyes, a pressure there but I stifled it back, I didn't cry. It hurt that he was leaving the investigation but I knew that sooner or later Jimmy would get to him. It hurt worse that he was leaving me. I was still pissed at him for the way he acted when he first came back, but I was starting to soften, I was starting to remember how much fun we used to have together. Before Anna or Sarah could ask anything, I went to my office, grabbed my skateboard, and headed for the door.

"You gonna be out long?" Anna asked.

"You two lock up," I said. "I just need to clear my head. I think best when I'm boarding."

I left the store and dropped my board to the ground. I jumped on it and started to build up speed. I didn't know where I was going to go, didn't have any kind of plan. That was my favorite way to skateboard, just go wherever I felt like. I didn't do any tricks, didn't do anything fancy as I moved along the sidewalks, past little shops and cafes. I realized I was heading right toward the gallery. I hadn't noticed any *no skateboarding* signs but the gallery would be a fun place to board. I figured I would have to give it a try.

As I was moving past the stores on the sidewalk, I happened to catch a glance of a car that didn't seem to be moving very fast. It was a black car with black windows. Even though I couldn't see to who was driving it, I could feel their eyes upon me, watching my every move. I quickly turned down a side street and the car followed. I turned into an alley, and the car followed. I picked up speed, and weaved through traffic, and the car followed.

I picked up as much speed as I could, flying down the sidewalk, praying I didn't hit anyone who was blindly coming out of one of the stores. I could see the entrance to the gallery and I hoped that I could get there before the car was able to cut me off. There was heavy traffic on the street, allowing me to get ahead of the car. I was almost to the gallery when I turned to look back, seeing three men in black suits jump out of the car and start to chase after me.

I turned to look forward right as I slammed into a man leaving the gallery, walking toward his car. I went flying off my skateboard, hitting the ground hard, scraping my arm on the cement sidewalk. I looked at the man, a mid-thirties man in a navy blue suit. He was carrying papers that were scattered on the ground. I quickly got to my feet to see the men in black suits running toward me.

"So sorry," I said, as I rushed to my board.

"Hey you stupid brat!" the man yelled. "Help me pick my stuff up."

"Next time I bang into you," I said, with a wink, "I'll make sure it's more pleasurable for both of us."

I got on my board and quickly built up as much speed as I could. I didn't dare look back as I blew through the mock main street. Once I was into the main open area of the gallery I looked back to see two of the men still in hot pursuit. I didn't know where to go. If I went into a store they would just wait for me to come out. I could try the mall but who knows what would happen in there. I tried to see another way out but I was moving so fast on my board that I couldn't pick anything out. As I was almost to the mall, the third man came around a corner in front of me, knocking me off my board and pinning me to the ground.

"Helps when you know all the shortcuts through the gallery," the man sneered as he held me down. "You've been causing a lot of trouble for us."

"HELP!" I screamed out, hoping that someone in the almost empty Gallery would hear me. There'd been so many people outside the gallery but almost no one inside. "What do you want?"

"Leave it alone," the man said, as his two friends ran up to us. "Just leave everything alone. This is your last warning. Next time we won't be so forgiving."

The man stood up as I started to cry. I tried everything to hold it in but between the pain of being slammed to the ground and the threat, there was nothing I could do but break down and cry. I watched as the man went over to my skateboard, picked it up, and smashed it in half across his knee. He threw the pieces at my feet as the men laughed while walking away.

Chapter #24

When there's No One Left to Buy

The police station felt like a zoo with animals that could only yell at each other. The stench of sweat and burnt coffee lingered in the air as Styrofoam cups half-full of steaming brew were scattered about on every desk. A main counter against a wall of office supplies had five different coffee pots brewing new batches to keep the caffeine-induced mayhem going. I was sitting next to a wooden desk in the large room full of wooden desks, trying to remember every little detail of the attack as an inconsiderate police officer continued to ask me questions.

"What did the man look like?" the officer asked. "The one who allegedly attacked you?"

I slowly turned and looked at the cop. *Allegedly attacked me?* There was no *allegedly* about it, I was physically assaulted and threatened. This officer must have been on the payroll of Jimmy, which is why he was assigned to question me. The cop was young, not older than twenty-five, and he still had his boyish looks. He worked out, a broad chest and big arms beneath his blue police uniform, but the kid couldn't grow a goatee even though he had a few stubbly hairs around his chin that made him look like a teenager trying to impress the girls.

"I asked," the cop repeated, "what did the man look like?"

"I don't know," I replied, having gone over this with him before. "He was in a black suit with a white shirt underneath. The man was shaved bald and his face was cleanly shaven. There were no distinguishing marks on his face. The rest of his body was covered with his suit."

"And he broke your skateboard?" the male cop asked.

"Yes," I replied. "After he threatened to kill me if I didn't stop looking into the disappearance of my father."

"I thought you were looking into the deaths of Mike and Cindy Garst?" the cop asked. "And that he was telling you to quit looking for the killer."

"That could be one of the things we are looking into," I replied. "There has to be security footage that got the license plate of the car they were in. They went through a number of traffic lights. Pull up the footage and you'll have them."

"We tried that," the cop said. "The car they were driving had no plates on it. The grill on the front is from a different model of car so it's hard to tell exactly what kind of car it is. All the identifiers have been removed...including the VIN."

"That car has been used before," I said. "It's the same people who..."

"Let us do the investigating," the cop said. "I'm just going to make sure that you are safe and that no one else can harm you."

"I doubt you could do that," I said, trying to remember what this cop said his name was. He was so forgettable that I couldn't even remember. "At this point I don't think there's anyone who could help me."

"There are good people out there," the cop said. "You just have to trust that one will appear in front of you."

"I'm quite tired of people appearing in front of me," I said, thinking back to Princess Aine's clothes-switching trick. "I'm ready for something more normal that than."

"I have to talk to a couple other guys," the cop said, giving me a confused look. "You wait here. If you want coffee or water or anything, please, help yourself."

"Thank you, Officer," I said, as he walked away.

I watched the cop as he moved out of the big room and into one of the side offices. The big room was for all the detectives and beat cops, the ones who worked the streets. The side offices were for those that stayed in the office and did the background work, double-checked the facts, and as it seemed tonight, collected the payoff money to make sure certain crimes didn't get solved. As I sat there I saw Anna and Sarah enter the room, Anna pushing her way past a cop that was trying to tell her she wasn't allowed to speak with me. Anna said something to the cop that made his face look like he was a little kid getting scolded for stealing a cookie. She rushed up to me and hugged me.

"You okay honey?" Anna asked.

"I think so," I said. "It was scary. I didn't know what they were going to do."

"Did you recognize any of them?" Anna asked.

"No," I said. "They were all new guys, not ones that have been tied up in this before. I just wonder how many people Jimmy has working for him. I'm pretty sure the cop who is taking my statements is on the payroll."

"I know when Jimmy will have his victory and truly be happy," Anna said.

"When?" I asked.

"When there's no one left to buy," Anna said, with a smirk. "He can run the entire police force and do whatever he wants."

"There's a question we need to ask," Sarah said, looking around the room to make sure no one was listening to our conversation. "How far will they let us go? I mean, they killed your parents...at what point are we so close to the truth that the only answer will be to kill us, too?"

We were all silent in a room raging with noise. With all the screaming and shouting and cops yelling into phones going on around me, I could only hear a soft ringing in my ears, everything else was pushed out as I contemplated Sarah's question. We were getting close to the point where we might just find the smoking gun and then we had Jimmy over a barrel, and I doubt that he was going to let us do that.

"I don't know about you," Anna said, "I am willing to push the limits, but I'm not willing to die for this cause. I've made a couple phone calls to people I've met overseas. I've given them all the information that we've discovered and told them we are all fearful for our lives. I did this on my cellphone and sent some documents from my personal e-mail accounts."

"Why would you do that?" Sarah asked. "If they are monitoring us then they know how close we really are."

"I didn't give them everything," Anna said, smiling, "I just sent enough so that connections could be made. I'm assuming that we are under surveillance and this shows we are covering our tracks. If something happens to us, they know that there will be people looking into it. It should provide us with some breathing room."

"Nice work," I said. "Have you spoken with Lund recently? Has he told you what's going on?"

"He hasn't returned my last couple phone calls," Anna said. "I think they are onto him...speak of the devil."

I turned to see that Lund had entered the room with Detective Travis Lukens. They both looked upset and were walking straight toward us. Detective Lukens had a pocket notebook open in his left hand and a pen in his right. He walked right up to me, pushing past both Anna and Sarah without saying a word to either of them.

"You just can't seem to keep yourself out of trouble," Detective Lukens said, staring me down. "Can you?"

"Seems like I've drawn some attention to myself," I said. "I guess since the store is taking off so well that someone may be jealous of me. That's the only thing that I can think of...is there something else that you can think of, Detective?"

"Now is not the time to start getting cute," Travis said. "You keep making things worse. We're looking into this but we have other cases that we're working on, too."

"You ever figure out why Christopher Trellis was buried in my father's grave?" Anna asked. "You ever figure out who killed my parents?"

"There is a lot of upset over that," Lund said. "The Trellis family has many ties in the community and we are working fast to piece together what happened. It's not good."

"That's not what we're here about," Detective Lukens said. "We are here to figure out what happened to Imara. I've gone over the notes from the other officer and I have a question. Why did you leave the store in the first place? It wasn't quitting time."

"I just wanted to think over some things," I said. "I've reached a point in my life where I have to decide what the next steps are going to be for me. I think best when I'm on my skateboard just cruising around without a care in the world."

"Really?" Detective Lukens asked with an accusatory tone. "Is that really the reason you were out and about?"

"It was," I replied.

"You had an encounter with this Malenko the magician earlier, correct?" Lund asked.

"I did," I replied. "He came to the store to order more outfits for the opening-night show. He has another assistant."

"How many assistants does a magician need?" Travis asked. "I swear he has so many people working on that stupid set and preparing for this show it's ridiculous. It better be the best damn magic show I've ever seen...Jimmy too, or he's going to cut his pay."

"What do you mean?" Anna asked.

"He asked for a large sum of money to perform," Lund said. "Jimmy loves magic shows, so he was all for having a world-renowned magician opening his Gallery. But he also asked for full reimbursement for the set and stage show. He's charged over one-hundred-thousand dollars to the gallery the way it is and he keeps bringing in more people. He's got his one assistant, this Princess Aine..."

"Which Princess Aine?" I asked, interrupting. "Was it the one with the glitter makeup all over her face or the one who was dressed for an office boardroom?"

"I don't understand," Lund said.

"When you've seen Princess Aine," I asked, "was it a woman wearing a leotard with glitter on her face, or was it one dressed in a business suit looking professional?"

"I've seen her dressed both ways," Lund said. "I don't understand what you're getting at."

"I've seen her switch between one and the other," I said. "In ways I cannot possibly explain."

"Well let's hope that the trick is good on the stage," Travis said. "Now he's brought his lover, Anna-Sophia, into the mix..."

"Lover?" Anna interrupted. "I thought he and Aine were romantic together."

"No," Travis said. "This woman," Travis flipped through his pocket notebook, "Anna-Sophia is his girlfriend, or romantically-linked woman, who knows what they call it. We've done some digging on her. She didn't appear in his shows right away, she's a recent addition."

"What the hell was that about he and Aine making love when he was Merlin and waiting for him to reincarnate?" Anna asked.

"Far as we can tell," Travis said, "he's only involved with Anna-Sophia. One thing we did learn, however, is sometimes when they arrive for a show it's Anna-Sophia who has been with him throughout time, other times it's Aine. They vary it depending on the show. We are pretty certain Anna-Sophia is Aine's mother, although it would mean that Anna-Sophia was about thirteen when Aine was born."

"*Aine*...is that her real name?" Anna asked.

"Not sure," Detective Lukens replied. "We can't find a real name on her."

"Then how can you think that it's a mother and daughter?" I asked.

"There are some subtle clues," Travis said. "At other shows there are certain things that give it away. If you see them standing next to each other, which is very rare, we only found one picture of them, no makeup, standing next to each other and the photo was from a few years back. I would safely say they are mother and daughter...but now that this Anna-Sophia is here with the show, Malenko wants more money. He's threatening to hold up the show and only do a partial if he doesn't get more pay for her. Jimmy has about had it with this guy."

"Do you have documented evidence that Malenko is married to Anna-Sophia or that Anna-Sophia and Aine are mother and daughter?" I asked. "I mean, Anna-Sophia looks Mediterranean, while Aine looks Scandinavian."

"Maybe more than one woman plays Aine," Travis said. "The picture we have of her from Europe shows a black-haired woman that looks like Anna-Sophia. That's what we're going off of, but we're not here to talk about them. Focus, Imara, what else can you tell us? There has to be something. We will find these men that attacked you and bring them to justice."

"I wish there was something else I could remember," I said. "I've told you everything. I've never seen them before and they told me to leave things alone."

"Well, we'll see what we can do," Detective Lukens said, with a sigh. "I can't promise you much. We don't have much to go on and no cameras have picked up anything useful."

I was about to ask another question when Eddie Hayes entered the room. He looked like a raging bull, his bulky body was sweaty and his large blockhead flushed red and dripping. His eyes looked intense enough to turn a person to stone with just a glance. He shouted loud enough to get everyone's attention. All the buzz and frenzy in the room came to a stop as everyone looked at Eddie, spittle flying from his mouth as he shouted.

"From this point out," Eddie shouted, "orders will be handed down from the police commissioner himself. You will no longer be receiving assignments from the department heads. The commissioner is looking over details right now and will be coming down within the hour to reassign anyone who isn't using their time effectively. If anyone has a problem with that I'll be waiting for you in the commissioner's office."

Before anyone could react, Eddie spun around and stomped out of the room. The room was quiet for a moment before the frenzy returned with a gusto. I tried to wrap my head around what I had just heard, how the hell does Eddie, a contractor, have the right to tell the police what to do? I quickly realized that I wasn't the only one thinking that.

"How the hell does a slob like Eddie," Sarah said, staring at Detective Lukens, "come in here and tell the police what to do? Shouldn't you arrest him for interfering in an investigation?"

"There's been a development I didn't tell you," Travis said. "Jimmy has hired Eddie as a police and city consultant. He's given him some power to take control over things. The paperwork was finalized this afternoon."

"Isn't someone going to stop him?" I asked. "I mean, can Jimmy really just steamroll over a few groups like that?"

"It was difficult," Lund said. "But Jimmy has his contacts in place and has certain...*controls* over the boards. He explained that with all that had happened, more force, having more cops on the ground wouldn't solve anything...they needed to better manage the police they already have."

"Translation, Jimmy wants complete control of the police force," Anna said. "They're going to destroy everything they can just so Jimmy can have his name immortalized and grab a higher office."

"As I've said," Detective Lukens said. "You three have bigger things to worry about. I want you three to be safe, stay sharp, and keep your noses clean. Just let this stuff go until everything calms down. We don't want any more bodies turning up, okay? Now get out of here."

I nodded as the detective and Lund walked away. I couldn't help but think how much they were stacking the deck against us. I wanted to get out of the station so that Anna, Sarah, and I could talk openly about this and try to figure out what it meant. I didn't know how we were going to be able to push forward if they kept burying us in the mix.

"There's something not right," Anna said. "I was certain that I had something figured out, certain I knew a truth that was being hidden, but now *Anna-Sophia* is his lover? I don't get how that works. How could they know that but not know anything about her?"

"Wait," I said. "You're more concerned with Malenko than with what is going on with the police?"

"He's the key," Anna said. "He knows about what happened here. I'm convinced your father sought out Malenko and hired him to come here."

"Why would Dad do that?" Sarah asked. "Dean Callan was a simple man. I never once saw him do things out of revenge."

"I don't know," Anna said. "Maybe he knew that the Trellis family was after him, if he did kill Chris."

"Dad was at the store that night," I said. "I talked to him when he was at the store."

"Did you call the store phone or his cellphone?" Anna asked.

"His cellphone," I replied. "I think."

"So he could have been anywhere," Anna said. "What if, just what if, my dad had twins before he met mom. For whatever reason, he and that woman couldn't be together but she kept a close eye on him. Your dad, I'm so sorry Imara, this part of the theory is going to hurt, your dad noticed this woman watching and they started a relationship."

"You saying that Dad cheated on mom?" Sarah asked. "How can you even think that?"

"Just hear me out," Anna said. "They had a relationship. The murder of my parents happens, your dad kills Chris but realizes that the evidence would point to him, which would also expose the affair. They run off together and get married. Together, they find Malenko and hire him to come here for this show."

"Okay," I said. "So what is the plan? Malenko has a great show that wows the world? Why go through all this trouble? What's the payoff?"

"I don't know," Anna said. "Maybe the woman is pissed that Jimmy killed Dad. Maybe she is the one pushing for this, wanting revenge for her love being taken away."

"I don't know," I said. "That's a big stretch. I'm not going to rule anything out, but can you give me one concrete piece of evidence that would lend credence to your story?"

"I have nothing," Anna said. "Just thinking out loud. I don't know...let's go."

I nodded as I stood up. I followed Anna and Sarah out of the wild room and into the main waiting room of the police station. As we entered my heart skipped a beat, Mark Lewis was waiting there for us. I walked up to him smiling, a smile that got even bigger than I ever thought possible. Every thought of murder and magic was pushed out of my head as I saw what was in Mark's hands; a brand new red skateboard with a red ribbon tied around it. Mark handed me the board as I walked up to him. A tear rolled down my cheek as I looked at the board. It wasn't a brand I would ever buy, or a color I would ever buy, but Mark knew exactly what I wanted more than anything else in the world right now. I smiled at Mark and without a word, I leaned in and kissed him.

Chapter #25

The Price of the Truth

Anna, Sarah, Mark, and I settled into the cramped living room of my apartment. It was cramped even before Anna moved her meager belongings into the place, but now it was almost unbearable. Anna insisted I stay in the bedroom and she would take the reclining chair, but now the living room was full of her clothes. I made tea for everyone and we all enjoyed our first few sips of delicious Earl Gray tea in silence. I knew many questions were going to be asked and much was going to be discussed, but just enjoying the silence after the mess at the police station was wonderful.

As I felt the warmth of the tea rushing through my body, overpowered with just a dash too much lemon added, I pondered Anna's theory of why Malenko was here. If my dad did hire him that would explain how he knew everything about the murders and what was going on in Prairie Rapids. I know that when I looked into his eyes it wasn't my dad, but it had been eight years, did I really remember what my father's eyes looked like? I didn't know if I could be sure. I couldn't ask Sarah, she was such a mess at the time, so strung out on drugs there would be no way for her to remember Dad's eyes. People can change, but could I forget my own father?

"There's been a lot of movement going on at the hospitals," Mark said. "Eddie was there before he was at the station. He's ordered a large number of files to be placed into locked files. They are beyond my reach."

"Why would he do that?" Anna asked. "I thought we'd gone through the files and saw everything they knew."

"There's a number I didn't look through," Mark said. "I have no idea why he would move them. There must be something in there to link everything together. I've tried to use hospital channels to find out anything I can on Malenko and Princess Aine but they seem to be ghosts. If I had real names to go off of it might be easier."

"That's a very good question," I said. "We've never gotten their real names but someone around here must have, right?"

"Jimmy might have their real names," Anna said. "Or he might just be writing the checks to a talent company so the real names aren't needed."

"When we go to the show," Sarah said, "and he picks one of us to help, should the others try to sneak around and find his wallet or papers? We could get a name and a social security number. That would go a long way in helping us."

"I don't think someone like Malenko is going to leave that lying around," Anna said. "The question is, what is the price of the truth? How far are we willing to push this?"

"I backed out once," Mark said. "And I felt horrible for doing it. They are holding my job over me. No one has directly said it but I've been reminded a number of times that I'm on probation and they have ninety days to decide if they want to keep me around or not."

"Sooner or later there has to be something," I said. "The show is soon. Malenko said he wanted one of us to perform with him. He was going to make the decision later. I think we should head there tonight and talk with them. Confront them and ask him what is going on. One of them, whether it's Malenko, Aine, or Anna-Sophia should be able to explain what is going on."

"Wait," Mark said. "Anna-Sophia? Who is that?"

"Don't ask," Sarah said. "It just makes this thing all the more confusing. She's the next assistant in the show. Imara has to get an outfit for her."

"I've got one that should work," I said. "The time period isn't exact but no one is going to know the difference. I just wish I knew what they were doing, the whole Count of the Highland trick. Something doesn't seem right with this."

"I've got that feeling too," Anna said. "I want to go down to the gallery tonight and talk with them...find out what's going on."

"Do you think they would tell you?" Mark asked. "Do you think they'll just open up and talk about all the magic? If there's one thing I know about magicians, they love keeping secrets. You ever have one reveal a trick to you?"

"No," Anna said. "I've made some good offers to them, too."

"They never will," Mark said. "I'm leery of even going to the show, who knows what trick is up this guy's sleeve. And here's another thing, we think Jimmy is behind all of this, that he killed your parents to get the land to build his Gallery, but who else did he screw over in the process of building the thing? You ever think of that? What if Malenko is a different land owner that got forced out?"

"That's a good point," Anna said.

"What if Malenko is related to, oh what was his name, the guy that Jimmy pushed out of the mayor's office in his first election then beat again the next time he was up?"

"Gary Wright," I said. "Gary was the mayor and Jimmy spread some pretty horrible rumors about him. Jimmy did some awful things to Gary...it almost cost Gary his marriage. I couldn't believe he ran again to get his office back but Jimmy trounced him the second time."

"What if Malenko is Gary," Mark said. "Or a brother or cousin or something. They would know about the murders but it would have nothing to do with us."

"We set out to find who killed my parents," Anna said. "I made a promise that I wasn't going to stop until I knew what happened that night. I'm not giving up. We know Jimmy is behind this…"

"We *think* Jimmy is behind this," Mark interrupted. "I'm sorry, Anna, but everything you have is circumstantial at best. You bring what we have to the police and they will laugh at you. Even if we could get Doctor Dumas to testify, we still don't have that great of a case. They could tear him apart on the witness stand."

"What are you saying we should do then?" I asked. "Is it time to simply give up or do you have an idea?"

"My only thought would be to hire someone to look into this," Mark said. "But we should have done that earlier, before they knew we were looking into the case. Any evidence we could have ever used is gone."

We all sat in silence for a moment. Mark was right, anything that could be used to prove our case would have been locked away. It seemed like Jimmy was always one step ahead of us, we were always playing catchup. And now, with all the weird friends of Malenko coming to the show, there was no way to even try and predict what was going to happen.

"I say we get Princess Aine alone," Anna said. "If the four of us corner her, separate her from Malenko, we might be able to get the truth."

"How?" I asked. "Malenko has told us nothing but lies since we first met him. I fail to see why that would change now."

"Malenko has," Anna said. "That's why we need to focus on Aine. If we could get her to crack, she might just tell us something useful...give us some real names to go off of."

"You haven't see her trick," I said. "I can't stand it. She changes in the blink of an eye. One second she's glittered up in her dance leotard and the next second she's in a business suit ready for a board meeting. It's infuriating. There's no reason to believe that she won't do the same thing. She's already lied to me twice about it, saying she doesn't know what I'm talking about when she does the switching. She denies what I just saw."

"It's part of the act," Anna said. "They have to keep the illusion going, that's what magic is about. In Malenko's show I saw in Europe, he talked a lot about Magic Eyes, how some people can see things and others can't. Malenko said life is all magic and we are just the props."

"See," I said. "He is buying into the bullshit he's talking about. Listen to that...magic eyes? Come on, Anna, don't tell me you believe that anything he's doing is real?"

"Wait until you've seen the show," Anna said. "You've seen the tricks; you know how fast it can happen. Sometimes you just have to wonder."

"I wonder how we fell for a scam like his," I said. "The more blocks that get set in front of us the more I want to get this mystery solved but I don't know what the price of the truth is. How far must we go with this?"

As Anna was about to reply, Mark's cellphone rang. We waited while he stepped out of the room to answer the phone. Mark moved from the kitchen to the hallway outside my apartment, not wanting us to hear what was being said. I couldn't understand why he would be that concerned with us hearing the conversation. Muffled voices from the hall is all I could hear. After about a minute, Mark finally reentered the room, a look of stone sadness on his face. Mark shuffled to his chair and almost fell into it, like something had completely deflated him.

"What happened?" Anna asked.

"Doctor Andrew Dumas," Mark said.

"What about him?" I asked as Mark paused.

"He's dead," Mark said. "Found shot, gunshot blast to the face. No discernable entry or exit points, no way to tell exactly what happened, no witnesses..."

"The doctor is dead?" Sarah asked. "Do you think they would have killed him for what he told us?"

"This is strange," Anna said. "He was killed the same way my parents, Tim Krause, and our attacker were killed. Jimmy wouldn't have killed Tim, which was a copycat of what they did to my parents. So the question is, did they kill Doctor Dumas or did the copycat kill him?"

"How do we know Jimmy and his people didn't kill Tim?" Sarah asked. "Maybe Tim knew too much and was threatening to tell someone unless he got money or power or something."

"Good point," Anna said. "What else did they say, Mark? Did they tell you anything else that could help us?"

"No," Mark said. "That was the hospital. I have to cover for Doctor Dumas in the morning. I was hoping for the day off but all the doctors need to pitch in while we get a new lead doctor. I'm sorry, I have to go. It's going to be an early morning and a long day tomorrow."

Mark stood up without another word and slowly walked out of the apartment. I wanted to say something, tried to think of a way to comfort him, but nothing came to mind. Doctor Dumas was someone Mark looked up to and hoped to emulate in his career. I knew the kind of pain that Mark was going through and wished there was something I could have done to help him.

"They told him something else," Anna said. "He wasn't telling us the whole story."

"What do you mean?" Sarah asked. "What do you think he was holding back on?"

"I don't know," Anna said. "If they know Doctor Dumas told us about the information and sent us the death certificate, why didn't they go after us instead of him? There has to be a reason."

"We don't know anything," I said. "We could take everything we've gotten to the police and they would laugh at us. We know nothing. They are taking out all the pieces of the puzzle that could lead to something...and there's something bothering me. That damn Aine. I'm going to get her to tell me how she made those switches or I'm going to die trying. They can't mess with my security footage like that. Come on, we're going to the theater."

"Really?" Anna said. "You want to go there and force them to tell us something?"

"You have a better idea?" I asked. "This was your idea. I doubt they will tell us anything but we are going to ask. And I'm going to tell them that if they don't tell us what's going on, then I'm not going to give them their costumes for the show. I'll sell them for something else. Come on, they are giving us something."

I stood up without waiting for anyone else to answer me. I walked to the door, put my shoes on, and opened the door, waiting for Anna and Sarah to follow me. They both sat in their chairs looking stunned for a moment before standing and getting their shoes on. I took one last look around my apartment, hoping a better plan would come to me before I marched into the theater and started making demands. Without a better thought, I closed and locked my door.

It didn't take the three of us long to walk the few blocks from my apartment to the gallery. Even at night, the gallery was an overwhelming place. There were so many decorative lights in the unique landscaping designs, and custom lighting in the water flowing through the fountains...I felt like I was transported to another world.

The night air was warm and humid, no need for a coat. There were very few people in the gallery, not more than a handful, as most of the stores had already shut down for the evening and it still wasn't time for the bars and nightclubs to really get going. It was that quiet evening lull where I thought we would be able to make it to the theater without being seen or having to stop for anyone. When I saw Darrel and Todd working security, I knew we were going to have to talk to them.

"Hey ladies," Darrel shouted out, spotting us as we were walking under a streetlight. "Hey Imara, Anna, what's up?"

The men approached us. They were both wearing black pants and black tee-shirts that said 'Security' in bright yellow letters. The men had belts that were loaded with security items, flashlights, nightsticks, mace, handcuffs, and two closed packs with who knows what loaded in them. I was glad neither of them carried a gun.

"Just out for a stroll," Anna said. "We have to visit someone in the theater tonight."

"I wouldn't go there," Todd said. "That Malenko character is very strict about who can go in. He's even yelled at Mayor Nelson and Eddie Hayes for going in there. Unless you have an invitation, I wouldn't go in. So, who's the other girl with you tonight?"

"This is my sister, Sarah," I said. "Sarah, this is Todd and Darrel, we told you about them, the security guards we went out on a date with."

"I think I remember," Sarah said, with a smile. "They were the ones who were really good at dancing."

"We still haven't finished our game of truth or dare yet," Darrel said. "We've got some really good truth questions and some excellent dares to give you."

"I'm sure you do," Anna said. "You get in any trouble for the dancing?"

"No," Todd said. "We were brought in to the head of security for the gallery. He gave us a tongue lashing, told us to be smarter next time and not drink so much. We kinda led him to believe we had more to drink than we actually did. Thought that would be better than telling him we were playing a kids' game with women who ran out on us."

"I said we were sorry," Anna said. "We were worried that it was moving too fast. You have to be gentle with us."

"Okay, whatever," Todd said. "I don't get you guys. Anna, we remember you from a long time ago, when we interviewed you after your parents' death. We know all about you, knew about the backseat arrest. We see you now and you want to play some innocent game...hey, we're down with that. You play the pretend game from the start and we'll go along with it. You two are 'virgins' who want to be treated gentle, not the first time we've played that game. You go with truth or dare, okay, that has lots of possibilities, but why did you run out on us? Spare me the *moving too fast* crap, what the fuck is going on?"

"All part of the game," Anna said, as she swallowed deeply. "All part of the game...ten points from security for breaking character...I'll give you some of the rules, the game ends with you, your security shirts on the floor next to our beds, and us in your handcuffs, if you get my drift." Anna moved in close to Todd, barely letting her lips touch his before pulling away. "Don't rush the game or you lose.

There's lots of levels of exploration this game takes...if you can use your imaginations."

"Fuck the game," Todd said. "No games. You three and the two of us, tonight, our shift is done in a couple hours."

"No way," Anna said. "That's not how we play."

"So, you bitches just used us to get information?" Darrel asked. "That's the truth of it, isn't it?"

"Yes, it is," Anna said, strongly. "You two dipshits told us everything we wanted to hear, not even realizing you were being played the entire time. We had no interest in ever touching you."

"Jokes on you, toots," Darrel said. "Double cross. We were warned about you before we got there. You don't know what was true from what was lies. Now for the real part of the game, you need to come with us and we're going to have a little fun, or we arrest you."

"For what?" Anna scoffed.

"We can drum up charges later on," Darrel said.

"I think we still have some weed we took off those teenagers," Todd said. "We can say it was yours. That would be a good start."

"You wouldn't dare," Anna said.

"If you're not getting down with me real damn quick, I would dare," Todd said. "You have to know that we're not going anywhere, we're not getting fired. You picked the wrong guys to mess with. Now come with us."

"Screw you," I said. "Come on, let's just walk away. They can't do anything."

I started to walk with Anna and Sarah following. Todd quickly took a step toward us and grabbed Anna's arm. Anna tried to move away but his grip was too strong. Anna screamed out and people started looking. I was about to move forward when someone startled us from nearby.

"Let her go this instant!" a voice boomed out. Todd instantly complied as Anna moved away from him. "Step away from the women."

Todd and Darrel took a step back as Princess Aine, in her business attire, stepped out from the shadows. She looked very professional in a black business suit and her amazing, let down hair.

"If you ever try to take advantage of one of these girls again," Aine said, getting right in Todd's face, "I swear it will be the last thing you ever do. Now beat it, punks."

Todd and Darrel looked at each other then took off running away. I breathed a sigh of relief, so thankful Aine showed up when she did.

"Thank you," Anna said.

"I didn't have time to properly deal with them," Aine said. "I'll do that later. As for now, I need you three to come with me."

Without another word, Aine started walking toward the theater. I looked at Anna and Sarah before we all shrugged our shoulders and began to follow her, wondering where this night was going to take us next.

Chapter #26

Magic in the Air

Princess Aine escorted Anna, Sarah, and myself toward the theater. I was thankful that she helped us with Darrel and Todd, and I wanted to call the real police about their behavior. I thought it strange they believed Anna with her innocent routine and I had doubts over whether those boys could be that naive–turned out I was right. They thought the entire act had been a game, which it was, just not with the outcome they thought they were going to get. The look on Anna's face, disappointment, meant she thought they had believed her. Now the question was to figure out which of what they told us was real, and which was fake.

Aine didn't say a word as we entered the grand double doors to the theater. The interior of the theater looked as grand as it did the first time I entered, a slice of Americana that took me back to the golden days of Hollywood when it was just starting out. I realized I was getting nervous, excited. The last time I was in the theater there was a mess of lumber and a super-structure that was starting to form on the stage. I was certain that whatever they were building would be finished, and judging by the size it had been before, it was bound to be grand.

We walked through the velvet-covered double doors that separated the theater from the lobby, walking into the dark theater where the only lights were small marker lights on the floor so that a person wouldn't trip while walking. The theater was silent, not a noise to be heard as Aine motioned us to stand where we were. The red curtains were drawn closed on the stage so we couldn't see what was behind them. As we waited, what little light there was disappeared, covering the entire theater into a blackness so dark I couldn't see Anna or Sarah, who were both just a step away from me.

"There's magic in the air!" Malenko's voice boomed out so loudly over the sound system that every word vibrated my bones. "And when the air is light in the depths of night, not a sound is heard nor voice is stirred, the day has waned yet we've had no gain, and despite the tragic, you see the color of magic!"

When Malenko said the word 'magic' the stage was bathed in cool blue light which took all of our breath away; sitting on the stage where the stacks of random lumber had been was a massive, intricate, detailed, majestic castle. The castle was white stone, with towers on both sides, turrets on the top level, and multiple doors and windows on the face. In the center was a great wooden door that looked like it could come down as a draw-bridge. It looked like something from a fairy tale. Malenko was nowhere to be seen on stage, but there was someone there. I turned, and to my surprise, Aine was still standing next to us, despite being on the stage as well.

"That's how you did it!" I exclaimed. "You have a twin."

"That woman on the stage is not my twin," Aine smiled. "Come, you will learn."

We started walking toward the stage as I studied the woman who was on the stage. She looked to be about five-foot-nine, with long, strawberry blonde curly locks that extended to her mid back, almost identical to Princess Aine's. The woman was wearing a black cat suit, with black gloves and dance slippers, covering her entire body in black spandex from the neck down. The woman was the same build as Aine, a fit dancer's body, who had her face painted in brilliant colors; blues, yellows, and greens, making her look like some kind of bizarre cat. Her outfit was topped off with a pair of furry cat ears on her head.

As we walked onto the stage, I got a closer look at the cat woman. Her eyes were set wide on her face, where Aine's were closer. The woman had a wide mouth where Aine's was very narrow, Aine had a much bigger chest and wider hips. The woman on the stage had a more rounded, flatter face while Aine's was narrow with sharp angles. From a distance, with these women's hair, height, and build, they looked like twins. Standing next to each other, I can tell they are not. My mind raced, was this how Aine was doing the switch? Each time I heard both of them talk, if the voices are close enough, I may have just realized the switching trick.

"This is a member of our team," Princess Aine said. "What do you think of the beginning of the show?"

"It was interesting," Anna said. "The sight of this castle alone should garner a grand wow factor for the opening, but if that is followed up with a woman dressed as a cat standing there doing nothing I think the opening is a little underwhelming."

"There will be more to it than that," Aine said. "But the speech and the revealing of the castle, you like that?"

"It was amazing," I said, before I turned to the cat woman. "What's your name?"

"She is called Felicity," Aine said. "She doesn't speak."

"Of course she doesn't," I said. "What does she do then?"

"She is a main player in the cast of our story," Aine said.

"Story?" Anna asked. "I thought this was just a magic show?"

"*Just* a magic show?" Malenko said, stepping through one of the doors on the castle in his black aristocrat suit, complete with top hat, cane, and mirrored sunglasses. "Just a magic show? No, my dear. Malenko isn't doing just a magic show. Malenko is creating an experience, telling a story...one of the greatest stories ever told. This stage will be the setting for a new movement in magic, a new day for theater. Gone is the time where simple magicians walk the streets hawking card tricks and slight of hands, this is grander, this is bigger. A company has been contracted to digitally record the entire event in high definition. No one will want to miss a moment of this. Malenko can bet that the people of this town will want to buy copies to watch again and again...magic in the air...can you feel it?"

"I feel something," Anna said. "How much did this set cost?"

"Money is no object," Malenko said. "When you've lived as long as I have you learn how to tuck money away, how to let it grow and compound. Money concerns me not...only magic."

"Show us a trick then," Sarah said. "Let's see some of this magic. I've been dying to see your show."

"Normally Malenko doesn't cater to whims," Malenko said, "but now Malenko's been meaning to show you some magic, been meaning to get you three here to demonstrate what Malenko can do and thereby get one of you three to participate in the show."

"If I have to wear an outfit like that," Sarah said, pointing to the cat woman, "or a leotard like Aine wears, count me out."

"I'm in," Anna said, excitedly. "That looks cool."

"Malenko hasn't decided on the final costume design just yet," Malenko said. "But when he does be assured that Malenko will find the perfect outfit for every participant. Anna, would you come with Malenko?"

"Sure," Anna said.

Malenko took Anna to a door on the castle. Malenko opened the door and looked inside. As he opened it, the area inside the door started to glow with a blue light that was hidden inside the room. The room was small, only about six-feet tall, three-feet wide, and not more than three-feet deep. Malenko ushered Anna into the room.

"Malenko wants you to look around this little space," Malenko said. "Tell the others if you find any way to get out of it other than the main door."

Anna looked around the space, looked through the door, looked on the walls, floors, and ceiling. Anna got into the small space and stomped her feet, the sound was solid.

"There's no way," Anna said, stepping out of the room. "There's no other way out besides the main door."

"Good," Malenko said. "Felicity, please be a dear and step into the space."

Felicity, dropping to all fours and walking like a cat, moved to the door, stood up, and backed herself in. The entire time she was making every movement cat-like. It was obvious this woman had studied cats, her actions were eerily similar to how cats move. It made for a very convincing setup to the upcoming trick.

"Malenko wants you to know Felicity," Malenko said, as he started to shut the door, "you will be perfectly safe inside. You know I would never do anything to hurt you."

Malenko closed the door and smiled at us. He raised his hands in the air, slowly, deliberately, making every movement with a structured purpose. Within the blink of an eye Malenko pulled a large dagger out of his jacket and in one fluid motion, stabbed the dagger through the door.

There was a yell from inside the little space and in the blink of an eye, the door opened, with thick white smoke pouring out.

I couldn't see inside due to all the heavy smoke coming out of the space. As the smoke started to dissipate, a figure emerged from the room; Princess Aine. Aine was wearing nothing but black briefs that went to her navel and a halter-cropped sequenced turquoise dancer's top. On her feet were black ballet slippers and opposite that, a tiara in her done-up hair. Aine's face was covered in glitter makeup. I turned around, but of course, the other Princess Aine, in the black business suit with her hair down, was nowhere to be seen.

Before we could start clapping for the trick, we heard a meowing in the theater. We all turned to look back and saw Felicity, crawling on top of the backs of theater seats near the rear doors. She was meowing, mock-licking her paws, and generally acting like a cat. I was stunned, beyond mystified as to how Aine changed clothes so quickly, how Felicity moved to the back of the theater so fast, and how she got out of the chamber in the first place.

"That was awesome," Anna said. "So cool. How the hell did she get out of the room? There's no way, I searched that chamber and there was no way out."

"How did she change so fast?" Sarah asked.

"That's a great question," I added before anyone else could say anything. "I've seen you do that trick a number of times now, Princess Aine. How *do* you switch clothing so fast?"

"One day you may learn," Malenko said. "But not today."

As I was about to press the issue, I noticed Felicity had come back on stage. She'd walked up to the stage on her hands and knees, walking like a cat would, and now she was snuggling herself around Malenko's feet. It was very strange, hard to watch—awkward. Here was a thirty-something-year-old woman acting like a kitten. I couldn't figure out what part this would play in his magic show, but Felicity made a very convincing cat.

"What's with her?" Anna asked. "Is it really necessary to act like that?"

"Felicity was saved by Malenko," Malenko said. "I saw a traveling carnival in the misty moors of Ireland. They had a trapeze artist that was without equal throughout the world. Felicity here could do tricks on the flying trapeze that most didn't think were possible. I made her an offer to come to my show but she refused. Years later, she showed up at my door in this condition, unable to speak. It turns out there was a very amateur magician who worked the carnival and he tricked Felicity into a relationship. The pair bonded but he only wanted her beauty for his act. He was going to have a kitten on stage, and after saying some magic words the kitten would disappear and Felicity would be there in the kitten's place...needless to say, magic was not in the air that night."

"So, what you're telling us," Anna said, trying to wrap her head around it, "is that Felicity here is a human woman that got crossed with a kitten?"

"Yes," Malenko said. "That is what Malenko is telling you."

"Because of incompetent magic?" Sarah asked.

"Yes," Princess Aine said. "We must care for Felicity now. She doesn't have the ability to take care of herself."

"Serious?" Anna asked.

"Why wouldn't Malenko and Princess Aine be serious?" Malenko asked as he stroked his black beard with one hand.

Anna smiled as she slowly approached Felicity. Anna crouched down, bringing her face to the same level as Felicity's face. Anna got close to Felicity and began to extend her hand out. Anna slowly brought her hand to Felicity's head and began to pet her. Felicity smiled and began to purr as Anna stroked her hair. Anna moved forward farther and hugged Felicity before standing up.

"Do you believe?" Aine asked.

"My beliefs are not for you to know," Anna said.

"Malenko has heard of the situations you girls are in," Malenko said. "Very difficult to lose family and even harder to lose family without gaining a sense of closure. Malenko has lost many families over the millennia, but always, there is new family. In time, friends become close enough to be family, even friends who were lost for long periods of time. Someday you will come to learn, as Malenko has, that there is truly only the here and now. What's in the past has happened and cannot be changed, and what's in the future is to come and will come no matter what path we take."

"We mustn't lose sight of what's important to us," Princess Aine said. "Throughout the many thousands of years I have walked this earth I have seen so much come and go. The destruction and damage humans can cause is incomprehensible, but so is the magical and healing power of love. I have seen empires rise and fall, I have seen dynasties born and wither, I have seen powerful men cut down in battle and I have seen brilliant men die penniless and alone. What's the point? Why do we get on this game called life? Magic in the air."

"Magic in the air," Malenko repeated. "All it takes is that one little speck of magic to turn the ordinary into something so much more. As you will see throughout my show, there is nothing that is truly for certain. Anything can happen."

"Who do you want in the show?" Anna asked. "Which one of us will get to perform with you?"

"I sense you want to be on the stage," Aine said.

"I do," Anna said. "But if Imara or Sarah want it more they can have it. I just think it would be really cool to be part of a magic show like this."

"Malenko realizes the size of the show will be larger than what anyone expected," Malenko said. "Malenko wants all three of you to join with him and share the stage for what will be a night to remember."

"I'm in," Anna said. "Imara?"

"Sure," I said. "I'm looking forward to this."

"Why not," Sarah said. "But no leotards for me...I don't have the body to pull one off in public."

"Don't worry," Aine said. "You will be able to decide what you want to wear...within reason, that is. We have something special planned for you."

"How special?" Sarah asked.

"A grand trick," Malenko said. "Something that will be remembered for all the ages, a spectacle that will be written in the annals of magic."

The next week almost seemed like a blur. Between getting properly-fitted costumes in the store to the right people, working with Malenko and Princess Aine on the show, and continuing to investigate what was going on with the murders, there was hardly time for anything else. Mark and I tried to schedule a date but our schedules were never able to match up.

All the costumes needed alterations, little adjustments, and fine tuning, but we got everything to fit. Jimmy, Eddie, and their families were all going to be dressed like movie stars from 1920s Hollywood. Everybody in Malenko's show had a number of costumes, ranging from Celtic warriors to futuristic stars. I'd worked with hundreds of different theater groups, many different directors, and I would venture to say that Malenko, with all his eccentricities, was one of the easiest to deal with. Any problem and he would simply smile and say something along the lines of, "It will either be fixed by opening night or we'll use it as it. If there's time, fix it, if not, we'll make it work." I wished that all customers could be as easy going as him.

Mark and I decided that the gallery opening would be our first official date, even though I was working with Malenko and his show. There was going to be something going on in every bar and nightclub, along with a band playing in the outdoor Gallery itself. Jimmy hired an entire carnival to be there for the opening few days, kids rides, games, and all sorts of events. The opening of the gallery was going to be the social event of the summer for Prairie Rapids.

With every new event planned for the opening, more and more media and news organizations were being invited to show up. The Front Street Gallery and Entertainment Complex was going to be seen around the world, and everyone would know that James Nelson was the man behind it...just in time for him to announce his intentions to seek the governorship of the state in next year's election.

Chapter #27

The Show Must Go On

I sat in a dressing room behind the stage of the theater, wondering how the show would turn out. I was in my costume, an elegant green dress, low cut at the neck, long-sleeved and hemmed just above the knees. My hair was down, flowing and shiny. Princess Aine had done my makeup, blush and enough black eyeliner to look like I was wearing a mask. My lips were a stunning ruby red and there was glitter sprinkled in my hair, face, and upper body. Sarah was dressed similarly, except she had a shimmering aqua blue dress. Anna was in a black leather tank top with shredded blue jeans and black biker boots with her hair teased out and stacked up like an '80s rocker chick.

Malenko had been very specific about our roles, even though we didn't need to do a lot of practice. Anna was going to be in the audience, waiting for her moment, while Sarah and I would be on stage, helping when indicated. I found it strange that Malenko didn't tell us exactly what we were going to be doing. He just kept saying that for the magic to be real, for it to be amazing, we needed to be kept in the dark. I was excited for the show. When I arrived at the gallery earlier in the day, I knew this show was going to be bigger than I'd thought.

I'd arrived with Anna and Sarah in the early afternoon to take in all the excitement of the opening of the gallery. Jimmy and Eddie didn't disappoint. In the open-air area of the gallery, a full-fledged carnival was going on. The area was packed with people as there were games, entertainers, bouncy houses for the kids, and a plethora of things that would normally be seen at a fair. Kids were running around with cotton candy in their hands and their faces painted. Couples were walking with stuffed animals won at the games. There were storytellers, jugglers, comedians, and even a firewalker.

Jimmy had truly outdone himself with the spectacle and grandeur of the event. It was something everyone was going to remember and Jimmy was making sure he was the center of attention. He was giving interviews, talking with everyone there, and he had people hired to start campaigning for him. That was the surprise though, everyone was certain Jimmy was going to announce that he was running for governor but he was campaigning for the senate. It was a move that took everyone by surprise but there were Senator Nelson signs hanging everywhere.

As we walked around the grounds, I couldn't help but notice all the security guards that were milling about. I kept my eyes open for Darrel and Todd, knowing they were still very upset with Anna and would most likely want to have words with us when they saw us, but I didn't see either of the men around. Even with all the people wearing security tee-shirts, I could tell there were other people who were dressed in plain clothes that were also security, blending in with the crowd.

I brought my attention back to the room when the door opened. Anna was walking in, her face almost glowing with the vast amounts of neon makeup that was caked on her face. She would have fit in perfectly at any head-banging metal rock concert. She pulled off the look very well. I thought that I fit my dress perfectly. Even though I still disliked wearing dresses after everything my mother had put me through, I liked this dress.

"You ready for all of this?" Anna asked as she took a seat.

"I think so," I said. "But I have a nagging concern. We've found out all this information, we know all that happened in the past...the gallery is opening but we are no closer to having any form of closure on the death of your parents nor are we any closer to finding out what happened to my father."

"I don't know," Anna said. "There's something about this whole event...this magic show, I mean. That Felicity, there's something about her. When I looked into her eyes, there was something there."

"She's a great actress," I said. "She was totally dedicated to the act of a cat while we were there. I just wonder how that is going to play into the show."

"I'm still stunned at that trick they pulled off," Anna said. "I mean, there was no way Aine could have changed that fast, not to mention how Felicity got out of that closet. I can't figure it out, you know?"

"I know," I said. "I watched Aine twice pull the switching clothes trick. I thought for sure that it was Felicity. The more I thought about it, Felicity, with all the glitter makeup on, would pass perfectly for Aine, but they were both standing there afterwards."

"I wonder what we'll be doing tonight?" Anna asked. "I'm sure Malenko is going to go all out for this show. With all the talk of things being remembered forever and whatnot."

"And Jimmy running for senate," I said. "Figured he would announce his candidacy today, but I thought it would be for Governor."

"I just wish we could bring him down and expose him for who he truly is," Anna said. "Show the world what he's really all about."

"Wishing to bring someone down isn't a noble cause," Princess Aine said, walking in the room. "Revenge isn't a just cause."

I studied Aine as she stood in the room, closing the door behind her, wondering if she'd been listening to our entire conversation or just caught the last part as she was coming in. Aine was in her black business suit with an indigo button-down shirt. She looked very professional with just the slightest bit of makeup on and her hair neatly done into a pair of braids. I wondered what kind of outfit she would change into when she did her switch trick.

"I don't want revenge," Anna said, looking over Aine. "I just want to expose what he did and show the world his true nature."

"Karma has a way of catching everyone," Aine said. "You can be sure that one day, karma will have her way with him. There's nothing that can stop that. I just wanted to check in and see how you were doing before the show."

"Great," I said. "I think everything is going good."

"Nervous?"

"A little," I said.

"Not at all," Anna said. "I have my reserved ticket for the front row...what am I going to be doing? Why did I have to dress like this?"

"That will be a surprise for later," Aine said. "You will be perfect for the role. You look perfect for it. When you're called on stage, just act natural and roll with it. The audience, when they see you, are going to assume that you're a plant, which you are, but you don't know what's coming up, and neither do they. It makes the trick all the more interesting. When the magic happens, your reactions will be natural and that enhances the show. Malenko has done this for many lifetimes. He's practiced and refined

297

what works and what doesn't. When this magic is finished, everyone will be talking about it."

"Sounds great," Anna said. "Are we going to see Malenko before the show?"

"The show goes on in about an hour," Aine said. "Malenko never appears before the show. He's resting, conserving his powers for the grandeur about to come. Ladies, just know that you will do great. Imara, you will start the show on the stage with me. I will be instructing you on what to do. Don't worry, everything will go smoothly. I'm sure you will do great."

The door opened and Sarah walked in. The little dressing room was tight with all four of us inside. Aine smiled, bowed, and rushed out of the room. I wasn't sure what had come up, why she left so fast, but I put it out of my head and looked over to Sarah. She looked so amazing in her dress, an absolutely stunning, beautiful woman. I was about to speak when the door opened again, Detective Travis Lukens and Officer Lund Grimes walked in.

"Again," Detective Lukens started sounding upset, "I find you three together, causing trouble."

"What trouble have we supposedly caused this time?" Anna asked.

"You were with the security guards the other day," Travis said. "Todd and Darrel, correct?"

"They stopped and talked to us," I said. "We brushed them off and made our way here. What's this about, Detective?"

"They were found dead today," Travis said. "They didn't show up for work this morning, so we sent someone to their houses to check on them. Both were shot in the face, shotgun blast. All the doors and windows were locked from the inside. I can't help but notice you three are in the magic show...magic...like getting through locks and windows, wouldn't you say?"

"No," Anna said, bluntly. "Not really. We don't even know our roles yet. Were there notes and letters left with them?"

"There were," Lund said.

"Does it implicate us?" I asked.

"It does," Lund replied.

"I have a question for you, Detective Lukens," Anna said. "If we killed these people, why would we implicate ourselves in the matter? I don't understand your logic on that one."

"It was sensitive to say the least," Travis said, pulling a piece of paper in a plastic baggie out of his jacket. "'Death was all around me but I survived. I was marked for death but being unlucky prevented my untimely demise. I will not stop until everyone has paid for their sins. Nothing can stop me. The show must go on.'"

"How do you think that's me?" Anna asked. "How does that implicate me?"

"Imara was the unlucky one," Travis said. "With everything that happened that night. You Anna, were unlucky that you got caught up in that mess. If you would have been in your house, you would have been killed. Death was all around you, your parents, and now you mistakenly think that Jimmy is behind it and you are going to extract revenge on him."

"If Jimmy isn't behind it," I said, standing up and putting my hands on my hips. "Who the hell is? All your great detective work and you are no closer to solving who killed Anna's parents, where my dad went, or who's really behind what's going on now."

"I'll take my shots," Travis said. "I don't have the best track record on this case but I will solve it. I'm watching you...all three of you. Now tell me, I know we went over this once, but what did you do after you left the guys?"

"We came here," Anna said. "We talked with Princess Aine and Malenko. They introduced us to Felicity."

"Ah, Felicity," Detective Lukens said. "The human cat. Such an interesting backstory. Once I saw Felicity I was certain that she's Anna-Sophia's daughter, not Aine. It was Felicity I saw in the picture taken in Europe, not Aine. It's strange how he has all these people around that just happen to appear when he wants them to."

"What do you mean?" I asked.

"I think there's more here than magic," Travis said. "This Malenko has his sights set on something else."

"What?" I asked.

"This is confidential, ladies," Travis said. "I'm not supposed to tell you, but I fear you are about to get blamed for something that you didn't do. There is a bank that is next to the theater. A lot of money has been placed in the bank and the security systems aren't fully up and running...there've been set backs. Now Malenko comes in, talking about doing magic and having a show, and he's bringing in trucks in the middle of the night, unloading something covered with black tarps. Why? What is he up to?"

"You think that the magic show is a diversion to rob a bank?" Anna asked.

"Exactly," Travis said. "We've been monitoring everything Malenko's been doing. Strange activity going on at night. There are men working for him at night that aren't seen during the day. They've been all over the gallery. We've never been able to catch one. I don't know what's going on but I'm certain that bank is going to be robbed...tonight. Do you know anything about this?"

"No," I said. "All they've told us is magical things. They only talk about the show to us. I don't know what else to tell you."

"I will tell *you* to be careful," Travis said. "Keep your eyes open. If you don't, you might end up in jail for a crime that these crooks committed."

Travis left the room but Lund waited. He closed the door and locked it, keeping Travis out. I couldn't tell if Travis walked away or waited, but Travis didn't try to get back into the room. Lund looked nervous...scared. He reached into his pants pocket and pulled out some papers, handing them to Anna.

"These are the official autopsy reports," Lund said. "There's an issue inside that you can figure out. Everyone involved in this, not saying that I know who it is, was very upset over that report. That's why everything was changed. The death certificate Doctor Dumas sent you was a fraud, made in his office that morning."

"Why would he do that?" Anna asked.

"I don't know," Lund said. "I swear to you that what you hold in your hand is the real report. All the notes from the doctors. You must understand, there will be two guards stationed in that bank tonight. They will be armed with instructions to defend the bank at all costs. James doesn't want a robbery on the opening night of his Gallery."

"Why give us this now?" Anna asked. "Why not before?"

"I didn't have access to it before," Lund said. "Travis had pulled it out to go over the details and I swiped it from his desk and copied it. He never knew. Don't let anyone know who gave this to you....it seems like everyone who helps you ends up dead."

Lund turned and quickly left the room, closing the door behind him. Anna wasted no time in opening up the papers and looking through them. She studied them, looking over every aspect, trying to figure out what the deal was. As Anna's eyes were scanning the pages, something caught her attention. Anna's eyes got huge, her jaw hung open and she remained silent for a moment.

"What is it?" Sarah asked.

"I can't believe this," Anna said. "This report says that they checked the blood type four separate times."

"Why would they need to check the blood type that many times?" I asked. "What was going on?"

Anna was about to speak when the lights went off in the room. We all shouted out in surprise, scared of what was going on. I braced myself, getting ready for something to happen, but when the lights came back on, Felicity was in the room, in her same cat outfit we'd seen her in before. She was curled up on the sofa that was against the back wall. Felicity didn't seem to be bothered with us at all, but I was dumbfounded as to how she got into the room without opening the door. There was no way she could have been hiding in the room before...at least I didn't think she could have been hiding there.

"Felicity," I said, causing her to turn and look at me. "What are you doing here?"

Felicity just stretched out on the sofa, mock-licking her paw, acting very similar to how a cat acts. Anna walked over to her, started to pet her hair. I was wondering what Anna was trying to do, why she was treating her like a cat. There was no way that story Malenko told about her could be true, no way could she have been magically crossed with a cat in a trick gone wrong.

Anna continued to pet her before moving her hand and starting to rub Felicity's stomach. Anna was rubbing her stomach just like she would a cat's. The whole situation was starting to get very weird, even for Anna. Felicity held her face, kept a happy expression on just like a cat would, never once showed any signs of discomfort or unpleasantness. As Anna was rubbing her stomach, Anna changed her hands, using her fingertips, and started tickling Felicity. Felicity instantly cracked up, laughing out. Anna started to tickle her harder, causing Felicity to laugh out more, squirming to get away from Anna's grip but Anna was keeping her pinned onto the sofa. Tears were coming out of Felicity's eyes as Anna finally got her to break character.

"Stop, stop, stop!" Felicity said, through her laughter. "Please stop."

"You can talk," Anna said. "Why don't you tell us something useful?"

"You're the worst kind," Felicity said, as she composed herself and sat upright like a normal person on the sofa. "I hate those people who force a magician to reveal their secrets...or in this case, deliberately cause a person to break character. My whole bit adds to the mystique of the show. Malenko tells the story of how he rescued me while I perform cat tricks. I've trained in gymnastics, yoga, and dance my entire life so I can do some pretty neat tricks. It's a fun part of the show that always gets people laughing...and wondering...*what if it's real?*"

Her voice was lower, for a woman, and rougher than Aine's. She could pass off as Aine from a distance or up close with the makeup on, but I heard both business Aine and leotard Aine speak so there was no way it could have been Felicity switching with Aine.

"Why did you keep the routine with us?" Sarah asked.

"Practice," Felicity said. "Sometimes I hang out after the show with Malenko in the crowd as they leave. We talk to people, let kids pet my hair, stuff like that."

"Why the hell did you come into our room?" I asked. "Why did you turn the lights out and appear instead of using the door like a normal person? How the hell did you get in here anyway?"

"All part of the magic," Felicity said. "Come on ladies, the show must go on. This is going to be Malenko's greatest show. I'm here to make sure you don't have any preshow jitters."

"You ever get preshow jitters?" Anna asked.

"I used to," Felicity said. "Now I've performed so many times it doesn't even bother me. Remember one thing, if you screw up, no one out there knows. They think it is part of the act. We even have tricks where we screw up, or at least make them think we screwed up, then hit everyone with an amazing trick. It's all part of the show."

"Part of the show," I said. "Still doesn't tell us how you got into this room in the first place."

"Part of the show," Felicity said. "*How* I got in, isn't important...why I'm here, is."

"Then why are you here?" Anna asked. "Are you guys planning to rob the bank?"

"Dearest me, no," Felicity said. "Robbing banks is the least of our concerns. When you get a rube like Jimmy Nelson who wants perfection, he's willing to pay for it. We've made more money off this gig than we could robbing a bank...well, maybe not more, but we're making a hell of a lot of money and we bought enough costumes and supplies to last us for the next couple years. Remember that we have enough to last for two, maybe three years."

"Okay," I said. "So, you're just here to make sure we don't have the preshow jitters?"

"Yes."

"If I hadn't tickled you," Anna said, "would you have ever revealed your true self?"

"No. I was just going to sit here for a bit and observe you...of course I was going to reveal myself. Now you girls aren't going to be walking around before the show, can't have you breathing a word of the magic to the people out there."

"Please tell me," I said. "Felicity, please, just tell me, what is going on here? How do you know about what happened to our parents and what is going on?"

"The show must go on," Felicity said.

The lights in the room went out, casting the room again into darkness. When the lights came back on, Felicity was gone, along with Anna. It was just Sarah and myself in the room. We were stunned. It took a second to realize it, but Anna had completely disappeared. Before we could say or do anything, the door opened and business-suit Princess Aine walked in.

"Come on," Princess Aine said. "It is time."

"But Anna just disappeared from the room," I said, still in shock over the matter. "What about Anna?"

"She's with Felicity," Aine said. "It's all part of the show. Anna is getting her final instructions. Come with me, I have to show you what you'll be doing for the show."

"Are you sure she's okay?" Sarah asked.

"She's better than okay," Aine said. "Come on, the show must go on."

I took one last look around the room before breathing a heavy sigh. It was now or never, we were going to be in a magic show.

Chapter #28

The Show Begins

"And the show begins!" said Princess Aine, her voice booming over the theater's sound system. "Get ready to be transported to the land of magic. For the rest of your lives, imagine pondering the feats of illusions, wondering, what's real and what isn't."

The crowd cheered wildly. I couldn't see them; the curtains weren't open yet. Princess Aine was standing just a few feet away from me, in front of the castle, center stage. I was to her left and had no clue where Anna or Sarah were. Princess Aine was in her black business suit, but I had a feeling she would be changing to start the show. Her instructions to me were simple, just follow her lead and don't be nervous.

I wasn't nervous until the curtains opened and the lights came up. At first I didn't think anything of it, the theater was cast in a darkness that didn't allow me to see what was going on, but as the cool blue lights on the stage illuminated the castle while ominous magical music blasted through the powerful sound system, and the bass rattled my bones, I realized just how full the theater actually was. The place was packed, not an empty seat in the house. The roar of the crowd was deafening, everyone cheering and yelling, ready for a grand show. I looked to Princess Aine, who was smiling, enjoying every moment of the crowd. Aine held her hands up to get the crowd to quiet down.

"Thank you," Aine said. "I'd like to introduce myself before we get started. You need to know a little about us before we begin the show. Please, my friends, sit back...relax...take a deep breath in...hold it for a moment...let it out...let me tell you a story...see, I was born well over three-thousand years ago." There was a murmur in the crowd, some laughing, some confused. "Don't be alarmed. You'd be amazed how many people like myself have lived for millennia.

"I was the only daughter of a humble sheep farmer in the highlands of Ireland. We had a fine flock of sheep that commanded the best prices for wool in the entire emerald isles. My father and mother worked hard and prospered. Every year we looked forward to Samhain, the Celtic New Year, which was on October 31st, the day you now call Halloween. That night, when the veil between the living and the dead is the thinnest, allowing our ancestors to cross back and forth, is the night my life changed forever.

"I was with the flock that day, getting ready to meet my betrothed, the man I was to marry. He was handsome and strong, with fire eyes and a mane of red hair so thick and lush that every girl in the village wished she could have him...but he was all mine. As I was tending the flock, a strange man came along looking for stones. He'd been all over the isle, to every corner, but he couldn't find the stones he was looking for.

"He told me he was building something grand, something that would stand for centuries and be very important to our religion and culture. He spoke of the grand castles that were being built, the circular churches where we worshiped the Pagan gods of old. He said this place would stand for all time as a symbol of our religion...even if future generations wouldn't understand.

"This man I speak of, I showed him the rock in our area but it wouldn't suffice. There was one thing that did, however...me. Even though I was to be married in less than a week, I made love to this man under a sky full of shooting stars. It was a magical night. I haven't aged a day since then.

This man, you know him as Merlin the wizard, from the Arthurian Legend, was building Stonehenge. I left Ireland with him the next morning, without a word of goodbye to my parents or future husband...I've never seen nor heard from them again."

There was a confused silence in the crowd. Princess Aine was a great talker. She knew just how to speak to pull a crowd in and get them to hang on every word. Aine was a natural in front of a crowd, and she seemed to be loving every second of it. She stared to motion me to move toward her as she walked to a door on the castle, the door that led to the chamber where the switch took place before.

"I did bring shame to myself," Aine said. "I admit that. But I love Merlin, who is now Malenko. You see, Malenko Pendragon lives his life and dies, to be instantly reincarnated. There are times when I must live hundreds of years before I find him again. I never know where he is going to be...what country he will be born in. Sometimes I find him right away, other times, I am very sad. That is the way of things. That is my story. Throughout the night I will tell you bits and pieces of the wisdom I have learned living so many lives, walking through so many lands, but to start with, my assistant, Imara, will close the door to this chamber, and the show begins."

Aine entered the chamber and I closed the door. The instant I closed the door, smoke billowed from the castle, the lights on the stage went wild, like the lighting show at a night club, and multi-colored shafts of light were dancing all around the room as the music blasted through the sound system. I stepped away from the door as it began to open. Aine stepped out, covered in glitter makeup, heeled boots that went to her knees, black sheer stockings, a black leotard with turquoise and indigo swirls, and a black and turquoise velvet cape. There was a tiara in her hair, which was loaded with glitter and cascading down her back. The crowd cheered.

"This is a much better outfit," Aine said, with a smile. "Forget the professional business stuff, who's ready to get down and dirty?"

The crowd roared with applause and cheers.

"You see," Aine said, as she paced in front of the crowd on the edge of the stage, "Malenko is by far the greatest magician who has ever walked this great planet we call Earth. The only problem is, he doesn't obey things like schedules and time. He's off in a faraway land and we need to bring him here. For that, I'm going to need my nemesis to come out, Anna-Sophia, please get out here."

The lights and smoke went crazy while the music blasted. The crowd cheered as the main drawbridge to the castle was lowered. There was an insane amount of lighting inside the tunnel of the castle. There was a figure moving, a voluptuous woman. Anna-Sophia emerged, not in the dress or skirt-and-top set I had gotten for her, but in nothing but an emerald green leotard. Anna-Sophia had her face painted the same shade of emerald green. She looked very stunning for her age.

"You see," Aine continued as the music quieted down, "Anna-Sophia and I are mortal enemies drawn to work together by that which makes us hate...Malenko. Anna-Sophia also made love to Malenko under a sky of falling stars, which is how we became immortal, but she was his first. When he came to my land, he thought that she was lost to him forever. They were reconciled and now we have a problem, can Malenko love enough to satisfy two women? It turns out his heart is big enough for the both of us but that still doesn't stop us from trying, from time to time, to kill each other."

As Aine finished speaking, all the lights in the theater went out, casting the theater into complete darkness, and a female scream was heard over the sound system. Everyone in the crowd was on edge until the lights came back on. Aine and Anna-Sophia were both on the stage, but a solid black, six-foot tall, three-feet wide, three-feet-deep box, was in the front of the castle. Next to the box was a table full of swords. Aine opened the front of the box, showing that it was empty inside.

"Anna-Sophia," Aine said. "Get in."

Anna-Sophia slowly got into the box and Aine closed the door. Aine hit each side of the box, showing that it was solid. Aine motioned to me to move to the table with the swords. I walked to it, looking over the pile of swords, all straight bladed, European-style swords.

"My assistant will hand me a sword," Aine said.

I complied. Aine took the sword and moved to the front of the box. She took a few moments to demonstrate some amazing sword-handling skills before she jammed the sword into the front of the box, right where Anna-Sophia's face would be.

"Another sword," Aine said, as the crowd gasped. "Now."

I handed her another sword. Again, she demonstrated some sword fighting skills before jamming the sword into the side of the box. I could see the tip sticking out of the other side, the sword was long enough to go all the way through. Aine kept demanding swords and I kept handing them to her until all twenty swords were in the box, tips sticking out the other end. Aine finished putting the last sword in and stepped away.

"Now that I have her trapped and skewered, "Aine said, "I wonder if Malenko will still want her? The only problem is this really isn't a magic trick. If you were paying attention, I told you that we are both immortal, we can't die, so really, I guess, what's the trick here? Imara, remove the swords from the box, quickly."

I quickly rushed to the box and started pulling swords out. I pulled them out as fast as I could, waiting to see what was going to happen. I expected, as I laid my hands on each one, that something amazing would happen, but I pulled each sword out and tossed it on the ground, nothing changed. When I pulled the last one out, the lights and music went wild, the door to the box opened, smoke rolled out, and Malenko stepped out of the box. I was stunned, not knowing how the hell he got in there or how Anna-Sophia got out. I looked inside the box but couldn't see anything.

"Malenko has arrived," Malenko said, in a booming voice as the crowd collectively gasped before breaking out in wild applause. He was wearing his black aristocrat suit, with top hat and cane. He looked very dignified as he walked over and kissed Aine. "You've done well," said Malenko as he looked over the castle and stage. "Malenko is very impressed with this setup."

"Thank you," Aine said, as she walked up and kissed Malenko before addressing the crowd. "Ladies and gentlemen, I give you Malenko Pendragon!"

The crowd cheered as Malenko took a bow. The lighting scheme on the castle slowly changed from a blue glow to a green glow. It was so subtle that I almost didn't notice. Most of the people were focused on Malenko and didn't notice the shift either.

"Thank you," Malenko said. "It's great to be here in this grand theater, this magical place of wonder and amazement. For only in the theater can you truly be transported, even if just for a little time, to a new world, see all the things that you want to see, experience what you never thought you could experience. It is here, on this stage, that men and women have immortalized themselves through the performances they give. Truly, the theater is a grand place to be. Tonight will be a night to remember...Malenko guarantees that. There is magic in the air and we will use all of our skills that Princess Aine has gained over the last three-thousand years and that Malenko has gained over hundreds of lifetimes to amaze you in ways you couldn't possibly imagine. First things first...Princess Aine, where's Anna-Sophia?"

"Well," Aine said, looking at the ground. "The thing about that is...you see...I wanted to start the show with a bang!"

"You put her in the box," Malenko said, like a father scolding a child. "Didn't you?"

"I did."

"And you used the swords?"

"Yes, Malenko."

"Then we will need to get her back," Malenko said. "Where did you send her?"

"She's safe," Aine said, still looking at the ground, "I can promise that."

"Folks," Malenko said. "Never get involved with two women, it's just too much of a headache. Malenko knows where she's at and how you sent her there, so the next question is, how do we get her back?"

"Take my cape," Aine said, taking off her cape and handing it to Malenko. "It's the quickest way."

"Very well," Malenko said, as he moved to the center of the stage and held the cape up like a matador taunting a bull. "Malenko calls out through time and space to bring my Anna-Sophia back to this theater."

As Malenko finished talking, the lights flickered for a couple seconds and smoke poured out of the stage.

Malenko dropped the cape and Anna-Sophia was standing on the stage with Felicity at her feet. Felicity was doing the cat act perfectly.

"Malenko sees that you brought a friend," Malenko said, as he kissed Anna-Sophia. "Why don't you tell the people her story?"

"This is Felicity," Anna-Sophia said. "Many years ago she was working for a traveling carnival, one of the best trapeze artists in the land. She was asked by a magician to help with an act. Because she fancied the magician, she instantly agreed. The magician was going to do a switching trick like you've seen us do already tonight, changing a kitten into a woman. The magician failed during the trick, and now, instead of a woman *and* a kitten, we have a woman who thinks she's a kitten. Even Malenko, with all his powers, cannot reverse the magic that took place that unfortunate night."

"She can't be changed back," Malenko said, "but she can perform magic for us. Malenko says to prepare the next miracle. Let's see if cats really do have nine lives."

Aine and Anna-Sophia rushed off the stage while Felicity acted like a cat, crawling around on her hands and knees, trying to get attention from Malenko and myself, and pausing to lick her paws. It only took a moment for Anna-Sophia and Aine to return, Aine pushing a large wheel on a pedestal, and Anna-Sophia pushing a table with knives.

Aine positioned the wheel on the left side of the stage and called Felicity to come to her. She petted Felicity and gave her a cat treat. Felicity was purring loud enough that the first few rows could hear her. Aine helped Felicity onto the wheel. Using the straps that were attached to the wheel, Aine strapped Felicity down, her arms and legs spread out. Malenko was looking over the table of knives, his back to Felicity. As Aine stepped away, Malenko turned and violently threw one of the knives at Felicity. The crowd gasped as the knife stuck into the wheel, not an inch from the top of Felicity's head.

"Far too easy," Malenko said. "People often ask Malenko how Malenko learned this power. Remember, Malenko has two lovers who are both immortal." Malenko threw another knife that struck the board, sticking into it not an inch below Felicity's groin. Again, the crowd gasped. "I could practice this without fear of harming them, knowing that if the knife struck them," Malenko threw another knife, this one sticking in the board not an inch from Felicity's right armpit, "they would be okay...but Felicity here, isn't immortal," another knife stuck not an inch from Felicity's left armpit. Felicity had yet to flinch once since Malenko started throwing knives. "Felicity *can* die, so I must be very careful as I do this...Aine, let's change the rules a bit. Let's see if a cat likes to spin."

Aine approached the wheel and started to spin it. Felicity was spinning on the wheel as Malenko was aiming to throw his next knife. My heart was racing and I was beginning to sweat. I knew it was possible to become an expert at throwing knives, what Malenko had done was impressive but not out of the norm—but to throw a knife at a spinning wheel with someone attached to it? I didn't know how he was going to be able to pull that one off.

"Malenko performed this very illusion for King Arthur when we christened the round table," Malenko said. "King Arthur, how I miss thee. There was a man that knew how to throw a party."

As Malenko finished talking he threw the knife. I didn't hear the knife hit the wooden wheel but I heard a thud, followed by a hiss and scream. There was a commotion on the stage as Anna-Sophia stopped the wheel from spinning. My heart almost stopped. The knife was sticking out of Felicity's chest, blood gushing down from her heart. Malenko seemed to be in a panic. I didn't know what to do, I was frozen on the stage. Felicity's eyes were closed and she didn't appear to be breathing. Anna-Sophia took the cape that was on the ground and tossed it on top of Felicity.

The second the cape hit Felicity, the music blared and the lights twinkled. Smoke filled the stage as the audience was petrified. No one was making a sound. The lights came back to normal and the music stopped. The wheel was empty. The cape had fallen to the ground. I looked around the stage, I couldn't see Felicity anywhere as a door on the far side of the castle started to open. Felicity walked out—not as a cat, but normally, wearing nothing but a black leotard with black dance slippers being followed by Princess Aine, but it was business-suit Princess Aine, with a clean face and professional makeup. I looked around the stage but didn't see leotard Princess Aine anywhere.

"Let's have a round of applause for my fearless cat, Felicity," Malenko shouted.

The crowd was confused but started to applause. The momentary belief that someone had died on the stage had thrown the crowd for a loop. Everyone thought this was going to be a family-friendly magic show, something everyone would enjoy but Malenko was turning it into something else—something darker.

"Now it's time for something really different," Malenko said. "Malenko is going to need a number of volunteers from the audience. Raise your hand if you would like to participate on stage, my ladies here will come out and pick while the stage hands bring some provisions."

A number of hands went up, far less than if he would have asked before the last trick. I noticed Sarah coming out on stage, pushing a cart with a shiny black casket on it.

When the people realized what was coming on stage, about half the hands went down. Sarah looked nervous, upset by something. I wasn't sure what but when she had pushed the casket to the center of the stage, she moved over and stood by me.

I saw Aine, Felicity, and Anna-Sophia coming back to the stage with Anna, Jimmy Nelson, Eddie Hayes, and Carla Nelson, Jimmy's fourteen-year-old, youngest daughter. Jimmy and Eddie were in black suits from the 1920s while Carla had a magnificent dress that would have been worn by a Hollywood starlet back in the day. Malenko looked very pleased as they came on the stage.

"No time to waste," Malenko said. "Young lady, please get in the box."

"That's a casket," Jimmy said.

"One could call it that," Malenko said. "Malenko calls it the axis of one of the greatest tricks you will ever see."

Aine and Anna-Sophia helped Carla in the casket. Once the lid was shut, the ladies took Eddie and Jimmy to the castle, where by removing a few bricks on the façade, they revealed cuffs. The ladies took both Jimmy and Eddie and cuffed them to the side of the castle, just like Felicity had been cuffed to the wheel moments before. Malenko paused and smiled before he drew a handgun, a small black pistol, from his jacket.

"Magic has been done since the beginning of time," Malenko said, as everyone got on edge from seeing a gun. "In every culture, in every kingdom. James Nelson, you want to be senator of this great state, correct?"

"I do," Jimmy said.

"And one of the greatest hallmarks of a great politician is honesty, correct?"

"That is true," Jimmy said.

"Then tell the crowd here tonight," Malenko said, as he leveled the gun to Jimmy's face, "have you ever paid someone to kill another?"

There was a stunned silence. Both Sarah and I were in states of utter shock. How could Malenko have the courage to ask that question? Who the hell was he?

"I have not," Jimmy replied right away. "You're quite good at the switching trick, Malenko. How did you do it?"

"I did it by hiding in the closet," Malenko said, as everyone looked around confused. "I did it by knowing that my whore of a wife was having an affair...an affair with *their* father!"

Malenko pointed the gun right at Sarah and me. I didn't know what to do, what did this mean? Our father *was* having an affair?

"You see," Malenko said, "it's time for some explanations. Eight years ago, I was being pressured by this man right here, James Nelson, and his lapdog Eddie Hayes to sell some property to create this Gallery."

I looked to Anna who had fallen onto her knees, crying. She was shaking as Malenko talked. I rushed to her and put my arm around her, trying to comfort her.

"There was so much money on the table to buy my land but I didn't want to sell," Malenko said. "I was warned they were going to kill me. James Nelson hired Christopher Trellis to come to my house and kill my wife and me as we were having sex in our bed."

"You can't prove any of that," Jimmy yelled out as he tried to break out of his cuffs. "There's no proof. Mike Garst is dead. The doctor's confirmed it."

"Doctor Andrew Dumas," Malenko said, "confirmed it after I threatened him, that's why the death certificate was changed. You see, it wasn't Mike and Cindy Garst in bed the night of the murders, it was Cindy Garst and Dean Callan."

My heart sank. I looked to Anna who was looking at me. There was anger, fear, and pain in her eyes. I did the only thing I could think of, I hugged her. "I'm sorry," I whispered into her ear.

"Don't be," Anna whispered back to me. "This can't be happening, can it?"

"I was in the closet," Malenko continued. "I knew this was going on but I didn't know it was with my neighbor and friend. Imara, Sarah, just know, I hold no ill-will toward you or your father. It was my wife who made the decision to breach the marriage vows. I was recording it. I was about to reveal that I was there, reveal and make some demands for silence, when Christopher Trellis came in with a shotgun.

"One of the biggest questions of the murders was why Mike Garst had a handgun in his headboard, but he didn't reach for it when a gunman entered the room. I saw Chris pull the trigger on them. I followed him out of the room, quickly swapping wallets with Dean before I left the room, hid in the house when Anna and Imara rushed in, then tracked Chris down, watching him get killed with a baseball bat before he was blasted with his own shotgun.

"I took some money from my accounts, and using the PIN information I got from Dean's wallet, I took some money from his accounts. Enough to fund a life of wandering around Europe, putting on magic shows. But then, damn it Jimmy, you had to go and build this fucking Gallery. All you ever cared about was your own damn ego. I know I'm going to burn in hell, not for what I'm about to do, but for what I did...I abandoned my daughter Anna. That was the cruelest of my crimes, and honey, for that I'm sorry."

Anna was a wreck, tears streaming down her face uncontrollably. She could barely nod as Malenko was talking to her.

"This story is false!" Jimmy yelled out. "I didn't order Chris Trellis to kill anyone. This man needs to be arrested. Police? Someone get the damn police up here."

"No," Malenko shouted as he pulled a remote control from his jacket. "I see one cop anywhere, see one laser sight on me, I push this button and that casket with your daughter inside burns."

"You wouldn't," Jimmy said.

"Yes, I would," Malenko said. "And the police are now going to be a little busy. I've spent the past few weeks loading every building in this gallery with explosives and napalm. In ten minutes, just enough time for everyone to leave in an orderly fashion, the Front Street Gallery and Entertainment Complex will be burned to the ground. No one needs to die...no one will die if you cooperate...but James, you must confess your sins."

"I didn't order him to kill you," Jimmy yelled. "I didn't."

"I was there," Eddie said. "I was there when he did it. James talked with Chris, paid him three million dollars. A million each for Mike, Cindy, and Anna. He was pissed when Anna didn't die and he didn't get his million for her back."

"You piece of shit, Eddie," James yelled. "You fucking rat bastard. How could you?"

"How many people have died?" Eddie yelled. "How many have we killed to keep this silent? You think this nut-job is going to stop until he has the truth?"

"Very good," Malenko said. "Folks, I know this show wasn't exactly what you thought it was going to be, but my point is valid. In ten minutes, starting now," Malenko pushed the button on the remote, "the entire Gallery will start burning. This place will be ash. Please make an orderly exit and move a safe distance away. I don't want anyone getting hurt. Let me leave you with one last trick."

Smoke filled the stage and the lights flickered on and off. When the lights came back on, Malenko, Aine, Anna-Sophia, and Felicity were gone. It was just Anna, Sarah, and me with Jimmy and Eddie chained up. Anna jumped up and opened the casket where Carla had been placed, but the casket was empty. Carla had been taken with Malenko.

Chapter #29

Magic of Murder

The crowd was starting to make their way to the exits of the theater, not in an orderly fashion, but more like a riotous mob. The sounds of panicked screams filled the air, people were climbing over seats, pushing people down, and generally acting like animals. I was frozen on the stage, Anna had fallen back to her knees, crying, and Sarah held a blank face of confusion. I couldn't see how Malenko and the ladies got away, where they could have taken Carla. Jimmy and Eddie were chained up to the castle walls, screaming for help but no one was listening to them.

My mind was swimming, our father having an affair with Anna's mother? He was unhappy with our mom, she wasn't in her right mind, and all the signs were there— being gone during strange hours, not showing a level of affection toward the woman he was married to. I never thought it possible when I was younger, that Dad could do something like that, but now as I look back, I understand what it was. The blinders were off my eyes and I was no longer looking at my father through magic eyes, I could see him for what he was, not a superhero as all kids see their fathers, but as a human, with human wants and desires.

"They can't die," Anna said, standing up. "We have to save those two bastards."

"What are you talking about?" Sarah said. "That fucker killed our father and he would have killed yours...and you too, Anna."

"That's why we have to save them," Anna said. "It's not up to us to deal out the punishment for their sins. Let him have his day in court. Let him go before the cameras and explain all this. Most importantly, let him watch this Gallery burn to the ground...letting them die here and now would be the easy way out for them. I want that bastard to suffer."

"She's right," I said. "I don't want anyone to suffer but it is not up to us to deal out their punishment. We have to save them."

I helped Anna stand up. We rushed over to Jimmy, looking over his cuffs. They were chained into the wall of the castle. On the backside, I could see that the chains had been cemented into the castle, which was itself cemented to the floor. Malenko had this castle built so sturdy that we couldn't cut it apart or easily break it. I looked at the cuffs, they were metal chains, with a locking system. There was no way to get the cuffs off the hands or feet without opening them up, and we didn't have the key. If only Aine were here, she could get through the locks for us, but I doubted she would be helping us with this.

"Why are you doing this?" Jimmy asked, looking at Anna.

"You need to watch this place burn," Anna said. "You need to face your peers in court. They'll lock you away forever for this."

"Not likely," Jimmy said. "There isn't a court in this state that would convict me. I'll use this as sympathy for my election, people are always trying to bring down successful people like me. I sweep into the senate and after one term I'll take the White House by storm. This place will be rebuilt, better than before. Your father will suffer for this...he'll be the only one."

"You really think...you arrogant prick," Anna said, slapping Jimmy, "that you'll get away with this? We could leave you here...save ourselves."

"That would be something you would have to live with your entire lives," Jimmy said. "I don't think you can do that. You have to save me."

"He's right," I said. "He has children. I can't let him die no matter how badly I want to walk away from this...but Jimmy, you could at least be slightly humble over the fact that we didn't leave you like everyone else did."

I looked back over the theater, it was almost empty now, with just the last few people, people who'd been pushed around and knocking down, limping out of the theater. There was a silence, a real silence, in the theater for the first time since the show had started. I looked toward Jimmy. I wanted to sympathize with him for what was being done, his life being destroyed, but after what he had done, I couldn't.

"Your father has just done more for me than any other person ever has," Jimmy said, as Anna and I kept looking over the chains, trying to find a way to break them. "I will be a national hero after this."

"And how do you expect that?" Anna asked. "After what was revealed here, how do you expect to get away?"

"Your father," Jimmy said. "He's killed everyone that was involved. He must have been the person killing everyone...the guards, the doctor, Tim Krause. Those were all the people who could have testified about what happened."

"Eddie made a pretty convincing confession," Anna said. "All the theater heard him."

"Made under duress," Jimmy said. "Saying whatever was needed to get the madman away."

"You don't think for one second that you're getting out of here alive you fucking prick," I heard Princess Aine's voice behind us.

I turned around and felt like I was hit in the face with a board. My mind reeled, trying to grasp what I was seeing. It took a moment for my senses to put everything together. Princess Aine was walking toward us, in her leotard and glitter, standing right next to Princess Aine, in her business suit. Identical twins. That's how the switches were being done.

"What the fuck?" Anna said. "Please tell me you're not my half-sisters."

"Felicity," Leotard Aine said. "Felicity and her twin Francis are your sisters. Felicity, the one who was acting as a cat, the one you met and spoke with in the dressing room, she is the sister who has your kidney. Francis is the one who came out at the end."

"I knew it," Anna said. "From the second I saw her, there was just something there. I knew she was my sister...and Anna-Sophia is her mother, correct?"

"You are right," Business Aine said.

"Hey," Jimmy yelled out. "You people can have your family reunion love-fest in jail. Get us the fuck out of here right now."

"You really think," Leotard Aine said, slapping Jimmy hard across the face, "for one damn second that we are going to let you live? Not going to happen. Even if the police get here, which they won't, they're too busy running all over the gallery, trying to find the explosives. The police won't save you."

"What about my daughter?" Jimmy asked. "Where is Carla?"

"She's safe," Leotard Aine said. "For now. She's outside of the gallery. Know one thing, there isn't some magic wire, some secret code, or some super computer than can stop the countdown. The place *will* burn to the ground with you inside."

"Please," Anna said. "Please don't kill him. Make him face his day in court."

"He's already said he'll get off," Business Aine said. "And he's right. Jimmy is so well connected that he can bribe a judge or get to a juror. There's no way he will ever face true justice. That's the magic of murder, we can take over when the courts and laws have failed."

"You're not God!" Jimmy yelled. "You don't have the authority to dispense justice."

"But you do?" Business Aine asked.

"You've got it all wrong," Jimmy said. "I'm doing good things. I'm an extraordinary person who can't be held to the same levels and law as others."

"So, that's why you killed everyone?" Aine asked.

"What are you talking about?" Jimmy scoffed. "I didn't kill anybody."

"Your orders did," Leotard Aine said. "We've not killed a person yet. You killed Tim Krause because he knew so much. He's been extorting you for money. He wanted all his family working in the gallery, in high-up positions. When it was just a little money here and there, it was okay, wasn't it, Jimmy? Everyone else who has been murdered, from the guards to the doctors, it was all because of you, wasn't it, Jimmy?"

"Fuck you, bitch!" Jimmy yelled, spitting at Aine's feet. "I didn't do anything. I didn't kill anyone. You people must have done it all."

"You were actually going to blame us," Leotard Aine said. "Weren't you? You were going to leave a trail of evidence that would point to us, mainly because of all the magic and mystery that was involved with the murders. It was a clever plan. Malenko told you he was going back to the Pacific after this opening, going to tour Japan and China.

Everything would have pointed our way...just admit it, that's all you have to do."

"You tell me how you did the switches so fast," Jimmy said. "Then I'll tell you what really happened."

"There's trap doors all over the stage," Leotard Aine said. "They drop on hydraulic cylinders. The spinning wheel is sitting on one. We used the smoke and lights to mask the fact that it drops. Stage hands underneath got Felicity off the wheel. In the castle, through that door where I did my switch, is a double layer elevator. She went in, the door closes, the system moves up, I walk out, once the door closes, it lowers down to let her out beneath the stage. The box for the swords was set on a platform as well. Nothing magic about it."

"That sucked the fun out of it," Jimmy said.

"You asked," Leotard Aine said. "Now tell us, you know that Malenko told the truth on stage. What is really going on? Who killed Christopher?"

"I hired Christopher to kill Anna and her family," Jimmy said. "But when Chris left, Mike didn't kill him, Eddie did. Eddie was supposed to bury the body, which he did, but it was dug up and moved...you want to know the truth? I killed everyone who knew about it. Eddie and I. He's going to be my vice when I run. We had everyone fooled."

"Including the police," Business Aine said.

Business Aine moved to the door on the castle and opened it, allowing Detective Travis Lukens and Officer Lund Grimes to walk out. Jimmy rolled his eyes and laughed as the detective smiled at him.

"I think that should be enough to convince a jury," Travis said.

"Never in a million years," Jimmy replied. "I was under duress and was forced to say certain things to make sure that I would survive this situation. The more you pile on me the better this will look when I run. Man alive, I really need to thank all of you for helping me out so much."

"Oh, you poor simpering fool," Leotard Aine said. "We have all the evidence that we need. You don't think for one second that we weren't stalking you the entire time? We weren't trailing you? Photographing your every move? We have video and pictures of you doing it. You were sloppy, thinking that you owned the police."

"We do own the police," Eddie said. "None of that will stand up in court...not even my confession to the crowd."

"You really think you're going to get out of this alive?" Leotard Aine asked. "Honestly? After all you've done, you think that we're going to let you simply walk out of here and face all of that?"

"What did you do with my daughter?" Jimmy asked. "Carla, where is she?"

"Do you want her to live or die?" Business Aine asked.

"Damn it, Grimes!" Jimmy shouted. "Arrest her. She's kidnapped my daughter."

"You don't know that," Aine said. "Your daughter was placed inside a casket for a magic trick. She disappeared. There's no reason to think she won't reappear when the time is right."

"Arrest them," Jimmy yelled.

"For what?" Lund asked. "They haven't done anything wrong yet."

"This is over," Detective Lukens said. "One of you, unlock them from those cuffs and get his daughter back here right now."

"Afraid I can't do that," Business Aine said. "No one is going anywhere until Jimmy and Eddie take full responsibility for what they have done. You must go to jail for the murders Jimmy. You cannot be allowed to walk a free man with this much blood on your hands."

"It's the magic of murder," Jimmy said. "No matter what I say here, no matter how many times I tell the story or who I tell it to, when I'm under oath all I say is that I said what I had to say to get free. I was tricked. I still have all the evidence that links the murders to Malenko. I still have my alibies."

"You may have them," Leotard Aine said. "But we have one thing that you will never have."

"What's that?"

"Magic."

The stage flooded with smoke as the lights flickered then went completely out. When they came back on there was a haze on the stage. It took a moment for the smoke to clear out, allowing everyone to see what had happened. Jimmy and Eddie had been released from their bindings and both Business and Leotard Aine were gone. It was very strange. I looked for a clock, trying to figure out what time it was, realizing that I didn't know the exact time the countdown started, so looking at the time wasn't going to help me any. Lund knew what I was doing as he glanced at his watch.

"We've got less than five minutes," Lund said. "We need to move."

"Not without knowing my daughter is safe," Jimmy said. "I don't want these nut jobs to kill her. Lund, go under the stage and see if she's trapped down there."

"It's a labyrinth down there," Lund said. "They have all sorts of stuff down there, chambers and rooms. There's no way we could search all of them in that amount of time."

"Go down there and look for her!" Jimmy yelled.

"Go down there yourself!" Lund shot back.

Lund didn't wait for a reply, he rushed toward the exits. Detective Lukens looked at his watch and his worried face told the story.

"I must insist," Travis said. "We all need to get out of here right now."

Anna grabbed my hand and started for the doors. I reached out for Sarah. The three of us ran for the doors, hand in hand, past all the fancy décor in the magnificent hallways. We ran as fast as we could, rushing to get to the exits. Once we passed the doors to the theater, Anna headed for the mock main street. There was no one there, under the glow of the street lamps.

As we went past the stores, it looked like there'd been a riot. Shelving was knocked over, merchandise was strewn over the floors and every store was deserted, completely empty. As we got past the stores we could see that police had already set up barricades and were holding people back in the parking lots. The crowd was on edge, nervous and jittery. The police were having problems keeping them back.

I looked back, saw Eddie and Jimmy running just steps behind us with Detective Lukens following. I had no idea where Malenko, the Aines, Felicity, Francis, or Anna-Sophia were. There hadn't been a sign of them since they'd disappeared from the theater. As we crossed the police barricade, Anna kept running, pushing her way through the crowd, doing everything she could to get past the mob of people who'd gathered to witness the destruction of the gallery.

"We need to keep moving," Anna said, once we were outside the group of people. "If there really are explosives and napalm and whatnot in there, I don't want to be anywhere near that crowd when it goes up. There can't be much time left."

"We need to get away from Eddie and Jimmy," Sarah said. "Who knows if they'll try to arrest us tonight? We have to keep moving."

I didn't know where we were going to run to, where we could go. Anna kept in the lead as we moved on. We ran down the deserted street that led toward the gallery, the street next to it, full of cars trying to get away. Cars were starting to jump the median, crossing into the lane we were running in. Everyone seemed to either want to get closer to watch or to get away as quickly as they could.

I ran with Anna and Sarah to a building near my shop. The building was five stories with a café on the roof. We ran up the stairs, not pausing at all for a breath. When we reached the top we burst out onto the roof, past the café and its wait staff, past the few people enjoying coffee and deserts, and ran right to the edge of the building, looking toward the gallery, waiting with baited breath for what was about to happen next.

It took another minute before anything happened. It started with a glowing near the center of the gallery that kept getting brighter and brighter. There were some small explosions, which sounded like small fireworks going off. It didn't take long after that for the flames to be seen. The air was filled with the sounds of fire truck sirens rushing toward the gallery as all the people at the rooftop café came over to the edge of the wall to join us in gawking at the spectacle of the fire.

In less than five minutes, we could feel the heat from the fires. The gentle winds were blowing toward us and I wondered if more than just the gallery was going to burn. The sky was full of helicopters, news, police, and firefighters, trying desperately to get control of the situation. Every fire house in Prairie Rapids had dispatched every truck they had, the lights of the trucks dancing around the gallery area, but it was no use. The gallery, the Mall, the sports arena and the theater were engulfed in flames. A towering inferno in the heart of Prairie Rapids.

"Do you think they all got away?" Sarah asked. "Do you think Malenko and Aine and the others got out of there?"

"I'm sure they did," I said. "I don't believe the remote control set off a timer. Malenko waited for everyone to leave, then he started the fire."

"I can't believe my father is still alive," Anna said. "And after this, I'll never be able to see him. He'll either have to flee the country or he'll be in jail. They'll pin him with all the murders."

"You don't know that," I said. "There's a chance Jimmy will do the right thing."

"Think about it," Anna said. "He's going to have all the sympathy in the world. He'll snake out of this like he snakes out of everything."

"Didn't you say karma had a funny way of dealing with everything?" I asked.

"It does," Anna said. "But this doesn't feel good. Jimmy should answer to the people for what he did, my dad shouldn't take the blame for it."

"He won't," a female voice said, behind us.

We turned around to see Aine, in her business suit, approaching us. She was nervously looking around, making sure she wasn't seen by anyone who knew what had happened.

"I don't have much time," Aine said, as she handed Anna a note. "Please, Anna, your father loves you. He always has and it tore him up inside that he had to leave. My sister and I met him right after everything happened and she fell in love with him. It was by chance he met up with Anna-Sophia again...strange chance. Please, all will be explained someday."

"What are we supposed to do now?" Anna asked. "Won't the police be looking for us? Are we going to get into trouble for anything that happened here?"

"They can't blame you for anything," Aine said. "You are clean. You were right in saying that Malenko didn't start the fire until everyone was out. He wouldn't hurt anyone. Carla is already back with her parents. Please, Anna, just read the note and know that everything will work out in the end."

Aine turned around and walked out before another word could be said. Anna opened the note and looked at it. All it said was, 'I love you, Anna. Dad.' Anna shed a tear as she looked the note over. There was nothing else. The three of us looked back over the raging inferno as I wondered how long the fire would burn. I looked to Anna, who had a confused look on her face. Her hand was in her left rear pocket.

"I never checked the pockets of these jeans," Anna said, as she pulled a folded piece of paper from her pocket. "My father always used to put notes in my pockets."

As Anna read the note to herself, her face lit up. She was glowing brighter than the fire consuming the gallery. As Anna looked back over the fire, the look on her face said it all...everything was going to be alright...someday.

Chapter #30

The Final Trick

Anna, Sarah, and I sat sipping coffee in a small café overlooking the Atlantic Ocean. The café was old, and had a quaint charm to it, a unique look that was derived from it being original, not some franchised coffee like we had in the states. I still couldn't believe where our journey had taken us; Casablanca, Morocco. We'd finally gone on our trip, the three of us together, just weeks after the magical ordeal back in the states. We'd flown to Madrid Spain, traveled by bus to Lisbon Portugal, before taking a boat to a country with no extradition treaties with the United States.

We weren't sure what to expect when we got here, not sure how Mike Garst expected to find us, all we knew was what was on the note in Anna's pocket; the name of a hotel, the name of the café, a specific, one-week time window, and the name *Casablanca*. I couldn't believe how quickly Malenko and his ladies had gotten out of the states, if they actually made it out—we'd been there for three days and hadn't see a single glimpse of them. Even if they didn't show up, I had confidence in Jack running the store for a month and we would enjoy our time across the pond.

"What do you think?" Anna asked as the sun was setting on the horizon. "How long do we wait here?"

"I'm not sure," I said. "I mean, what if they didn't get out?"

"We should have heard about it by now," Anna said. "If they were captured or killed it would have been front page news."

"I would think so," Sarah said. "But with all that's gone on, who knows?"

It was then that a woman caught my attention. She was watching us from a different table and, try as I might, I couldn't quite remember when she'd sat down. The woman had large black sunglasses covering her eyes, black tights with a billowy black top that covered her body. Her long, straight black hair danced in the wind; black hair that had just a little bit of blonde coming out from the hairline...a wig. I stared at her, realizing she was staring back at me. She lowered her sunglasses and that's when I knew; Princess Aine.

I didn't say anything, didn't notify the others. Aine put her hand under the table, out of sight from others, and slowly motioned for us to follow. Anna and Sarah hadn't even noticed her yet. Aine stood up and started slowly walking toward the hotel that was just across the street.

"We need to go," I said, standing up.

"Maybe we should wait," Anna said.

"No," I said, quickly winking at Anna. "We need to go now...I'm suddenly not feeling well."

Anna and Sarah exchanged a glance as they stood and followed me. I rushed to catch up to Aine, falling in step about twenty feet behind her. There were enough people moving around that Anna and Sarah didn't realize who I was following. Through the street and the grand entrance of the hotel, Anna and Sarah kept looking around, realizing that something was going on but not realizing the person I was following.

Through the magnificent lobby, decorated for tourists to resemble the Morocco of old, I followed Aine up a flight of stairs and down a hallway. As we entered the hallway, Aine was gone. I slowly walked the hallway, with Anna and Sarah close behind. When we got to the first set of doors I stopped; one was propped slightly open, having the deadbolt extended before the door was closed. Hanging on the knob was a 'Do Not Disturb' card with 'The Final Trick' spelled out in black magic marker.

I slowly opened the door and walked in, Anna and Sarah following close behind. The room was amazing, a deep red covered the walls and the plush carpet. Magnificent dark wood furniture adorned a parlor with tapestry hangings separating the other room. A bottle of wine and a few glasses were on a chocolate-covered table. I looked back, motioned for Sarah to close and lock the door. Once the lock had been secured, Aine walked out from behind a tapestry, taking her glasses and black wig off.

"So good to see you again," Aine said, giving each one of us a hug. "Mike hoped you would figure out the message and be able to get here."

"What happened?" Anna asked. "How did you get out of the country?"

"That was the easiest part of the act," Mike said, as he emerged, his hair now dyed blonde, his face cleanly shaven, and having dropped about fifty pounds from before. "This deception was planned long ago."

"Dad," Anna said, looking at her father. "I don't...what happened to you?"

"This is my real body," Mike said. "What you saw in Prairie Rapids was thanks to bulk sewn into the clothing I was wearing. I kept lifts in my shoes and always wore platforms or heels so my true height was never revealed. Contacts to conceal my eye color along with my hair and beard dyed."

"I hardly recognize you," Anna said. "Are you sure you're safe?"

"What can they charge me with?" Mike said, "Arson? Most countries aren't going to go through the red tape of extradition for a petty arson charge dear. I never killed anyone."

"Where's the others?" Anna asked. "I want to see my sisters."

The other Aine, in jeans and a tank top, Felicity, Francis, both in sundresses, and Anna-Sophia, in black tights and a black tee-shirt, emerged from a side room. They all looked normal; normal clothing, normal makeup, and normal smiles on their faces. They could all pass as standard American Tourists. Anna rushed up and hugged her half-sisters.

"I'm glad to be able to meet you," Anna said.

"Thank you so much for the sacrifice you gave to me," Felicity said. "I can never repay you for what you've done for me. You saved my life."

"You're welcome," Anna said. "What happened, Dad? How did everything go astray?"

"There was a scandal," Mike said. "Your grandparents, my parents, had a pretty nice summer home up in lakes country to the north of Prairie Rapids. I would spend the summers there. When I was eighteen, wild as a dog, I met Anna-Sophia, who was, shall we say, younger than I was. We spent the summer together, just swimming, hiking, making out by the campfire, stuff like that. By the end of the summer, she was pregnant...she was only thirteen."

"WHAT?" Anna shouted.

"I looked older than I was," Anna-Sophia said. "Plus...I didn't have a lot of friends. I was picked on a lot. My family had a cabin not far from his and when we met, it was amazing, just to have someone there with me. I told him I was seventeen, turning eighteen at the end of the summer. I was developed enough that he didn't question it. It was wrong of me to do but I wanted more than anything, a friend of my own."

"Her family threw a fit when they found out," Mike continued, "as did mine. I was looking at real jail time for what happened. I don't regret it; it was the best summer I ever had. Anna-Sophia and I had something special. I wouldn't call it love, we were a bit young to say that, but there was a connection there. An agreement was made...I would never contact or have anything to do with Anna-Sophia or her twins, plus my family would pay the sum of one-hundred-thousand dollars, to be put in trust to cover the girls' college educations, plus another hundred grand to be used for expenses growing up, and her father wouldn't press charges, wouldn't throw me in jail...I had no choice, I took the deal.

"I had to pay my father back by working for him, but when he died, I inherited all the family property. The first thing I did was sell the family lake cabin. I met your mom and we had you, Anna. She even let me pick the name, but she never knew I'd named you after my first love. Every day my heart ached for them, to know that I had twins out there but not even able to see a picture of them broke my heart.

"The accident is where things started to unravel. Anna-Sophia called me, knowing that you were the only one who could save Felicity. I had to tell my wife that I had two daughters from another woman. It didn't matter that it happened years before I'd even met her, after that your mother never trusted me again. That's when she started cheating."

"This is incredible, Dad," Anna said. "I can't imagine the pain you must have gone through."

"It was bad," Mike said. "I knew about the affair, so I hid in the closet. I didn't know it was Dean. I recorded it and was going to step out of the closet, give my wife a choice, either make things work with me and no one else, or leave and get nothing. It was pure happenstance that the murder took place that night. What I had over Jimmy, what he feared the most, I had a video of Eddie killing Christopher Trellis with Jimmy standing there watching. I sent that to him when I left. For all these years I don't think they knew who had sent it.

"When I took your father's wallet, Imara, I found his bank account numbers with passwords and PINs to access the accounts. I took about a hundred grand and fled the country. In Eastern Europe I got access to fake documents...an entirely new identity that allowed me to travel anywhere in the world as a citizen of Austria.

"I always had a love of magic, always had a secret desire to be a magician, so when the opportunity to create a new life came, I studied everything I could about magic, touring the world learning the oldest and best tricks, putting my spin on them, and building a reputation as a great performer. In Bucharest, I met Aine, the one in black who led you here today, the one you always saw in leotards and glitter. We fell in love as I started my magic act.

"Using Aine and her twin sister, Aspin, we developed a very successful magic show. Aine and Aspin had been traveling circus performers, as their parents were. They grew up traveling all around Europe in a show, performing since they could walk, always looking for a way out, wanting a normal lifestyle, not what their parents had. Aine and I made a home in Bucharest, never marrying but loving each other all the same.

"Fate has a strange way of playing games. We were doing a show, traveling to bigger cities for the weekends, spending the week in our little cottage in the foothills, when we found ourselves flying to Paris. We had four shows scheduled in Paris before flying home. One day, we were sitting in a café next to a lady with twin daughters who looked so beautiful, yet so familiar. We started talking and boom, Anna-Sophia and our daughters. Anna-Sophia's parents had passed away and she was using some of the inheritance money to take her daughters on a cultural trip, not knowing what she was going to do with her life."

"I was a mess," Anna-Sophia interrupted. "I hated my father for taking Mike away from me. I know, I was so young, but I loved him and had twins with him. I swore that I would never love another man again. I was stunned to see Mike in Europe, let alone hear his story."

"Aine and I had always had an agreement that our relationship would be open," Mike said, "although neither of us had ever spent time with others since we started dating. Aine was very open to me speaking with Anna-Sophia and even starting to date her. I know that it's unconventional, and most people would think it wrong or immoral on some level, but the three of us have done very well."

"I don't think it's wrong, Dad," Anna said. "If it works for you then no one else is to judge. I just wish I knew about this before. I don't know, I mean, this is a lot to process. I wish you would have told me something before the show, let me know so I wasn't blindsided like that on the stage."

"The theater can have an effect on people," Mike said. "When I heard the gallery was opening I knew I had to stop it. Together we formulated a plan to burn the place to the ground while at the same time, exposing Jimmy for what he was. It was by pure chance that we saw you Anna, remember, at the magic show in Romania?"

"I remember being blown away by your magic," Anna said.

"I knew you right away," Mike said. "I could never forget my daughter. I told the others here that it was you but you were gone before we could talk off stage. I was so happy when you were back in Prairie Rapids. I was glad to get to see you and explain all of this to you. All the money that I charged for the show and the design of the set will keep us funded for a long time. We were well off before but I wanted to make sure that our lives would be set.

"I knew just how to get Jimmy enticed and I never thought he would start killing off the people that knew, but when he did, it became obvious he was going to point the finger at us, travelling freaks that are drifting through town...is he going to face his day in court?"

"No," Anna said. "Karma is a harsh mistress...Tim Kraus's alcoholic, anger-prone daughter tried to gun him down leaving the courthouse. He was dumb enough to state publicly that he wouldn't be charged and he would be winning the senate. He didn't die, thankfully, and she's required to serve two years in an institution and complete rehab, but he's finally accepted responsibility...although it was his wife and kids pleading with him to get the violence to stop that made him agree...plus the video of him and Eddie killing Christopher surfaced...somehow."

"The final trick," Mike smiled.

"What's your next move then?" Anna asked. "What happens from here?"

"I wanted to explain everything to you Anna," Mike said. "You deserve that much. From here, the sky's the limit. Aspin has been studying at university for a business degree and will be starting a job in London in just a couple weeks. Felicity and Francis are going back to Paris. With their gymnastics and yoga training, they are opening a fitness studio. As for Anna-Sophia, Aine, and myself, well, the less I say about where we are the better, but just know, I'm settling down. We've bought a small farm. We'll raise some sheep and chickens, vegetables that we'll sell at the local farmer's markets, along with raising some wheat. I'll be writing poetry and maybe a novel or two, while Anna-

Sophia and Aine start a crafts business, sewing projects and whatnot to sell at craft fairs."

"Where are you going to be?" Anna asked. "I just want to know...will you be safe?"

"We'll be safe," Mike said. "Far away from big city prying eyes. I doubt anybody will even be looking for me, there are bigger fish to fry out there."

"Will I be able to see you again?" Anna asked.

"In time," Mike said. "When you first arrived here, we were monitoring your every move, not to look at you, but to see if someone was watching you. For three days we waited and when I was certain that no one had a tail on you, we brought you here. I still have some contacts in Interpol and the FBI...if my name is brought up, I'll know."

"But I will be able to visit?" Anna asked. "Right?"

"Yes," Mike said. "Give it a few months, but I'll get word to you...what's your plans?"

"We're going to continue to explore the city," Anna said. "Before we see some more of Europe. We took a month for this. Once we get back, I'm helping Imara run the store."

"Imara and Sarah," Mike said, turning his attention to us. "I am sorry. I saw your dad get murdered that night. I should have told you, somehow, instead of letting you wonder all those years. It was wrong of me, I admit, but necessary for my positon. From the look of your store, you've carved out a good life for yourself."

"I have," I said. "I'm really looking forward to running the store with Sarah and Anna. We've been discussing expansion plans and maybe some real estate deals."

"Shoot for the stars, girls," Mike said. "Anything you want you can have. Imara, you've taken to anyone yet? I noticed that you and Doctor Mark were speaking again."

"Mark and I are spending some time together," I said. "It's nice but we haven't labeled anything yet."

"Be glad you've got good friends," Mike said. "Anna, I love you but we need to go. I will get word to you soon as to where you can find us...I'm proud of you, Anna, I really am."

Mike hugged Anna, both of them tearing up. After they let go, Anna hugged both Felicity and Francis. All the girls were crying as Mike, Anna-Sophia, Aine, Aspin, Felicity, and Francis left the room, leaving just the three of us alone. After so many years of wondering, after so many years of a burst bubble, everything had come together. The blinders were off. I could see without the need of magic eyes. I didn't know what the future would hold for the three of us, but as Anna, Sarah, and I left the room, I knew the world was at our feet and no magic could stop us from getting what we wanted.